Five Nights at Freddy's™

THE TWISTED ONES

The Graphic Novel

BY SCOTT CAWTHON AND
KIRA BREED-WRISLEY

ADAPTED BY CHRISTOPHER HASTINGS

ILLUSTRATED BY CLAUDIA AGUIRRE
COLORS BY LAURIE SMITH
AND EVA DE LA CRUZ

ISBN 978-1-338-62976-7 (paperback)
ISBN 978-1-338-64109-7 (hardcover)

10 9 8 7 6 5 4 3 2   21 22 23 24 25

Printed in the U.S.A.   40

First printing 2021

Edited by Michael Petranek and Chloe Fraboni

Book design by Betsy Peterschmidt

Inks by Claudia Aguirre

Colors by Laurie Smith and Eva de la Cruz

Letters by Mike Fiorentino

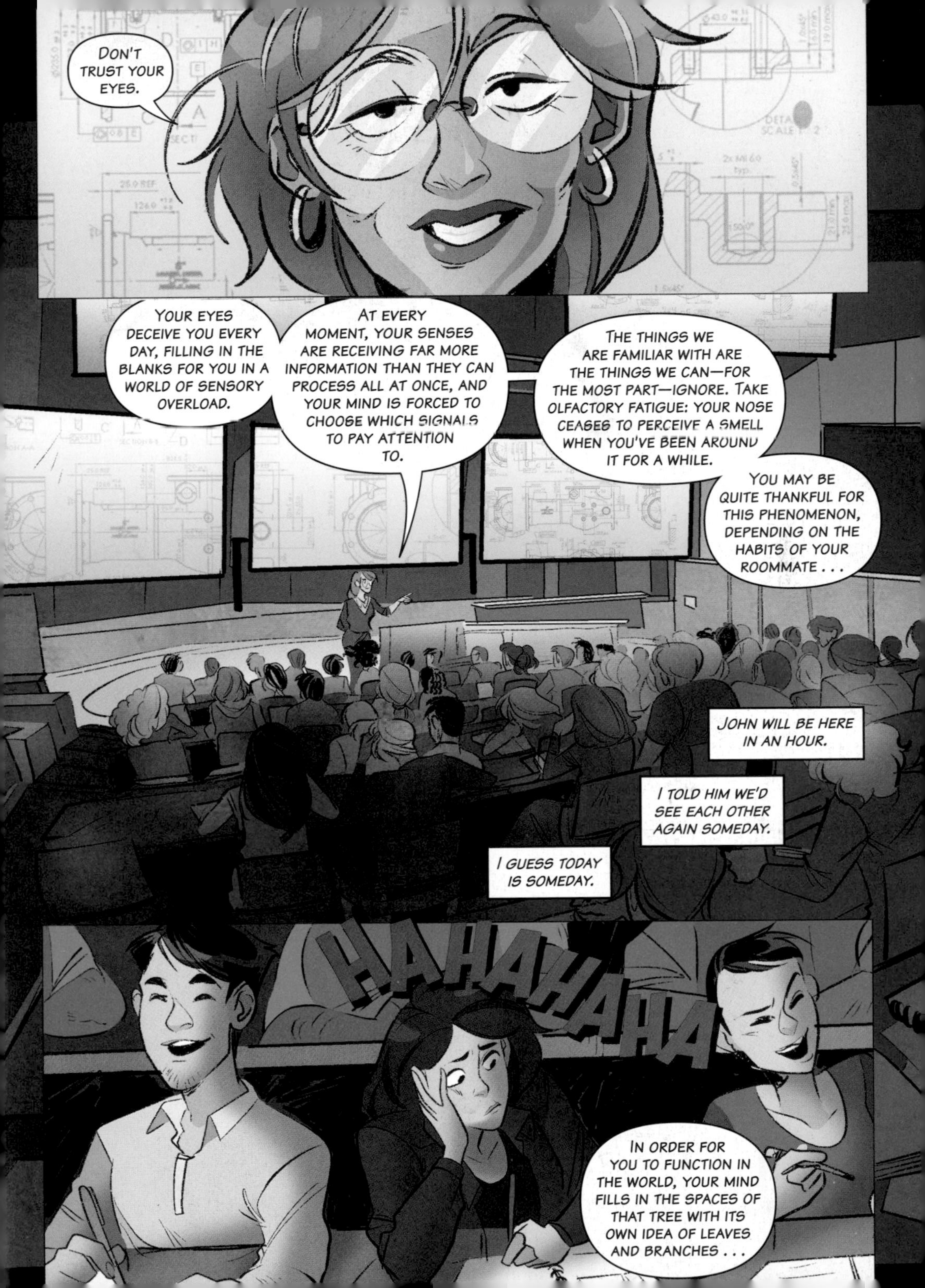
DON'T TRUST YOUR EYES.
YOUR EYES DECEIVE YOU EVERY DAY, FILLING IN THE BLANKS FOR YOU IN A WORLD OF SENSORY OVERLOAD.
AT EVERY MOMENT, YOUR SENSES ARE RECEIVING FAR MORE INFORMATION THAN THEY CAN PROCESS ALL AT ONCE, AND YOUR MIND IS FORCED TO CHOOSE WHICH SIGNALS TO PAY ATTENTION TO.
THE THINGS WE ARE FAMILIAR WITH ARE THE THINGS WE CAN—FOR THE MOST PART—IGNORE. TAKE OLFACTORY FATIGUE: YOUR NOSE CEASES TO PERCEIVE A SMELL WHEN YOU'VE BEEN AROUND IT FOR A WHILE.
YOU MAY BE QUITE THANKFUL FOR THIS PHENOMENON, DEPENDING ON THE HABITS OF YOUR ROOMMATE . . .
JOHN WILL BE HERE IN AN HOUR.
I TOLD HIM WE'D SEE EACH OTHER AGAIN SOMEDAY.
I GUESS TODAY IS SOMEDAY.
HAHAHAHAHA
IN ORDER FOR YOU TO FUNCTION IN THE WORLD, YOUR MIND FILLS IN THE SPACES OF THAT TREE WITH ITS OWN IDEA OF LEAVES AND BRANCHES . . .

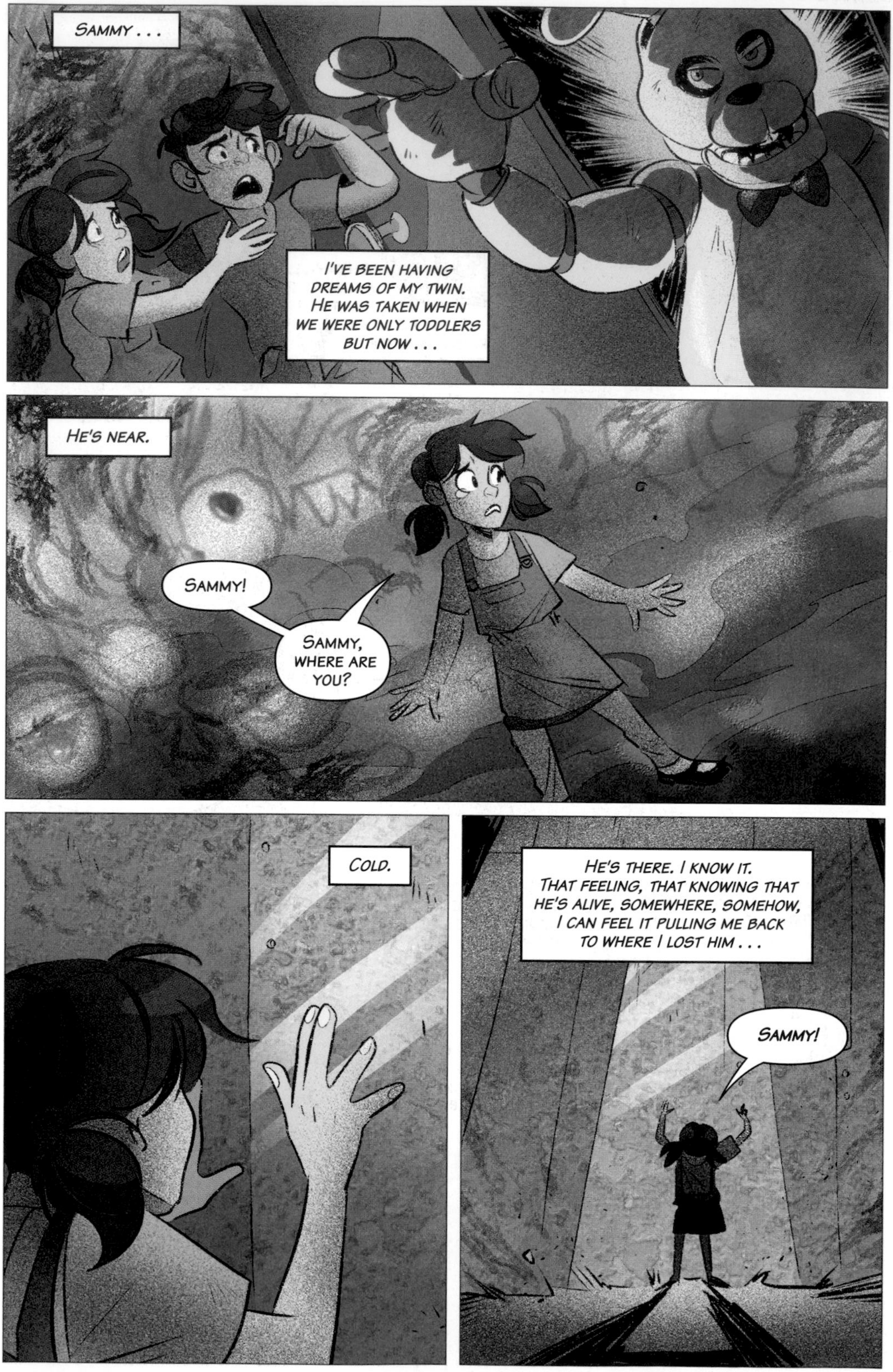
SAMMY . . .
I'VE BEEN HAVING DREAMS OF MY TWIN. HE WAS TAKEN WHEN WE WERE ONLY TODDLERS BUT NOW . . .
HE'S NEAR.
SAMMY!
SAMMY, WHERE ARE YOU?
COLD.
HE'S THERE. I KNOW IT. THAT FEELING, THAT KNOWING THAT HE'S ALIVE, SOMEWHERE, SOMEHOW, I CAN FEEL IT PULLING ME BACK TO WHERE I LOST HIM . . .
SAMMY!

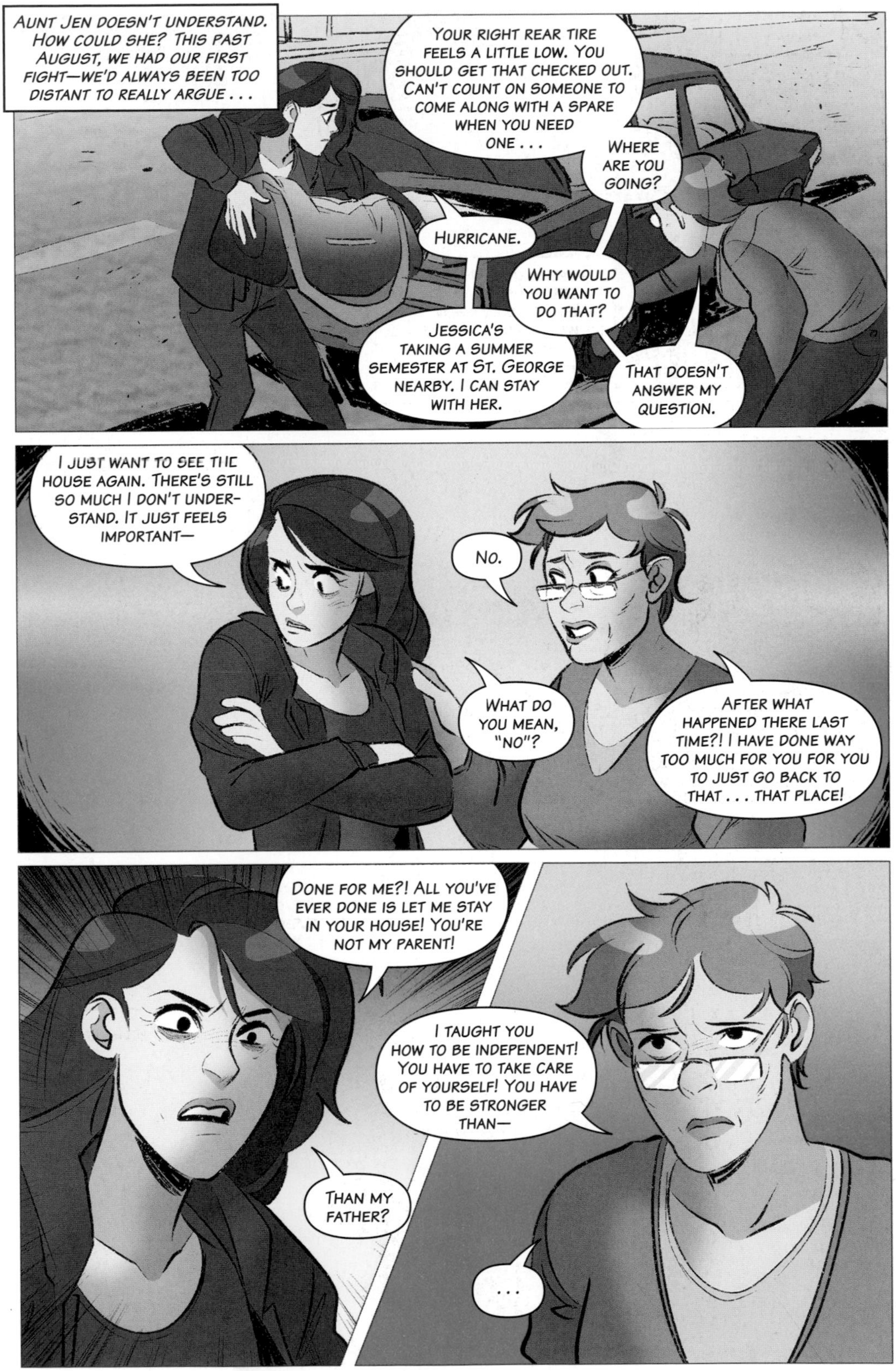
AUNT JEN DOESN'T UNDERSTAND. HOW COULD SHE? THIS PAST AUGUST, WE HAD OUR FIRST FIGHT—WE'D ALWAYS BEEN TOO DISTANT TO REALLY ARGUE . . .
YOUR RIGHT REAR TIRE FEELS A LITTLE LOW. YOU SHOULD GET THAT CHECKED OUT. CAN'T COUNT ON SOMEONE TO COME ALONG WITH A SPARE WHEN YOU NEED ONE . . .
WHERE ARE YOU GOING?
HURRICANE.
WHY WOULD YOU WANT TO DO THAT?
JESSICA'S TAKING A SUMMER SEMESTER AT ST. GEORGE NEARBY. I CAN STAY WITH HER.
THAT DOESN'T ANSWER MY QUESTION.
I JUST WANT TO SEE THE HOUSE AGAIN. THERE'S STILL SO MUCH I DON'T UNDER-STAND. IT JUST FEELS IMPORTANT—
NO.
WHAT DO YOU MEAN, "NO"?
AFTER WHAT HAPPENED THERE LAST TIME?! I HAVE DONE WAY TOO MUCH FOR YOU FOR YOU TO JUST GO BACK TO THAT . . . THAT PLACE!
DONE FOR ME?! ALL YOU'VE EVER DONE IS LET ME STAY IN YOUR HOUSE! YOU'RE NOT MY PARENT!
I TAUGHT YOU HOW TO BE INDEPENDENT! YOU HAVE TO TAKE CARE OF YOURSELF! YOU HAVE TO BE STRONGER THAN—
THAN MY FATHER?
. . .

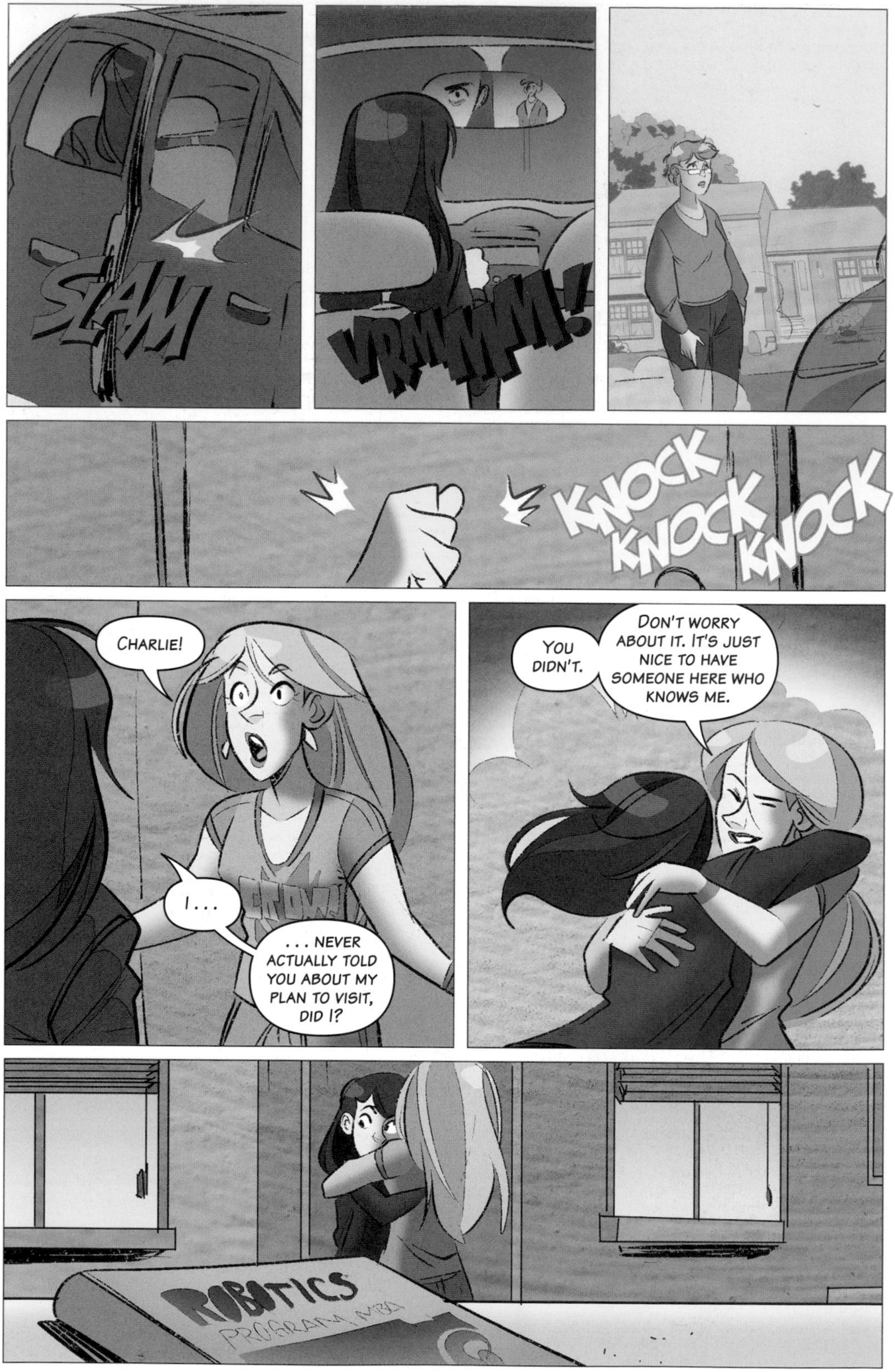
SLAM
VRMMMM!
KNOCK KNOCK KNOCK
CHARLIE!
I . . .
. . . NEVER ACTUALLY TOLD YOU ABOUT MY PLAN TO VISIT, DID I?
YOU DIDN'T.
DON'T WORRY ABOUT IT. IT'S JUST NICE TO HAVE SOMEONE HERE WHO KNOWS ME.
ROBOTICS

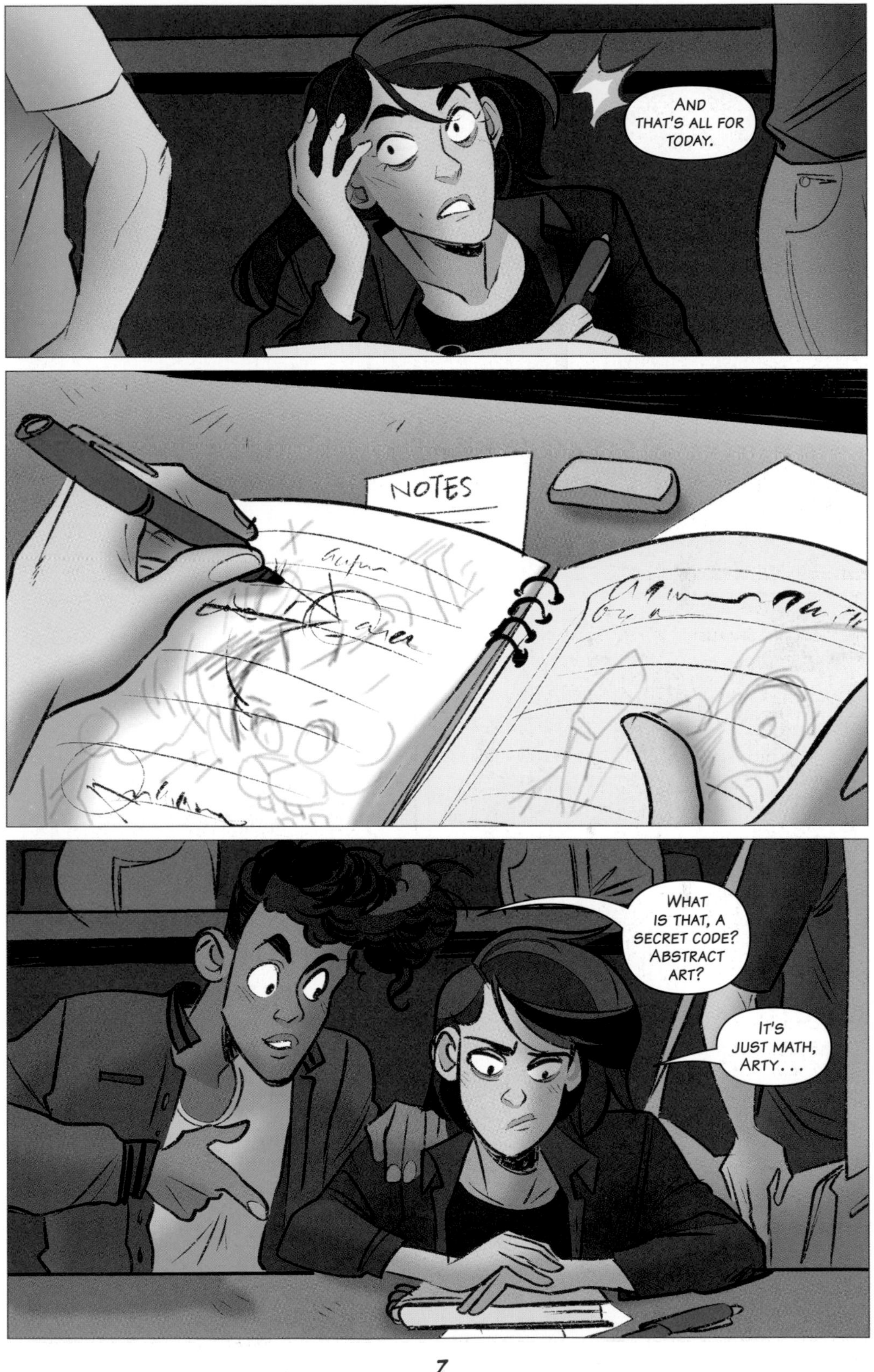
AND THAT'S ALL FOR TODAY.
NOTES
WHAT IS THAT, A SECRET CODE? ABSTRACT ART?
IT'S JUST MATH, ARTY...

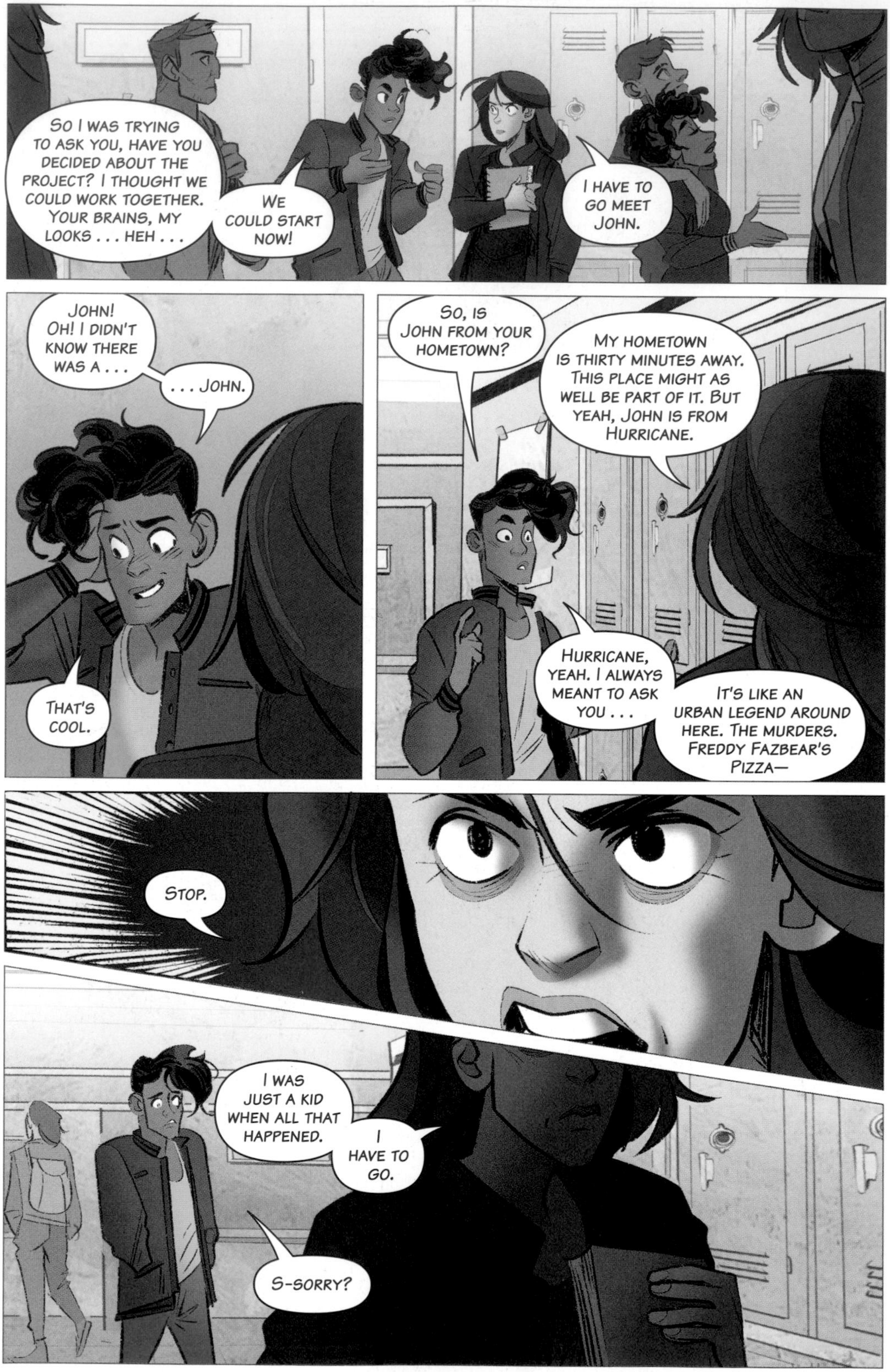
So I was trying to ask you, have you decided about the project? I thought we could work together. Your brains, my looks . . . heh . . .
We could start now!
I have to go meet John.
John! Oh! I didn't know there was a . . .
. . . John.
That's cool.
So, is John from your hometown?
My hometown is thirty minutes away. This place might as well be part of it. But yeah, John is from Hurricane.
Hurricane, yeah. I always meant to ask you . . .
It's like an urban legend around here. The murders. Freddy Fazbear's Pizza—
Stop.
I was just a kid when all that happened.
I have to go.
S-sorry?

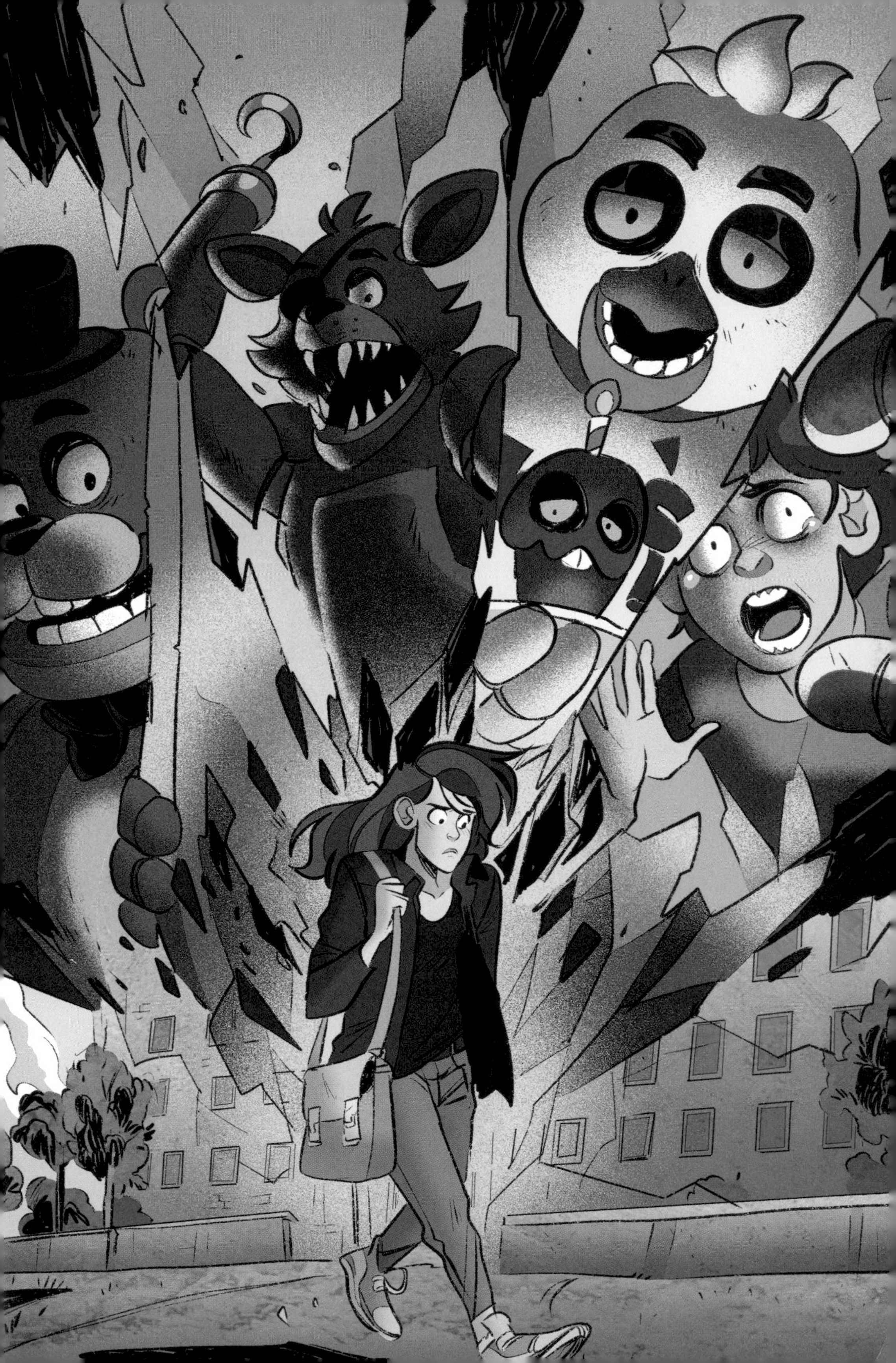

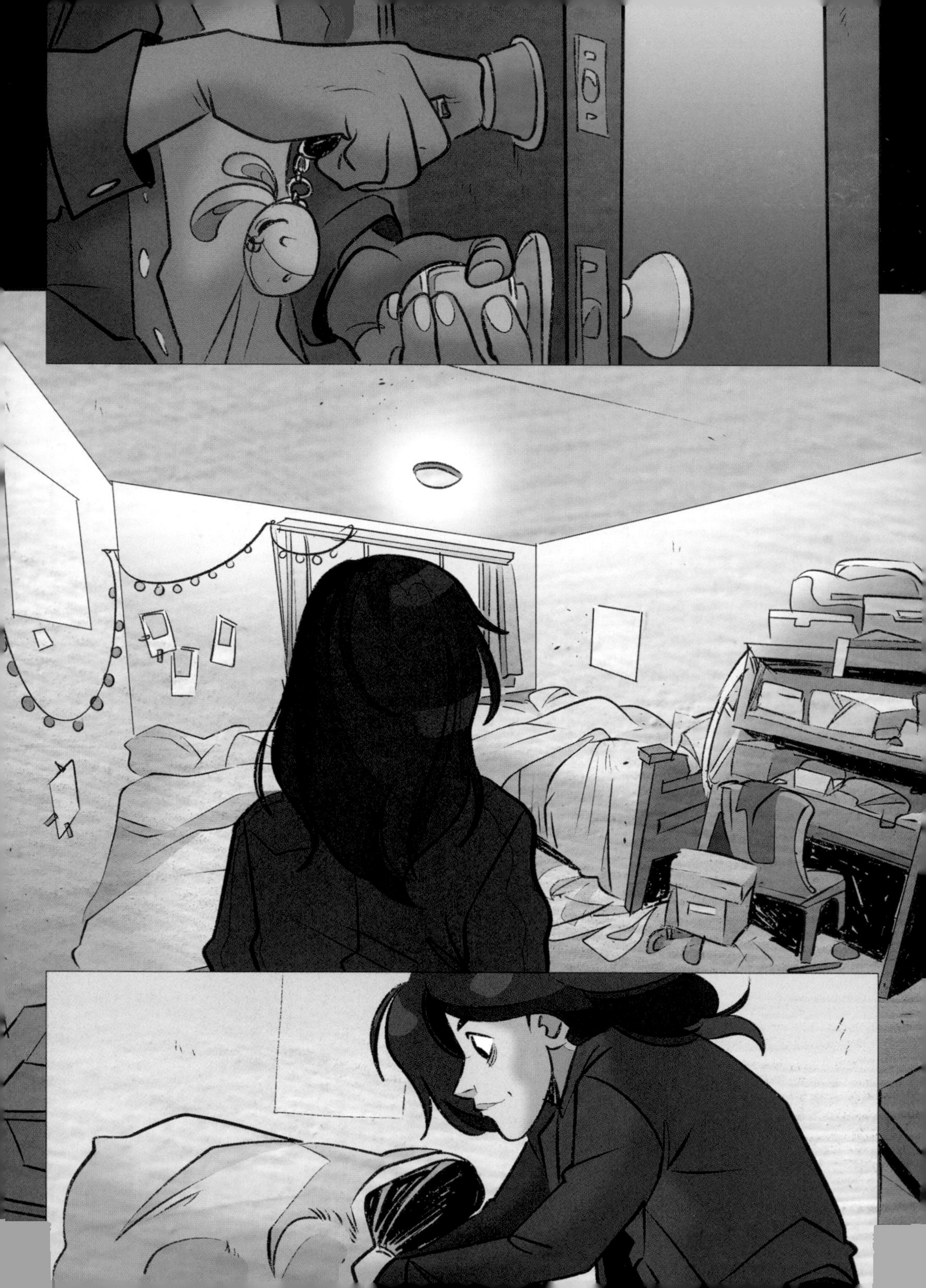

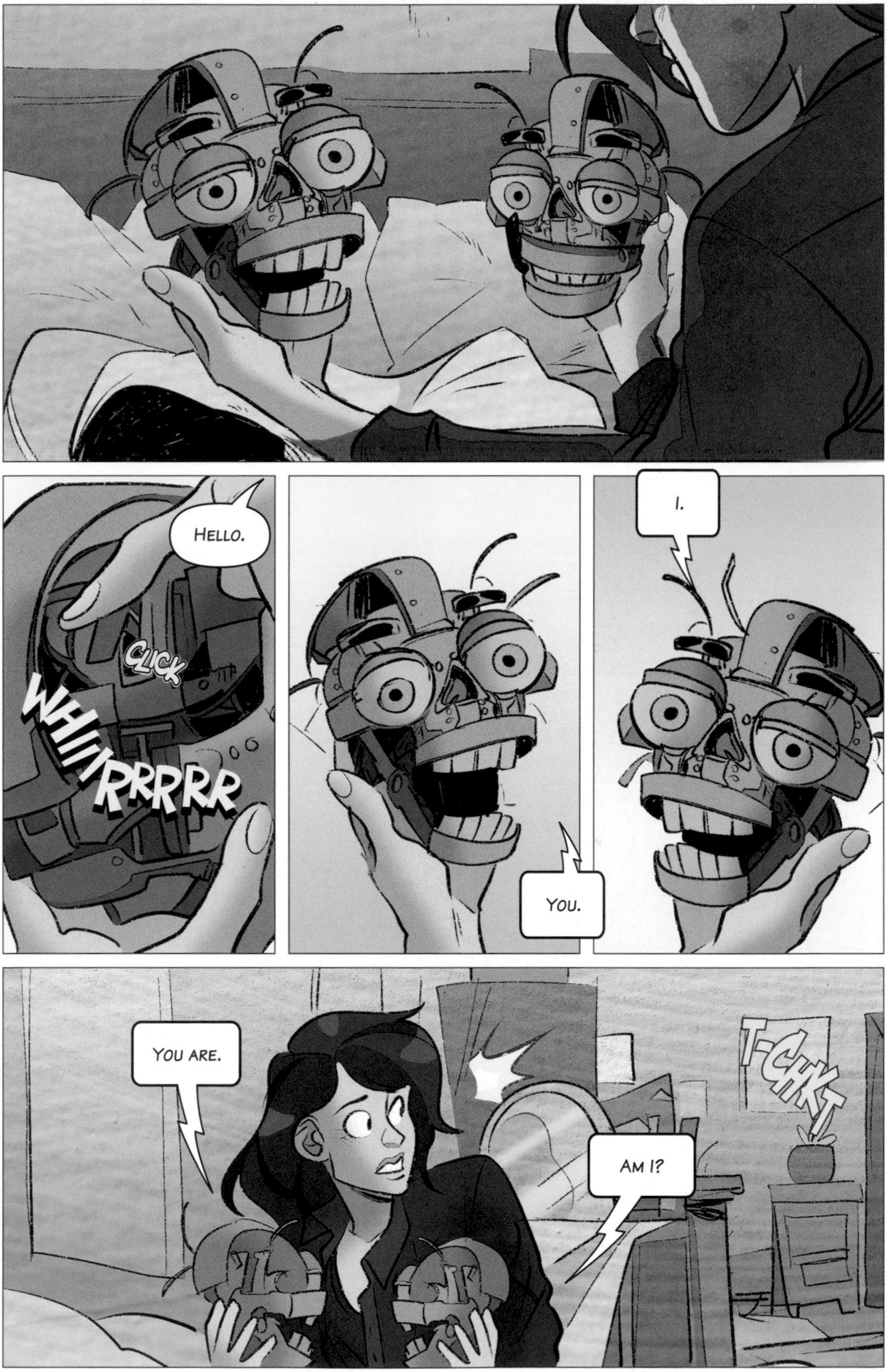
Hello.
CLICK
WHIIIRRRRR
You.
I.
You are.
Am I?
T-CHKT

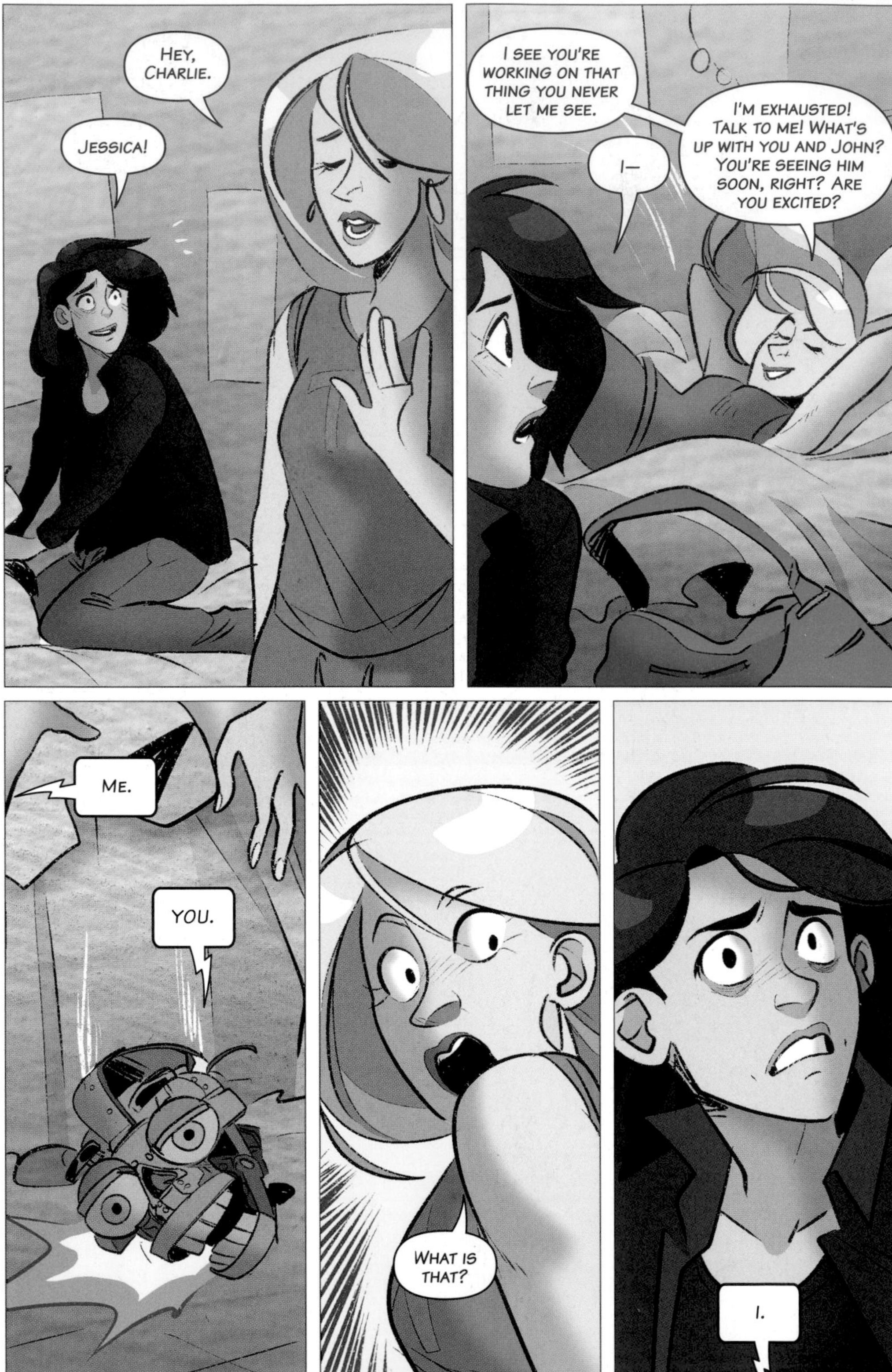
Hey, Charlie.
Jessica!
I see you're working on that thing you never let me see.
I—
I'm exhausted! Talk to me! What's up with you and John? You're seeing him soon, right? Are you excited?
Me.
You.
What is that?
I.

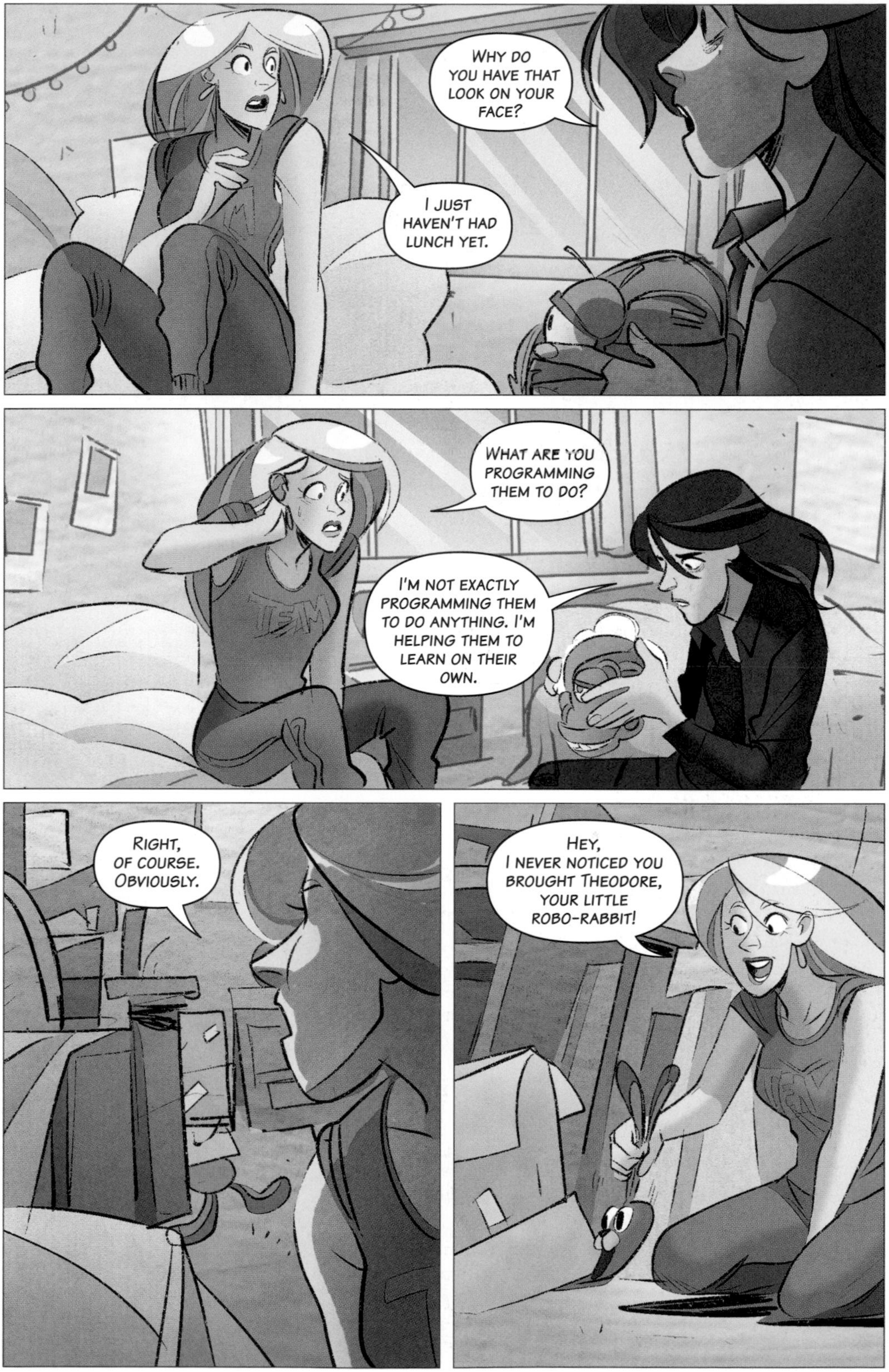
WHY DO YOU HAVE THAT LOOK ON YOUR FACE?
I JUST HAVEN'T HAD LUNCH YET.
WHAT ARE YOU PROGRAMMING THEM TO DO?
I'M NOT EXACTLY PROGRAMMING THEM TO DO ANYTHING. I'M HELPING THEM TO LEARN ON THEIR OWN.
RIGHT, OF COURSE. OBVIOUSLY.
HEY, I NEVER NOTICED YOU BROUGHT THEODORE, YOUR LITTLE ROBO-RABBIT!

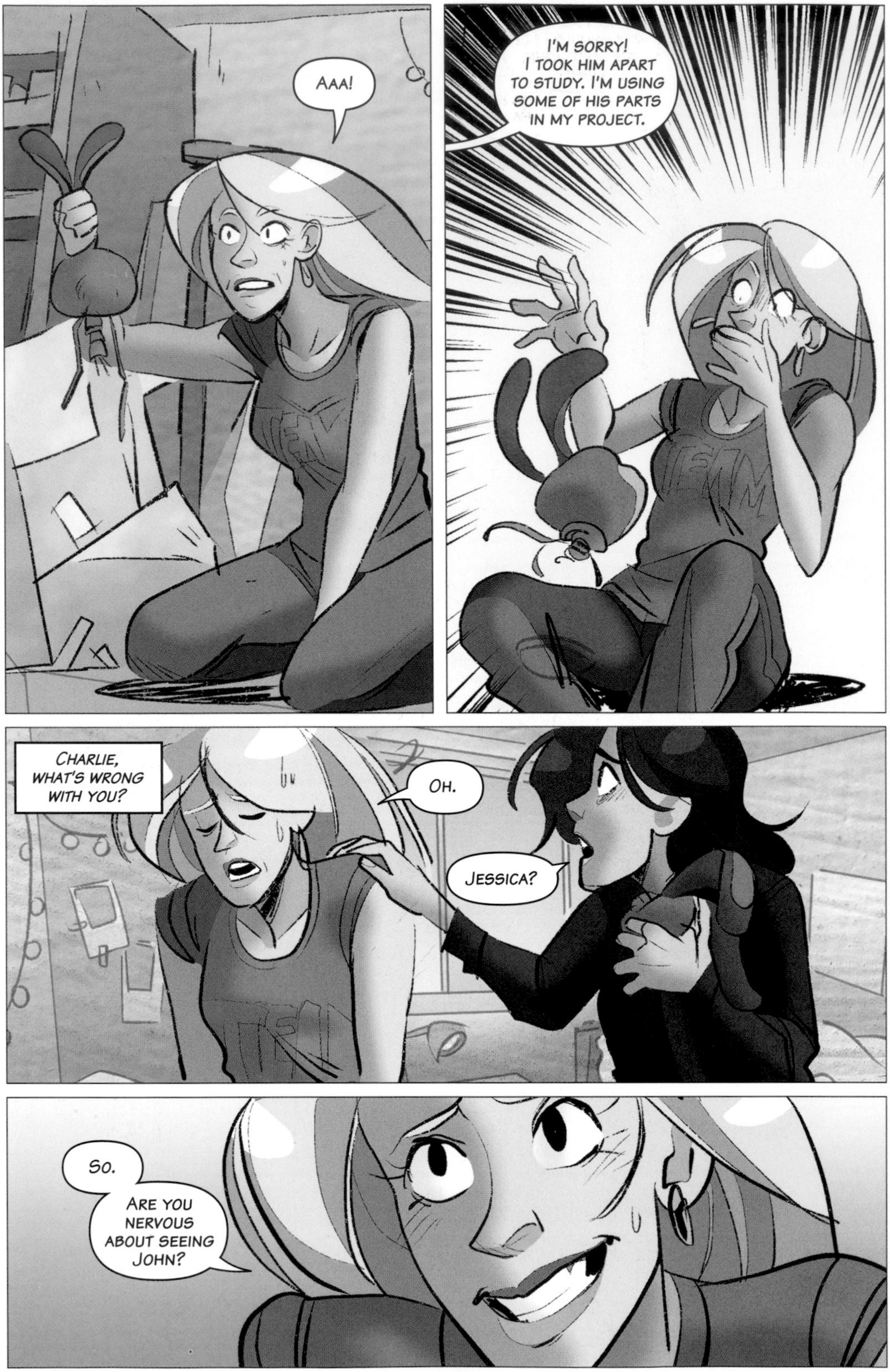
AAA!
I'M SORRY! I TOOK HIM APART TO STUDY. I'M USING SOME OF HIS PARTS IN MY PROJECT.
CHARLIE, WHAT'S WRONG WITH YOU?
OH.
JESSICA?
SO.
ARE YOU NERVOUS ABOUT SEEING JOHN?

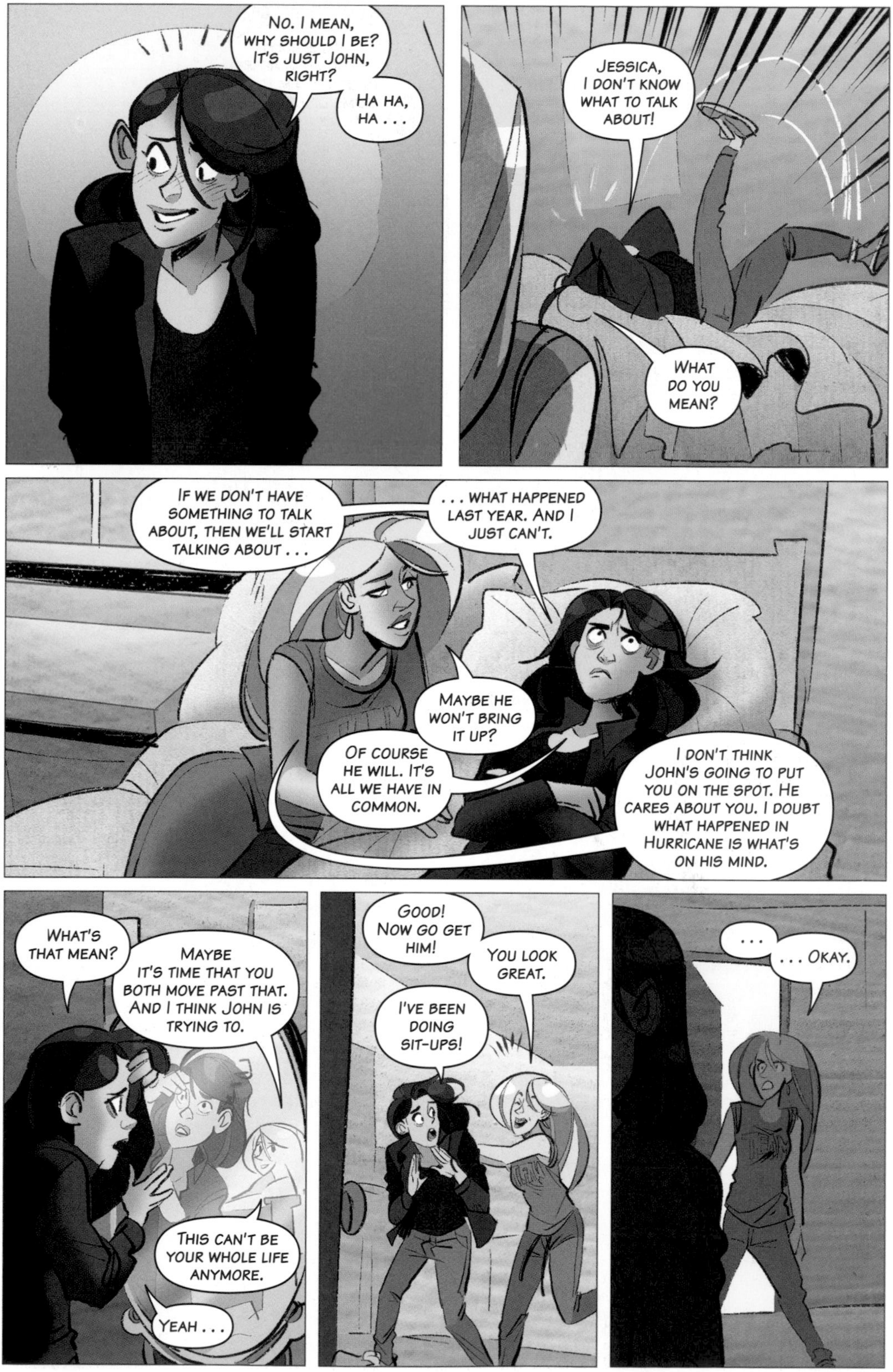
No. I mean, why should I be? It's just John, right?
Ha ha, ha . . .
Jessica, I don't know what to talk about!
What do you mean?
If we don't have something to talk about, then we'll start talking about . . .
. . . what happened last year. And I just can't.
Maybe he won't bring it up?
Of course he will. It's all we have in common.
I don't think John's going to put you on the spot. He cares about you. I doubt what happened in Hurricane is what's on his mind.
What's that mean?
Maybe it's time that you both move past that. And I think John is trying to.
This can't be your whole life anymore.
Yeah . . .
Good! Now go get him!
You look great.
I've been doing sit-ups!
. . .
. . . Okay.

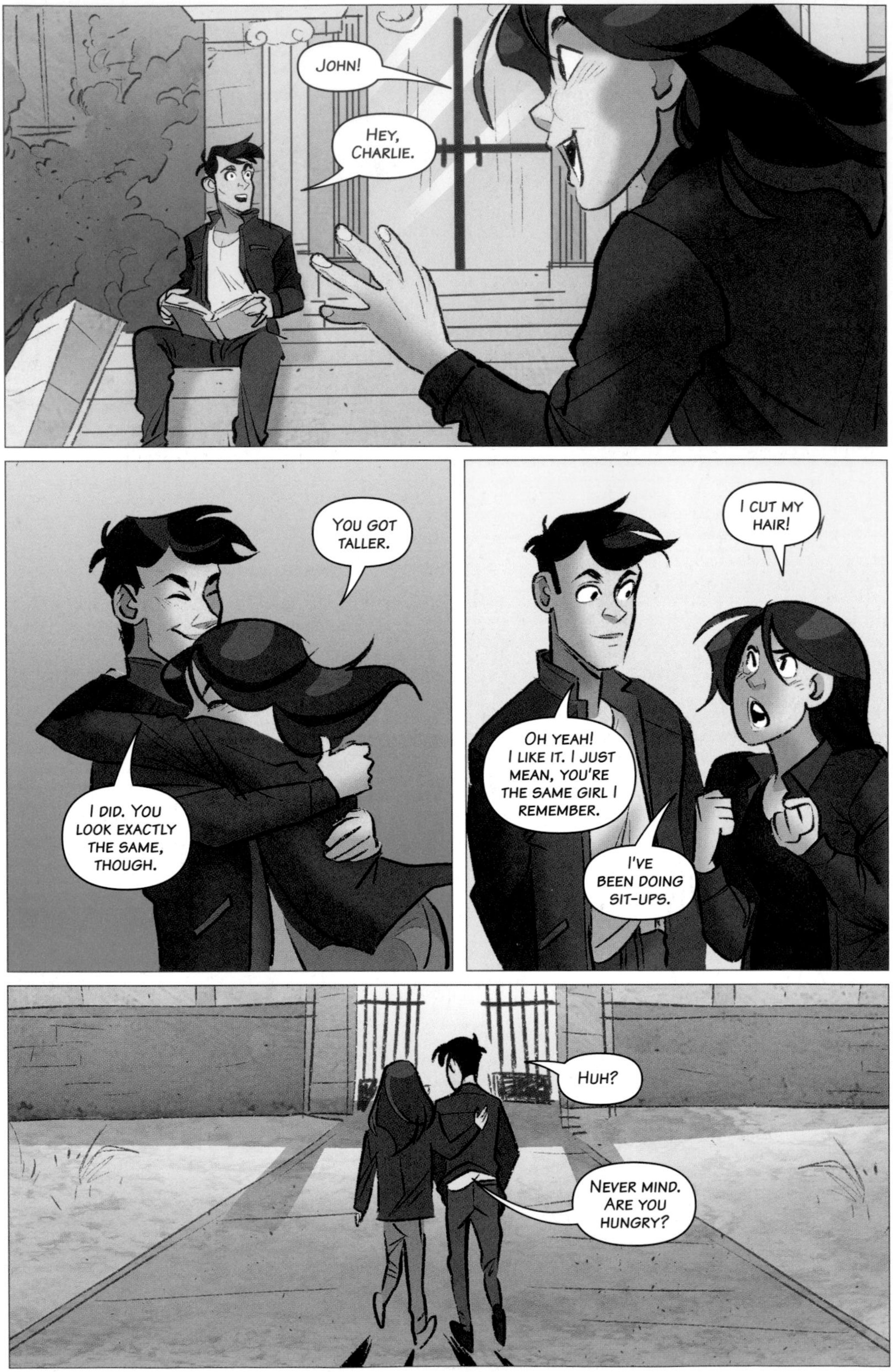
John!
Hey, Charlie.
You got taller.
I did. You look exactly the same, though.
I cut my hair!
Oh yeah! I like it. I just mean, you're the same girl I remember.
I've been doing sit-ups.
Huh?
Never mind. Are you hungry?

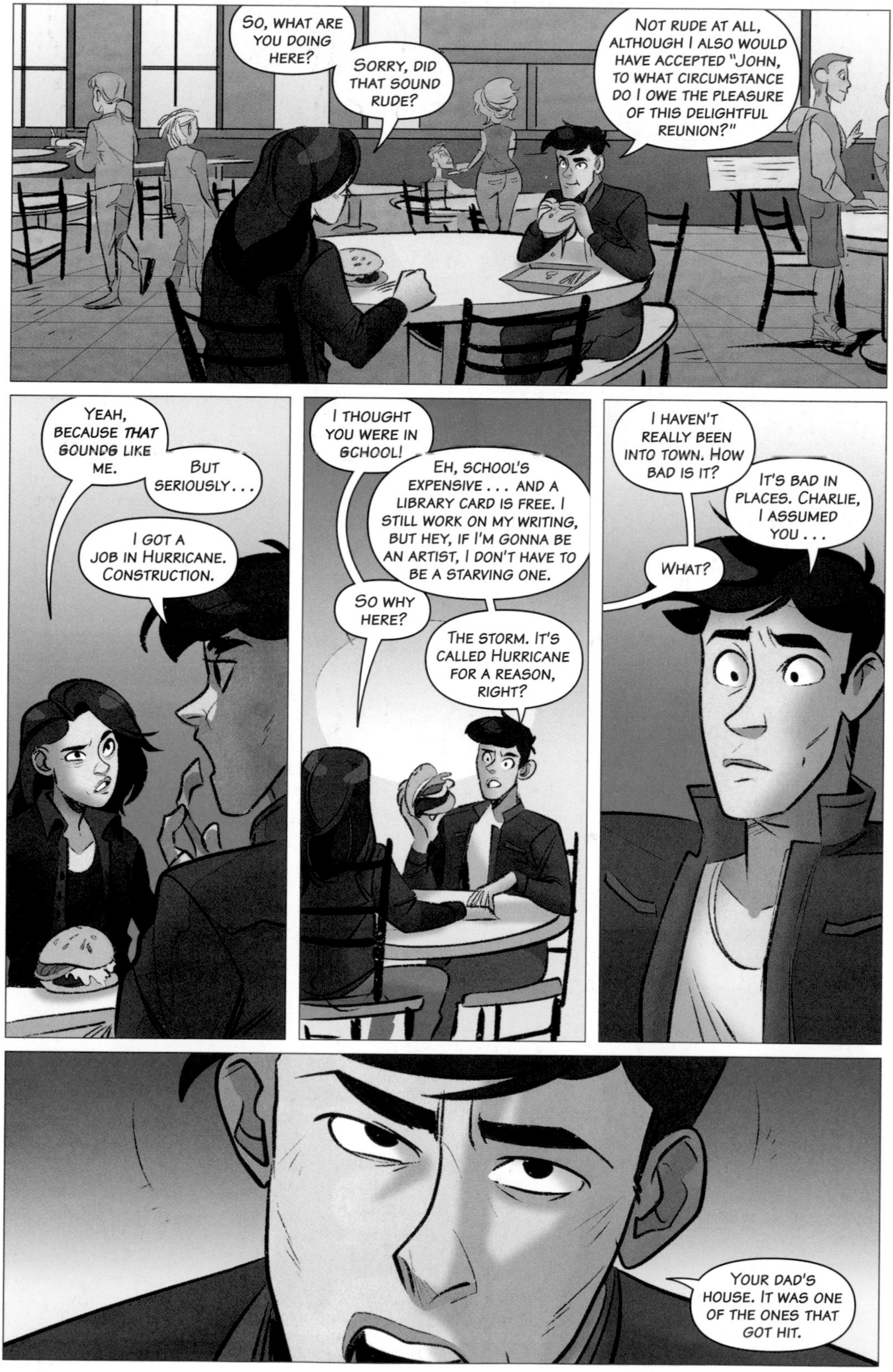
So, what are you doing here?
Sorry, did that sound rude?
Not rude at all, although I also would have accepted "John, to what circumstance do I owe the pleasure of this delightful reunion?"
Yeah, because *that* sounds like me.
But seriously . . .
I got a job in Hurricane. Construction.
I thought you were in school!
Eh, school's expensive . . . and a library card is free. I still work on my writing, but hey, if I'm gonna be an artist, I don't have to be a starving one.
So why here?
The storm. It's called Hurricane for a reason, right?
I haven't really been into town. How bad is it?
It's bad in places. Charlie, I assumed you . . .
What?
Your dad's house. It was one of the ones that got hit.

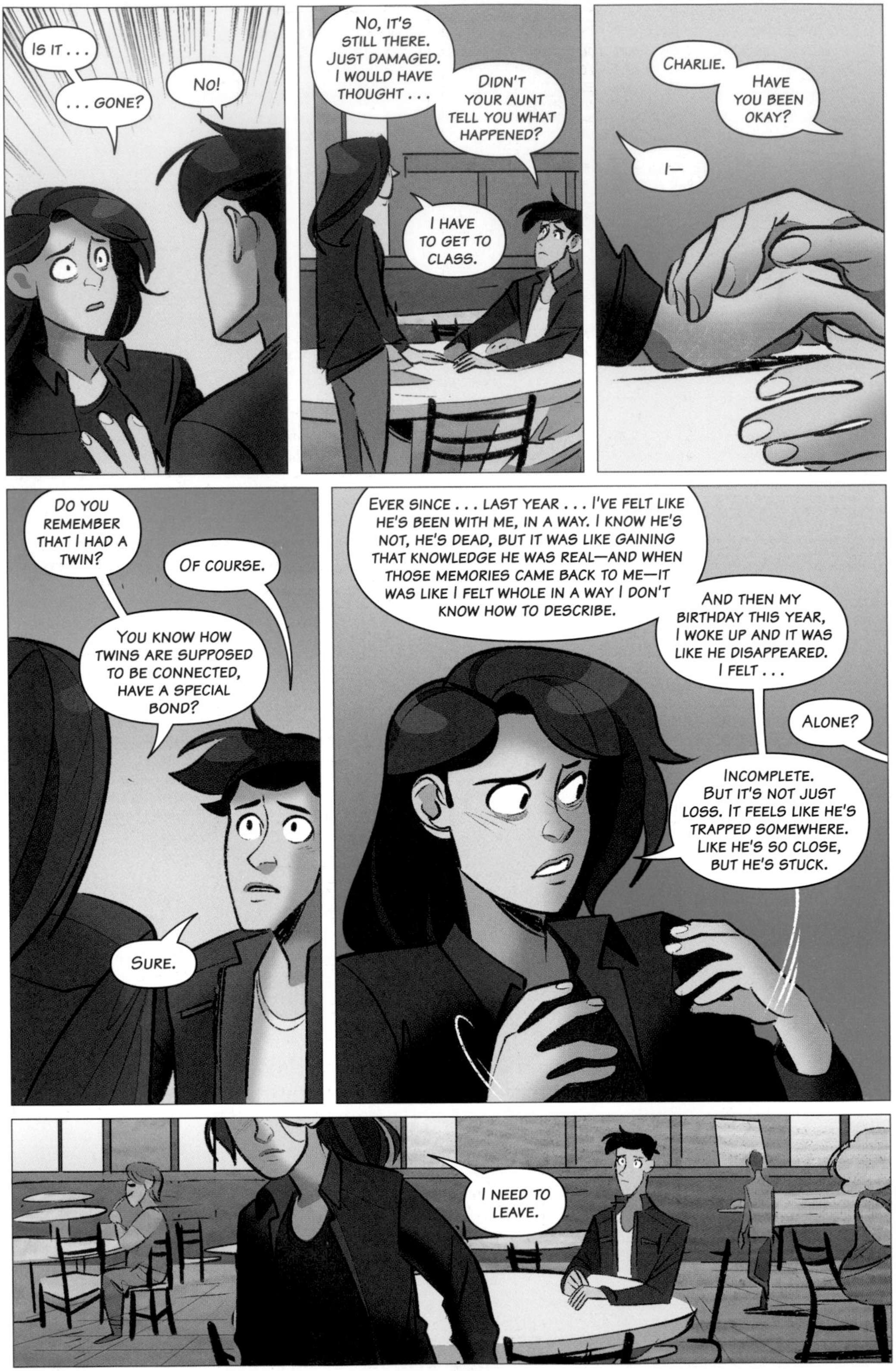
Is it . . .
. . . gone?
No!
No, it's still there. Just damaged. I would have thought . . .
Didn't your aunt tell you what happened?
I have to get to class.
Charlie.
Have you been okay?
I—
Do you remember that I had a twin?
Of course.
You know how twins are supposed to be connected, have a special bond?
Sure.
Ever since . . . last year . . . I've felt like he's been with me, in a way. I know he's not, he's dead, but it was like gaining that knowledge he was real—and when those memories came back to me—it was like I felt whole in a way I don't know how to describe.
And then my birthday this year, I woke up and it was like he disappeared. I felt . . .
Alone?
Incomplete. But it's not just loss. It feels like he's trapped somewhere. Like he's so close, but he's stuck.
I need to leave.

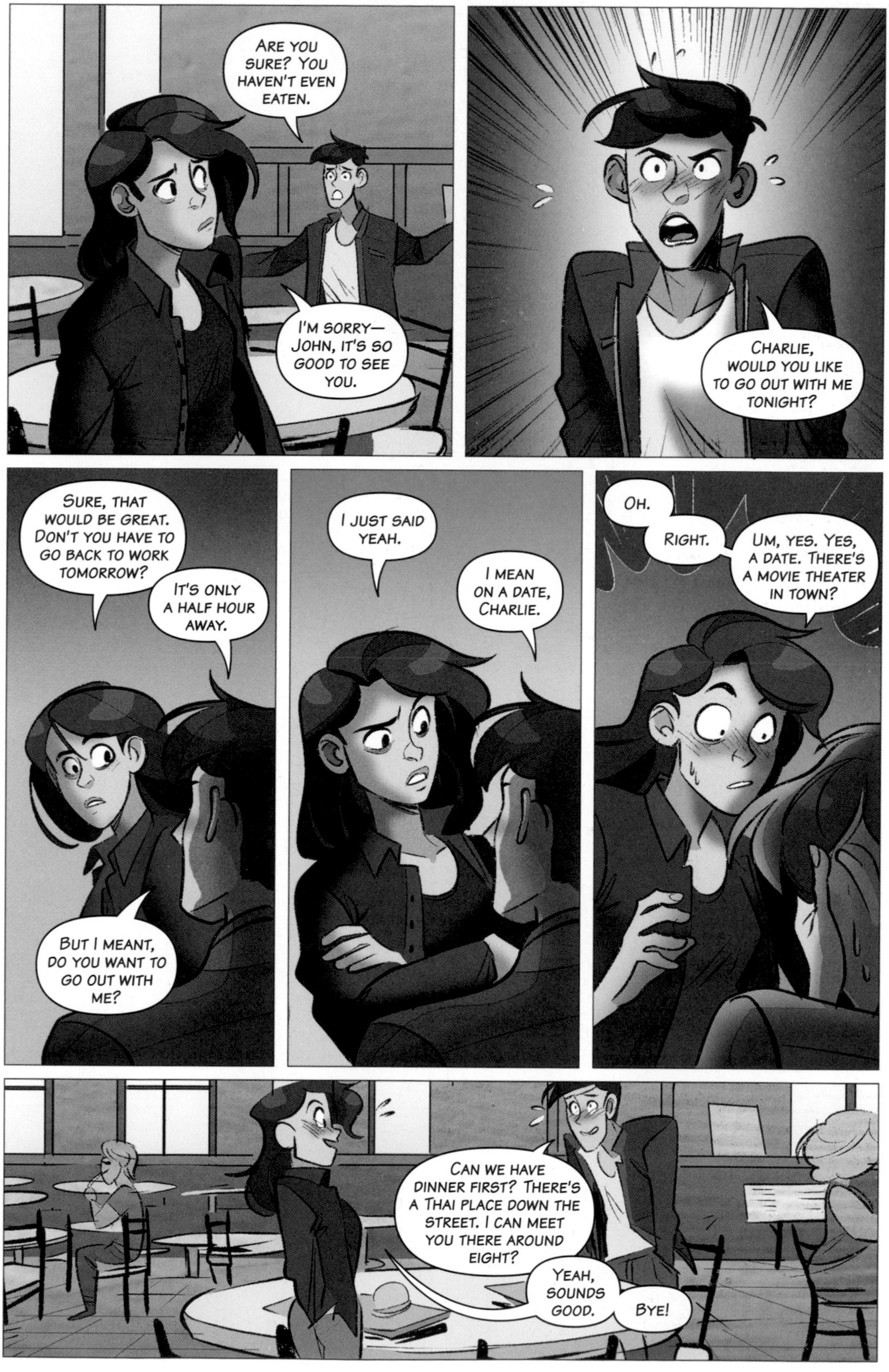

Are you sure? You haven't even eaten.
I'm sorry— John, it's so good to see you.
Charlie, would you like to go out with me tonight?
Sure, that would be great. Don't you have to go back to work tomorrow?
It's only a half hour away.
But I meant, do you want to go out with me?
I just said yeah.
I mean on a date, Charlie.
Oh.
Right.
Um, yes. Yes, a date. There's a movie theater in town?
Can we have dinner first? There's a Thai place down the street. I can meet you there around eight?
Yeah, sounds good.
Bye!

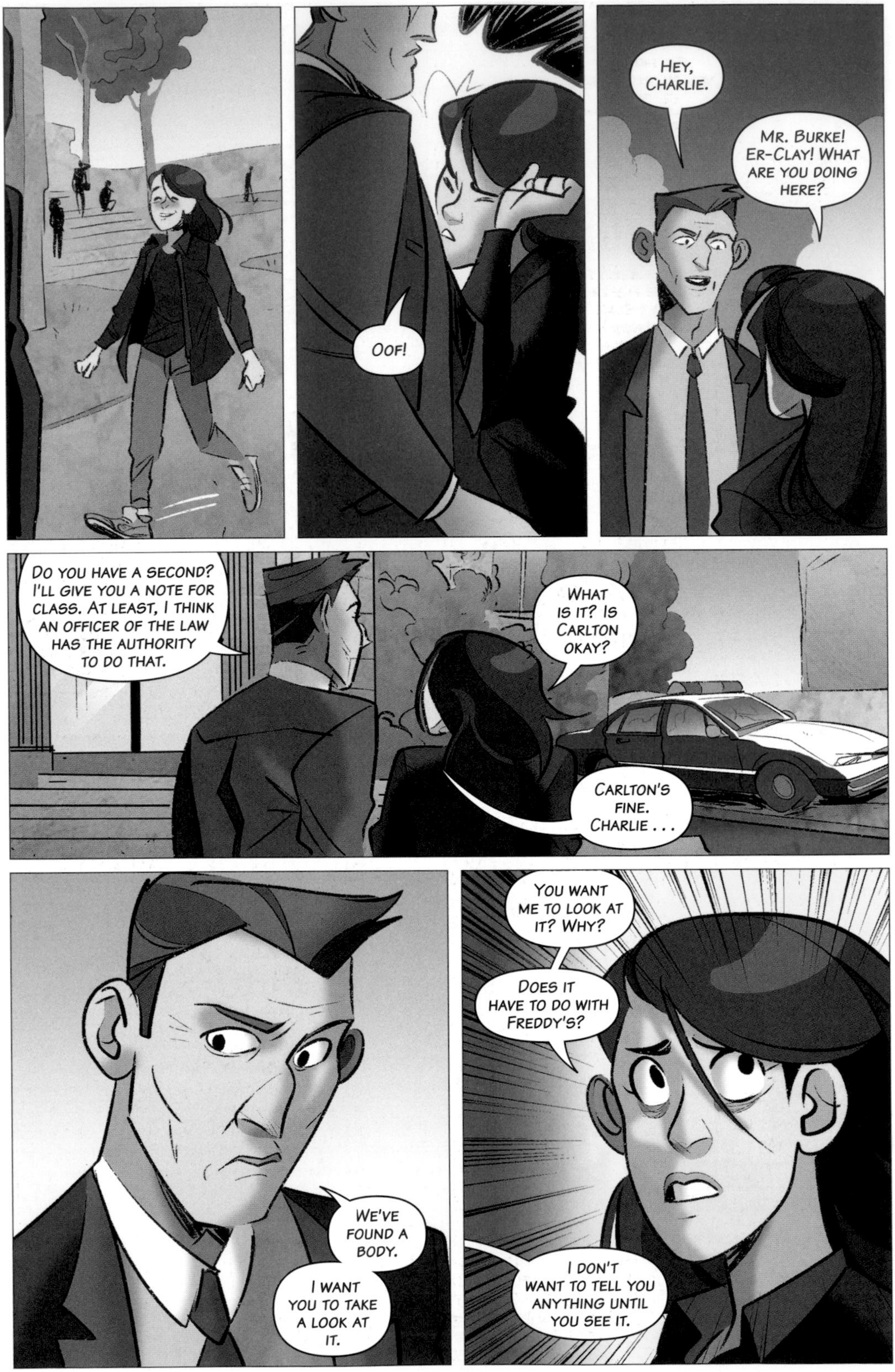
Oof!
Hey, Charlie.
Mr. Burke! Er–Clay! What are you doing here?
Do you have a second? I'll give you a note for class. At least, I think an officer of the law has the authority to do that.
What is it? Is Carlton okay?
Carlton's fine. Charlie . . .
We've found a body.
I want you to take a look at it.
You want me to look at it? Why?
Does it have to do with Freddy's?
I don't want to tell you anything until you see it.

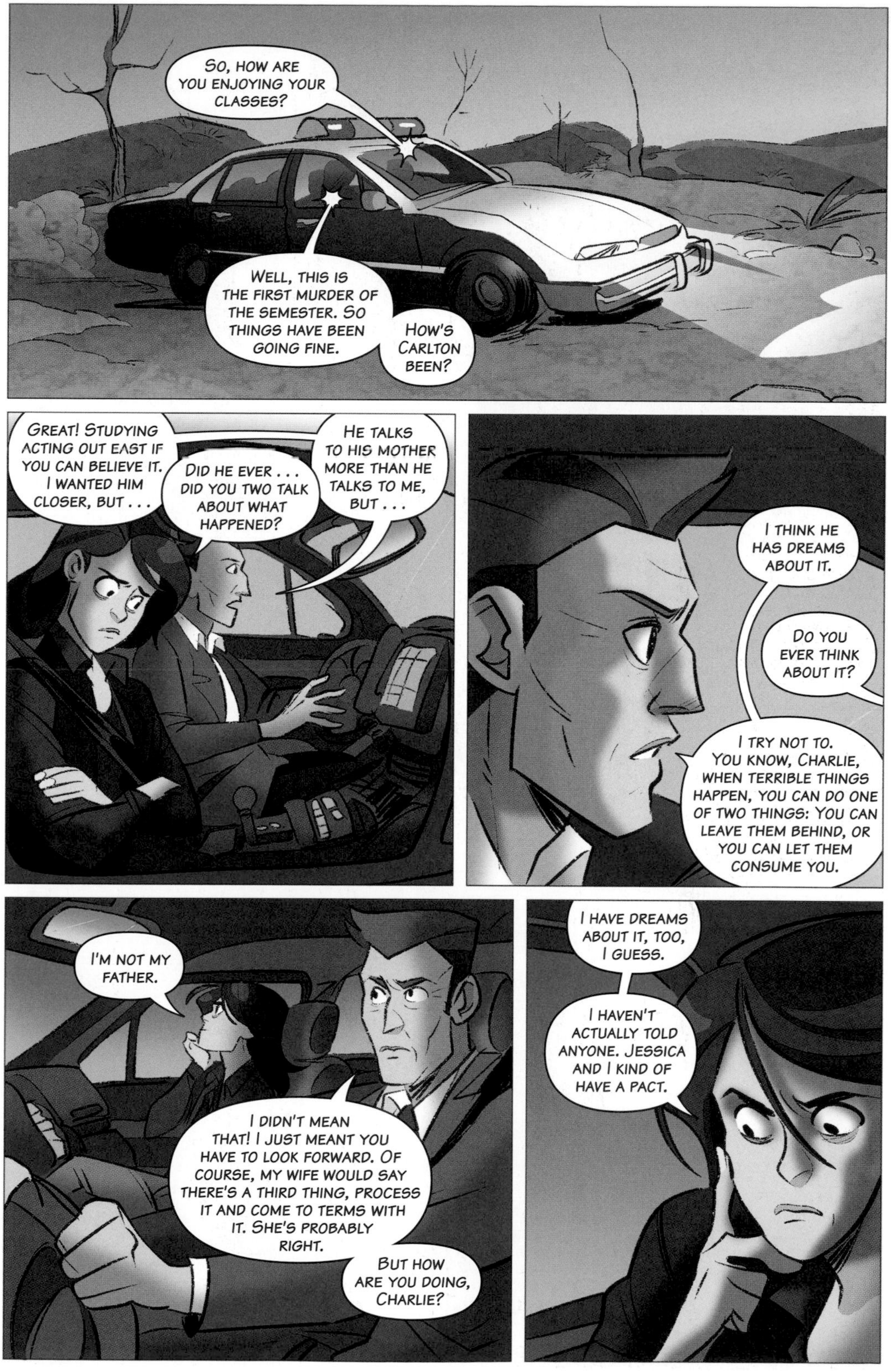
So, how are you enjoying your classes?
Well, this is the first murder of the semester. So things have been going fine.
How's Carlton been?
Great! Studying acting out east if you can believe it. I wanted him closer, but . . .
Did he ever . . . did you two talk about what happened?
He talks to his mother more than he talks to me, but . . .
I think he has dreams about it.
Do you ever think about it?
I try not to. You know, Charlie, when terrible things happen, you can do one of two things: You can leave them behind, or you can let them consume you.
I'm not my father.
I didn't mean that! I just meant you have to look forward. Of course, my wife would say there's a third thing, process it and come to terms with it. She's probably right.
But how are you doing, Charlie?
I have dreams about it, too, I guess.
I haven't actually told anyone. Jessica and I kind of have a pact.

YOU GUESS? WHAT KIND OF DREAMS?

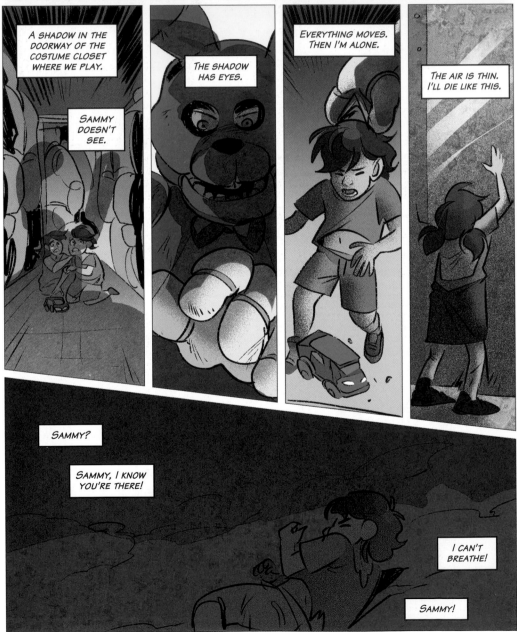

A SHADOW IN THE DOORWAY OF THE COSTUME CLOSET WHERE WE PLAY.

SAMMY DOESN'T SEE.

THE SHADOW HAS EYES.

EVERYTHING MOVES. THEN I'M ALONE.

THE AIR IS THIN. I'LL DIE LIKE THIS.

SAMMY?

SAMMY, I KNOW YOU'RE THERE!

I CAN'T BREATHE!

SAMMY!

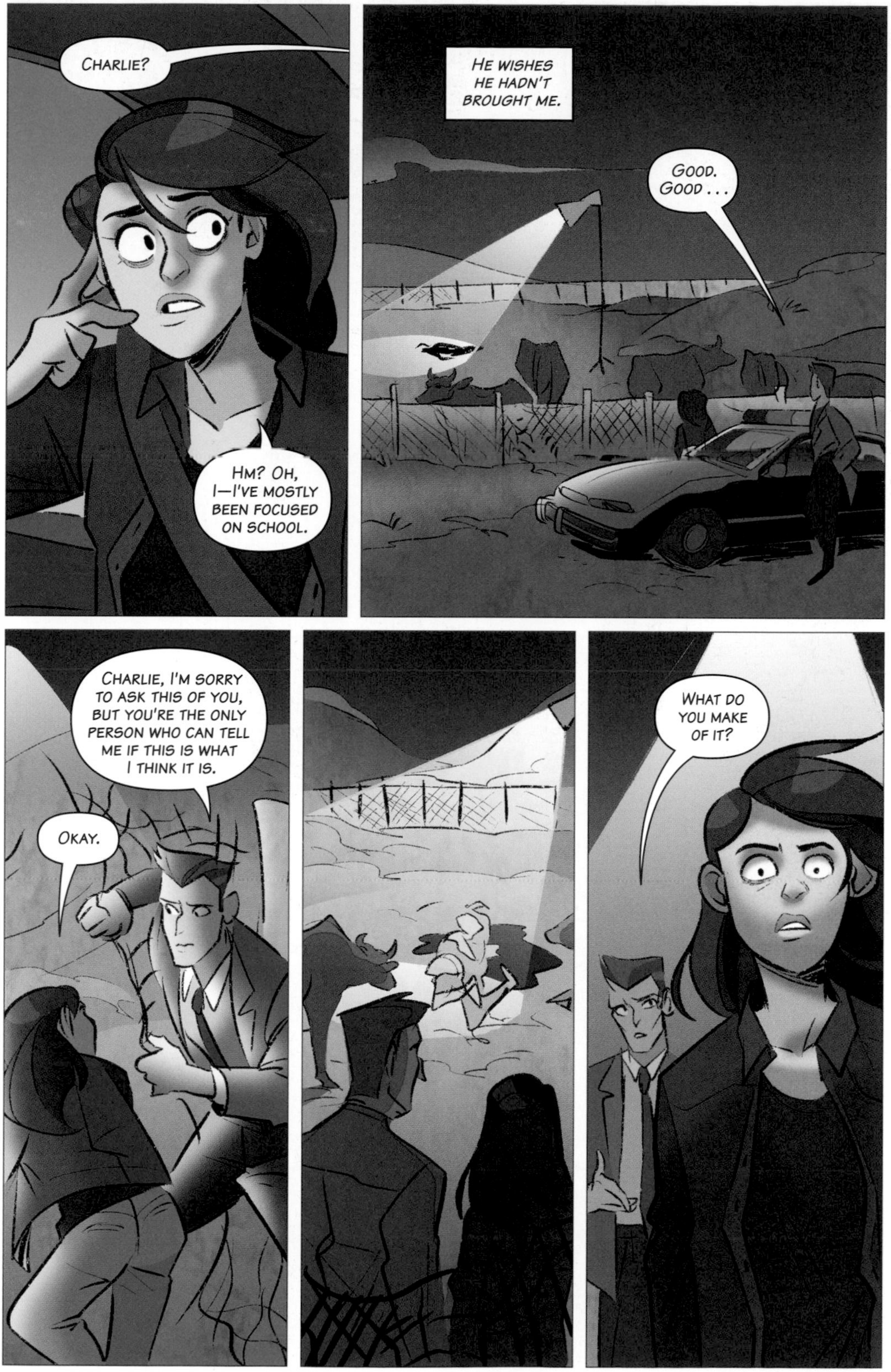
CHARLIE?
HM? OH, I—I'VE MOSTLY BEEN FOCUSED ON SCHOOL.
HE WISHES HE HADN'T BROUGHT ME.
GOOD. GOOD . . .
CHARLIE, I'M SORRY TO ASK THIS OF YOU, BUT YOU'RE THE ONLY PERSON WHO CAN TELL ME IF THIS IS WHAT I THINK IT IS.
OKAY.
WHAT DO YOU MAKE OF IT?

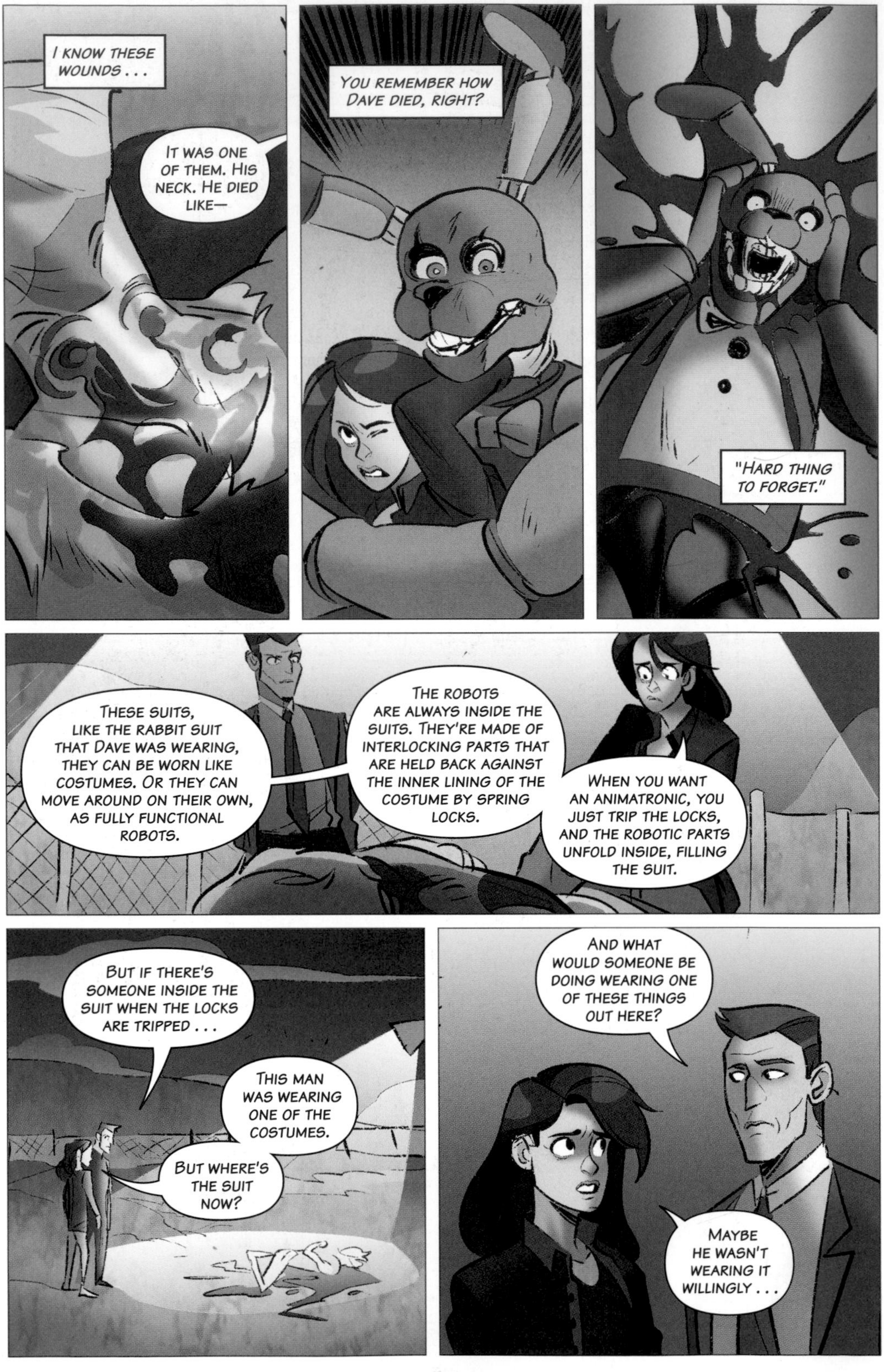
I KNOW THESE WOUNDS . . .
IT WAS ONE OF THEM. HIS NECK. HE DIED LIKE—
YOU REMEMBER HOW DAVE DIED, RIGHT?
"HARD THING TO FORGET."
THESE SUITS, LIKE THE RABBIT SUIT THAT DAVE WAS WEARING, THEY CAN BE WORN LIKE COSTUMES. OR THEY CAN MOVE AROUND ON THEIR OWN, AS FULLY FUNCTIONAL ROBOTS.
THE ROBOTS ARE ALWAYS INSIDE THE SUITS. THEY'RE MADE OF INTERLOCKING PARTS THAT ARE HELD BACK AGAINST THE INNER LINING OF THE COSTUME BY SPRING LOCKS.
WHEN YOU WANT AN ANIMATRONIC, YOU JUST TRIP THE LOCKS, AND THE ROBOTIC PARTS UNFOLD INSIDE, FILLING THE SUIT.
BUT IF THERE'S SOMEONE INSIDE THE SUIT WHEN THE LOCKS ARE TRIPPED . . .
THIS MAN WAS WEARING ONE OF THE COSTUMES.
BUT WHERE'S THE SUIT NOW?
AND WHAT WOULD SOMEONE BE DOING WEARING ONE OF THESE THINGS OUT HERE?
MAYBE HE WASN'T WEARING IT WILLINGLY . . .

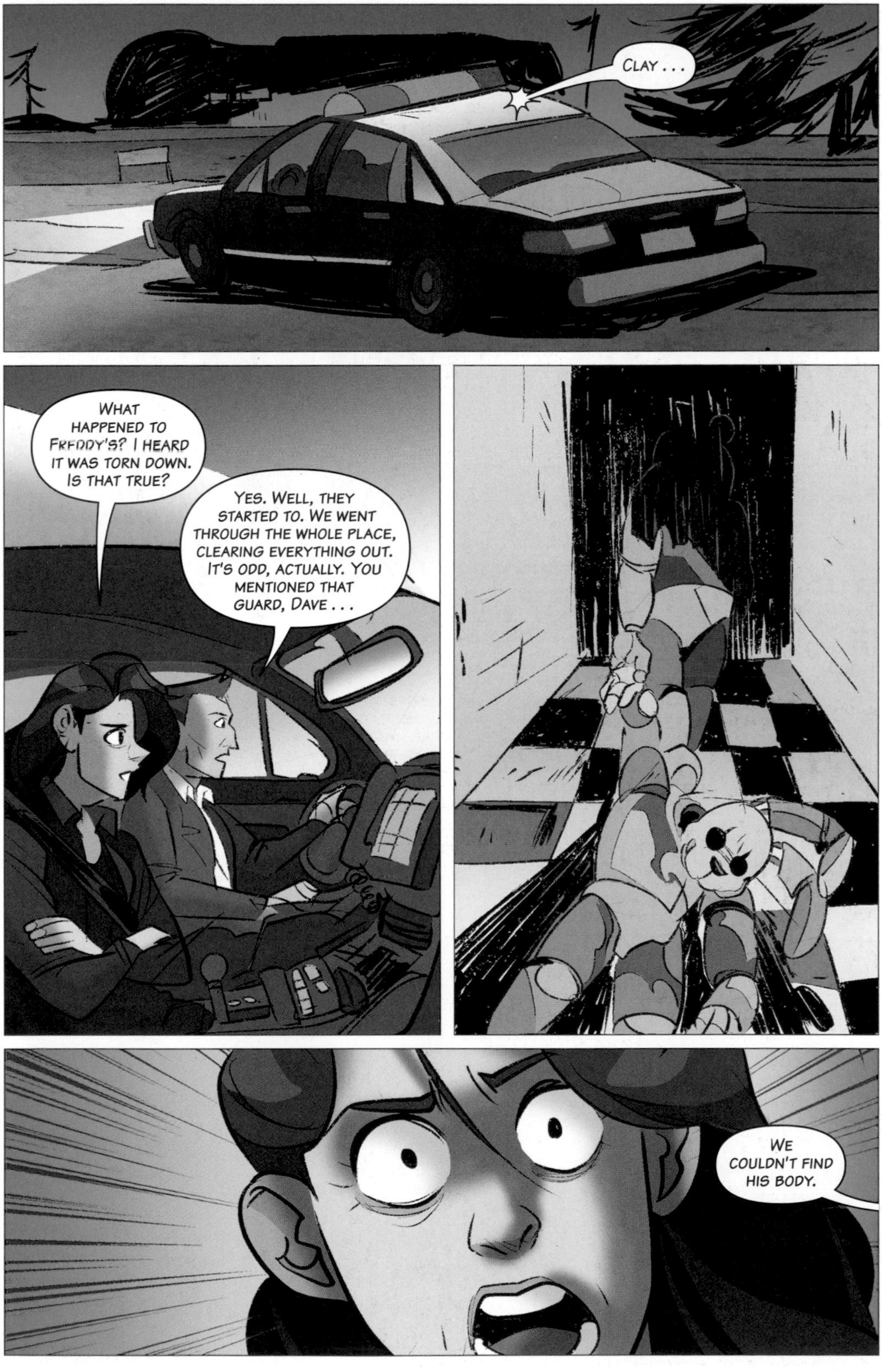

CLAY . . .
WHAT HAPPENED TO FREDDY'S? I HEARD IT WAS TORN DOWN. IS THAT TRUE?
YES. WELL, THEY STARTED TO. WE WENT THROUGH THE WHOLE PLACE, CLEARING EVERYTHING OUT. IT'S ODD, ACTUALLY. YOU MENTIONED THAT GUARD, DAVE . . .
WE COULDN'T FIND HIS BODY.

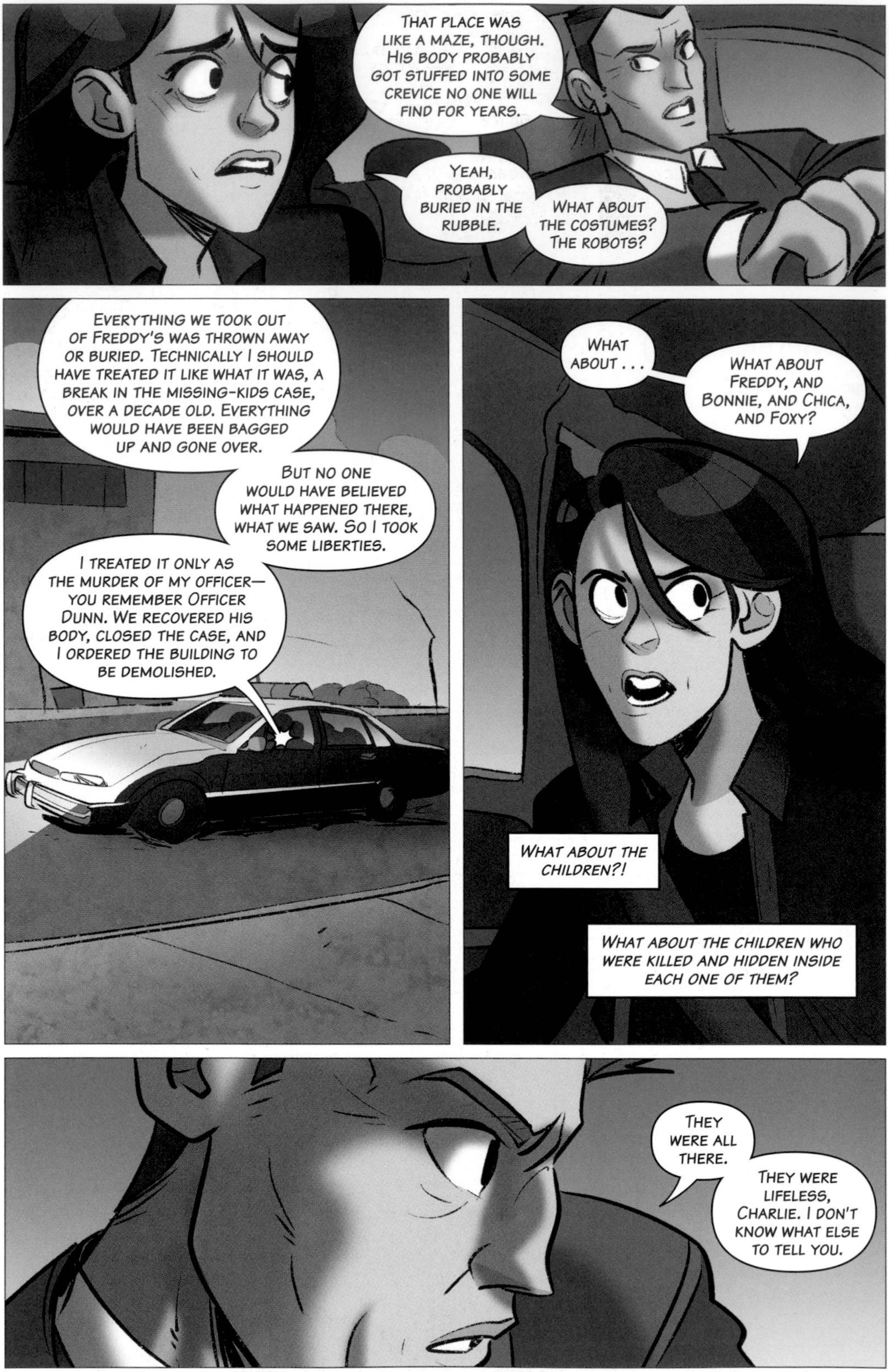
THAT PLACE WAS LIKE A MAZE, THOUGH. HIS BODY PROBABLY GOT STUFFED INTO SOME CREVICE NO ONE WILL FIND FOR YEARS.
YEAH, PROBABLY BURIED IN THE RUBBLE.
WHAT ABOUT THE COSTUMES? THE ROBOTS?
EVERYTHING WE TOOK OUT OF FREDDY'S WAS THROWN AWAY OR BURIED. TECHNICALLY I SHOULD HAVE TREATED IT LIKE WHAT IT WAS, A BREAK IN THE MISSING-KIDS CASE, OVER A DECADE OLD. EVERYTHING WOULD HAVE BEEN BAGGED UP AND GONE OVER.
BUT NO ONE WOULD HAVE BELIEVED WHAT HAPPENED THERE, WHAT WE SAW. SO I TOOK SOME LIBERTIES.
I TREATED IT ONLY AS THE MURDER OF MY OFFICER—YOU REMEMBER OFFICER DUNN. WE RECOVERED HIS BODY, CLOSED THE CASE, AND I ORDERED THE BUILDING TO BE DEMOLISHED.
WHAT ABOUT . . .
WHAT ABOUT FREDDY, AND BONNIE, AND CHICA, AND FOXY?
WHAT ABOUT THE CHILDREN?!
WHAT ABOUT THE CHILDREN WHO WERE KILLED AND HIDDEN INSIDE EACH ONE OF THEM?
THEY WERE ALL THERE.
THEY WERE LIFELESS, CHARLIE. I DON'T KNOW WHAT ELSE TO TELL YOU.

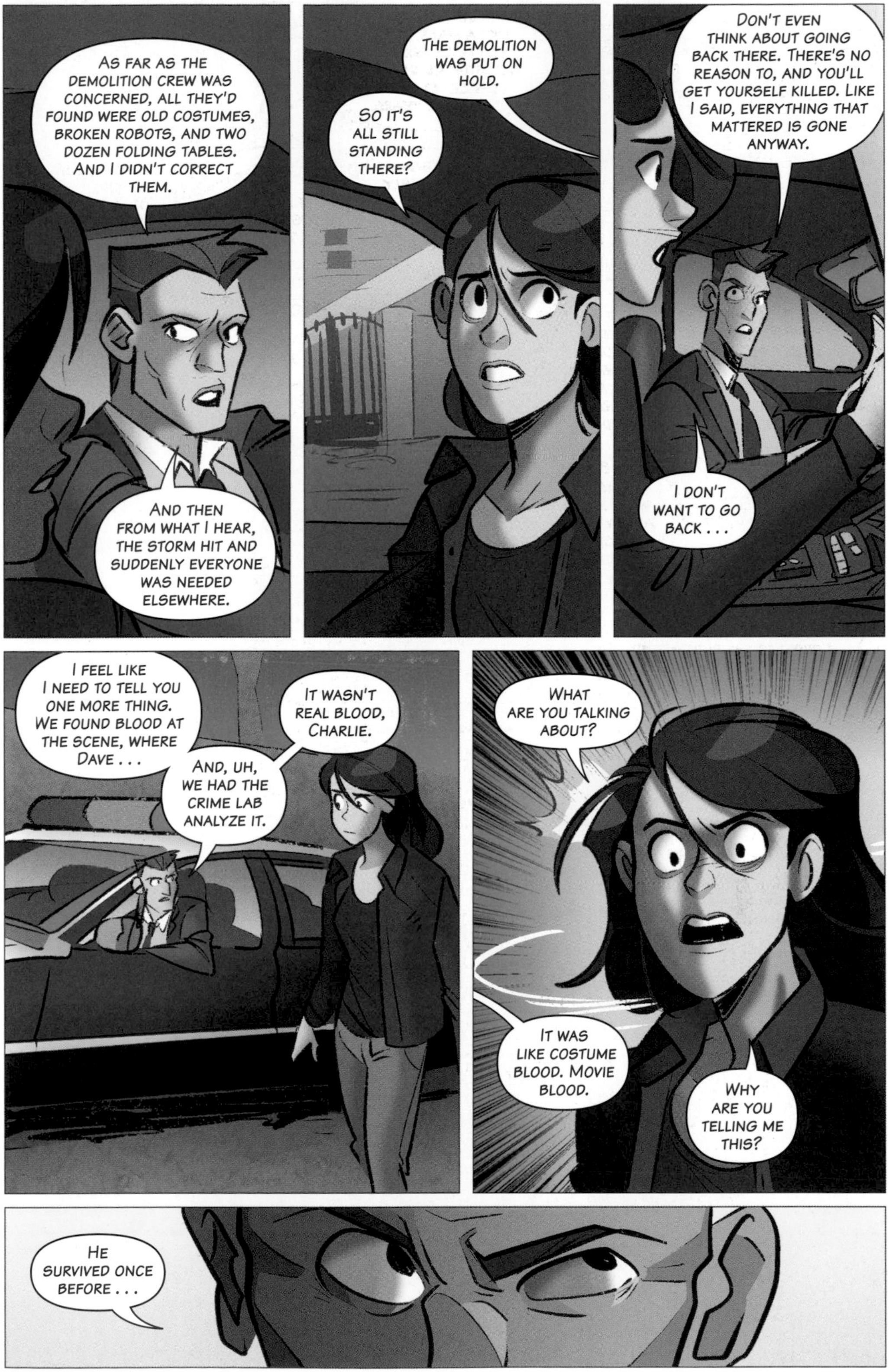

As far as the demolition crew was concerned, all they'd found were old costumes, broken robots, and two dozen folding tables. And I didn't correct them.
And then from what I hear, the storm hit and suddenly everyone was needed elsewhere.
The demolition was put on hold.
So it's all still standing there?
Don't even think about going back there. There's no reason to, and you'll get yourself killed. Like I said, everything that mattered is gone anyway.
I don't want to go back . . .
I feel like I need to tell you one more thing. We found blood at the scene, where Dave . . .
And, uh, we had the crime lab analyze it.
It wasn't real blood, Charlie.
What are you talking about?
It was like costume blood. Movie blood.
Why are you telling me this?
He survived once before . . .

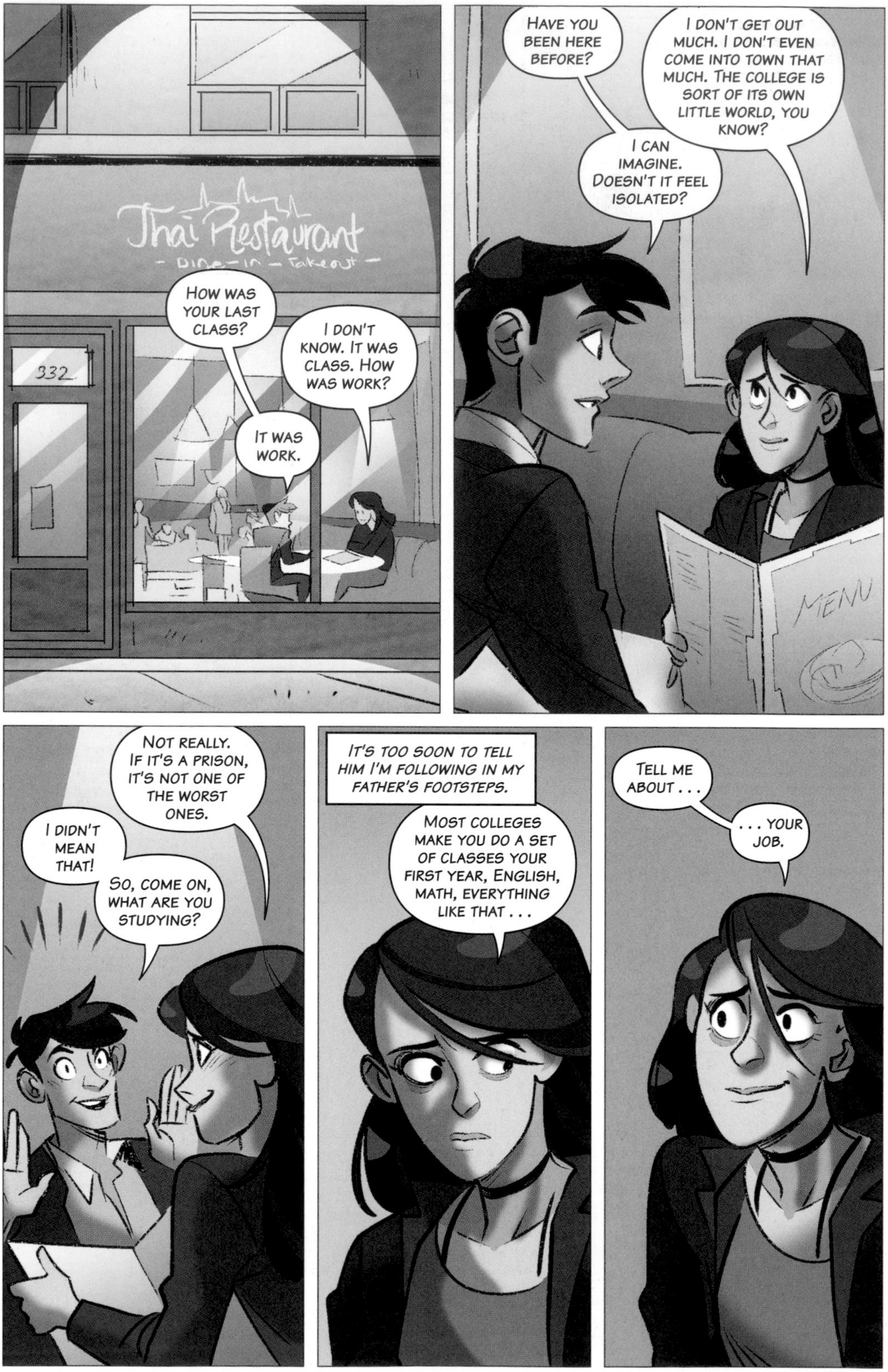
Thai Restaurant
- Dine-in - Takeout -
332
HOW WAS YOUR LAST CLASS?
I DON'T KNOW. IT WAS CLASS. HOW WAS WORK?
IT WAS WORK.
HAVE YOU BEEN HERE BEFORE?
I DON'T GET OUT MUCH. I DON'T EVEN COME INTO TOWN THAT MUCH. THE COLLEGE IS SORT OF ITS OWN LITTLE WORLD, YOU KNOW?
I CAN IMAGINE. DOESN'T IT FEEL ISOLATED?
MENU
NOT REALLY. IF IT'S A PRISON, IT'S NOT ONE OF THE WORST ONES.
I DIDN'T MEAN THAT!
SO, COME ON, WHAT ARE YOU STUDYING?
IT'S TOO SOON TO TELL HIM I'M FOLLOWING IN MY FATHER'S FOOTSTEPS.
MOST COLLEGES MAKE YOU DO A SET OF CLASSES YOUR FIRST YEAR, ENGLISH, MATH, EVERYTHING LIKE THAT . . .
TELL ME ABOUT . . .
. . . YOUR JOB.

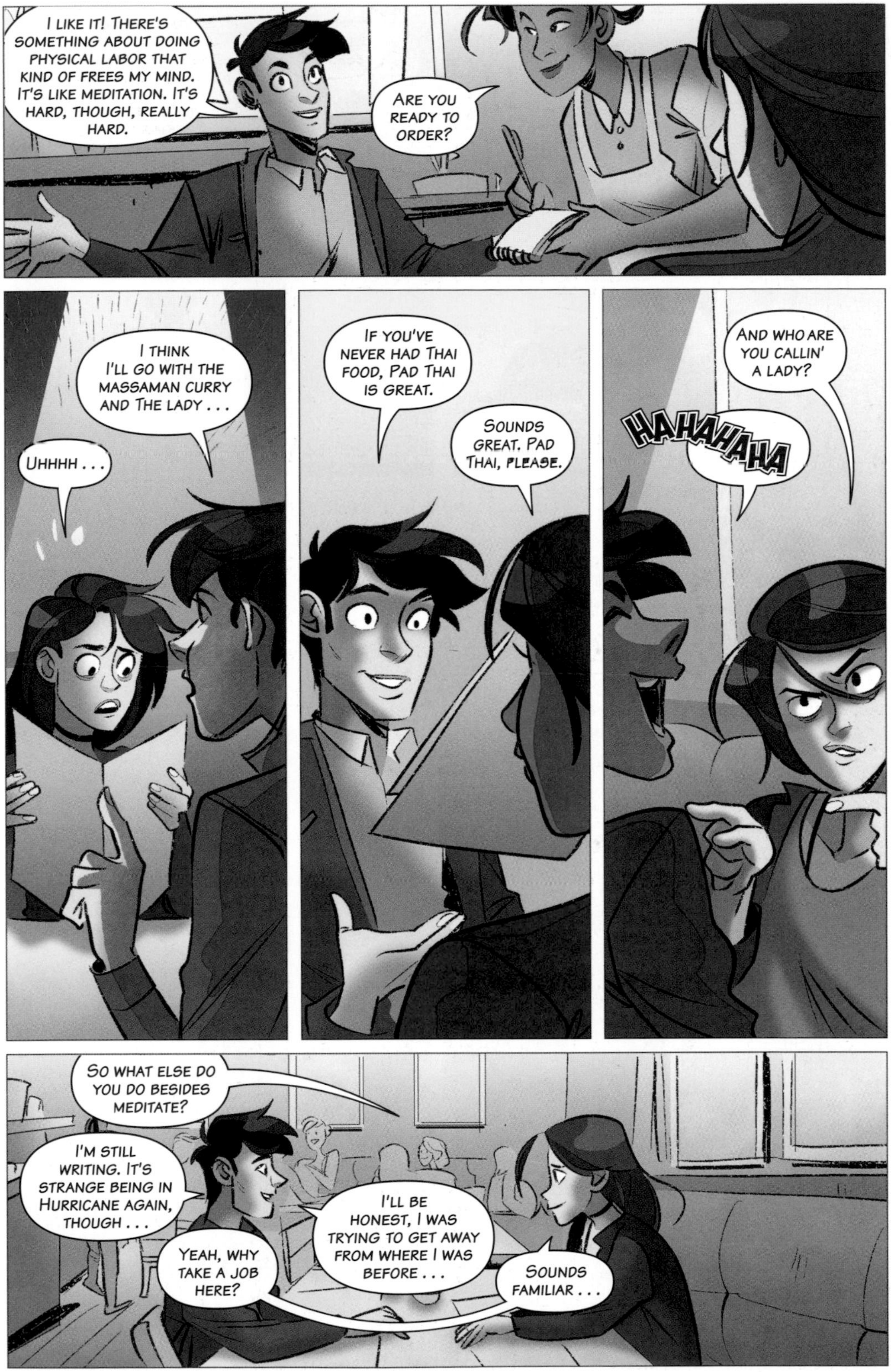
I LIKE IT! THERE'S SOMETHING ABOUT DOING PHYSICAL LABOR THAT KIND OF FREES MY MIND. IT'S LIKE MEDITATION. IT'S HARD, THOUGH, REALLY HARD.
ARE YOU READY TO ORDER?
I THINK I'LL GO WITH THE MASSAMAN CURRY AND THE LADY . . .
UHHHH . . .
IF YOU'VE NEVER HAD THAI FOOD, PAD THAI IS GREAT.
SOUNDS GREAT. PAD THAI, PLEASE.
AND WHO ARE YOU CALLIN' A LADY?
HAHAHAHA
SO WHAT ELSE DO YOU DO BESIDES MEDITATE?
I'M STILL WRITING. IT'S STRANGE BEING IN HURRICANE AGAIN, THOUGH . . .
YEAH, WHY TAKE A JOB HERE?
I'LL BE HONEST, I WAS TRYING TO GET AWAY FROM WHERE I WAS BEFORE . . .
SOUNDS FAMILIAR . . .

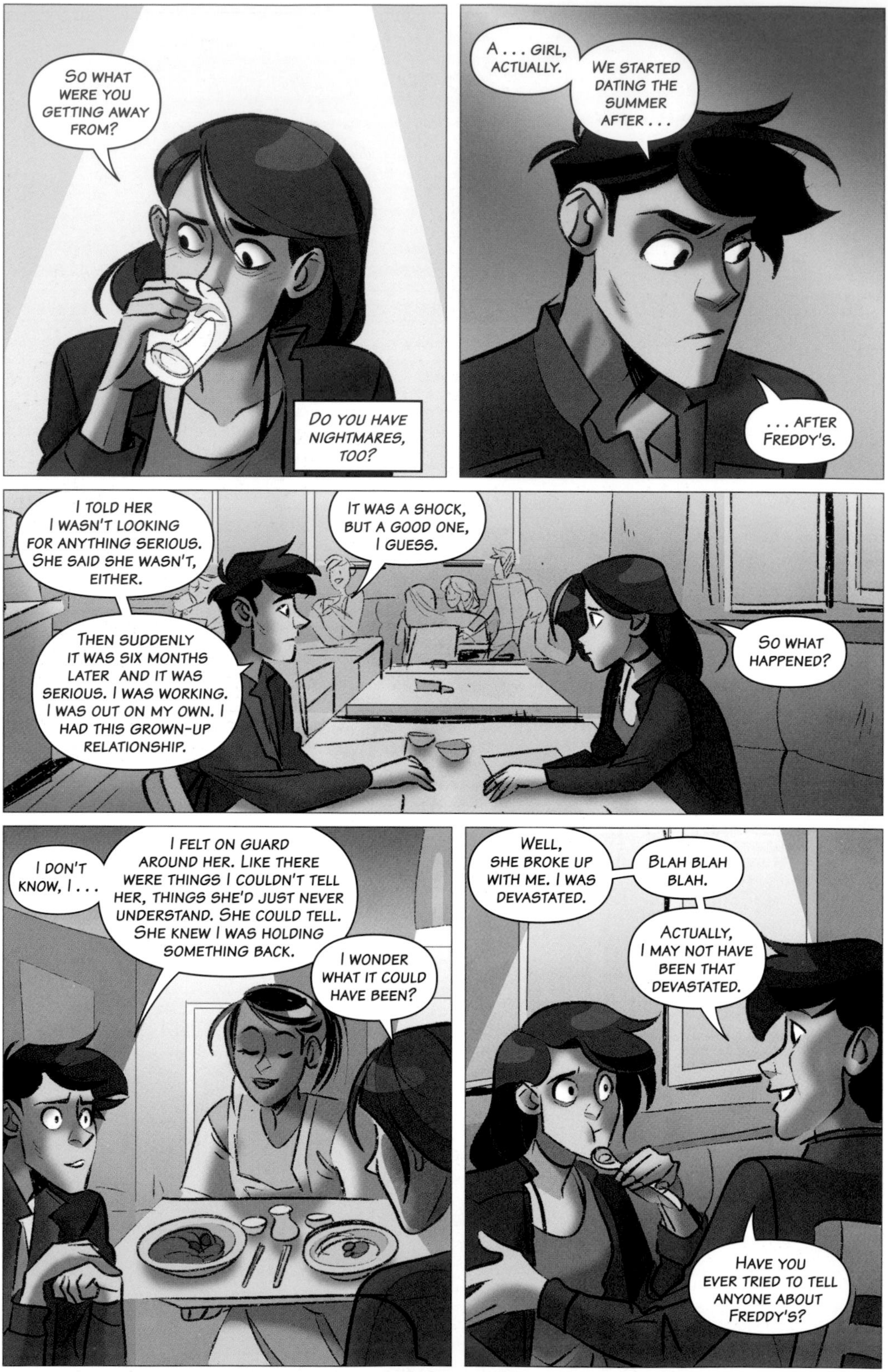
SO WHAT WERE YOU GETTING AWAY FROM?
DO YOU HAVE NIGHTMARES, TOO?
A . . . GIRL, ACTUALLY.
WE STARTED DATING THE SUMMER AFTER . . .
. . . AFTER FREDDY'S.
I TOLD HER I WASN'T LOOKING FOR ANYTHING SERIOUS. SHE SAID SHE WASN'T, EITHER.
THEN SUDDENLY IT WAS SIX MONTHS LATER AND IT WAS SERIOUS. I WAS WORKING. I WAS OUT ON MY OWN. I HAD THIS GROWN-UP RELATIONSHIP.
IT WAS A SHOCK, BUT A GOOD ONE, I GUESS.
SO WHAT HAPPENED?
I DON'T KNOW, I . . .
I FELT ON GUARD AROUND HER. LIKE THERE WERE THINGS I COULDN'T TELL HER, THINGS SHE'D JUST NEVER UNDERSTAND. SHE COULD TELL. SHE KNEW I WAS HOLDING SOMETHING BACK.
I WONDER WHAT IT COULD HAVE BEEN?
WELL, SHE BROKE UP WITH ME. I WAS DEVASTATED.
BLAH BLAH BLAH.
ACTUALLY, I MAY NOT HAVE BEEN THAT DEVASTATED.
HAVE YOU EVER TRIED TO TELL ANYONE ABOUT FREDDY'S?

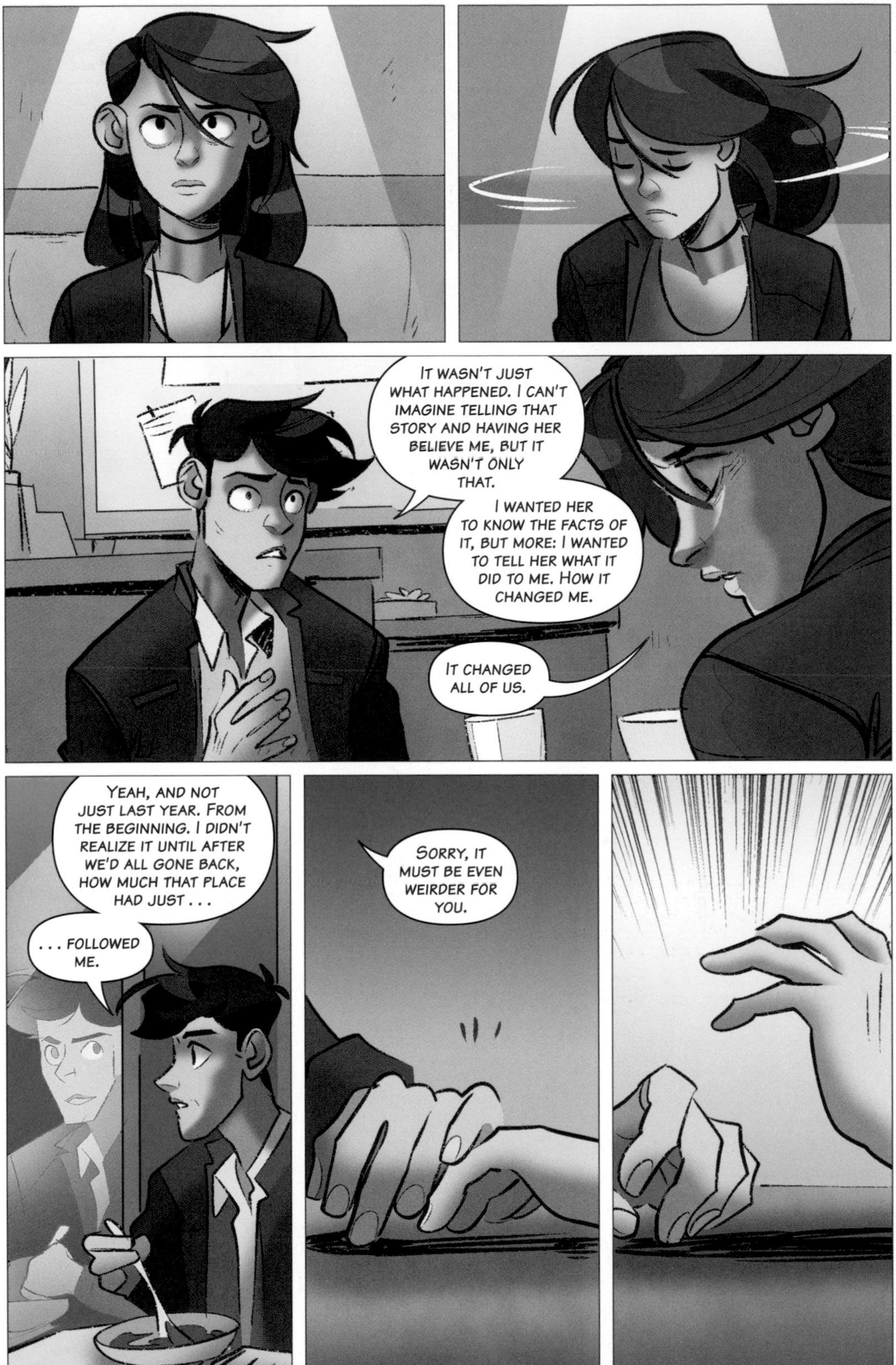
It wasn't just what happened. I can't imagine telling that story and having her believe me, but it wasn't only that.
I wanted her to know the facts of it, but more: I wanted to tell her what it did to me. How it changed me.
It changed all of us.
Yeah, and not just last year. From the beginning. I didn't realize it until after we'd all gone back, how much that place had just . . .
. . . followed me.
Sorry, it must be even weirder for you.

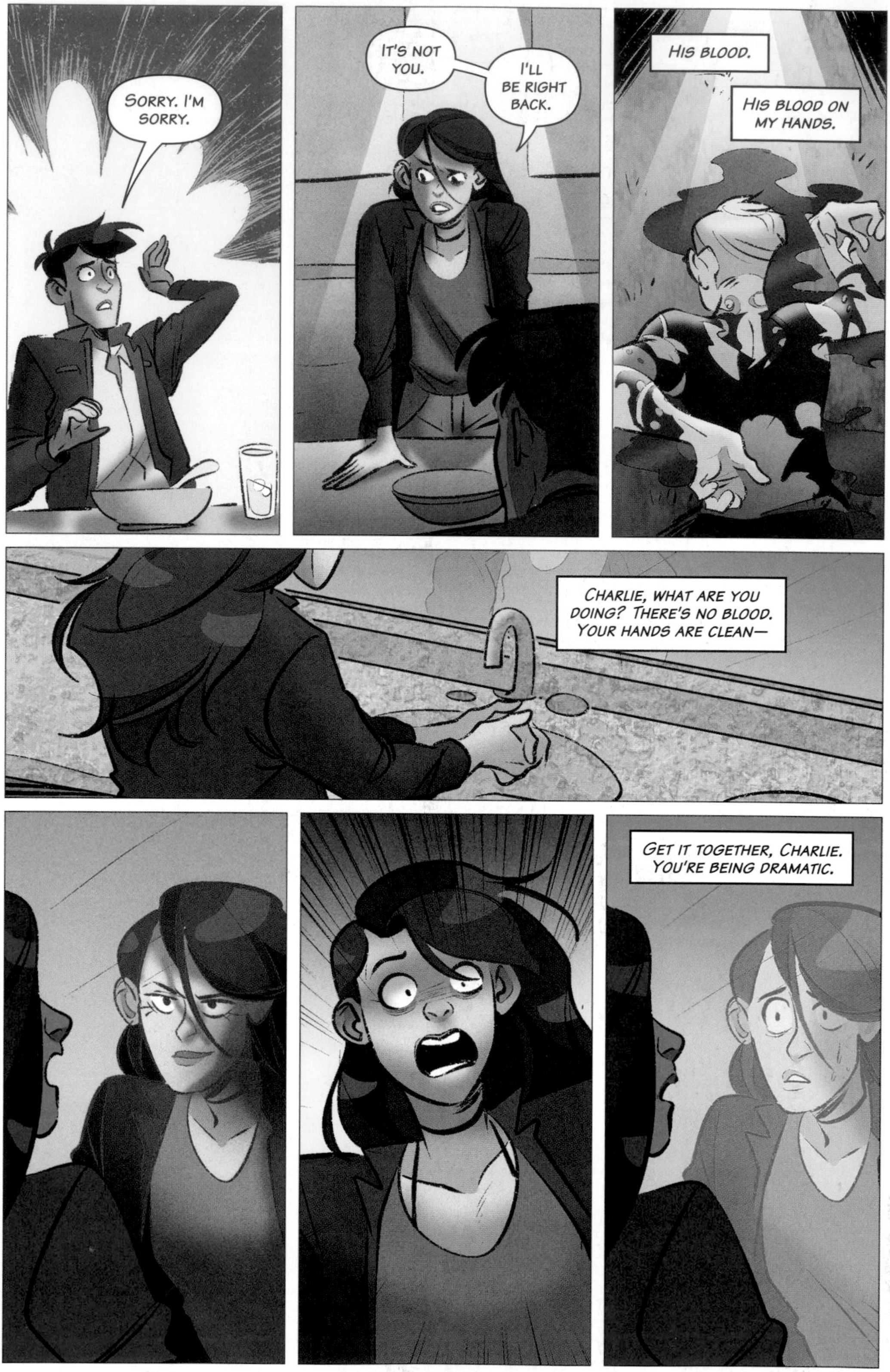
SORRY. I'M SORRY.
IT'S NOT YOU.
I'LL BE RIGHT BACK.
HIS BLOOD.
HIS BLOOD ON MY HANDS.
CHARLIE, WHAT ARE YOU DOING? THERE'S NO BLOOD. YOUR HANDS ARE CLEAN—
GET IT TOGETHER, CHARLIE. YOU'RE BEING DRAMATIC.

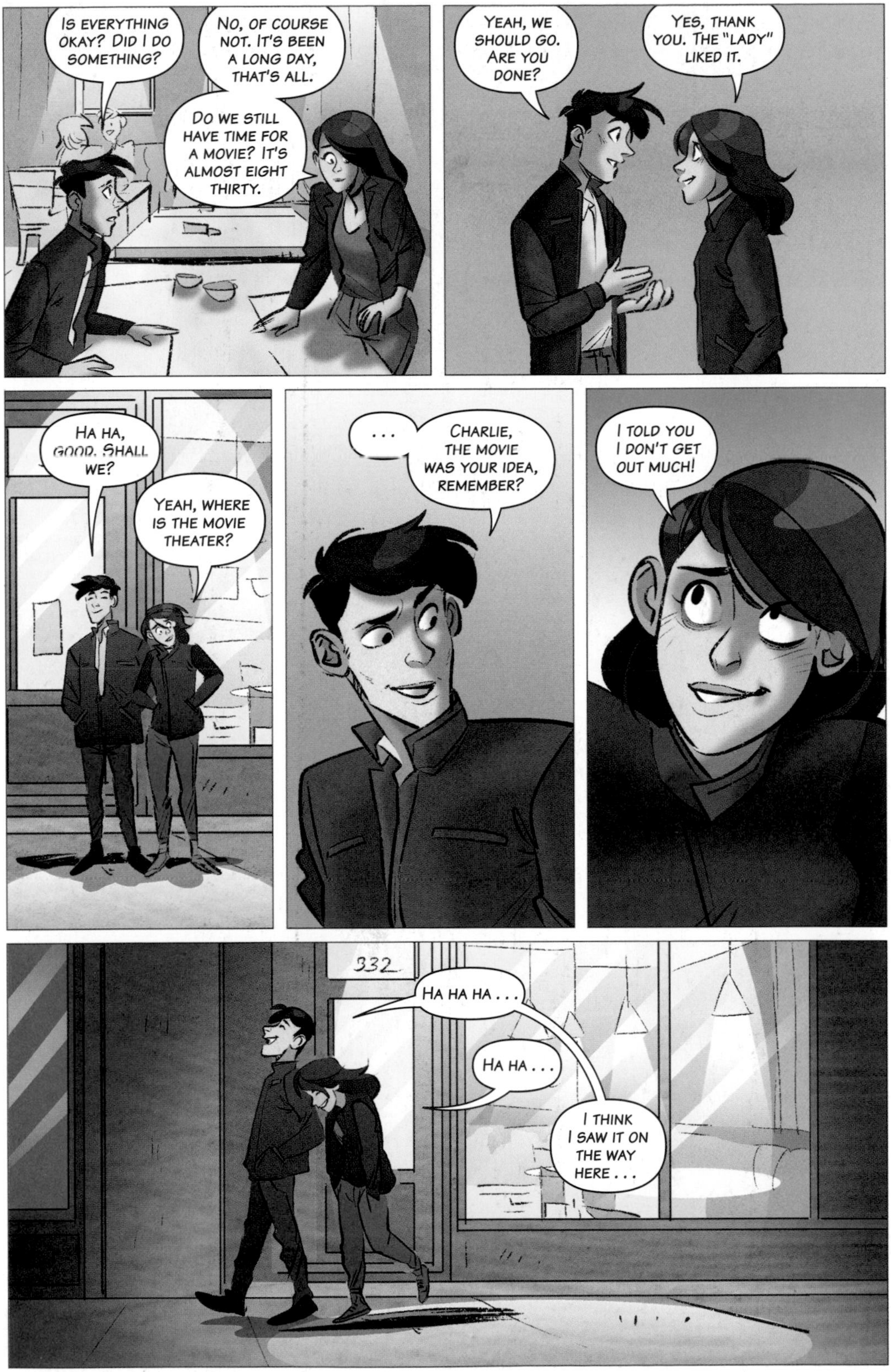
Is everything okay? Did I do something?
No, of course not. It's been a long day, that's all.
Do we still have time for a movie? It's almost eight thirty.
Yeah, we should go. Are you done?
Yes, thank you. The "lady" liked it.
Ha ha, good. Shall we?
Yeah, where is the movie theater?
. . .
Charlie, the movie was your idea, remember?
I told you I don't get out much!
332
Ha ha ha . . .
Ha ha . . .
I think I saw it on the way here . . .

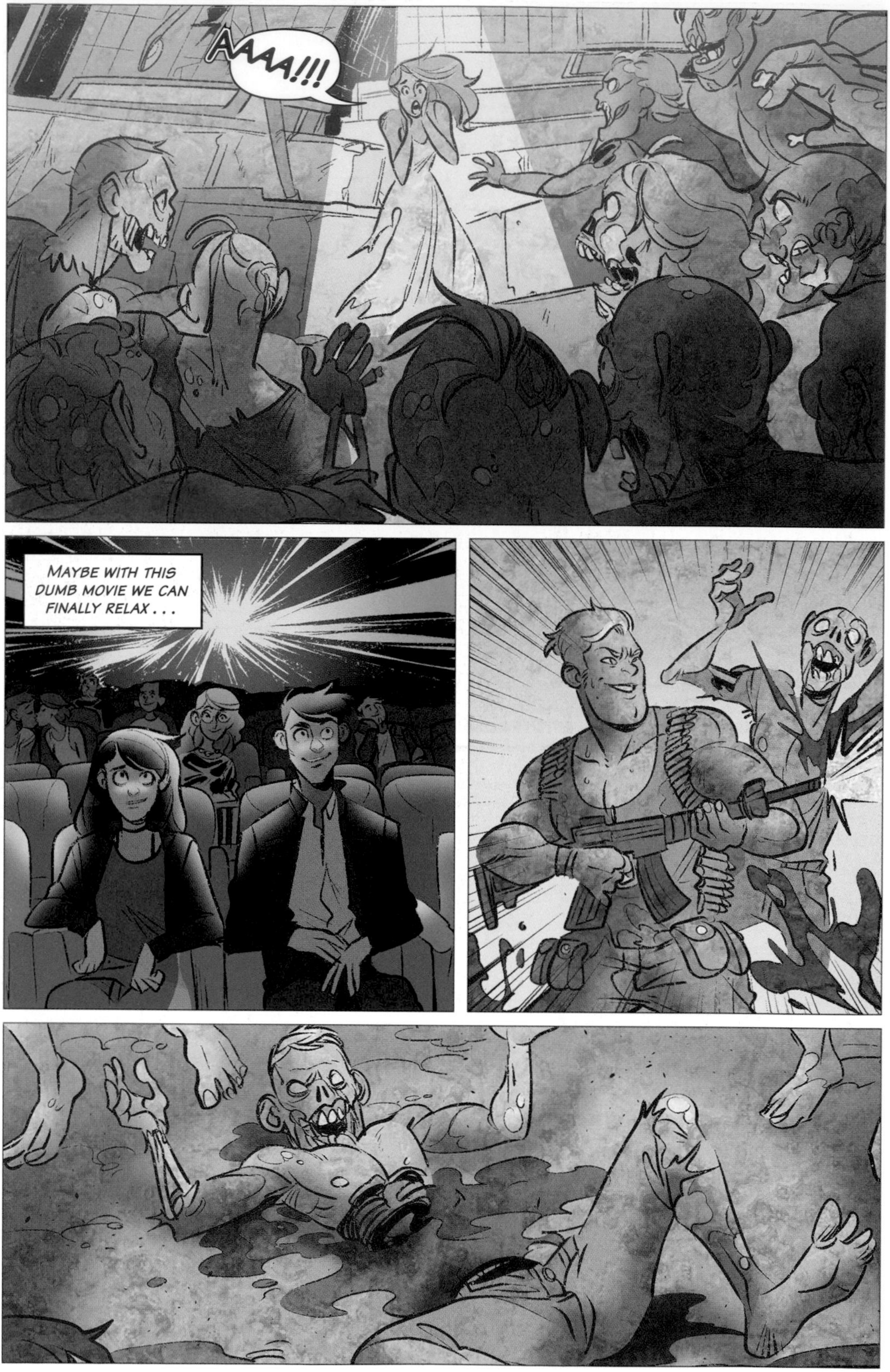
AAAA!!!
MAYBE WITH THIS DUMB MOVIE WE CAN FINALLY RELAX . . .

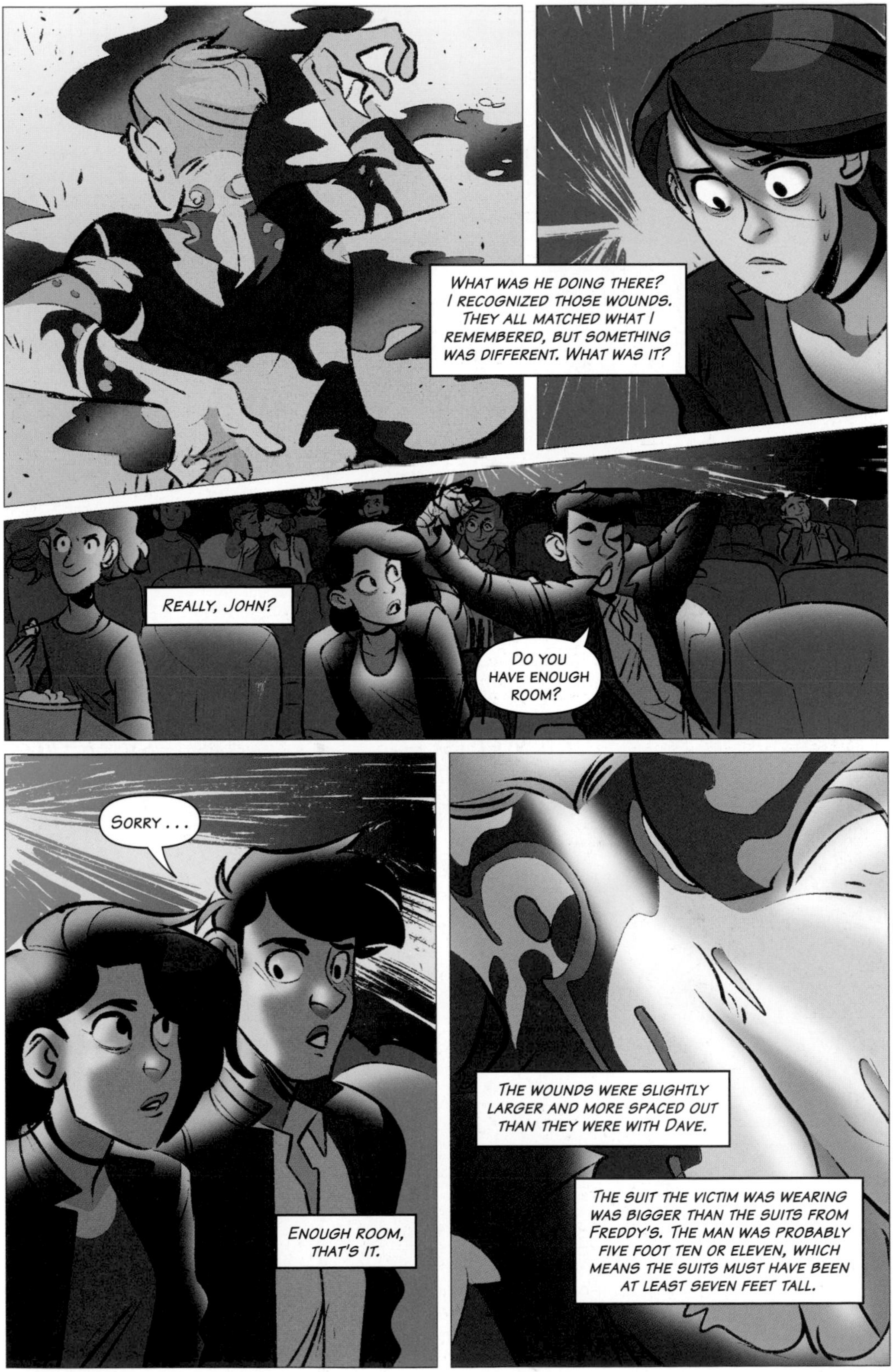
WHAT WAS HE DOING THERE? I RECOGNIZED THOSE WOUNDS. THEY ALL MATCHED WHAT I REMEMBERED, BUT SOMETHING WAS DIFFERENT. WHAT WAS IT?
REALLY, JOHN?
DO YOU HAVE ENOUGH ROOM?
SORRY . . .
ENOUGH ROOM, THAT'S IT.
THE WOUNDS WERE SLIGHTLY LARGER AND MORE SPACED OUT THAN THEY WERE WITH DAVE.
THE SUIT THE VICTIM WAS WEARING WAS BIGGER THAN THE SUITS FROM FREDDY'S. THE MAN WAS PROBABLY FIVE FOOT TEN OR ELEVEN, WHICH MEANS THE SUITS MUST HAVE BEEN AT LEAST SEVEN FEET TALL.

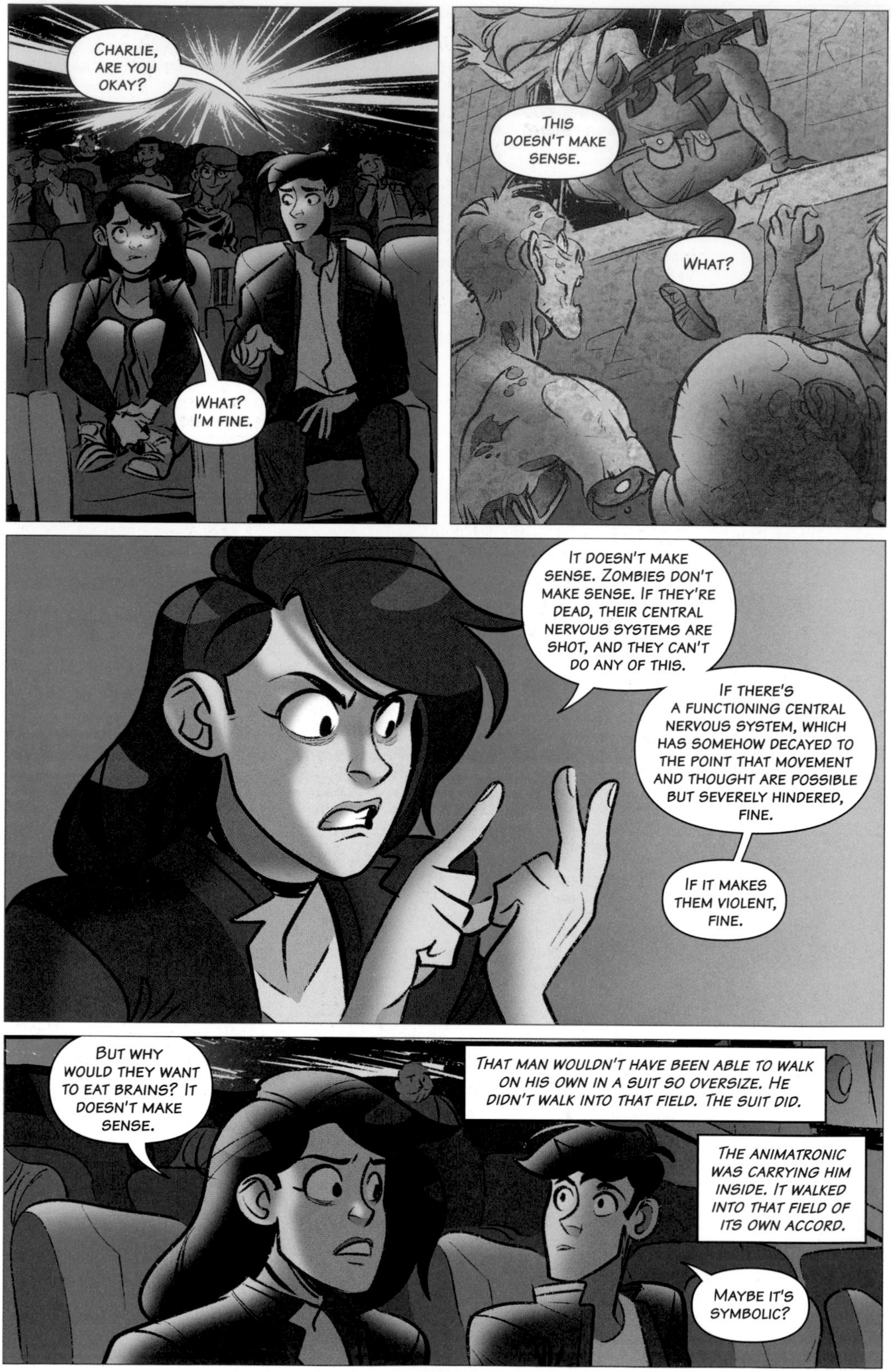
CHARLIE, ARE YOU OKAY?
WHAT? I'M FINE.
THIS DOESN'T MAKE SENSE.
WHAT?
IT DOESN'T MAKE SENSE. ZOMBIES DON'T MAKE SENSE. IF THEY'RE DEAD, THEIR CENTRAL NERVOUS SYSTEMS ARE SHOT, AND THEY CAN'T DO ANY OF THIS.
IF THERE'S A FUNCTIONING CENTRAL NERVOUS SYSTEM, WHICH HAS SOMEHOW DECAYED TO THE POINT THAT MOVEMENT AND THOUGHT ARE POSSIBLE BUT SEVERELY HINDERED, FINE.
IF IT MAKES THEM VIOLENT, FINE.
BUT WHY WOULD THEY WANT TO EAT BRAINS? IT DOESN'T MAKE SENSE.
THAT MAN WOULDN'T HAVE BEEN ABLE TO WALK ON HIS OWN IN A SUIT SO OVERSIZE. HE DIDN'T WALK INTO THAT FIELD. THE SUIT DID.
THE ANIMATRONIC WAS CARRYING HIM INSIDE. IT WALKED INTO THAT FIELD OF ITS OWN ACCORD.
MAYBE IT'S SYMBOLIC?

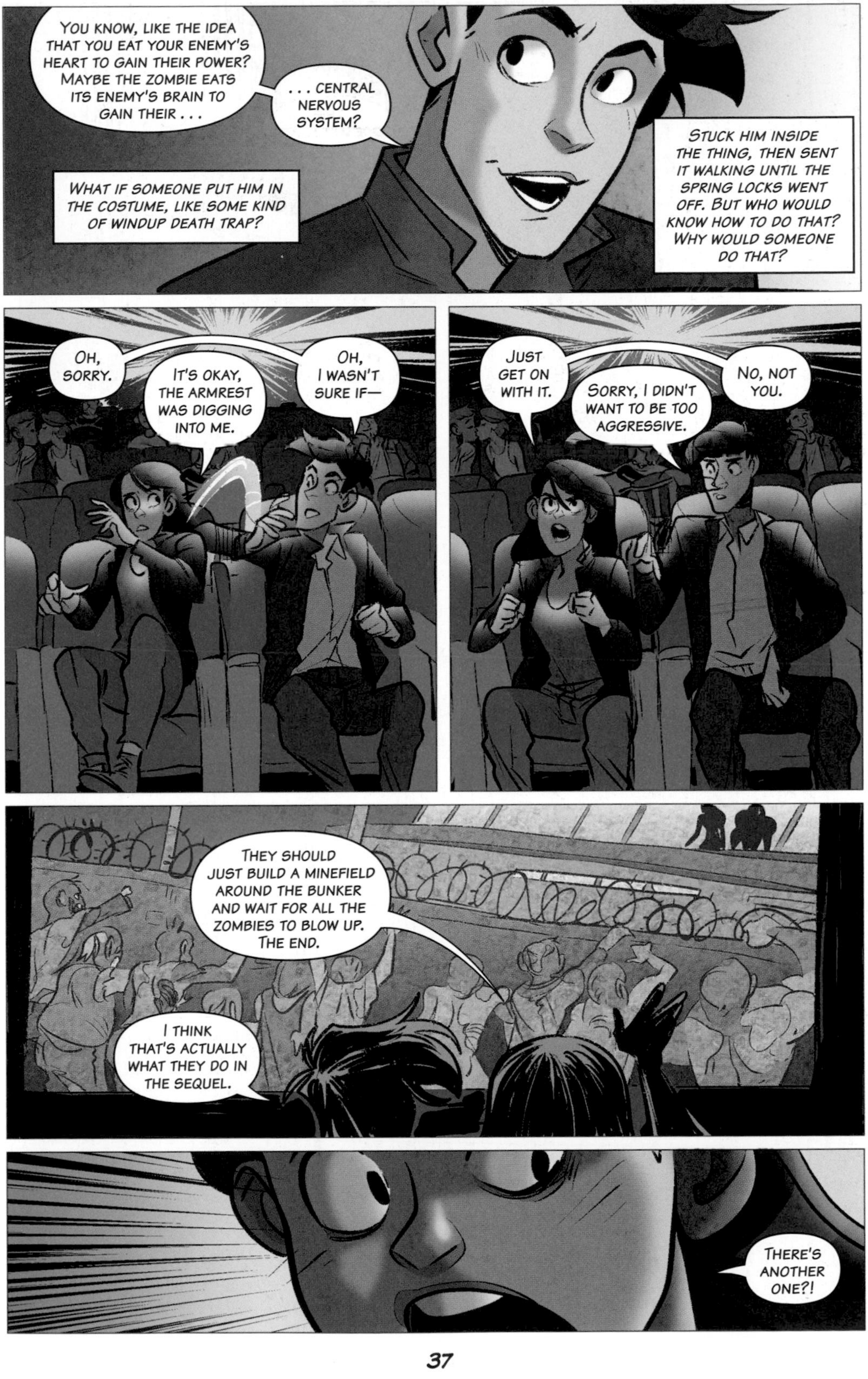

YOU KNOW, LIKE THE IDEA THAT YOU EAT YOUR ENEMY'S HEART TO GAIN THEIR POWER? MAYBE THE ZOMBIE EATS ITS ENEMY'S BRAIN TO GAIN THEIR . . .
. . . CENTRAL NERVOUS SYSTEM?
WHAT IF SOMEONE PUT HIM IN THE COSTUME, LIKE SOME KIND OF WINDUP DEATH TRAP?
STUCK HIM INSIDE THE THING, THEN SENT IT WALKING UNTIL THE SPRING LOCKS WENT OFF. BUT WHO WOULD KNOW HOW TO DO THAT? WHY WOULD SOMEONE DO THAT?
OH, SORRY.
OH, I WASN'T SURE IF—
IT'S OKAY, THE ARMREST WAS DIGGING INTO ME.
JUST GET ON WITH IT.
NO, NOT YOU.
SORRY, I DIDN'T WANT TO BE TOO AGGRESSIVE.
THEY SHOULD JUST BUILD A MINEFIELD AROUND THE BUNKER AND WAIT FOR ALL THE ZOMBIES TO BLOW UP. THE END.
I THINK THAT'S ACTUALLY WHAT THEY DO IN THE SEQUEL.
THERE'S ANOTHER ONE?!

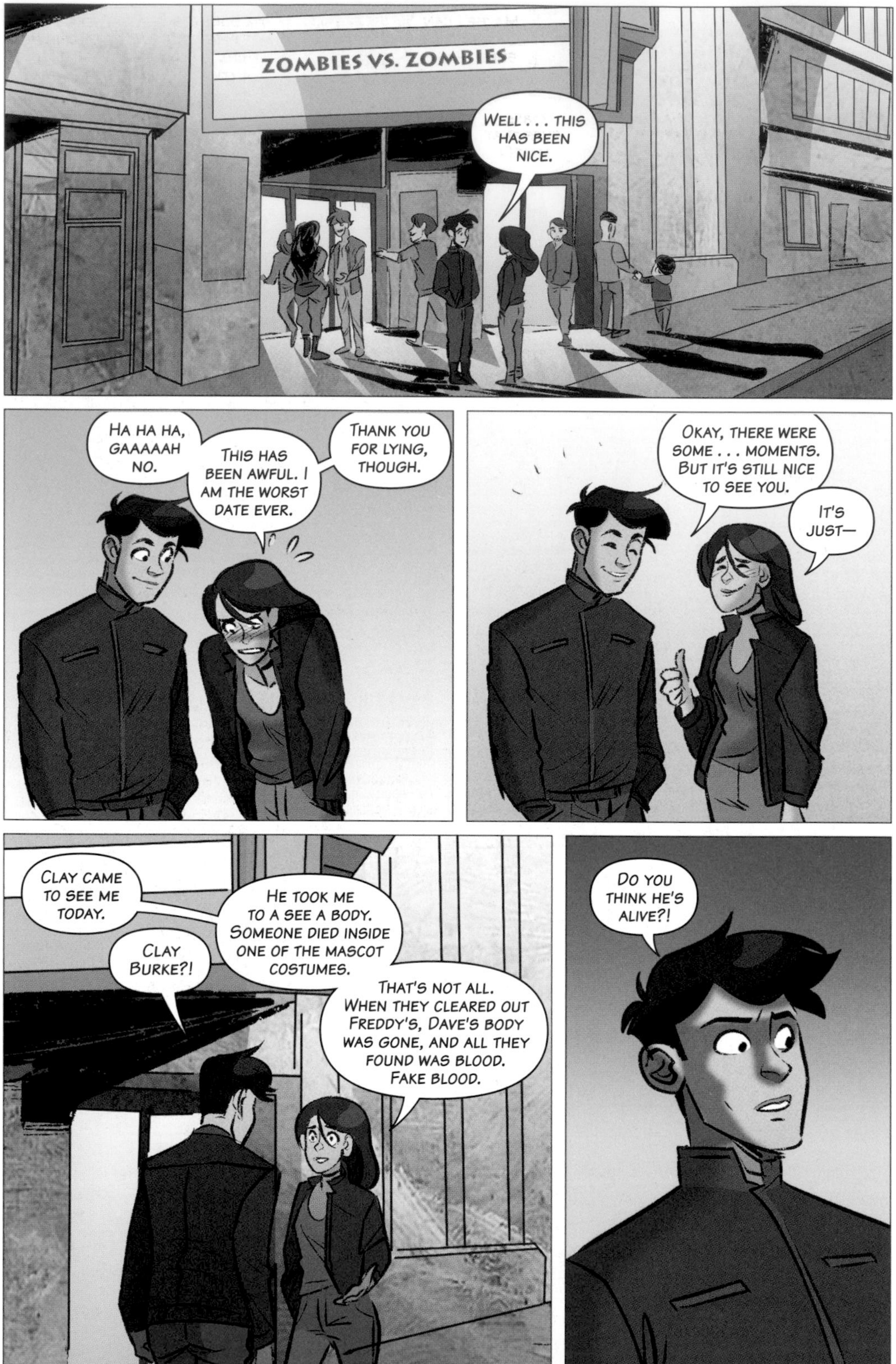
ZOMBIES VS. ZOMBIES
WELL . . . THIS HAS BEEN NICE.
HA HA HA, GAAAAAH NO.
THIS HAS BEEN AWFUL. I AM THE WORST DATE EVER.
THANK YOU FOR LYING, THOUGH.
OKAY, THERE WERE SOME . . . MOMENTS. BUT IT'S STILL NICE TO SEE YOU.
IT'S JUST—
CLAY CAME TO SEE ME TODAY.
CLAY BURKE?!
HE TOOK ME TO A SEE A BODY. SOMEONE DIED INSIDE ONE OF THE MASCOT COSTUMES.
THAT'S NOT ALL. WHEN THEY CLEARED OUT FREDDY'S, DAVE'S BODY WAS GONE, AND ALL THEY FOUND WAS BLOOD. FAKE BLOOD.
DO YOU THINK HE'S ALIVE?!

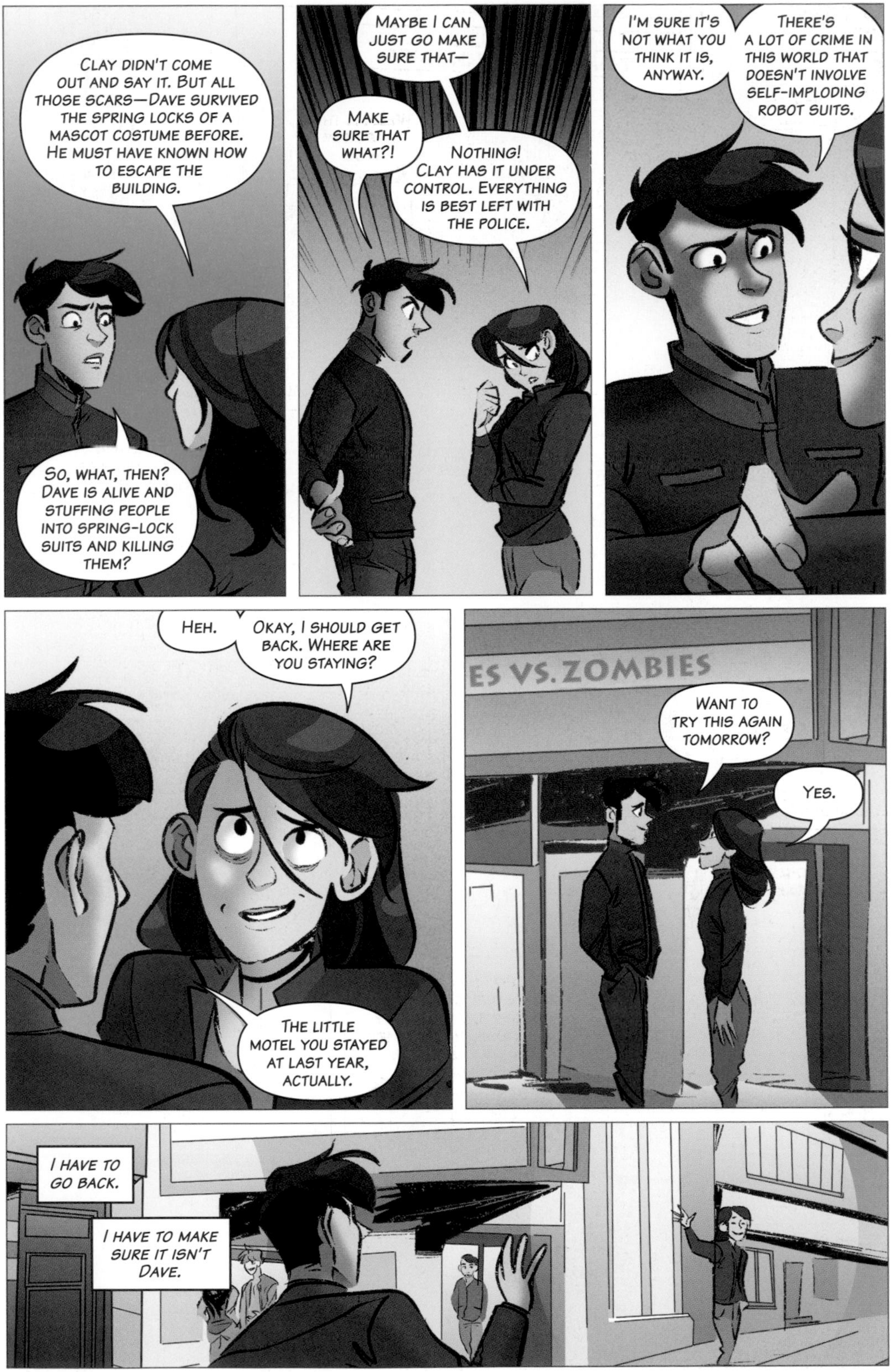
Clay didn't come out and say it. But all those scars—Dave survived the spring locks of a mascot costume before. He must have known how to escape the building.
So, what, then? Dave is alive and stuffing people into spring-lock suits and killing them?
Maybe I can just go make sure that—
Make sure that what?!
Nothing! Clay has it under control. Everything is best left with the police.
I'm sure it's not what you think it is, anyway.
There's a lot of crime in this world that doesn't involve self-imploding robot suits.
Heh.
Okay, I should get back. Where are you staying?
The little motel you stayed at last year, actually.
ES VS. ZOMBIES
Want to try this again tomorrow?
Yes.
I have to go back.
I have to make sure it isn't Dave.

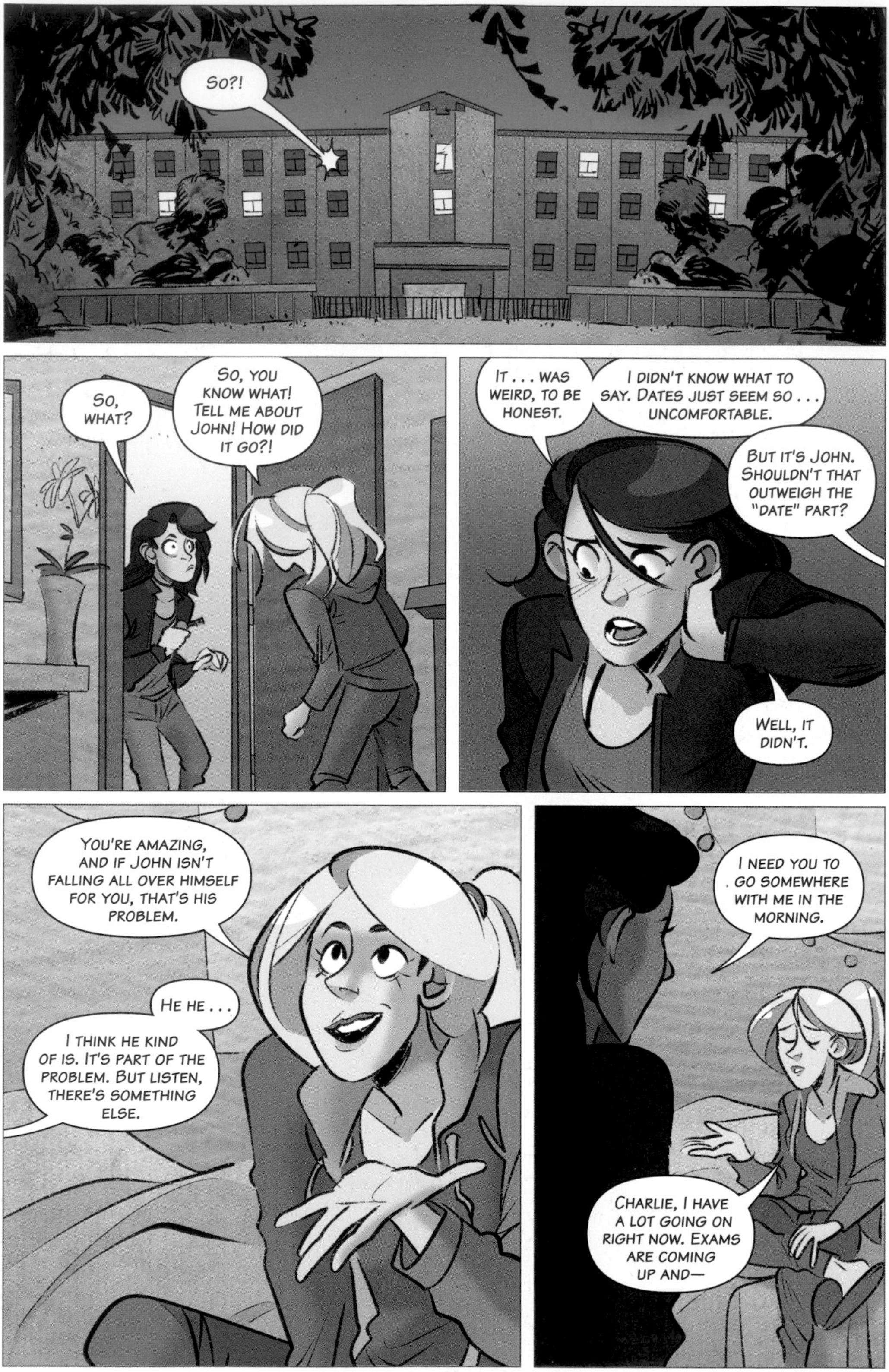
So?!
So, what?
So, you know what! Tell me about John! How did it go?!
It . . . was weird, to be honest.
I didn't know what to say. Dates just seem so . . . uncomfortable.
But it's John. Shouldn't that outweigh the "date" part?
Well, it didn't.
You're amazing, and if John isn't falling all over himself for you, that's his problem.
He he . . .
I think he kind of is. It's part of the problem. But listen, there's something else.
I need you to go somewhere with me in the morning.
Charlie, I have a lot going on right now. Exams are coming up and—

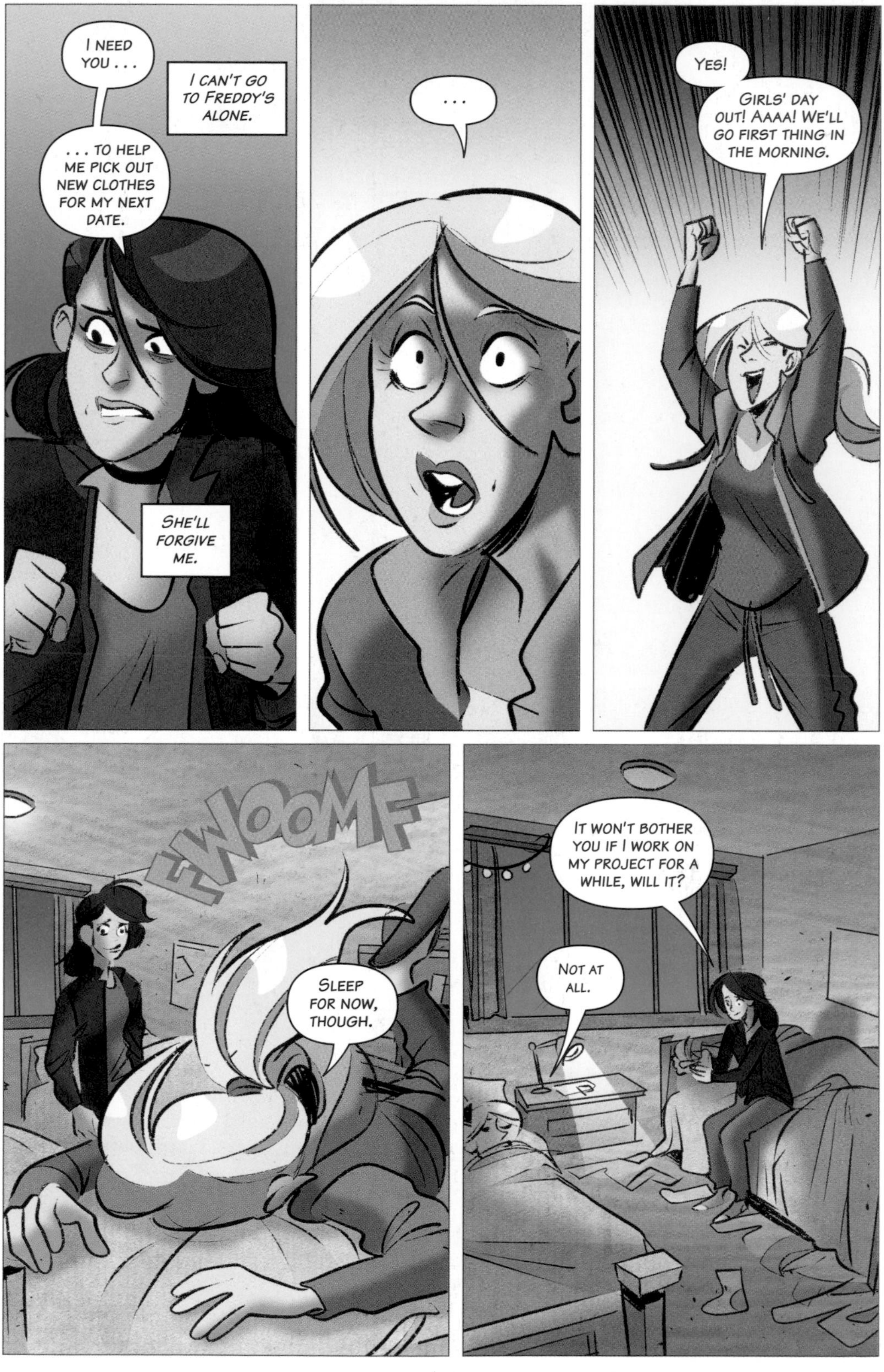
I NEED YOU . . .
I CAN'T GO TO FREDDY'S ALONE.
. . . TO HELP ME PICK OUT NEW CLOTHES FOR MY NEXT DATE.
SHE'LL FORGIVE ME.
. . .
YES!
GIRLS' DAY OUT! AAAA! WE'LL GO FIRST THING IN THE MORNING.
FWOOMF
SLEEP FOR NOW, THOUGH.
IT WON'T BOTHER YOU IF I WORK ON MY PROJECT FOR A WHILE, WILL IT?
NOT AT ALL.

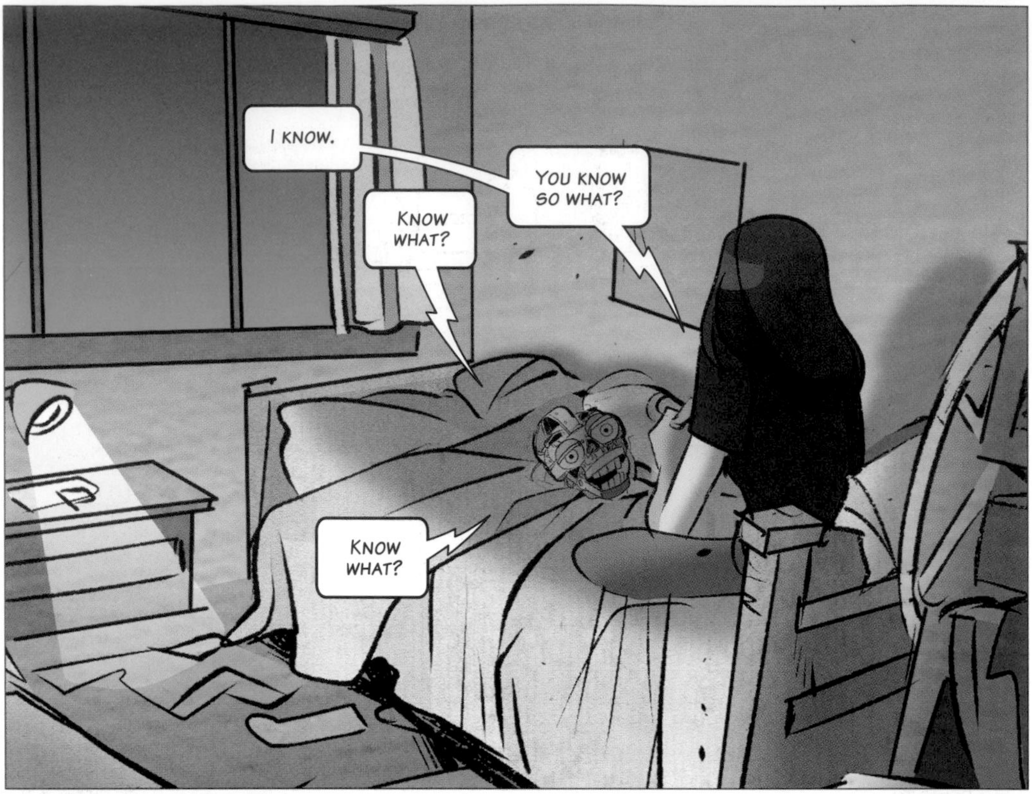
I KNOW.
YOU KNOW SO WHAT?
KNOW WHAT?
KNOW WHAT?

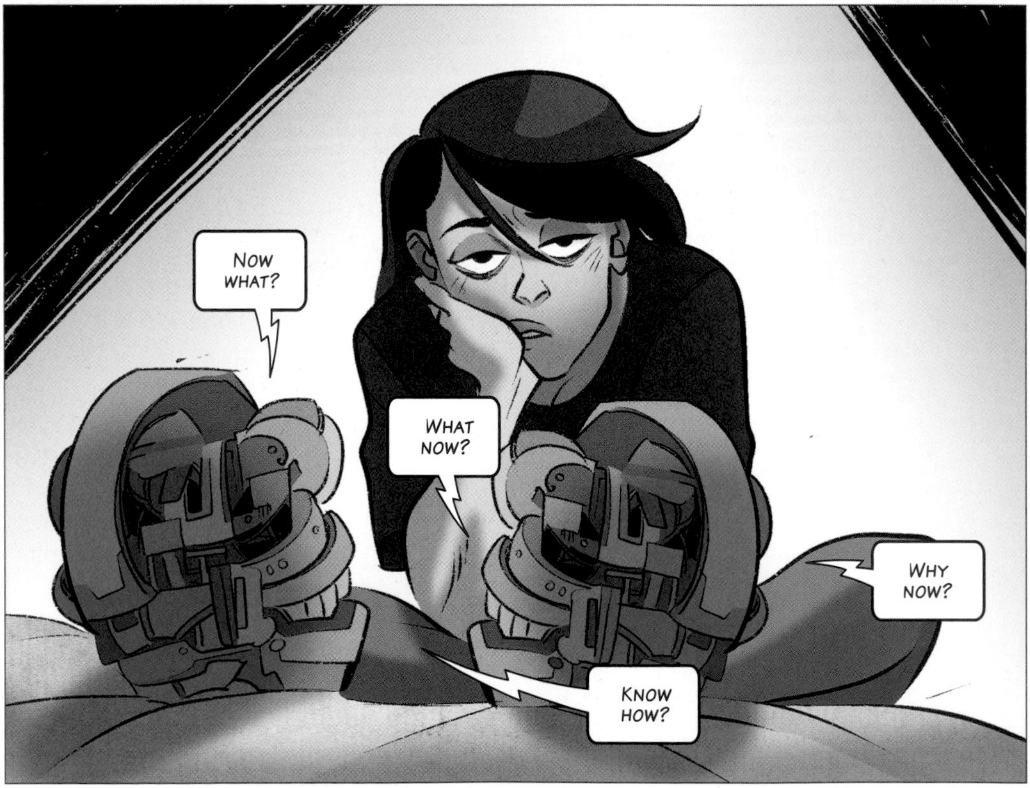
NOW WHAT?
WHAT NOW?
WHY NOW?
KNOW HOW?

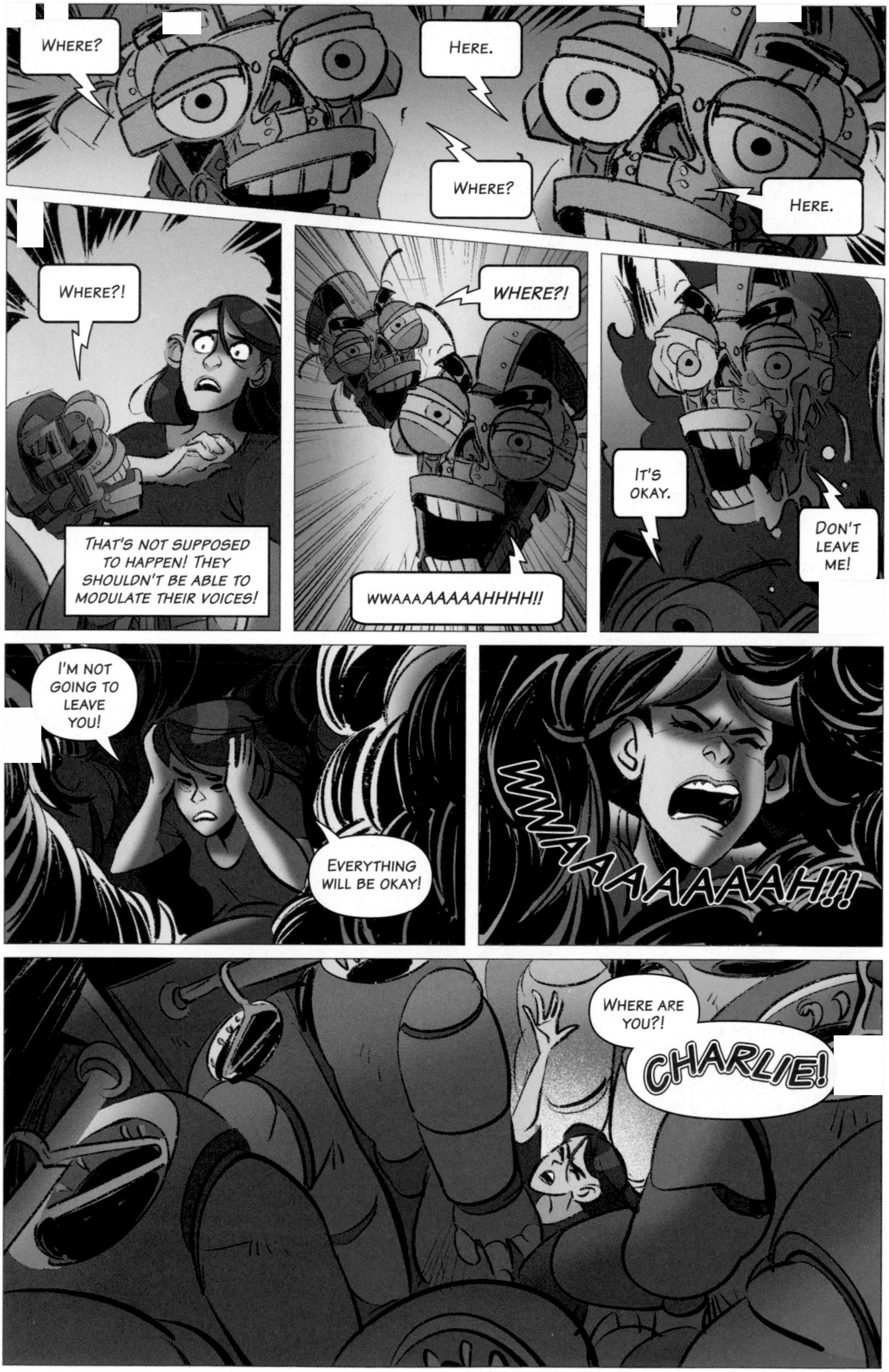
WHERE?
HERE.
WHERE?
HERE.
WHERE?!
WHERE?!
THAT'S NOT SUPPOSED TO HAPPEN! THEY SHOULDN'T BE ABLE TO MODULATE THEIR VOICES!
WWAAAAAAAAHHHH!!
IT'S OKAY.
DON'T LEAVE ME!
I'M NOT GOING TO LEAVE YOU!
EVERYTHING WILL BE OKAY!
WWAAAAAAAAAH!!
WHERE ARE YOU?!
CHARLIE!

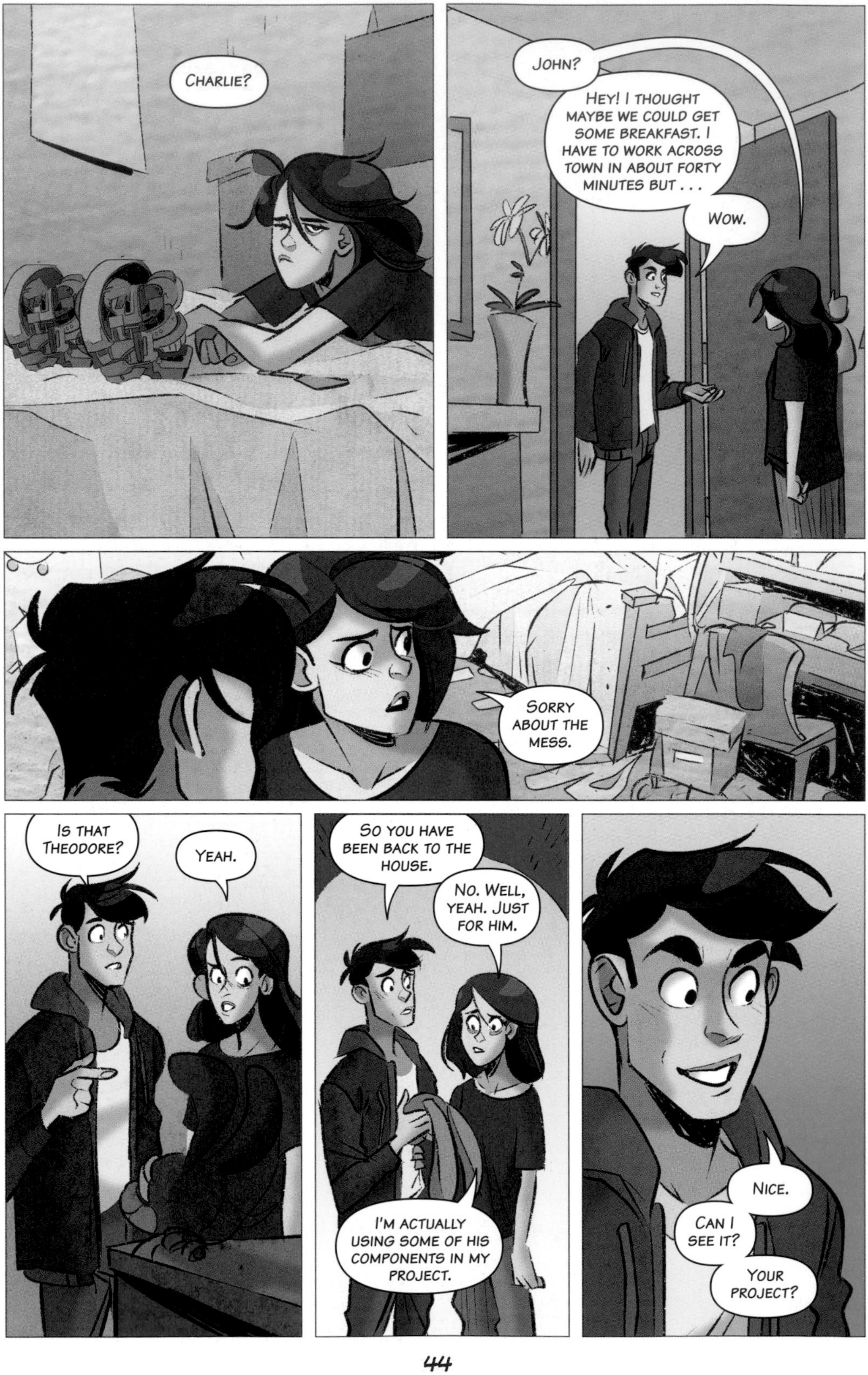
CHARLIE?
JOHN?
HEY! I THOUGHT MAYBE WE COULD GET SOME BREAKFAST. I HAVE TO WORK ACROSS TOWN IN ABOUT FORTY MINUTES BUT . . .
WOW.
SORRY ABOUT THE MESS.
IS THAT THEODORE?
YEAH.
SO YOU HAVE BEEN BACK TO THE HOUSE.
NO. WELL, YEAH. JUST FOR HIM.
I'M ACTUALLY USING SOME OF HIS COMPONENTS IN MY PROJECT.
NICE.
CAN I SEE IT?
YOUR PROJECT?

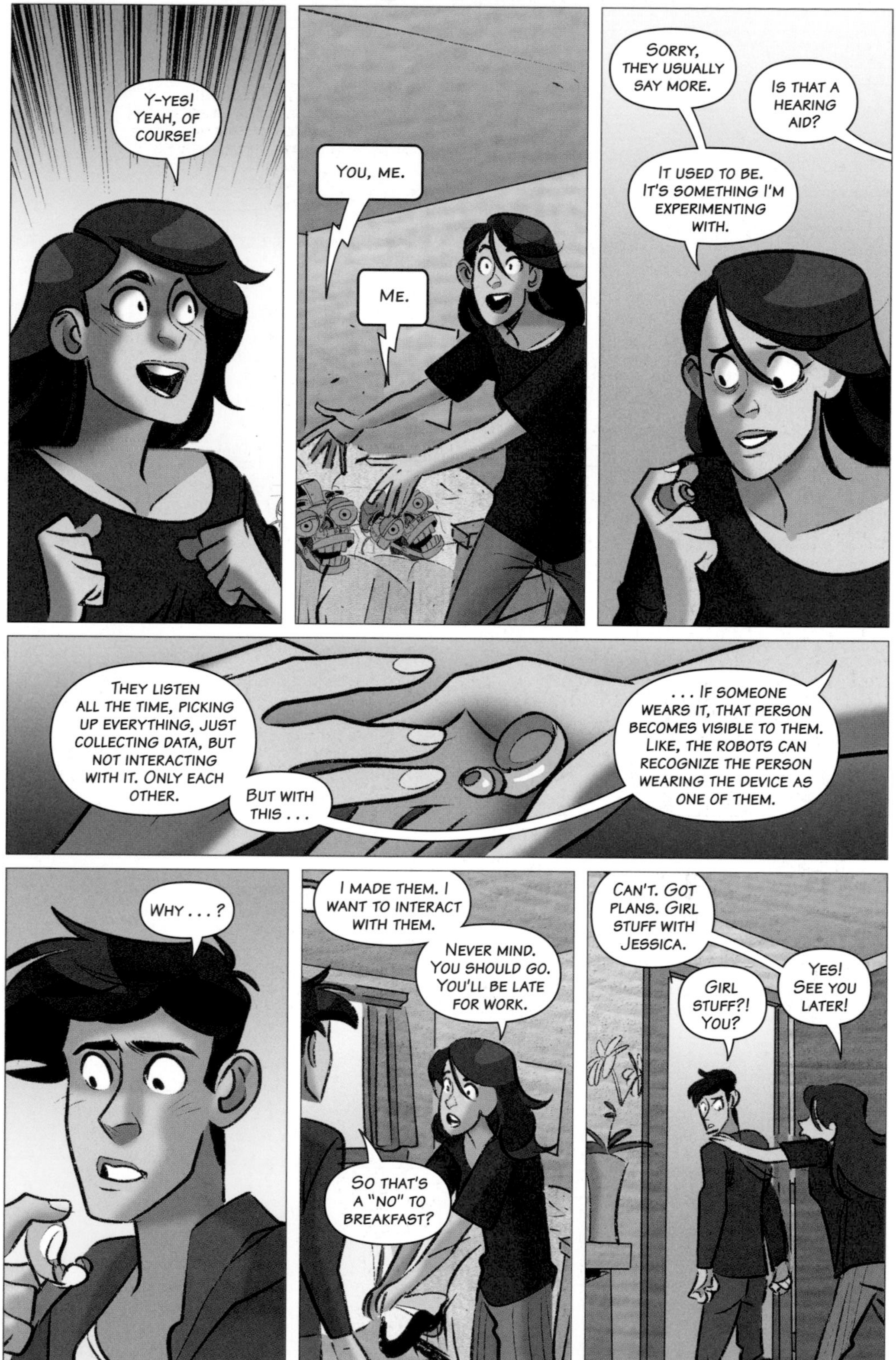
Y-YES! YEAH, OF COURSE!
YOU, ME.
ME.
SORRY, THEY USUALLY SAY MORE.
IS THAT A HEARING AID?
IT USED TO BE. IT'S SOMETHING I'M EXPERIMENTING WITH.
THEY LISTEN ALL THE TIME, PICKING UP EVERYTHING, JUST COLLECTING DATA, BUT NOT INTERACTING WITH IT. ONLY EACH OTHER.
BUT WITH THIS . . .
. . . IF SOMEONE WEARS IT, THAT PERSON BECOMES VISIBLE TO THEM. LIKE, THE ROBOTS CAN RECOGNIZE THE PERSON WEARING THE DEVICE AS ONE OF THEM.
WHY . . . ?
I MADE THEM. I WANT TO INTERACT WITH THEM.
NEVER MIND. YOU SHOULD GO. YOU'LL BE LATE FOR WORK.
SO THAT'S A "NO" TO BREAKFAST?
CAN'T. GOT PLANS. GIRL STUFF WITH JESSICA.
GIRL STUFF?! YOU?
YES! SEE YOU LATER!

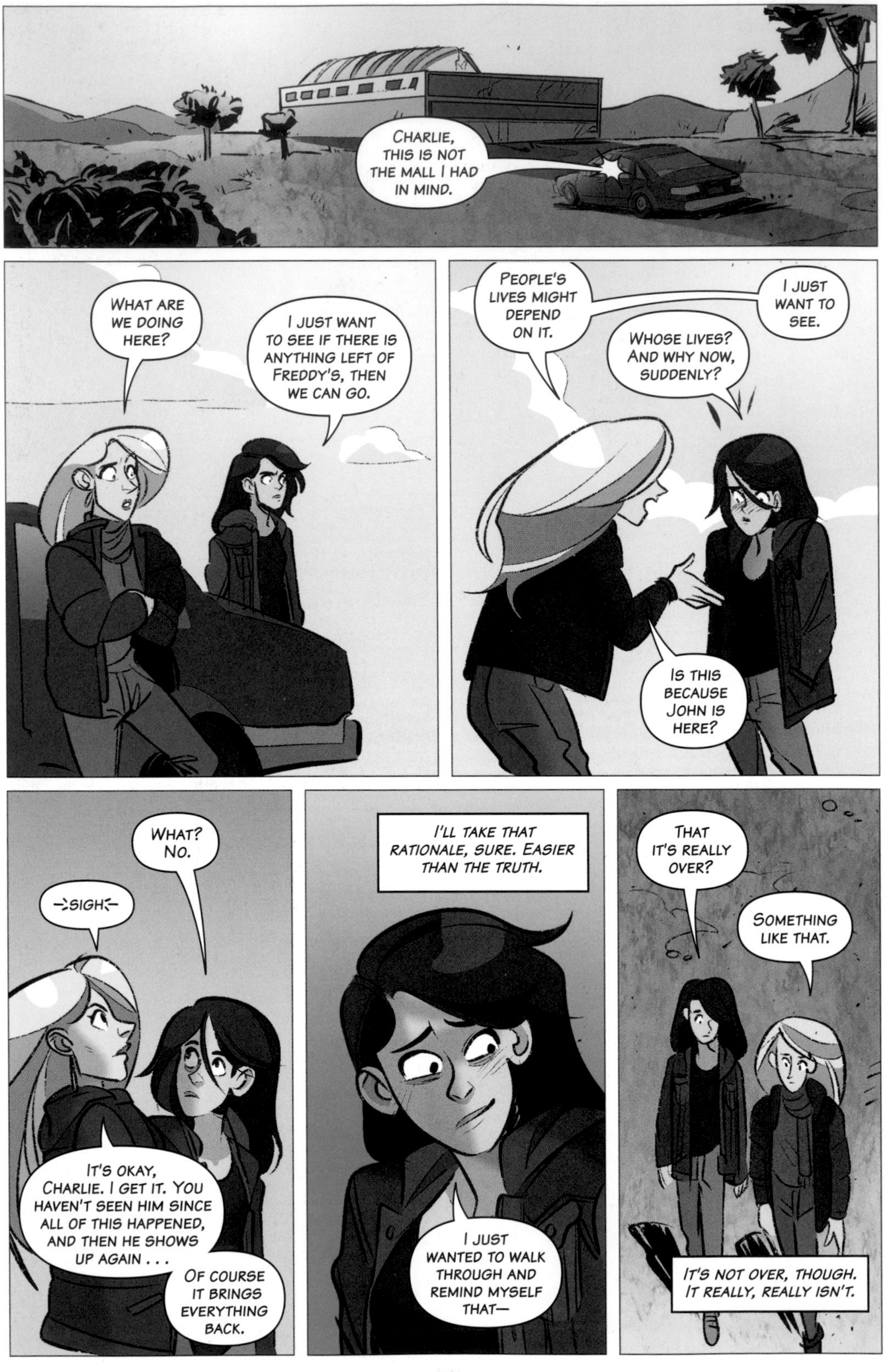
CHARLIE, THIS IS NOT THE MALL I HAD IN MIND.
WHAT ARE WE DOING HERE?
I JUST WANT TO SEE IF THERE IS ANYTHING LEFT OF FREDDY'S, THEN WE CAN GO.
PEOPLE'S LIVES MIGHT DEPEND ON IT.
I JUST WANT TO SEE.
WHOSE LIVES? AND WHY NOW, SUDDENLY?
IS THIS BECAUSE JOHN IS HERE?
WHAT? NO.
SIGH
IT'S OKAY, CHARLIE. I GET IT. YOU HAVEN'T SEEN HIM SINCE ALL OF THIS HAPPENED, AND THEN HE SHOWS UP AGAIN . . .
OF COURSE IT BRINGS EVERYTHING BACK.
I'LL TAKE THAT RATIONALE, SURE. EASIER THAN THE TRUTH.
I JUST WANTED TO WALK THROUGH AND REMIND MYSELF THAT—
THAT IT'S REALLY OVER?
SOMETHING LIKE THAT.
IT'S NOT OVER, THOUGH. IT REALLY, REALLY ISN'T.

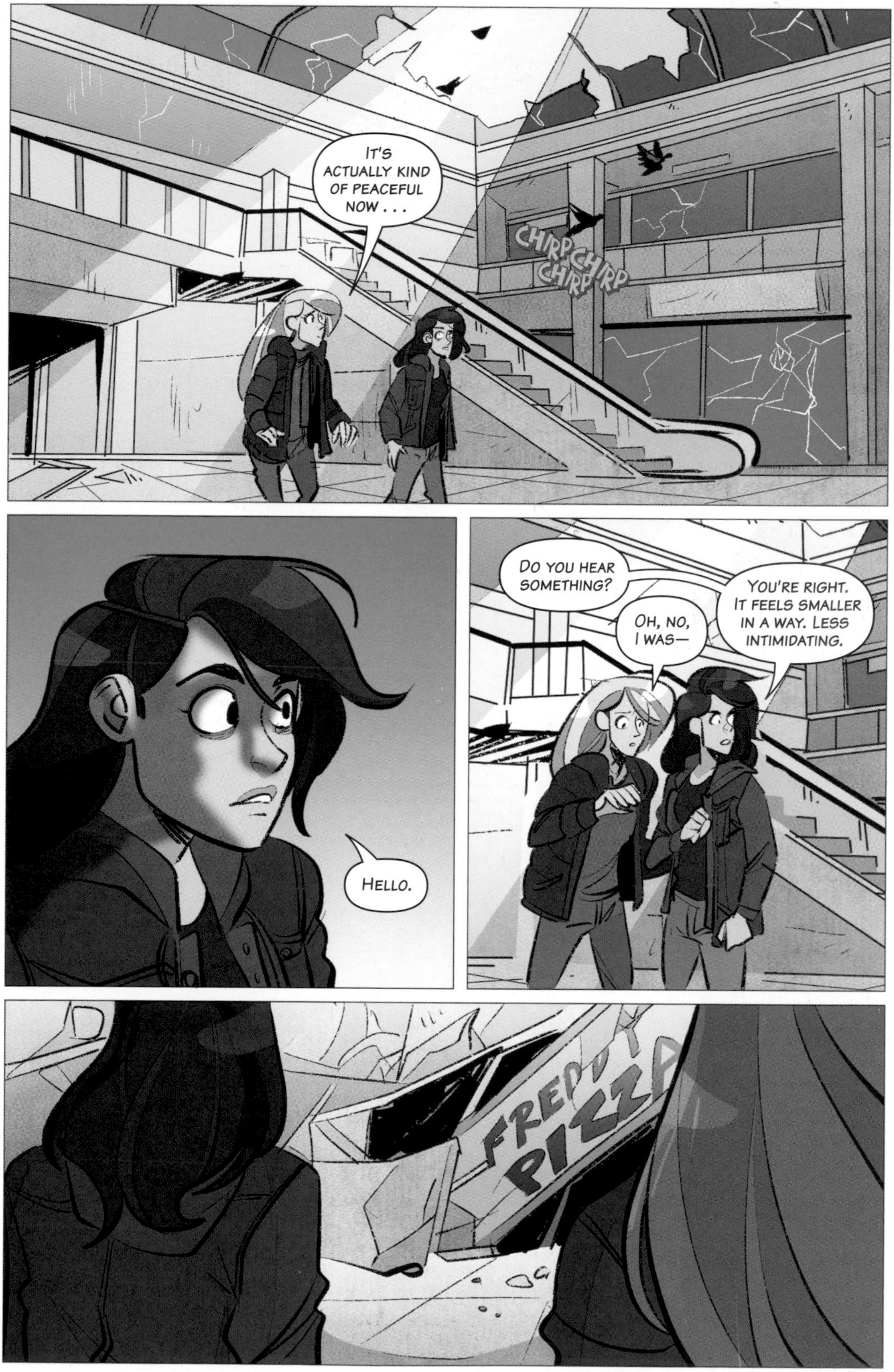
It's actually kind of peaceful now . . .
CHIRP CHIRP CHIRP
Hello.
Do you hear something?
Oh, no, I was—
You're right. It feels smaller in a way. Less intimidating.
FREDDY PIZZA

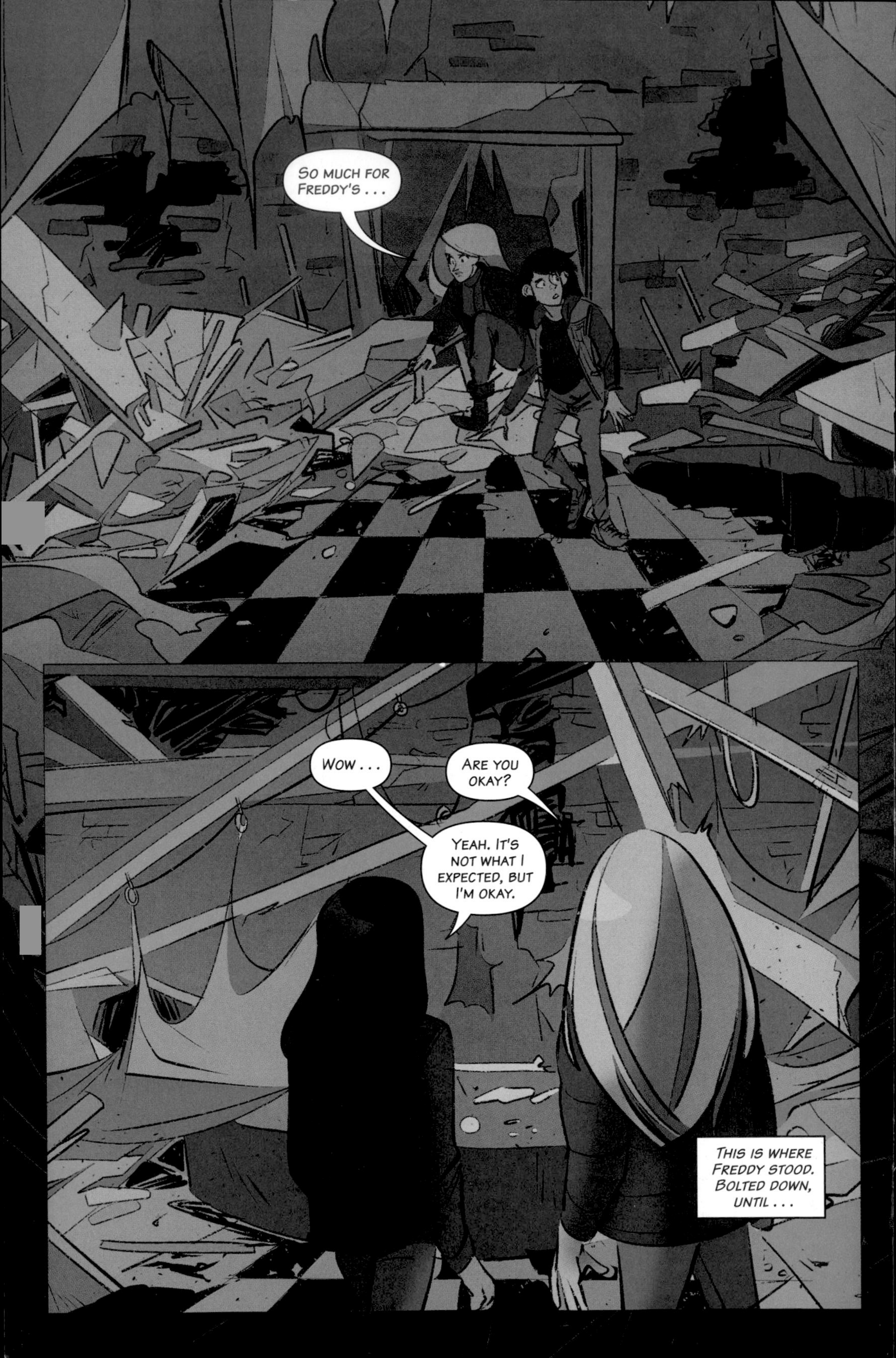
SO MUCH FOR FREDDY'S . . .
WOW . . .
ARE YOU OKAY?
YEAH. IT'S NOT WHAT I EXPECTED, BUT I'M OKAY.
THIS IS WHERE FREDDY STOOD. BOLTED DOWN, UNTIL . . .

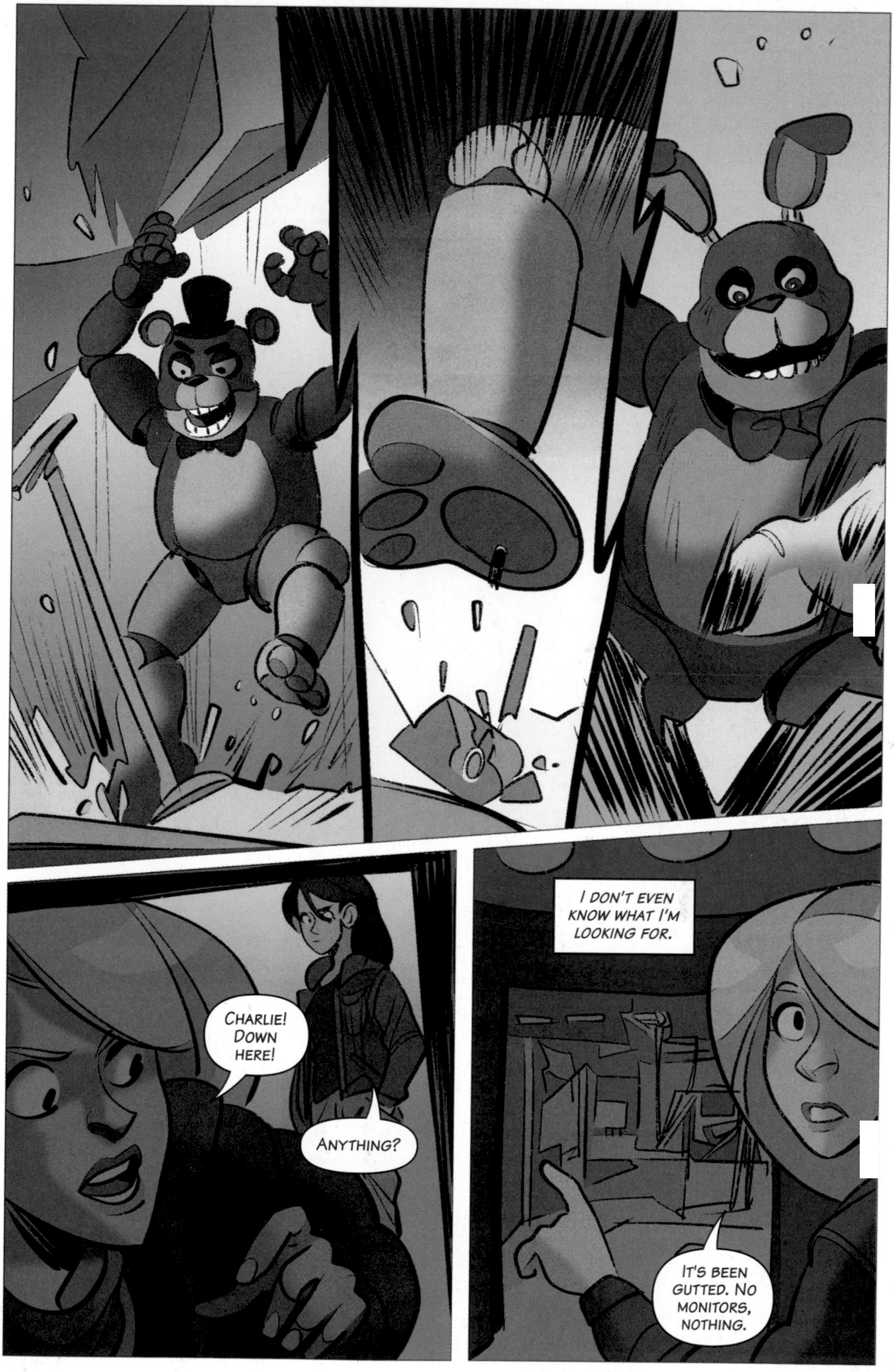
CHARLIE!
DOWN
HERE!
ANYTHING?
I DON'T EVEN
KNOW WHAT I'M
LOOKING FOR.
IT'S BEEN
GUTTED. NO
MONITORS,
NOTHING.

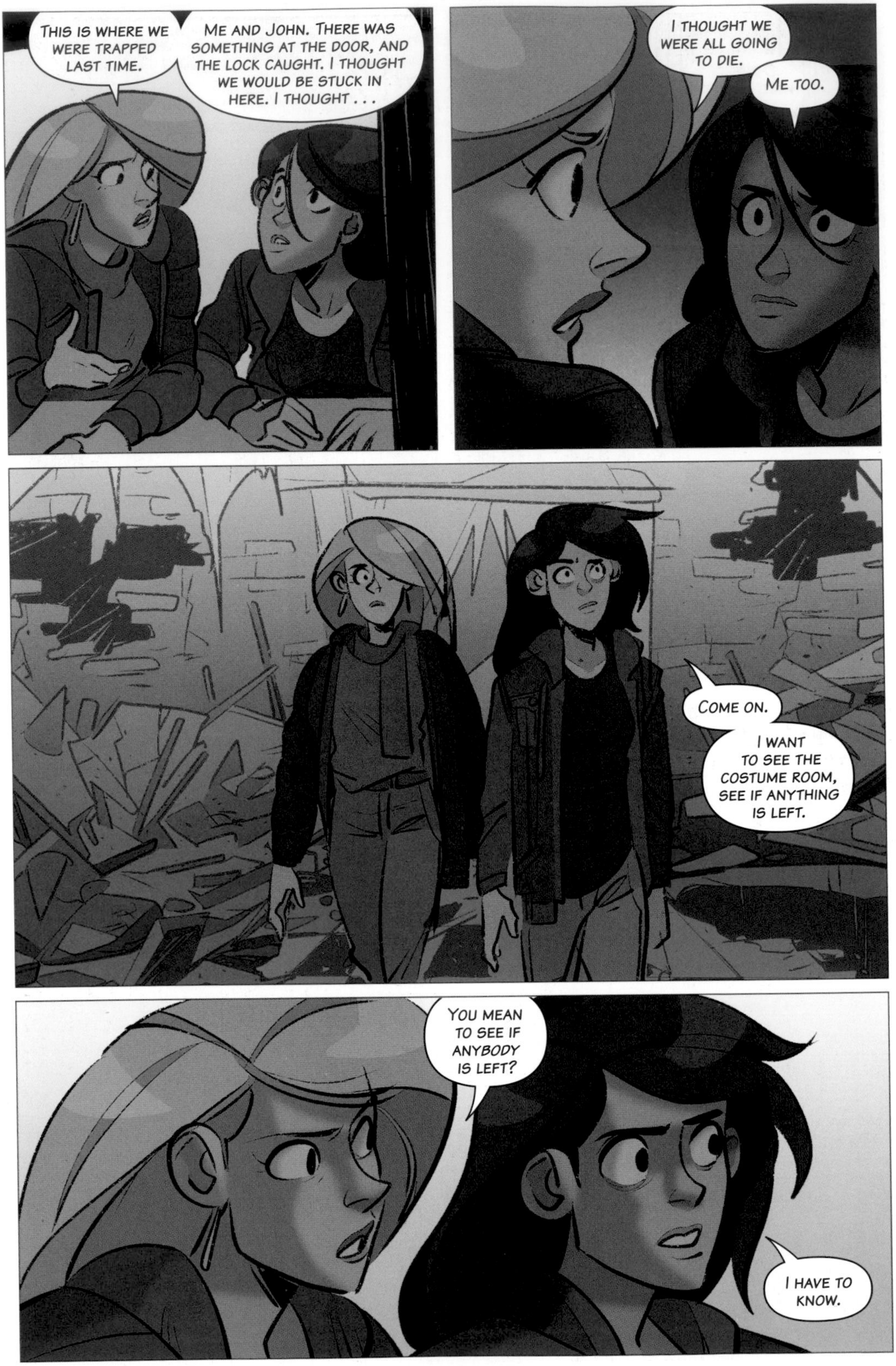
This is where we were trapped last time.
Me and John. There was something at the door, and the lock caught. I thought we would be stuck in here. I thought . . .
I thought we were all going to die.
Me too.
Come on.
I want to see the costume room, see if anything is left.
You mean to see if anybody is left?
I have to know.

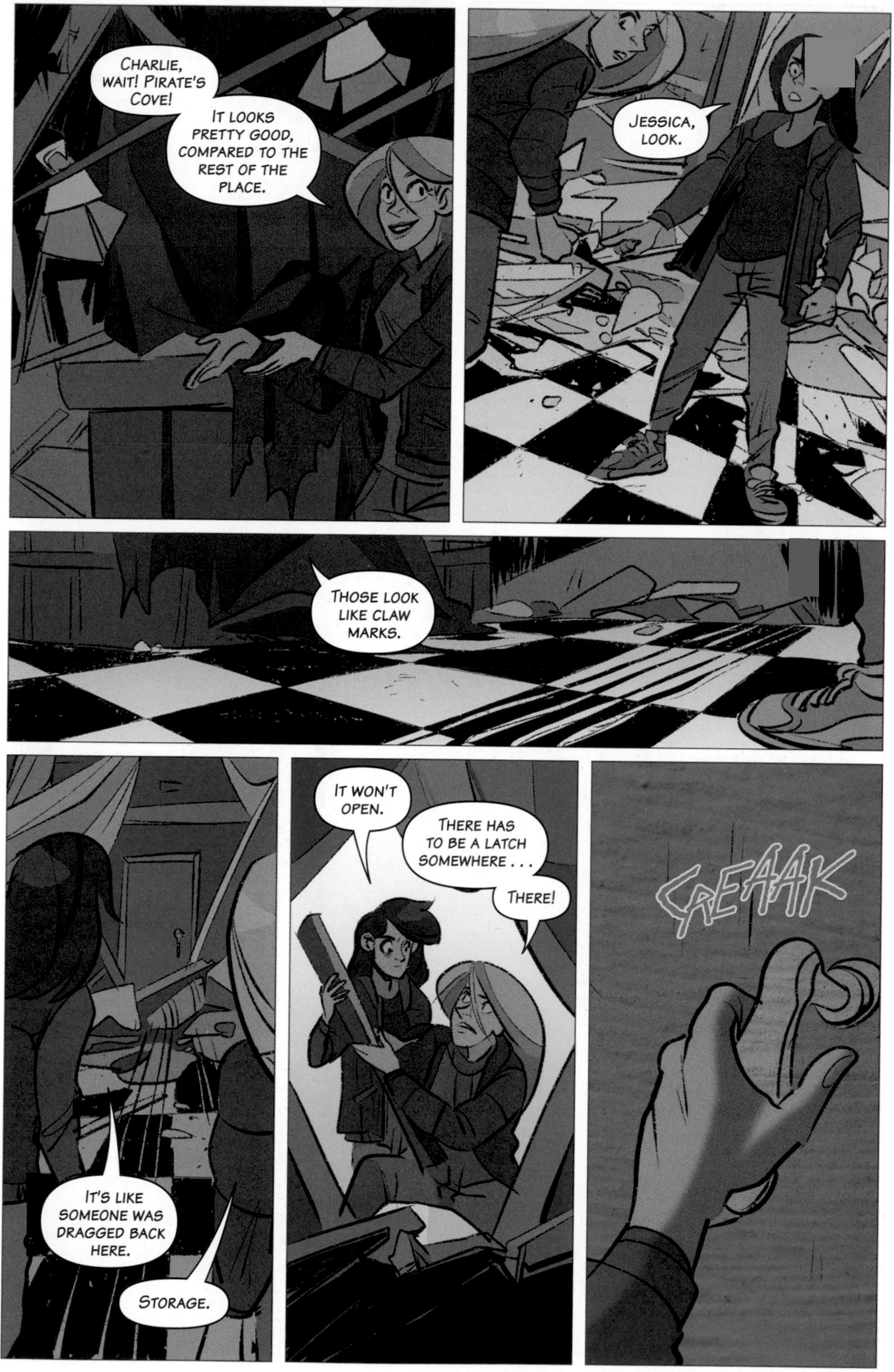
Charlie, wait! Pirate's Cove!
It looks pretty good, compared to the rest of the place.
Jessica, look.
Those look like claw marks.
It's like someone was dragged back here.
Storage.
It won't open.
There has to be a latch somewhere . . .
There!
CREAAK

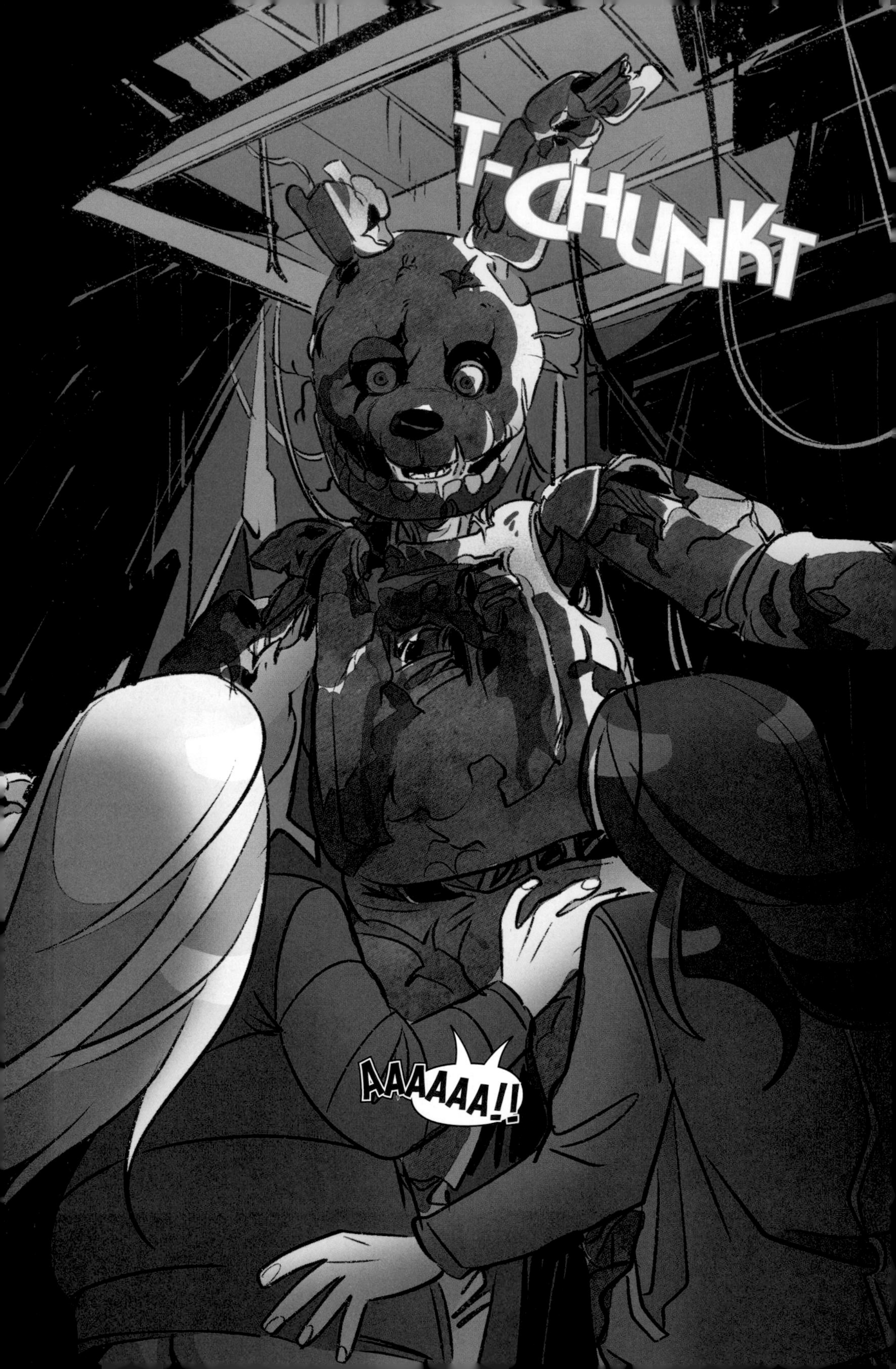
T-CHUNKT
AAAAAA!!

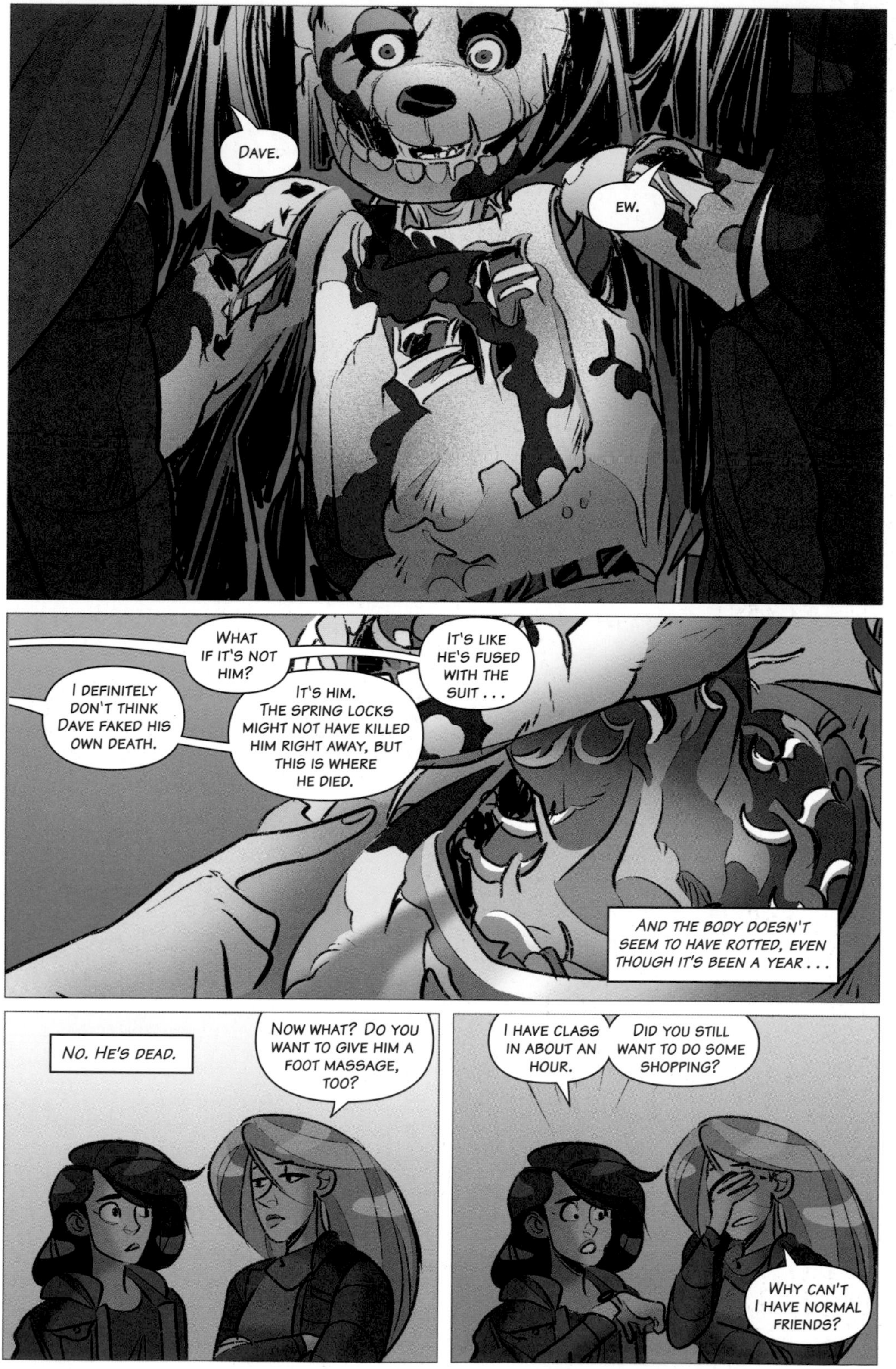
Dave.
Ew.
What if it's not him?
I definitely don't think Dave faked his own death.
It's like he's fused with the suit . . .
It's him. The spring locks might not have killed him right away, but this is where he died.
And the body doesn't seem to have rotted, even though it's been a year . . .
No. He's dead.
Now what? Do you want to give him a foot massage, too?
I have class in about an hour.
Did you still want to do some shopping?
Why can't I have normal friends?

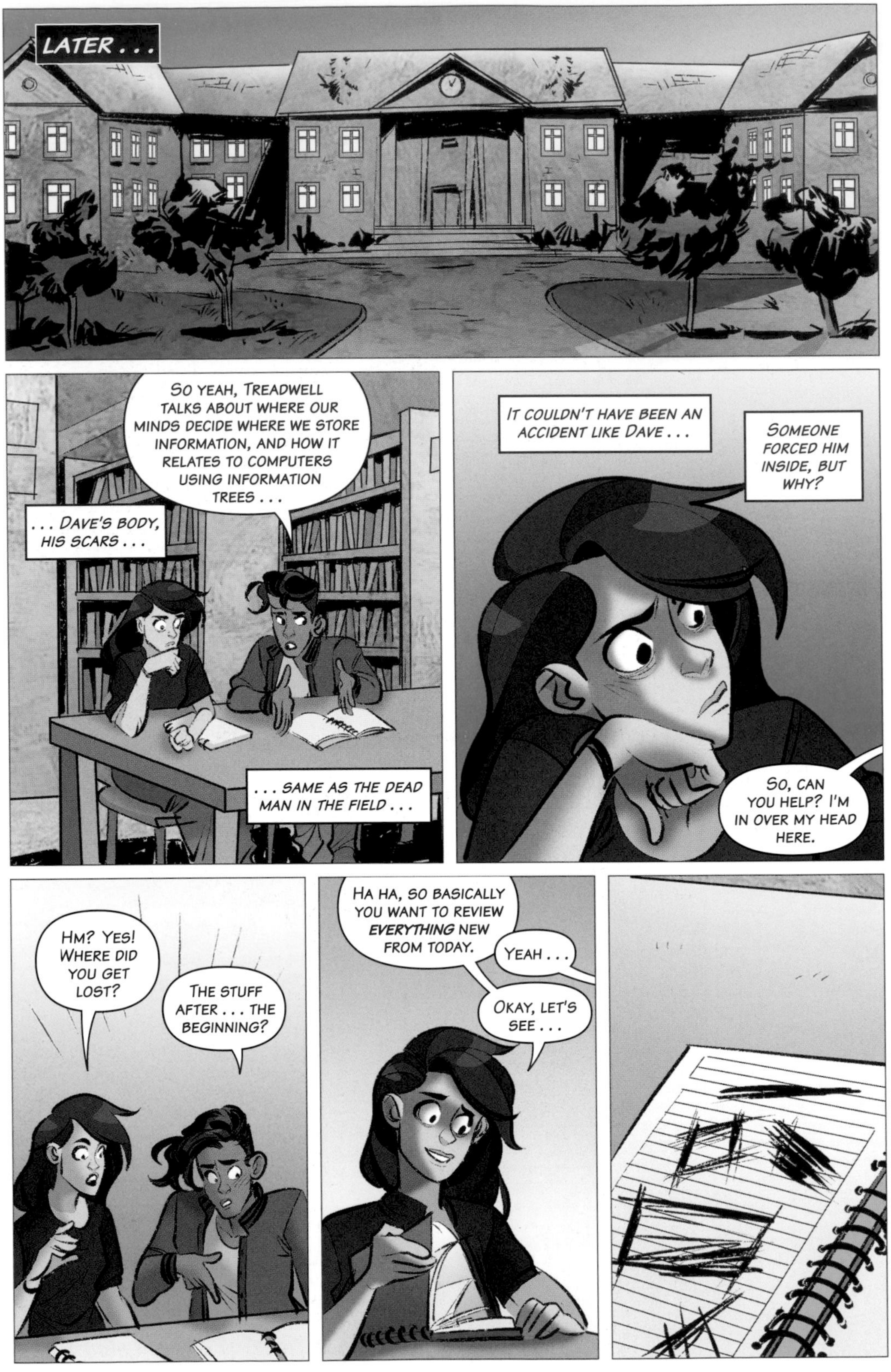
LATER . . .
So yeah, Treadwell talks about where our minds decide where we store information, and how it relates to computers using information trees . . .
. . . Dave's body, his scars . . .
. . . same as the dead man in the field . . .
It couldn't have been an accident like Dave . . .
Someone forced him inside, but why?
So, can you help? I'm in over my head here.
Hm? Yes! Where did you get lost?
The stuff after . . . the beginning?
Ha ha, so basically you want to review **everything** new from today.
Yeah . . .
Okay, let's see . . .

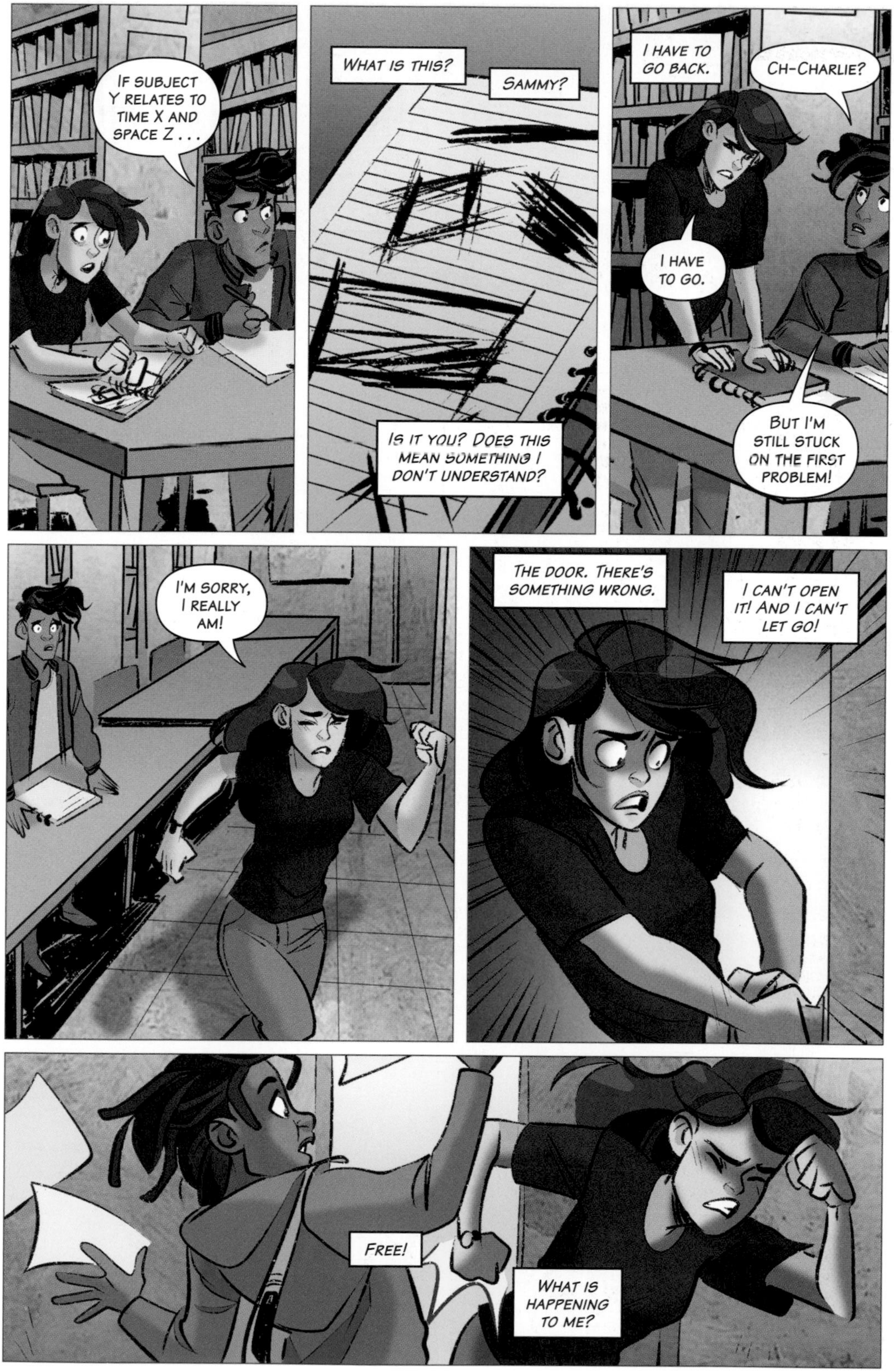
IF SUBJECT Y RELATES TO TIME X AND SPACE Z . . .
WHAT IS THIS?
SAMMY?
IS IT YOU? DOES THIS MEAN SOMETHING I DON'T UNDERSTAND?
I HAVE TO GO BACK.
CH-CHARLIE?
I HAVE TO GO.
BUT I'M STILL STUCK ON THE FIRST PROBLEM!
I'M SORRY, I REALLY AM!
THE DOOR. THERE'S SOMETHING WRONG.
I CAN'T OPEN IT! AND I CAN'T LET GO!
FREE!
WHAT IS HAPPENING TO ME?

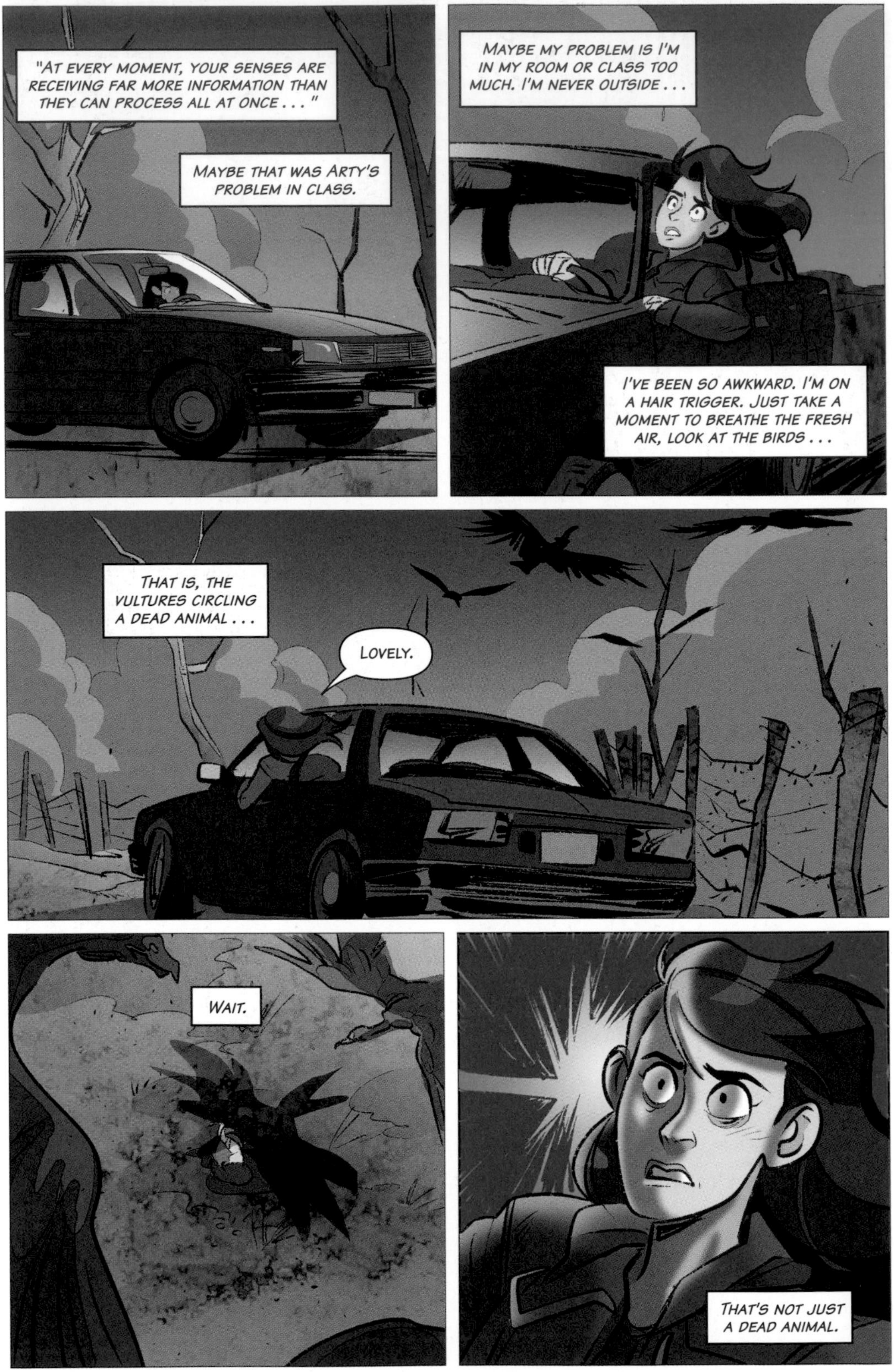
"At every moment, your senses are receiving far more information than they can process all at once . . ."
Maybe that was Arty's problem in class.
Maybe my problem is I'm in my room or class too much. I'm never outside . . .
I've been so awkward. I'm on a hair trigger. Just take a moment to breathe the fresh air, look at the birds . . .
That is, the vultures circling a dead animal . . .
Lovely.
Wait.
That's not just a dead animal.

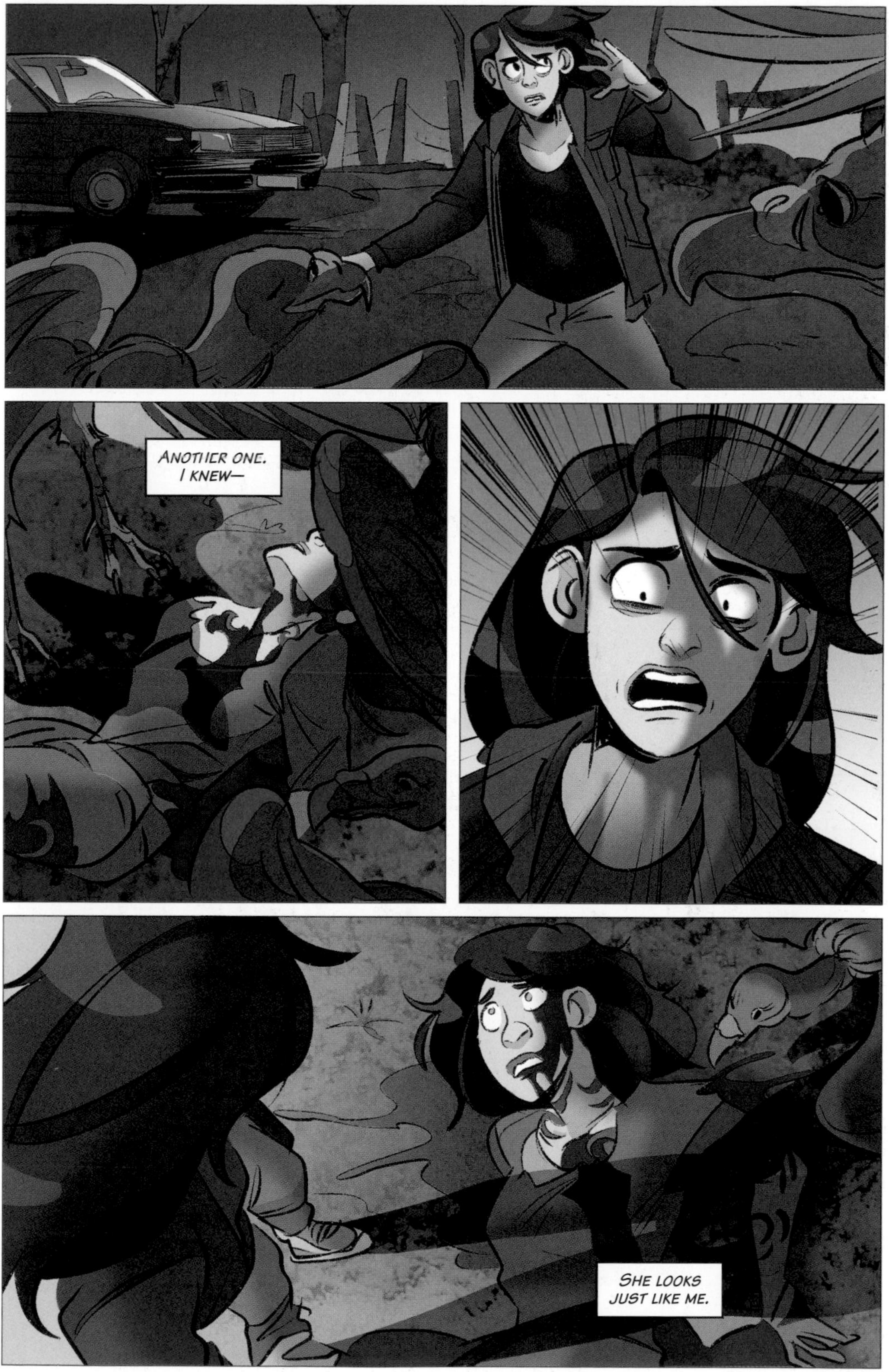
ANOTHER ONE.
I KNEW—
SHE LOOKS
JUST LIKE ME.

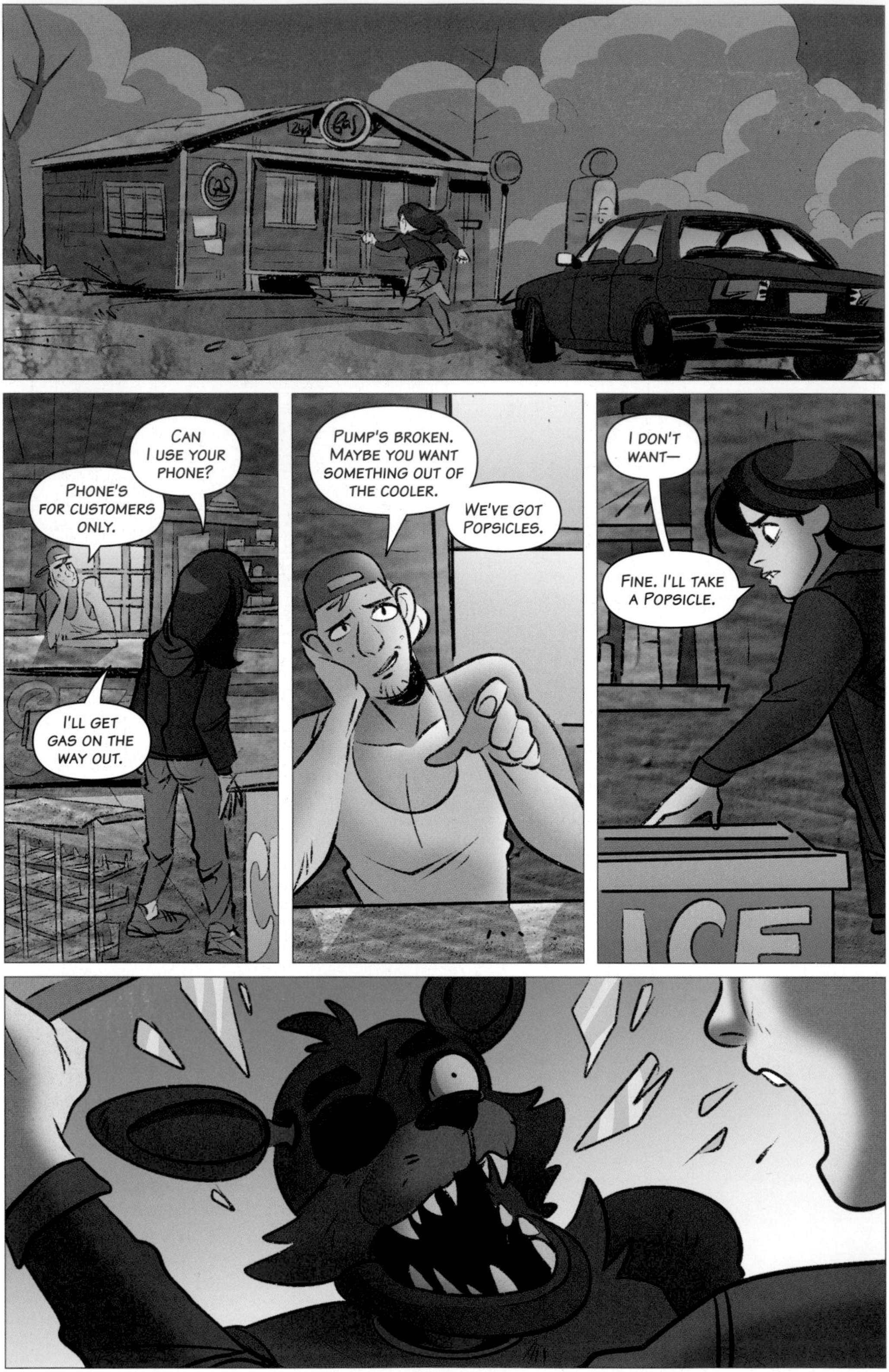
CAN I USE YOUR PHONE?
PHONE'S FOR CUSTOMERS ONLY.
I'LL GET GAS ON THE WAY OUT.
PUMP'S BROKEN. MAYBE YOU WANT SOMETHING OUT OF THE COOLER.
WE'VE GOT POPSICLES.
I DON'T WANT—
FINE. I'LL TAKE A POPSICLE.
ICE

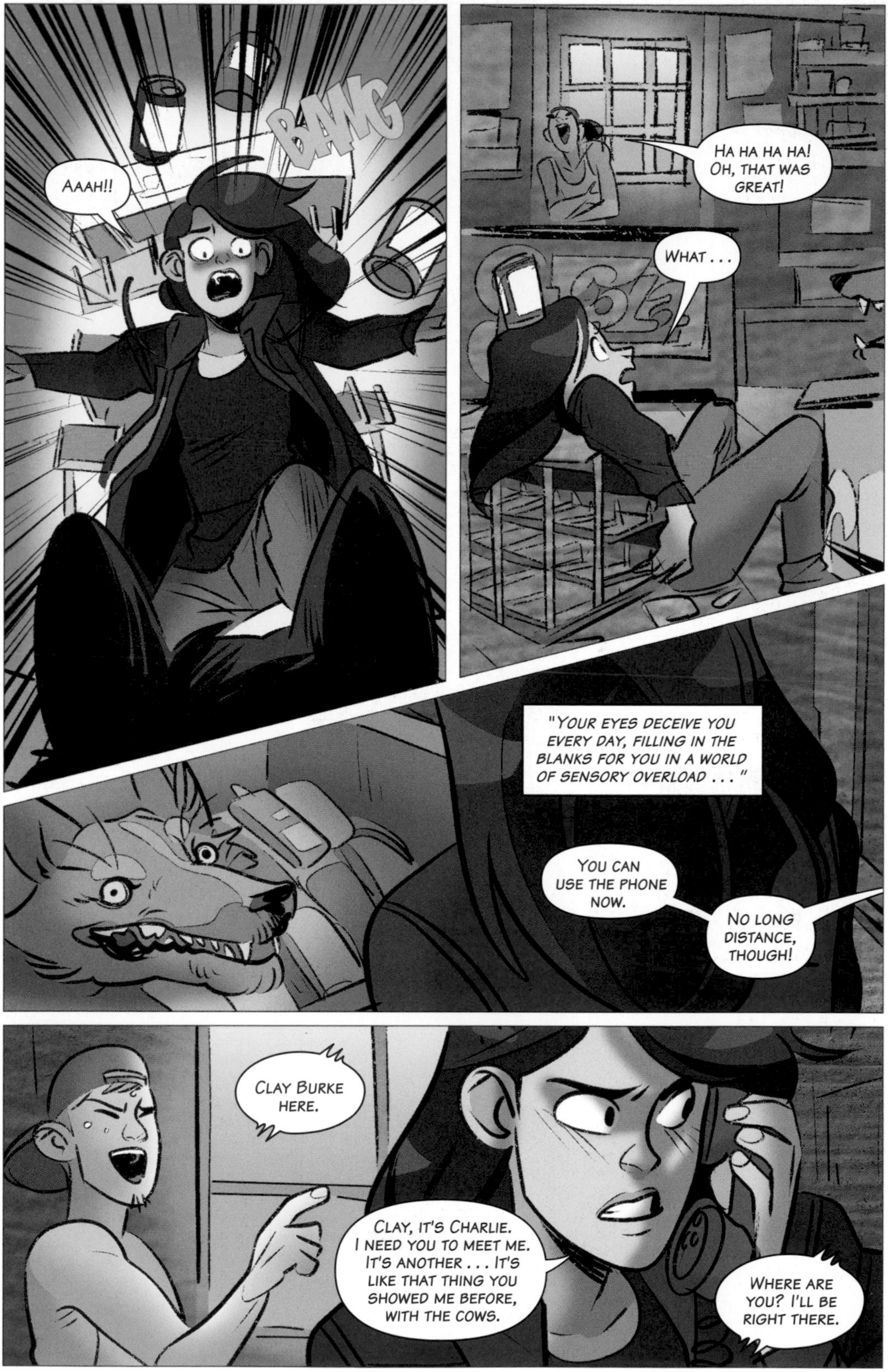
BAMG
AAAH!!
HA HA HA HA!
OH, THAT WAS GREAT!
WHAT . . .
"YOUR EYES DECEIVE YOU EVERY DAY, FILLING IN THE BLANKS FOR YOU IN A WORLD OF SENSORY OVERLOAD . . ."
YOU CAN USE THE PHONE NOW.
NO LONG DISTANCE, THOUGH!
CLAY BURKE HERE.
CLAY, IT'S CHARLIE. I NEED YOU TO MEET ME. IT'S ANOTHER . . . IT'S LIKE THAT THING YOU SHOWED ME BEFORE, WITH THE COWS.
WHERE ARE YOU? I'LL BE RIGHT THERE.

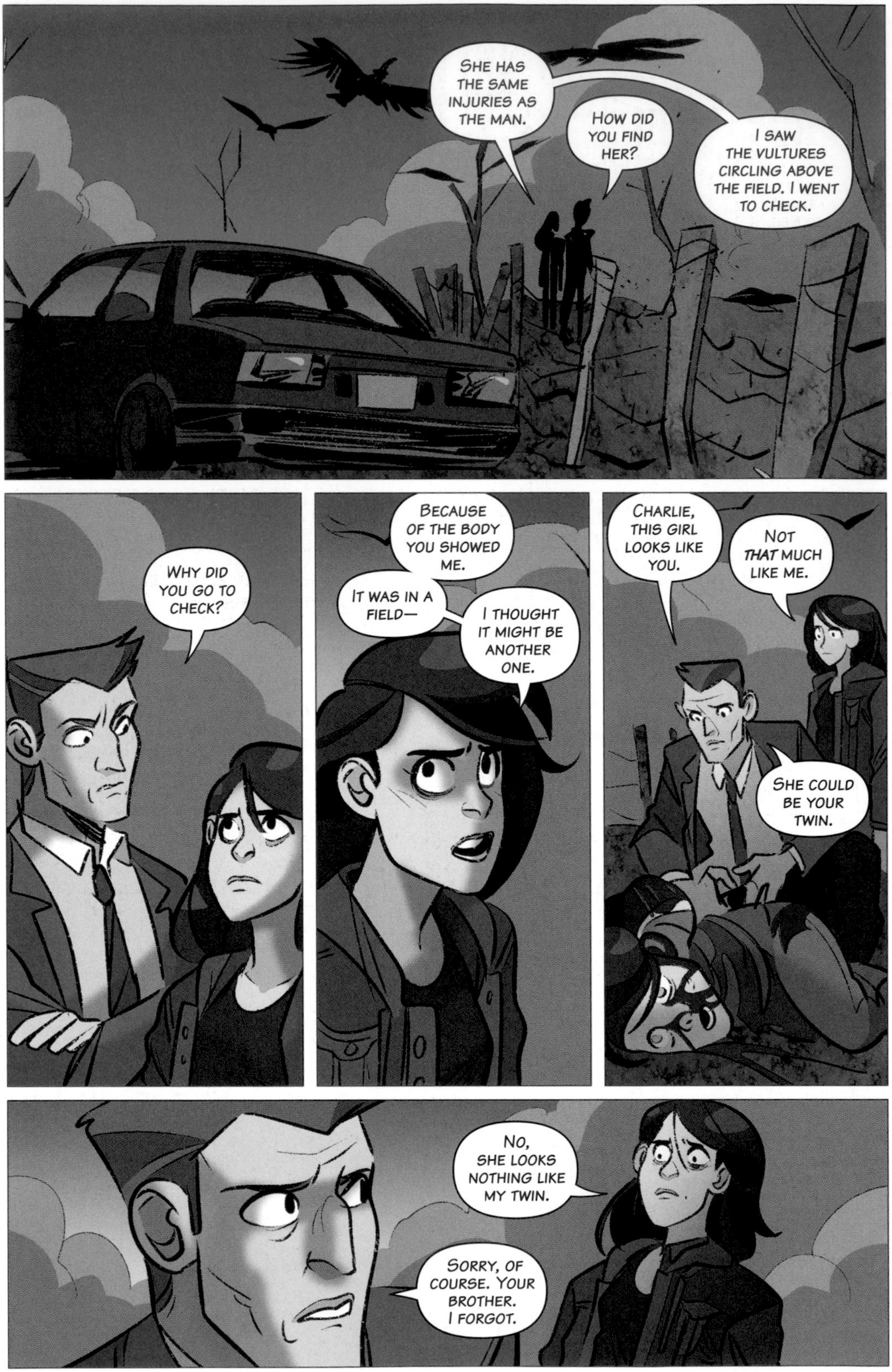
SHE HAS THE SAME INJURIES AS THE MAN.
HOW DID YOU FIND HER?
I SAW THE VULTURES CIRCLING ABOVE THE FIELD. I WENT TO CHECK.
WHY DID YOU GO TO CHECK?
BECAUSE OF THE BODY YOU SHOWED ME.
IT WAS IN A FIELD—
I THOUGHT IT MIGHT BE ANOTHER ONE.
CHARLIE, THIS GIRL LOOKS LIKE YOU.
NOT *THAT* MUCH LIKE ME.
SHE COULD BE YOUR TWIN.
NO, SHE LOOKS NOTHING LIKE MY TWIN.
SORRY, OF COURSE. YOUR BROTHER. I FORGOT.

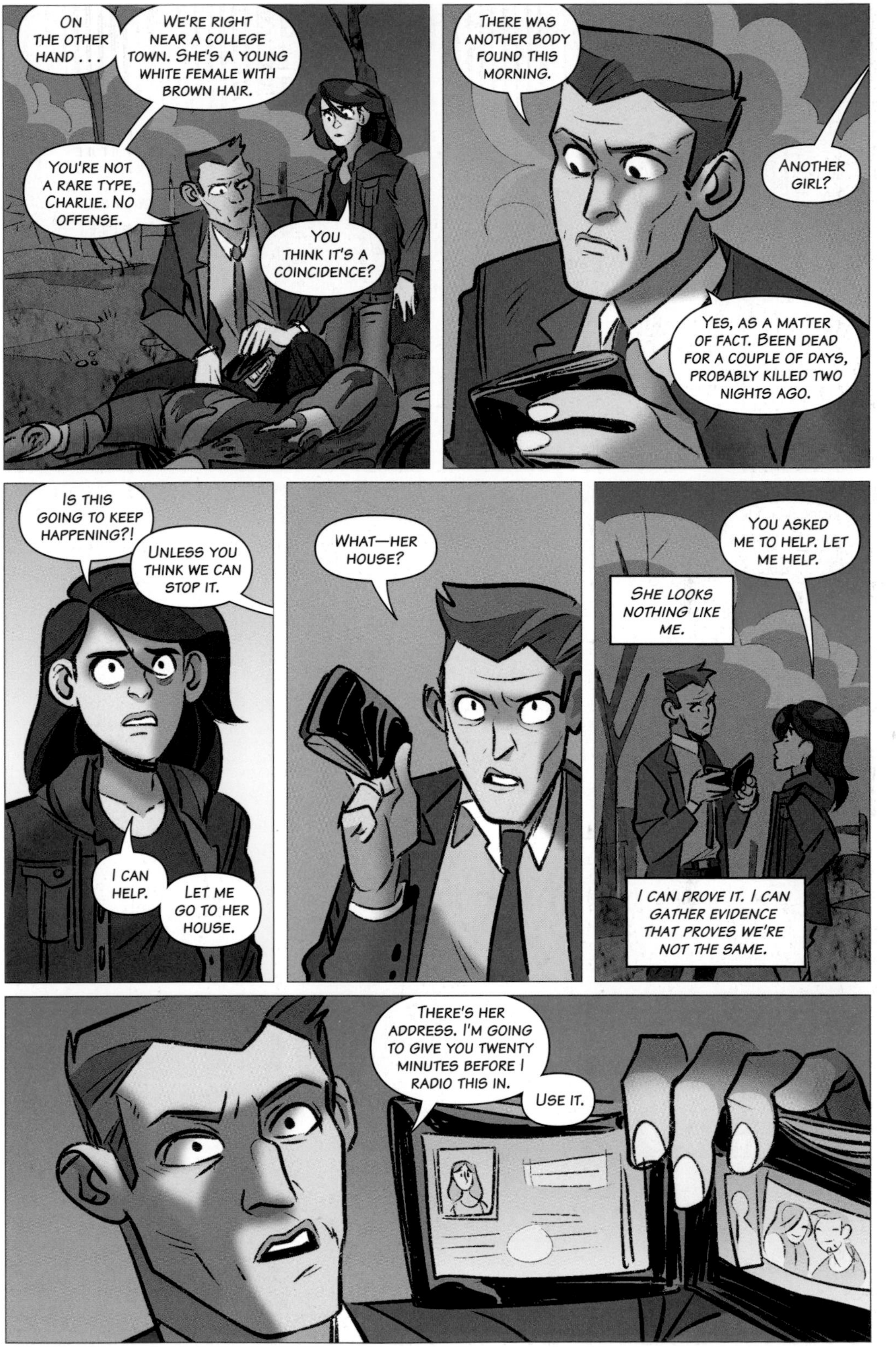
On the other hand . . .
We're right near a college town. She's a young white female with brown hair.
You're not a rare type, Charlie. No offense.
You think it's a coincidence?
There was another body found this morning.
Another girl?
Yes, as a matter of fact. Been dead for a couple of days, probably killed two nights ago.
Is this going to keep happening?!
Unless you think we can stop it.
I can help.
Let me go to her house.
What—her house?
You asked me to help. Let me help.
She looks nothing like me.
I can prove it. I can gather evidence that proves we're not the same.
There's her address. I'm going to give you twenty minutes before I radio this in.
Use it.

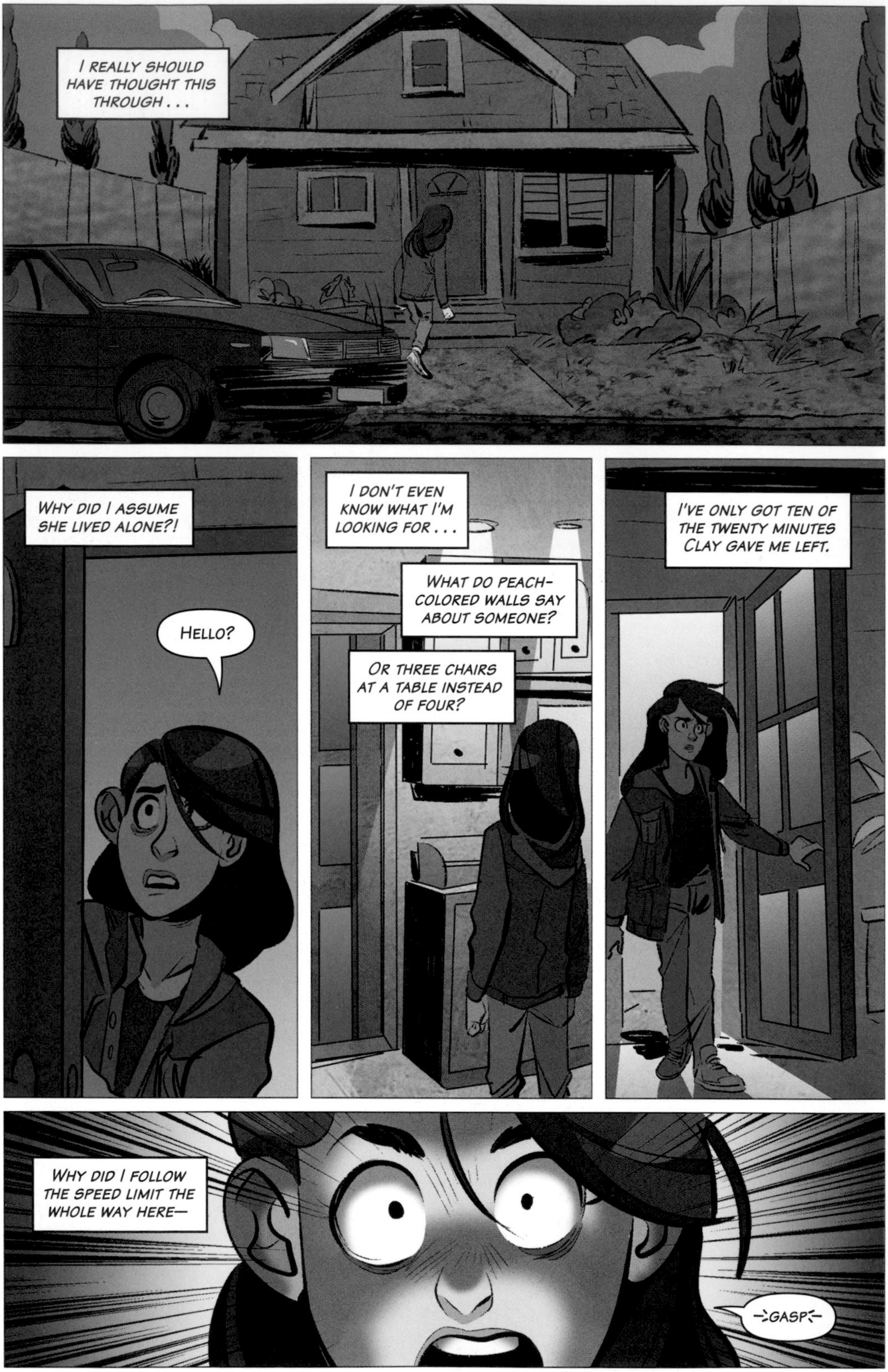
I REALLY SHOULD HAVE THOUGHT THIS THROUGH . . .
WHY DID I ASSUME SHE LIVED ALONE?!
HELLO?
I DON'T EVEN KNOW WHAT I'M LOOKING FOR . . .
WHAT DO PEACH-COLORED WALLS SAY ABOUT SOMEONE?
OR THREE CHAIRS AT A TABLE INSTEAD OF FOUR?
I'VE ONLY GOT TEN OF THE TWENTY MINUTES CLAY GAVE ME LEFT.
WHY DID I FOLLOW THE SPEED LIMIT THE WHOLE WAY HERE—
GASP

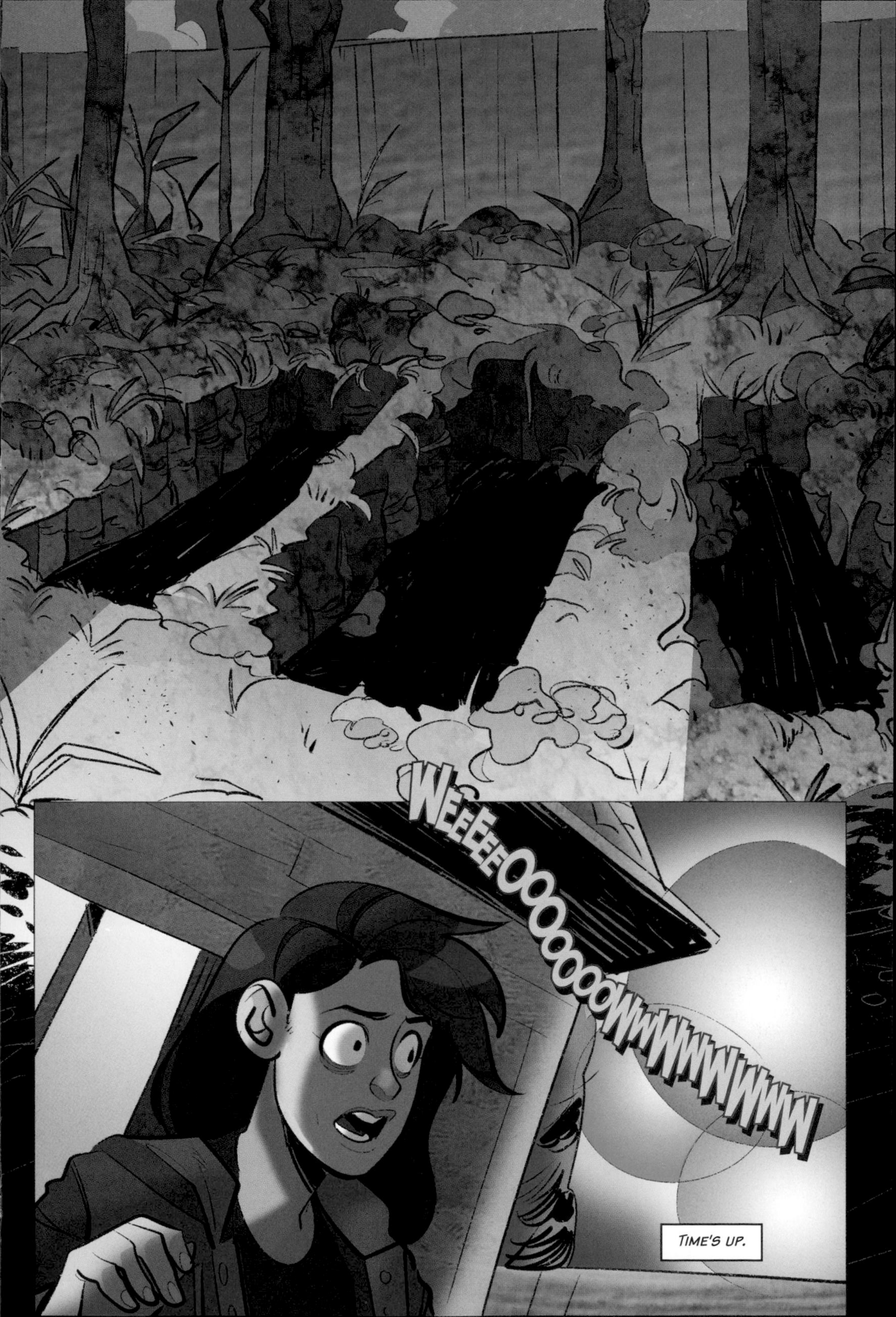
WEEEEEOOOOOOOWWWWWWWWWW
TIME'S UP.

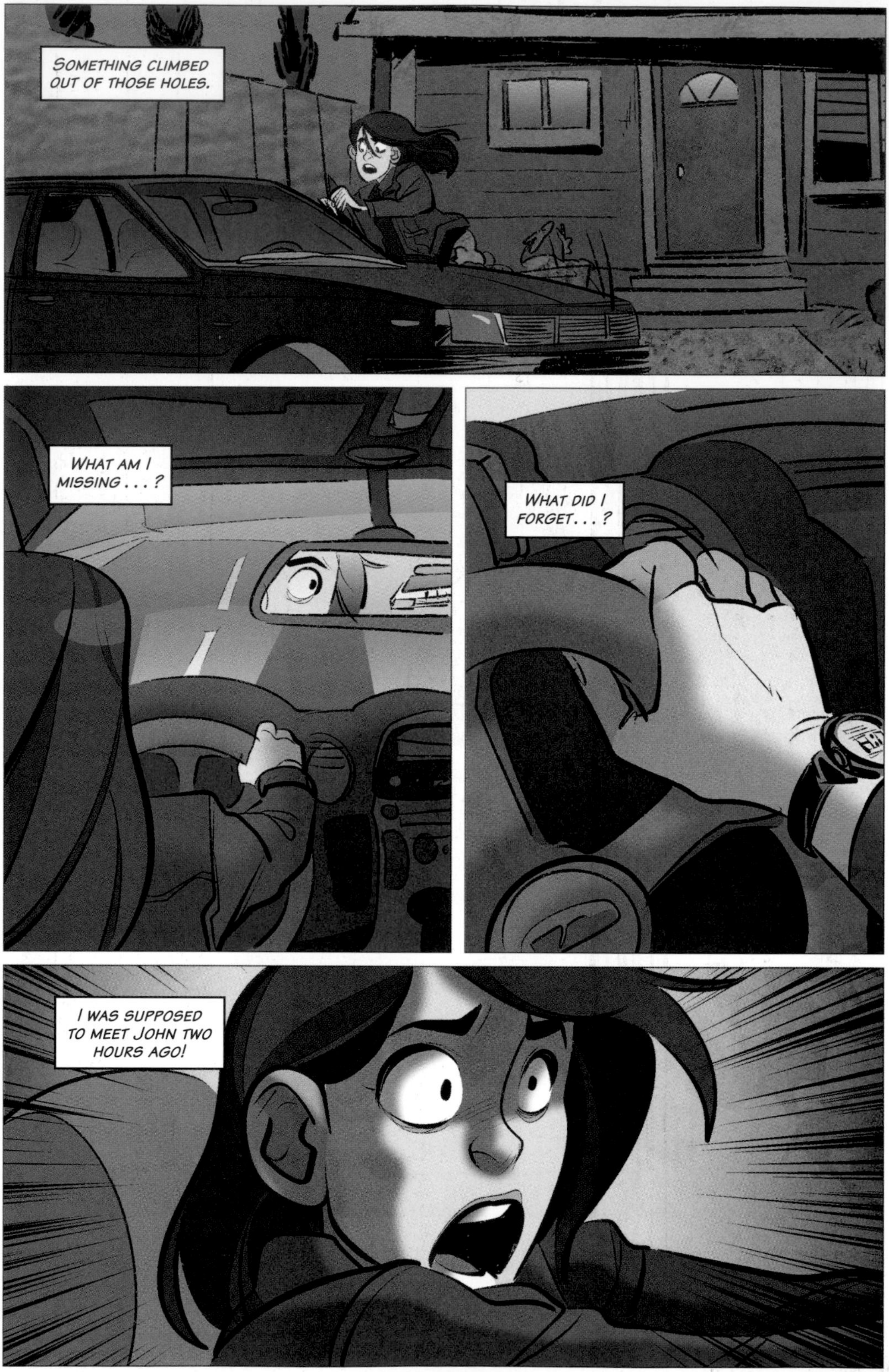
SOMETHING CLIMBED OUT OF THOSE HOLES.
WHAT AM I MISSING . . . ?
WHAT DID I FORGET . . . ?
I WAS SUPPOSED TO MEET JOHN TWO HOURS AGO!

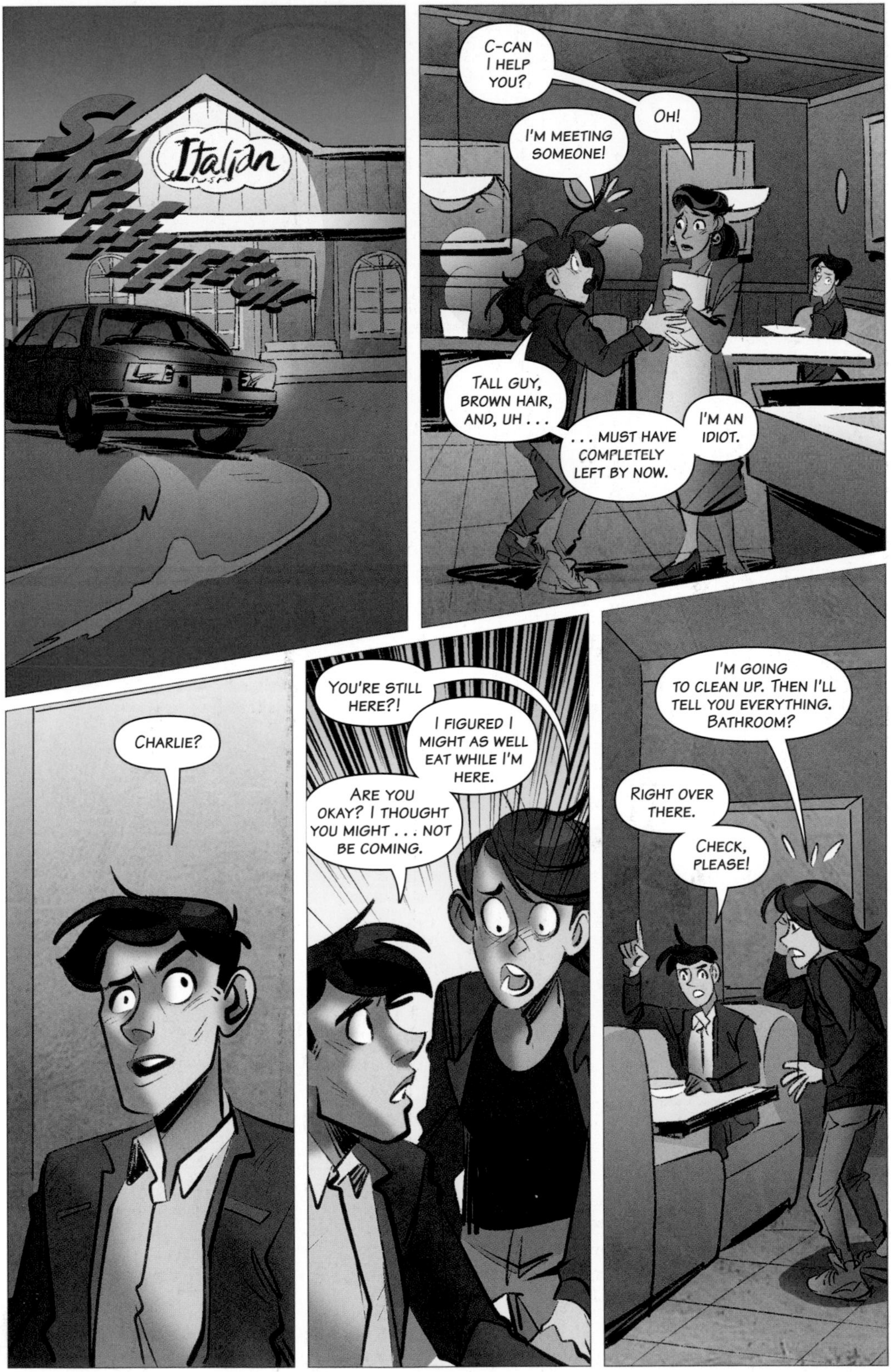
SKREEEEEEEECH!
Italian
C-CAN I HELP YOU?
OH!
I'M MEETING SOMEONE!
TALL GUY, BROWN HAIR, AND, UH . . .
. . . MUST HAVE COMPLETELY LEFT BY NOW.
I'M AN IDIOT.
CHARLIE?
YOU'RE STILL HERE?!
I FIGURED I MIGHT AS WELL EAT WHILE I'M HERE.
ARE YOU OKAY? I THOUGHT YOU MIGHT . . . NOT BE COMING.
I'M GOING TO CLEAN UP. THEN I'LL TELL YOU EVERYTHING. BATHROOM?
RIGHT OVER THERE.
CHECK, PLEASE!

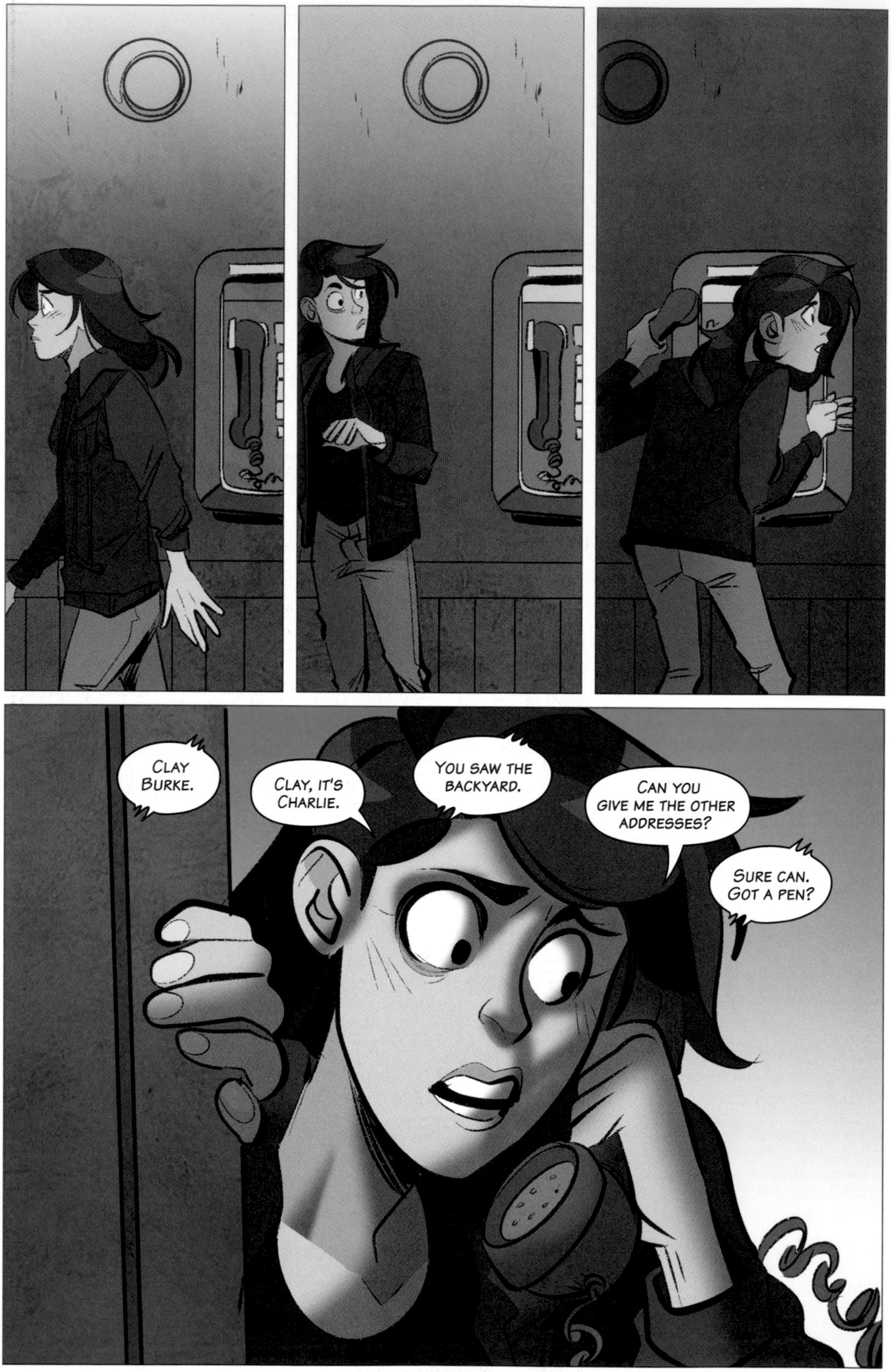
CLAY BURKE.
CLAY, IT'S CHARLIE.
YOU SAW THE BACKYARD.
CAN YOU GIVE ME THE OTHER ADDRESSES?
SURE CAN. GOT A PEN?

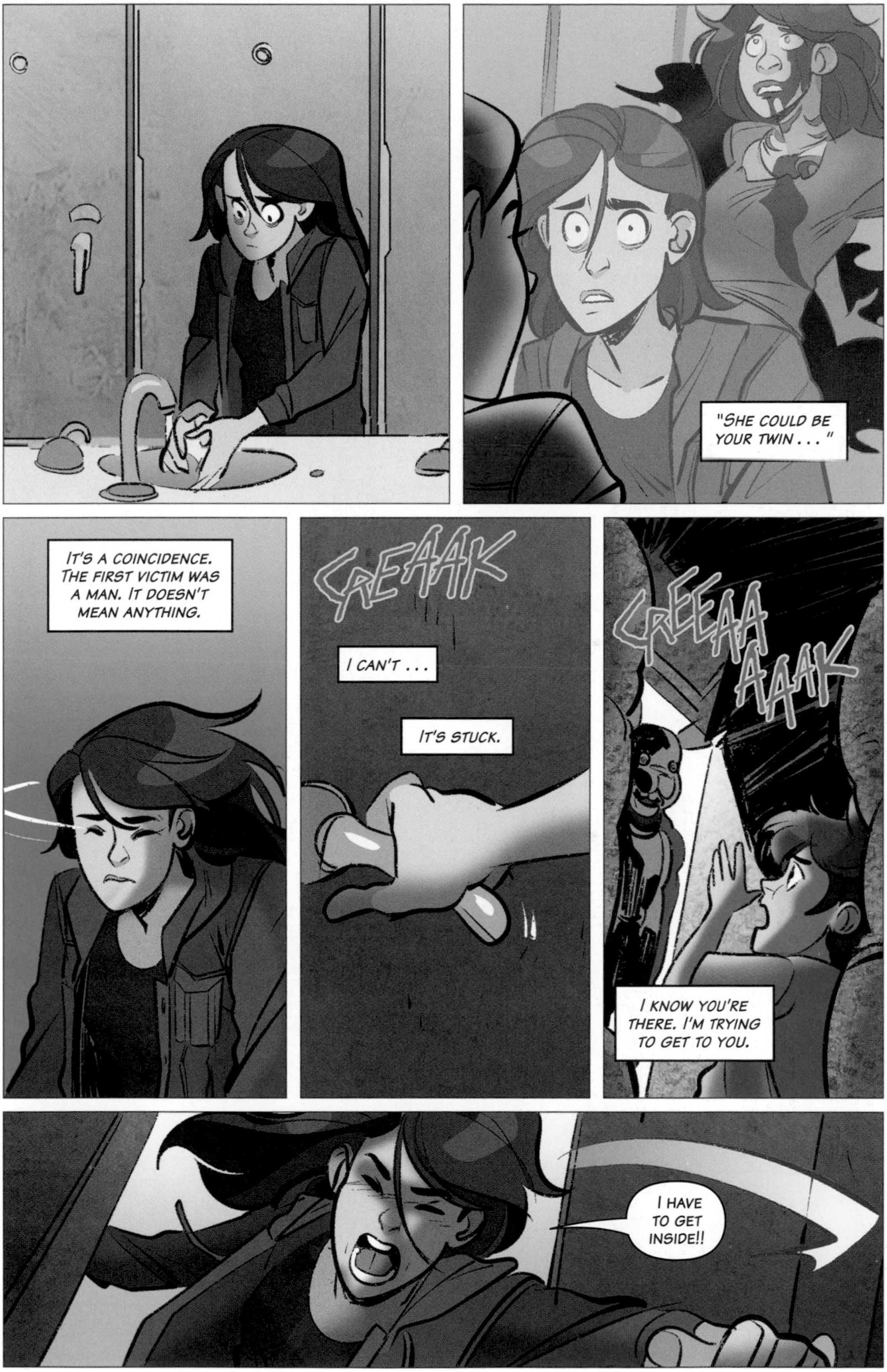
"SHE COULD BE YOUR TWIN . . ."
IT'S A COINCIDENCE. THE FIRST VICTIM WAS A MAN. IT DOESN'T MEAN ANYTHING.
CREAAK
I CAN'T . . .
IT'S STUCK.
CREEAAAAAK
I KNOW YOU'RE THERE. I'M TRYING TO GET TO YOU.
I HAVE TO GET INSIDE!!

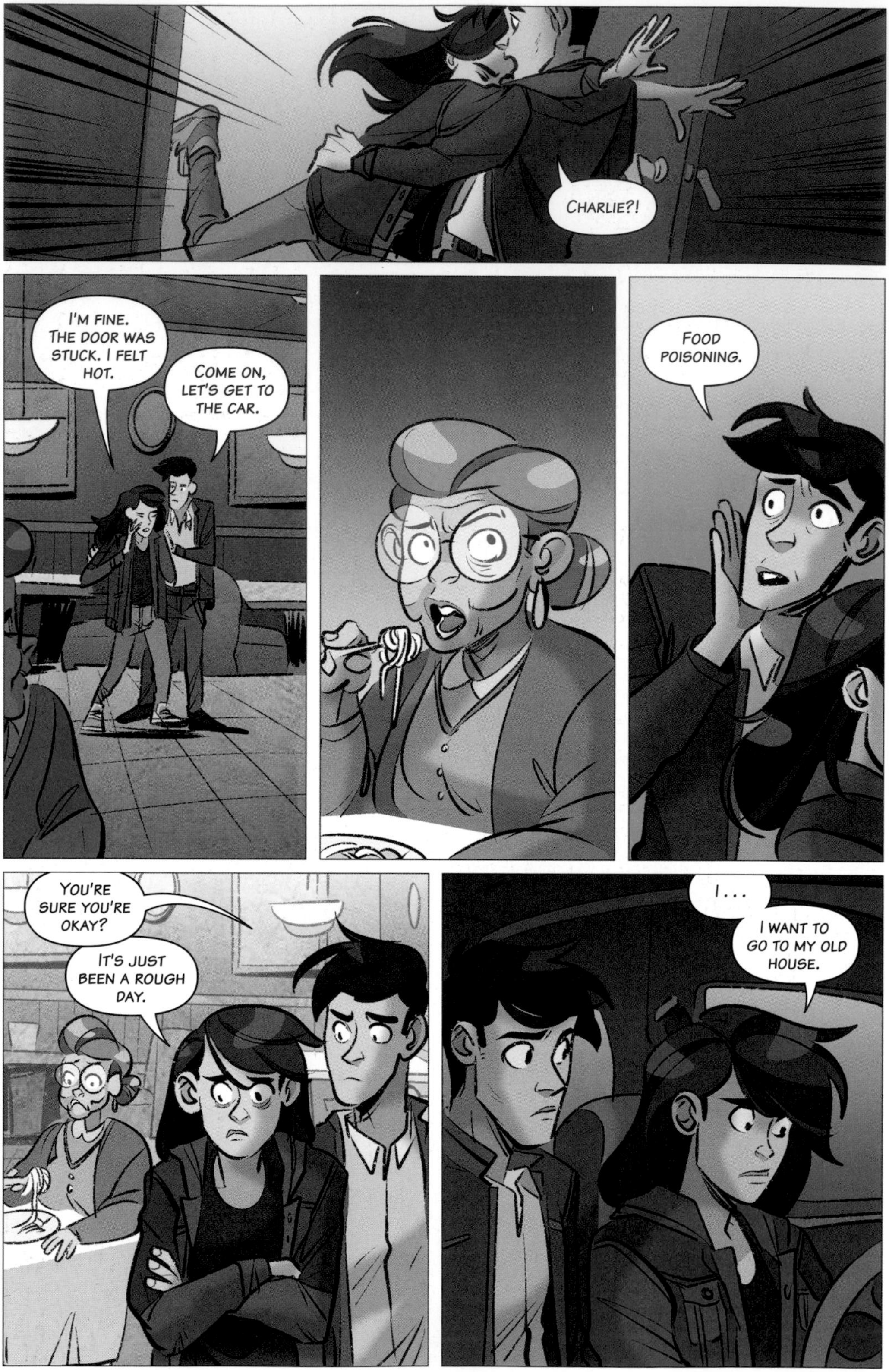
CHARLIE?!
I'M FINE. THE DOOR WAS STUCK. I FELT HOT.
COME ON, LET'S GET TO THE CAR.
FOOD POISONING.
YOU'RE SURE YOU'RE OKAY?
IT'S JUST BEEN A ROUGH DAY.
I...
I WANT TO GO TO MY OLD HOUSE.

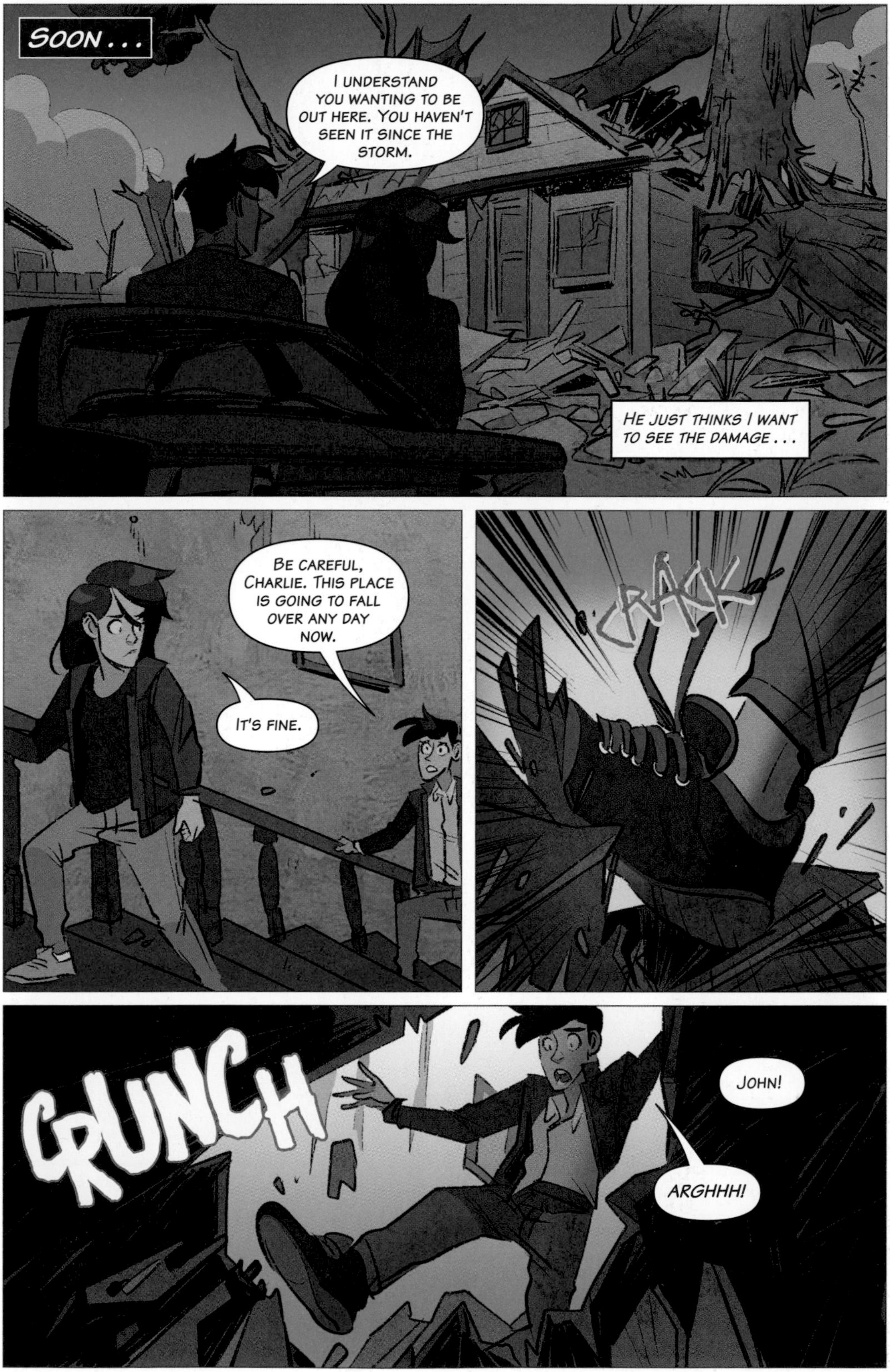
Soon . . .
I understand you wanting to be out here. You haven't seen it since the storm.
He just thinks I want to see the damage . . .
Be careful, Charlie. This place is going to fall over any day now.
It's fine.
CRAKK
CRUNCH
John!
ARGHHH!

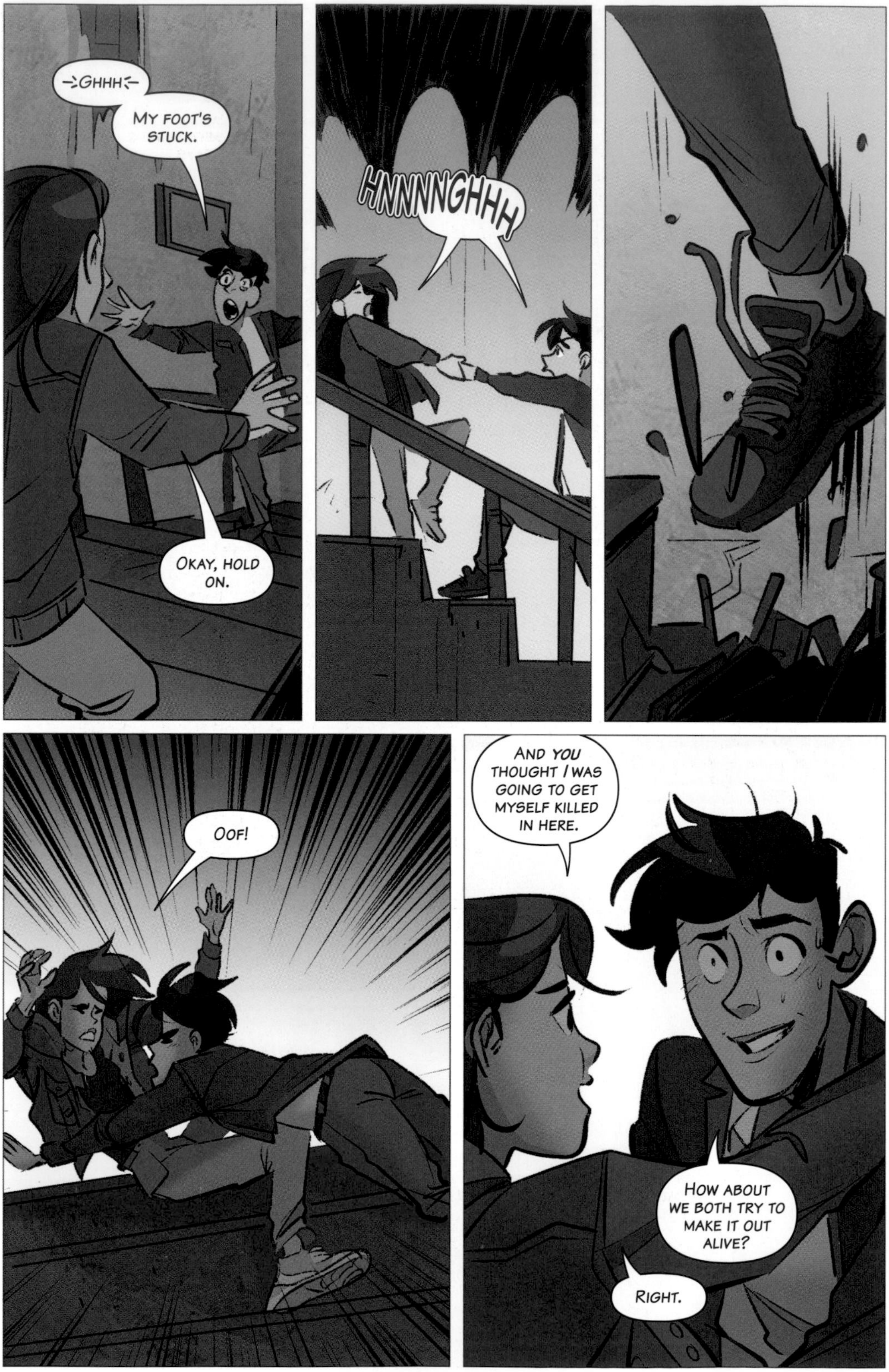
-GHHH-
MY FOOT'S STUCK.
OKAY, HOLD ON.
HNNNNGHHH
OOF!
AND YOU THOUGHT I WAS GOING TO GET MYSELF KILLED IN HERE.
HOW ABOUT WE BOTH TRY TO MAKE IT OUT ALIVE?
RIGHT.

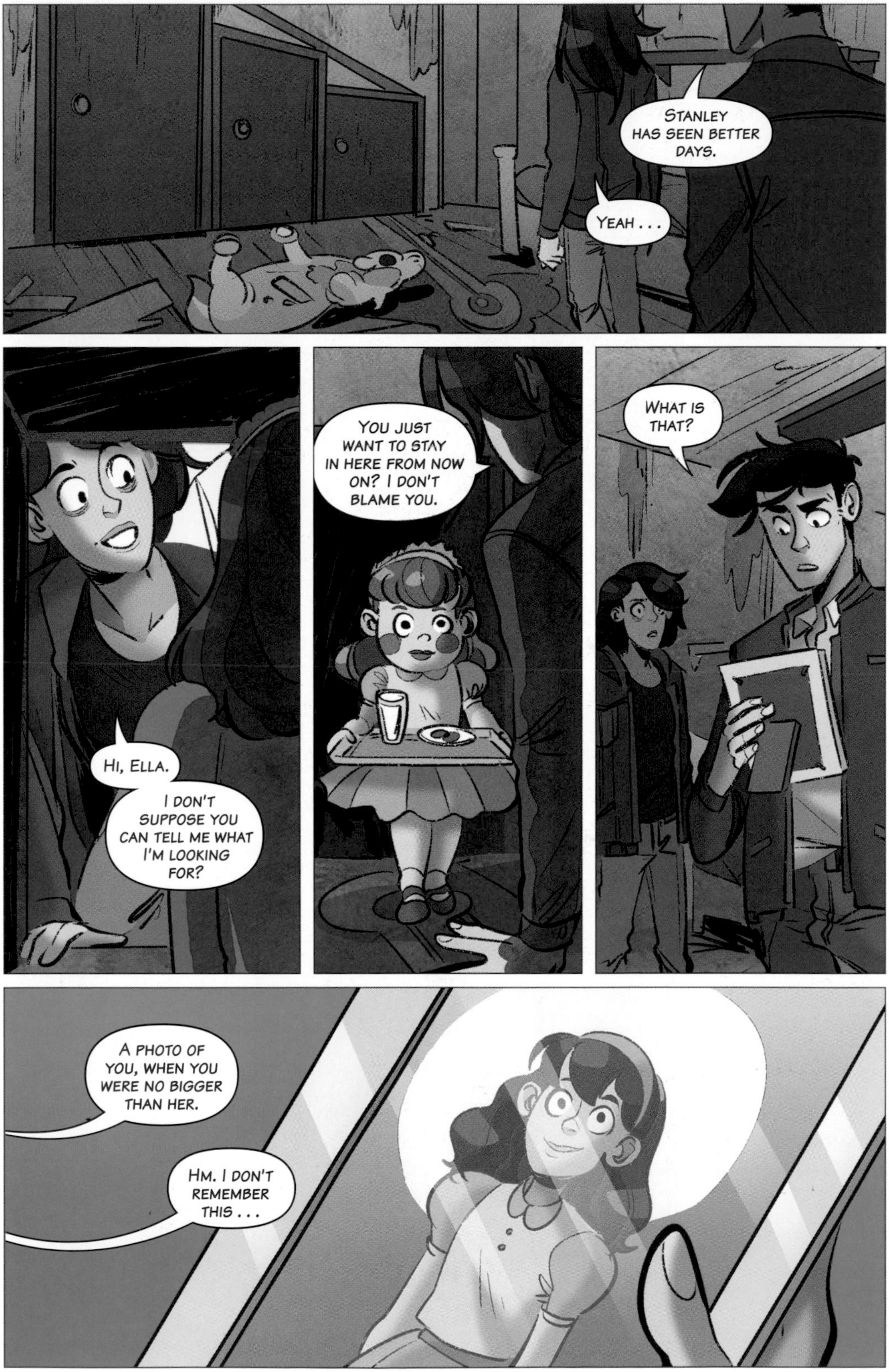
STANLEY HAS SEEN BETTER DAYS.
YEAH . . .
HI, ELLA.
I DON'T SUPPOSE YOU CAN TELL ME WHAT I'M LOOKING FOR?
YOU JUST WANT TO STAY IN HERE FROM NOW ON? I DON'T BLAME YOU.
WHAT IS THAT?
A PHOTO OF YOU, WHEN YOU WERE NO BIGGER THAN HER.
HM. I DON'T REMEMBER THIS . . .

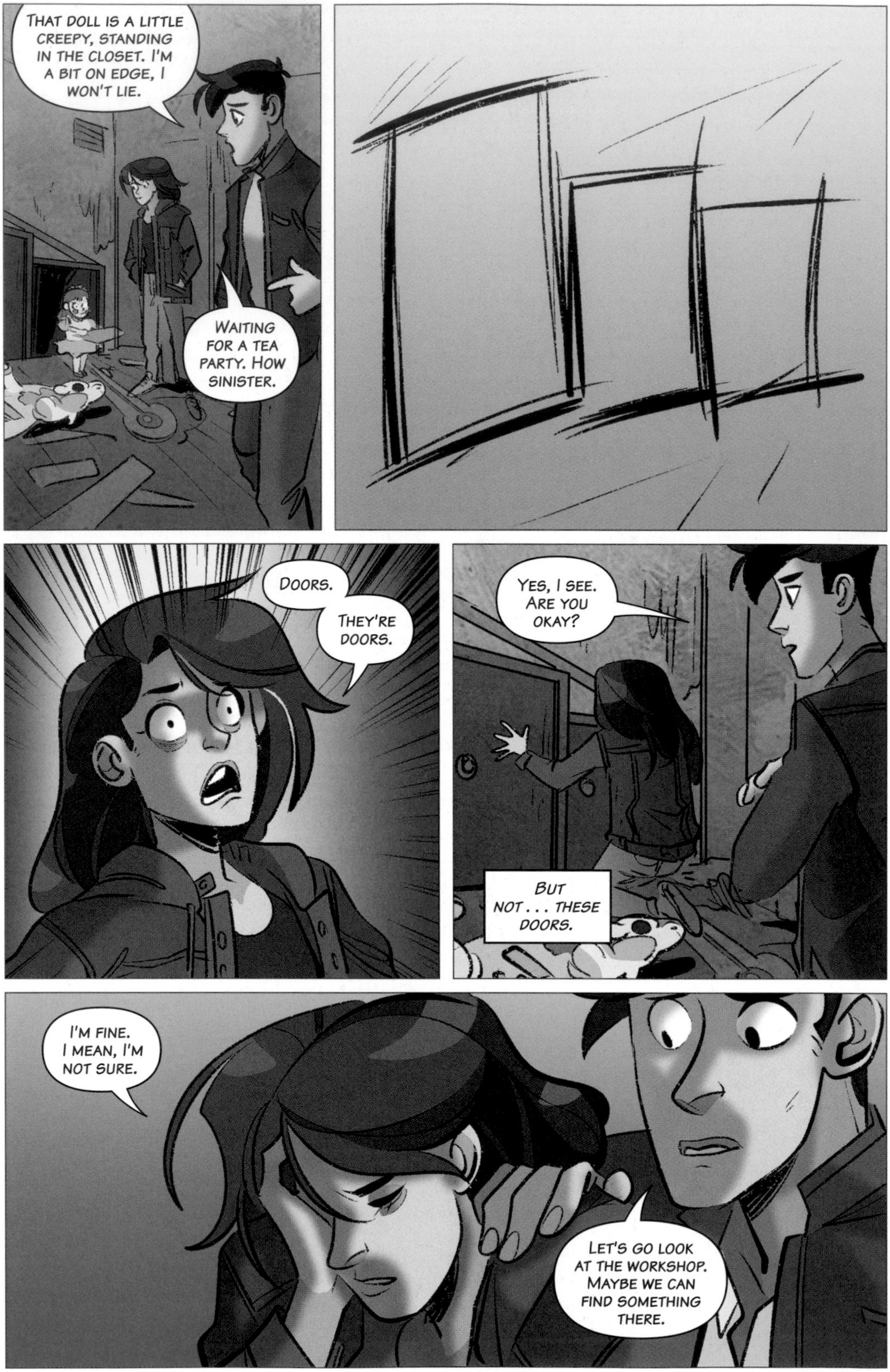
THAT DOLL IS A LITTLE CREEPY, STANDING IN THE CLOSET. I'M A BIT ON EDGE, I WON'T LIE.
WAITING FOR A TEA PARTY. HOW SINISTER.
DOORS.
THEY'RE DOORS.
YES, I SEE. ARE YOU OKAY?
BUT NOT . . . THESE DOORS.
I'M FINE. I MEAN, I'M NOT SURE.
LET'S GO LOOK AT THE WORKSHOP. MAYBE WE CAN FIND SOMETHING THERE.

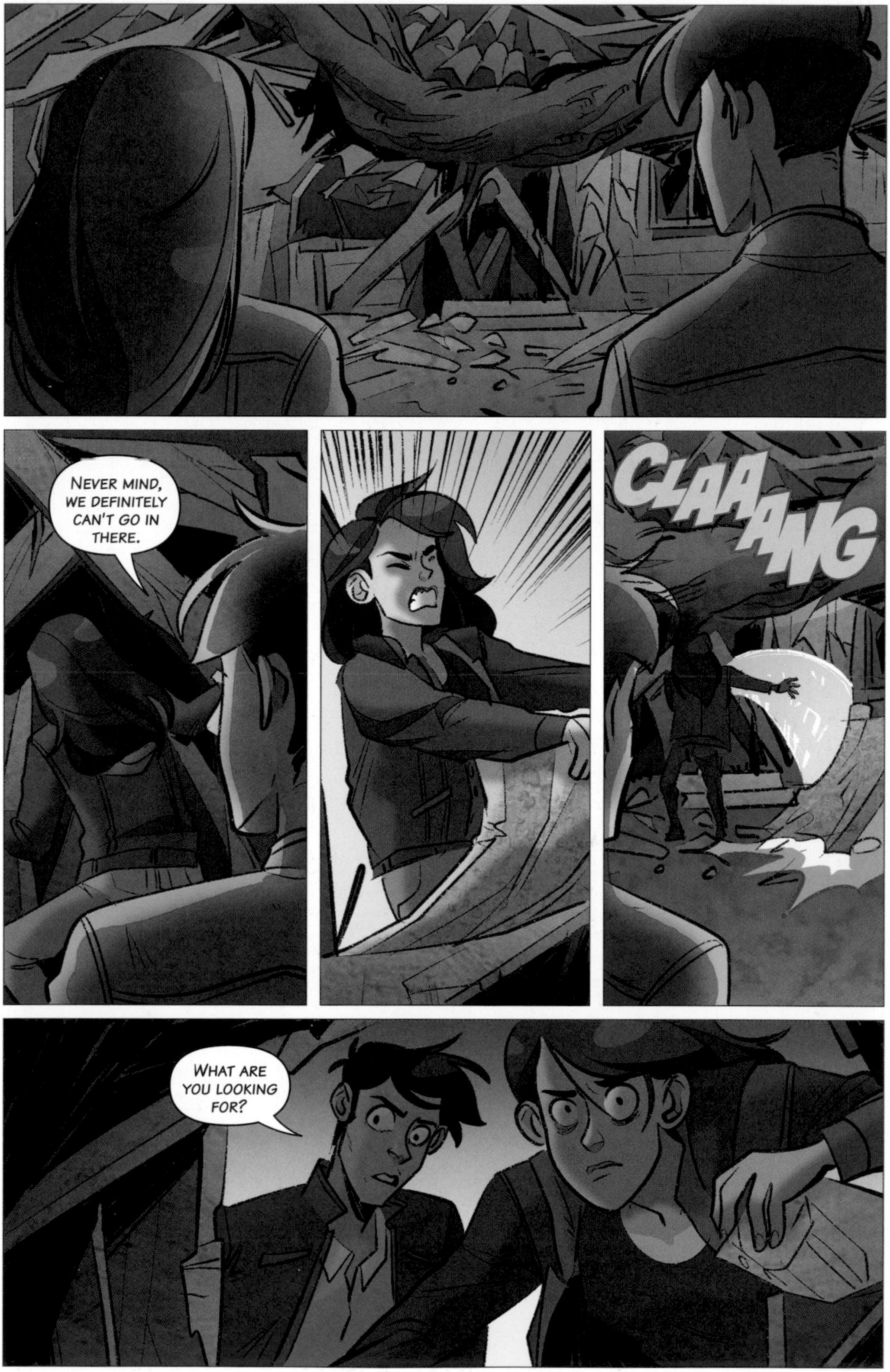
NEVER MIND, WE DEFINITELY CAN'T GO IN THERE.
CLAAAANG
WHAT ARE YOU LOOKING FOR?

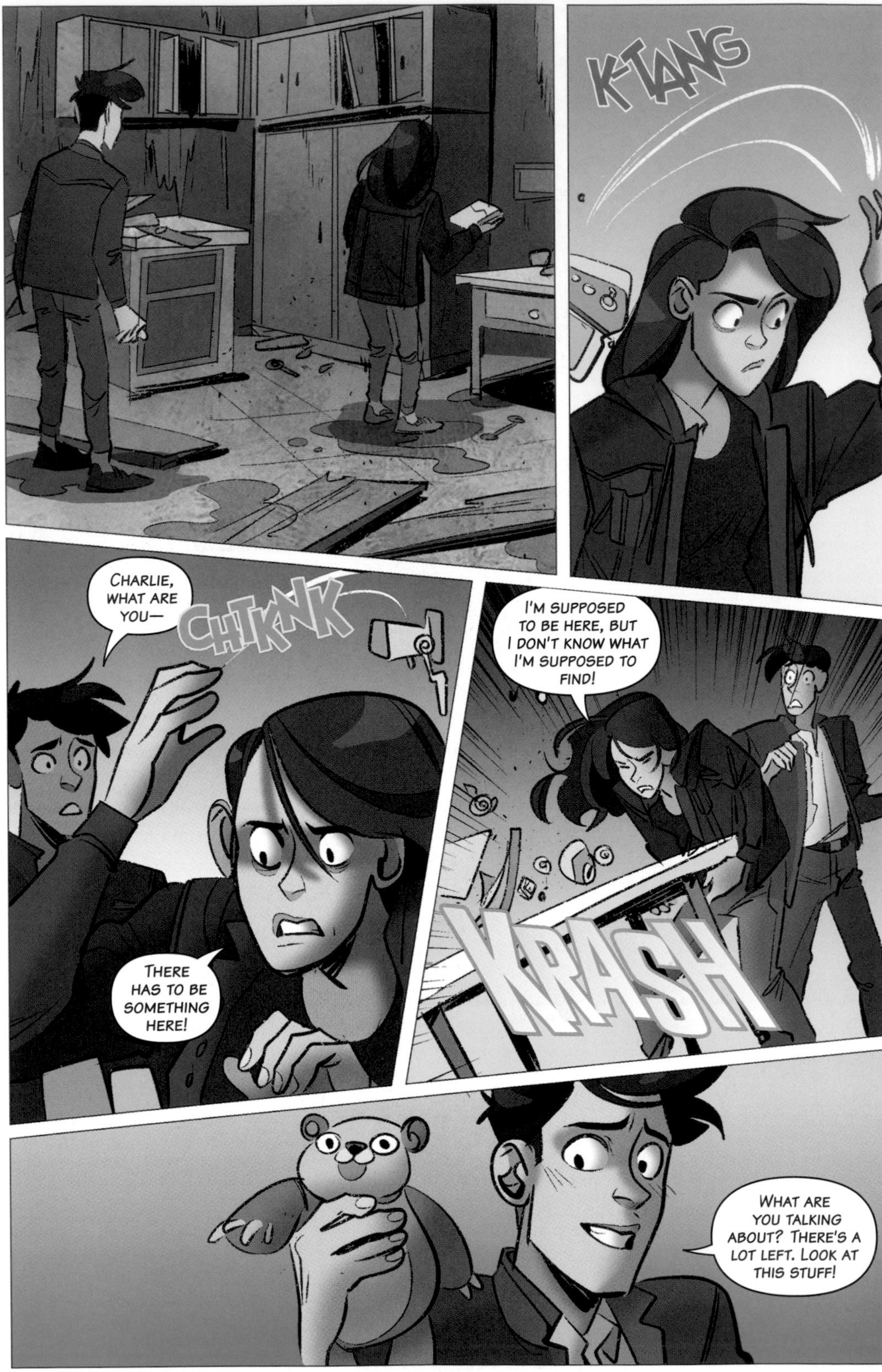
K-TANG
CHARLIE, WHAT ARE YOU—
CHTKNK
THERE HAS TO BE SOMETHING HERE!
I'M SUPPOSED TO BE HERE, BUT I DON'T KNOW WHAT I'M SUPPOSED TO FIND!
KRASH
WHAT ARE YOU TALKING ABOUT? THERE'S A LOT LEFT. LOOK AT THIS STUFF!

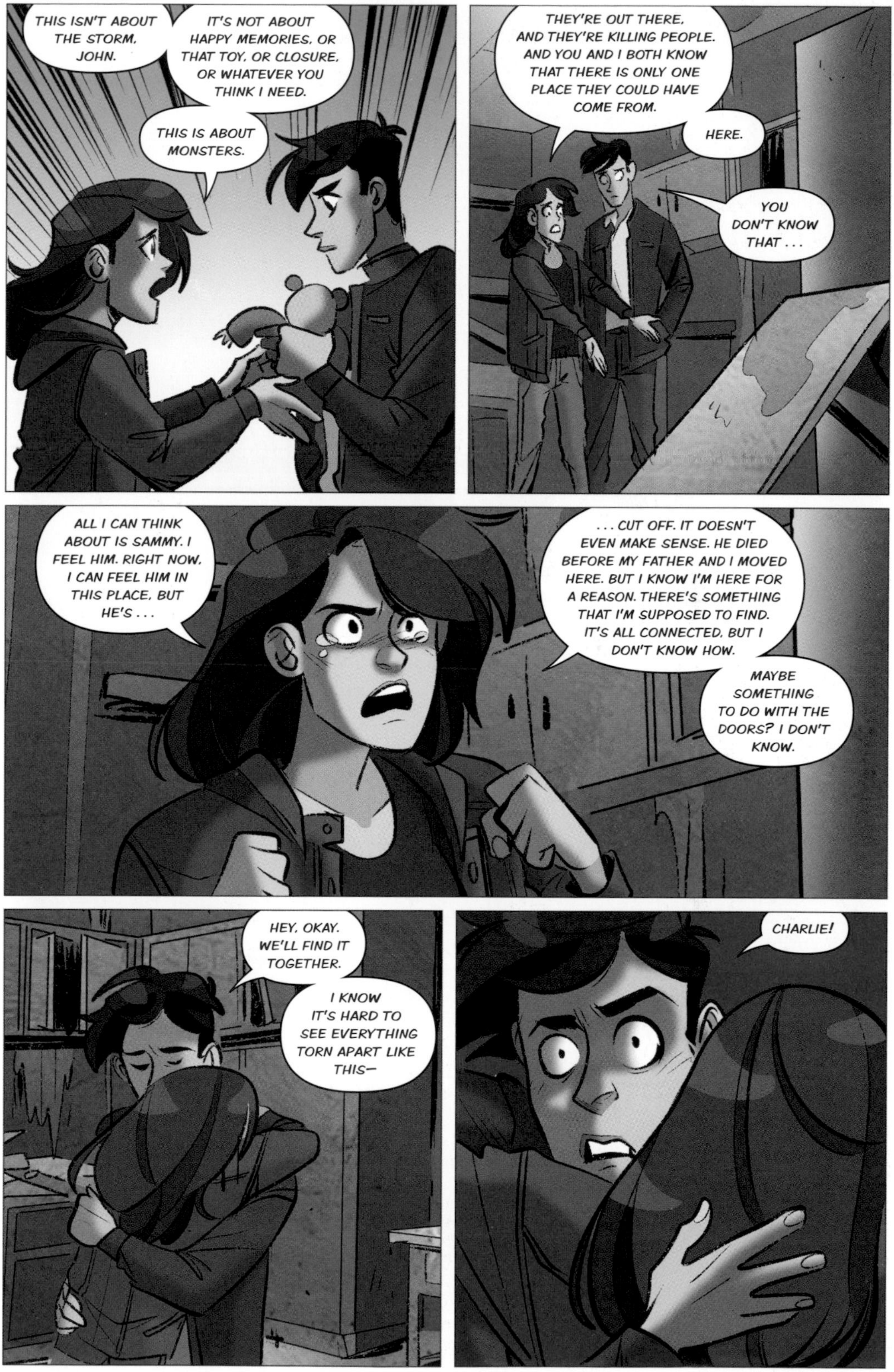
THIS ISN'T ABOUT THE STORM, JOHN.
IT'S NOT ABOUT HAPPY MEMORIES, OR THAT TOY, OR CLOSURE, OR WHATEVER YOU THINK I NEED.
THIS IS ABOUT MONSTERS.
THEY'RE OUT THERE, AND THEY'RE KILLING PEOPLE. AND YOU AND I BOTH KNOW THAT THERE IS ONLY ONE PLACE THEY COULD HAVE COME FROM.
HERE.
YOU DON'T KNOW THAT . . .
ALL I CAN THINK ABOUT IS SAMMY. I FEEL HIM. RIGHT NOW, I CAN FEEL HIM IN THIS PLACE, BUT HE'S . . .
. . . CUT OFF. IT DOESN'T EVEN MAKE SENSE. HE DIED BEFORE MY FATHER AND I MOVED HERE. BUT I KNOW I'M HERE FOR A REASON. THERE'S SOMETHING THAT I'M SUPPOSED TO FIND. IT'S ALL CONNECTED, BUT I DON'T KNOW HOW.
MAYBE SOMETHING TO DO WITH THE DOORS? I DON'T KNOW.
HEY, OKAY. WE'LL FIND IT TOGETHER.
I KNOW IT'S HARD TO SEE EVERYTHING TORN APART LIKE THIS—
CHARLIE!

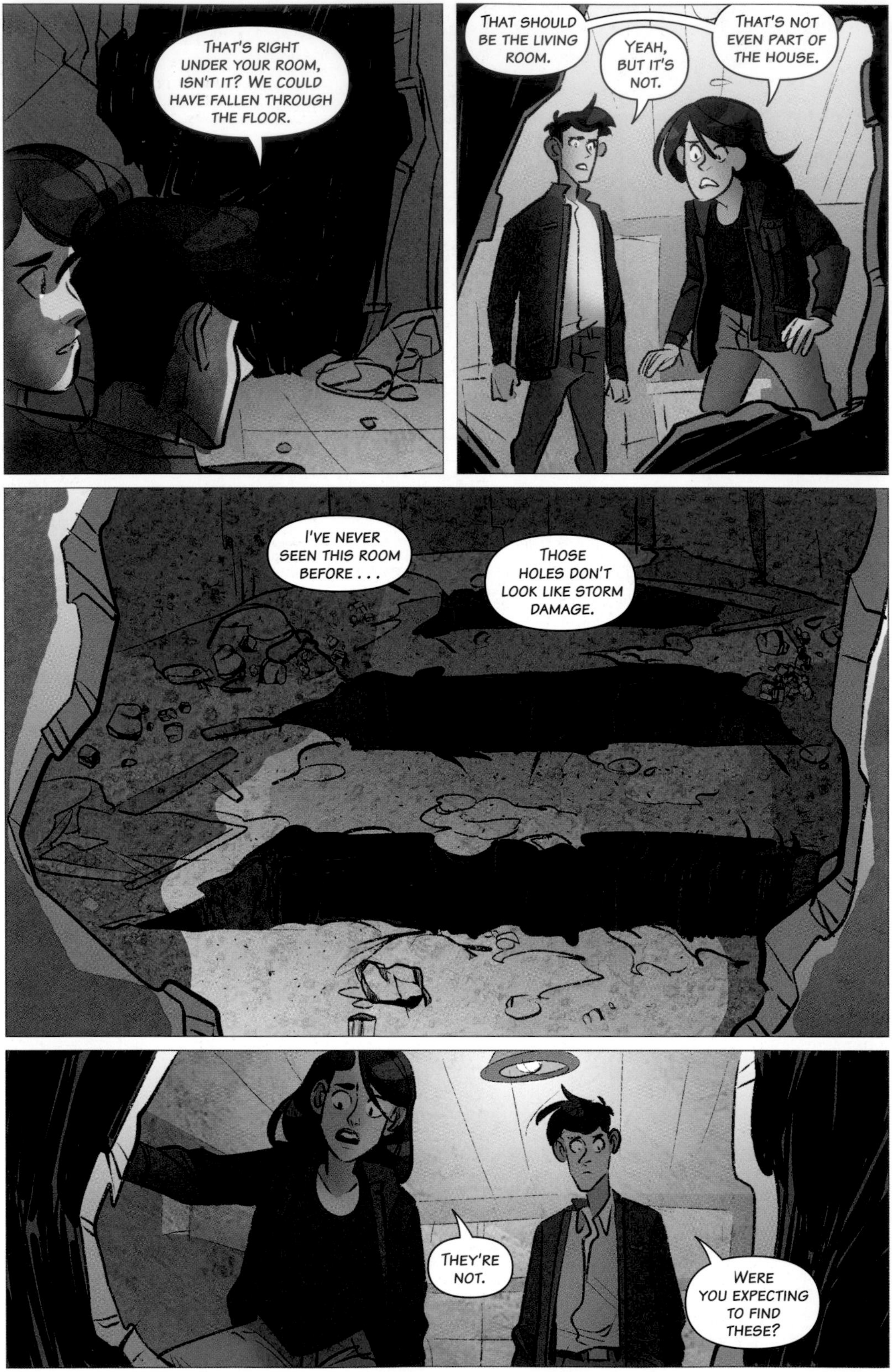
THAT'S RIGHT UNDER YOUR ROOM, ISN'T IT? WE COULD HAVE FALLEN THROUGH THE FLOOR.
THAT SHOULD BE THE LIVING ROOM.
YEAH, BUT IT'S NOT.
THAT'S NOT EVEN PART OF THE HOUSE.
I'VE NEVER SEEN THIS ROOM BEFORE . . .
THOSE HOLES DON'T LOOK LIKE STORM DAMAGE.
THEY'RE NOT.
WERE YOU EXPECTING TO FIND THESE?

I'VE SEEN THEM BEFORE. BEHIND THE HOUSE OF A DEAD WOMAN.

WHAT ARE YOU TALKING ABOUT?

-:SIGH:-

THERE WAS ANOTHER BODY. I FOUND HER TODAY, IN A FIELD. I CALLED CLAY, AND THEN I WENT TO HER HOUSE WHILE HE WAITED FOR THE REST OF THE COPS TO SHOW UP. THERE WERE HOLES LIKE THIS IN HER BACKYARD.

THAT'S WHAT YOU WOULDN'T TELL ME? ANOTHER BODY?!

THAT, AND THE FACT THAT SHE LOOKED LIKE ME.

IS THAT . . .

DO I KNOW THAT WALL?

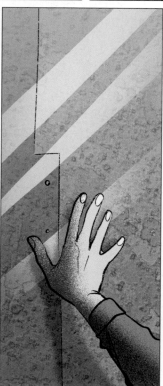

HEY! OVER HERE!

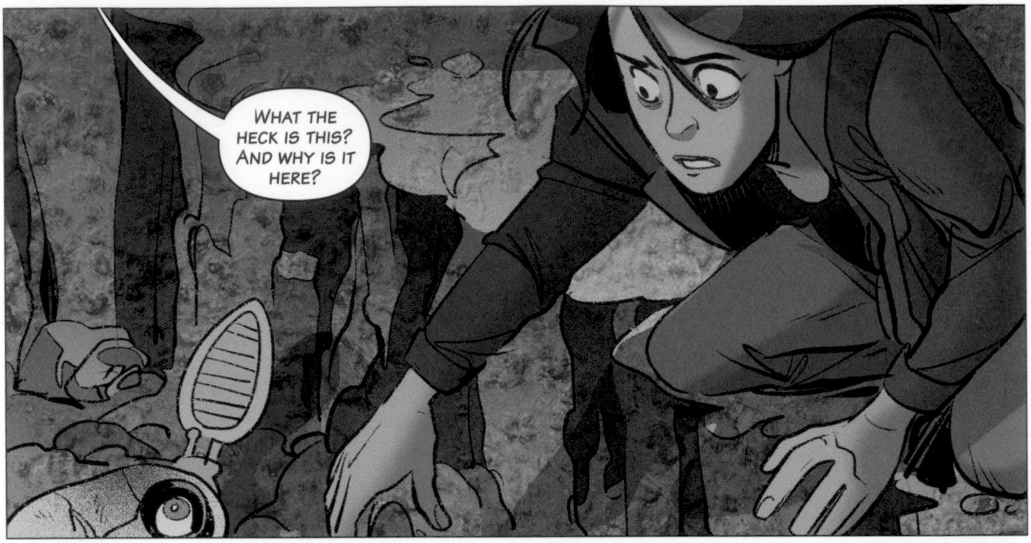
WHAT THE HECK IS THIS? AND WHY IS IT HERE?

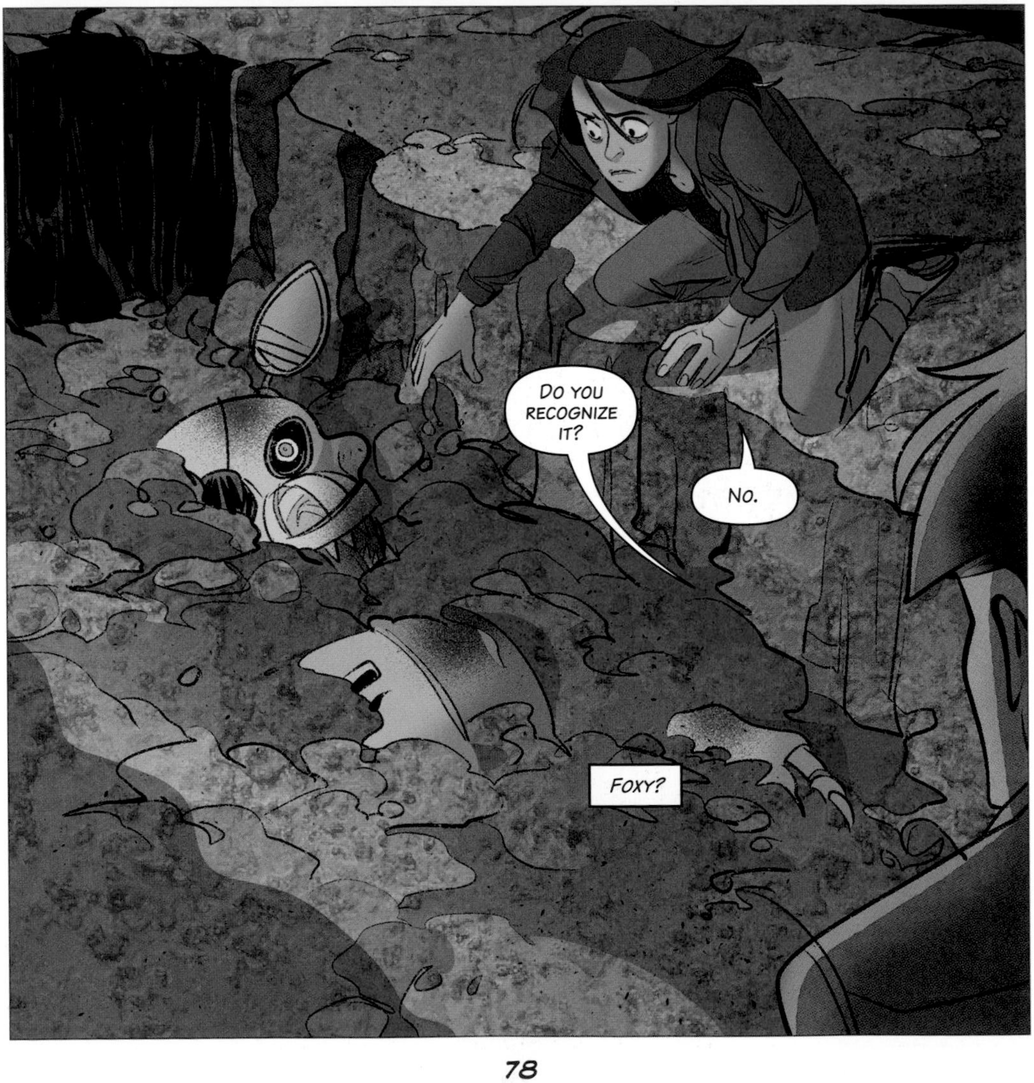
DO YOU RECOGNIZE IT?
NO.
FOXY?

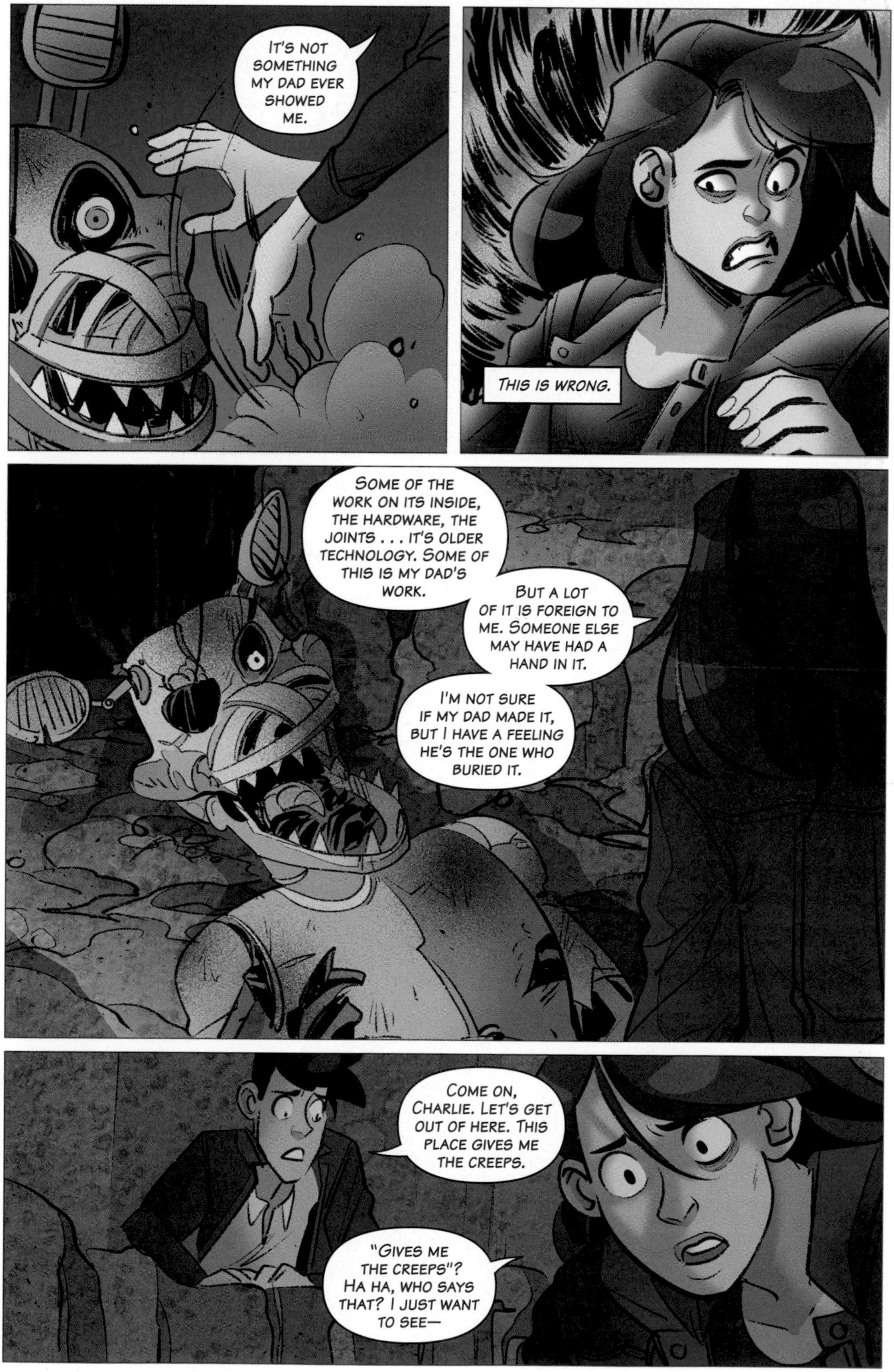
IT'S NOT SOMETHING MY DAD EVER SHOWED ME.
THIS IS WRONG.
SOME OF THE WORK ON ITS INSIDE, THE HARDWARE, THE JOINTS . . . IT'S OLDER TECHNOLOGY. SOME OF THIS IS MY DAD'S WORK.
BUT A LOT OF IT IS FOREIGN TO ME. SOMEONE ELSE MAY HAVE HAD A HAND IN IT.
I'M NOT SURE IF MY DAD MADE IT, BUT I HAVE A FEELING HE'S THE ONE WHO BURIED IT.
COME ON, CHARLIE. LET'S GET OUT OF HERE. THIS PLACE GIVES ME THE CREEPS.
"GIVES ME THE CREEPS"? HA HA, WHO SAYS THAT? I JUST WANT TO SEE—

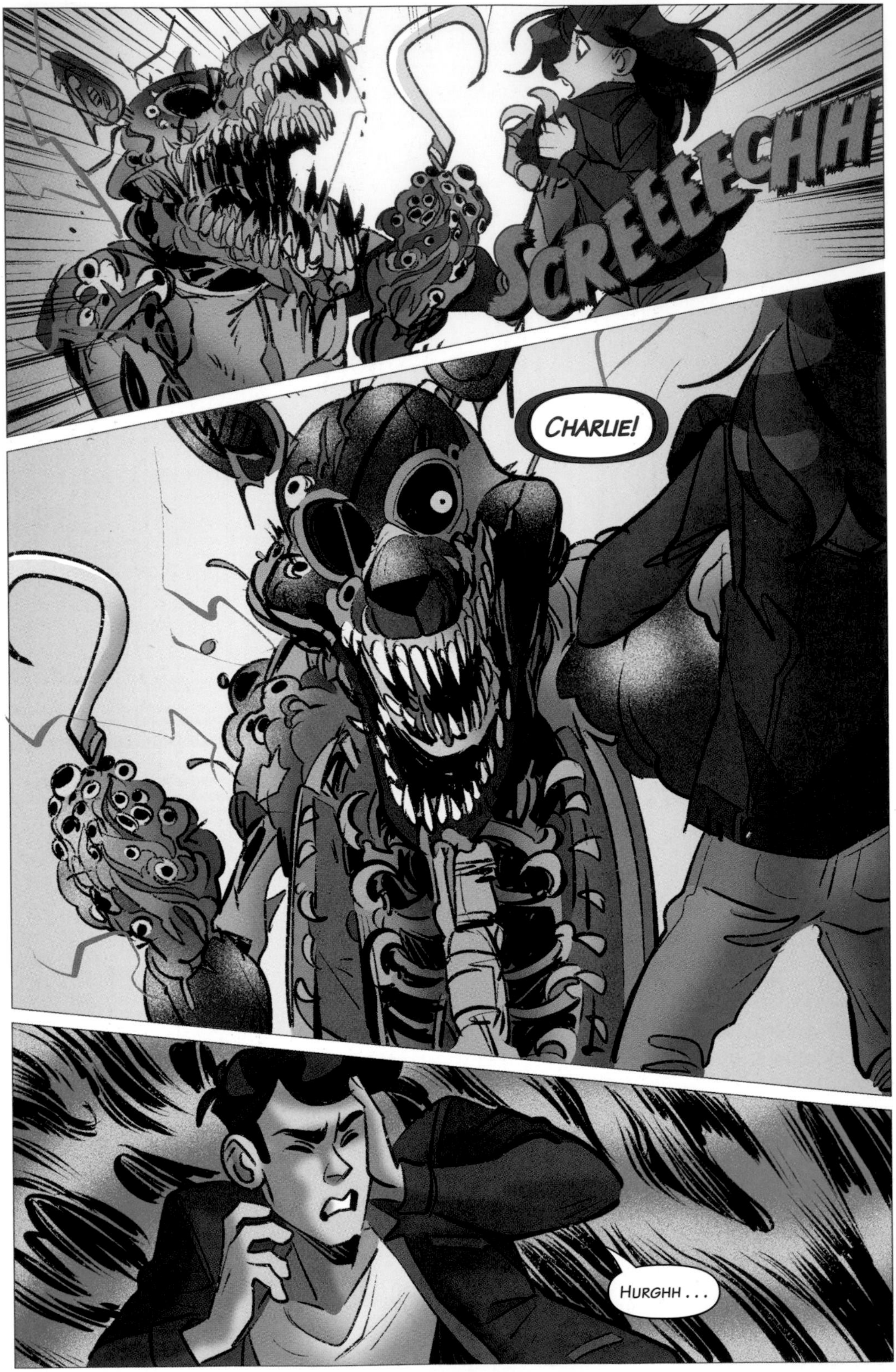
SCREEEECHH
CHARLIE!
HURGHH . . .

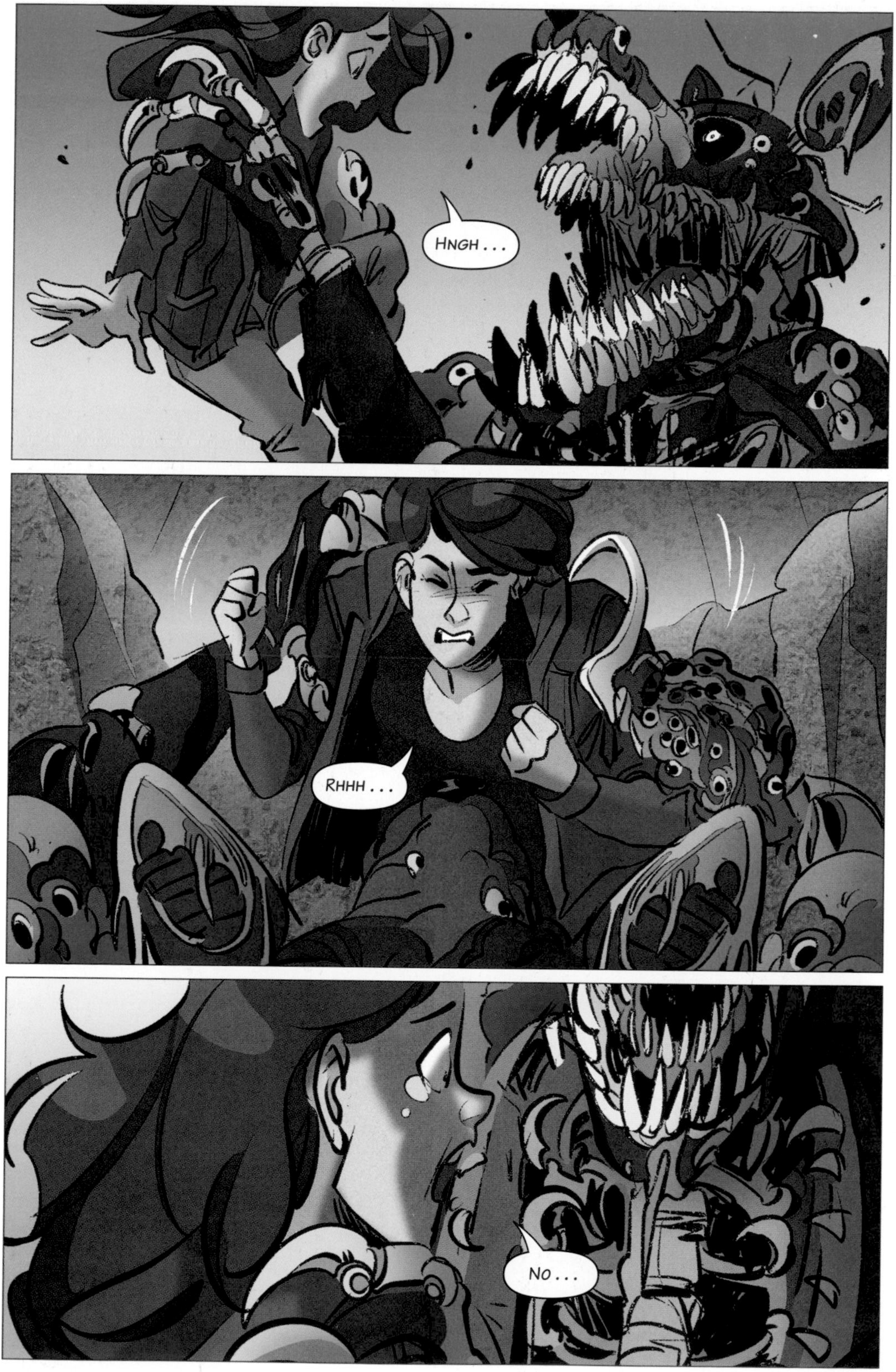
HNGH . . .
RHHH . . .
NO . . .

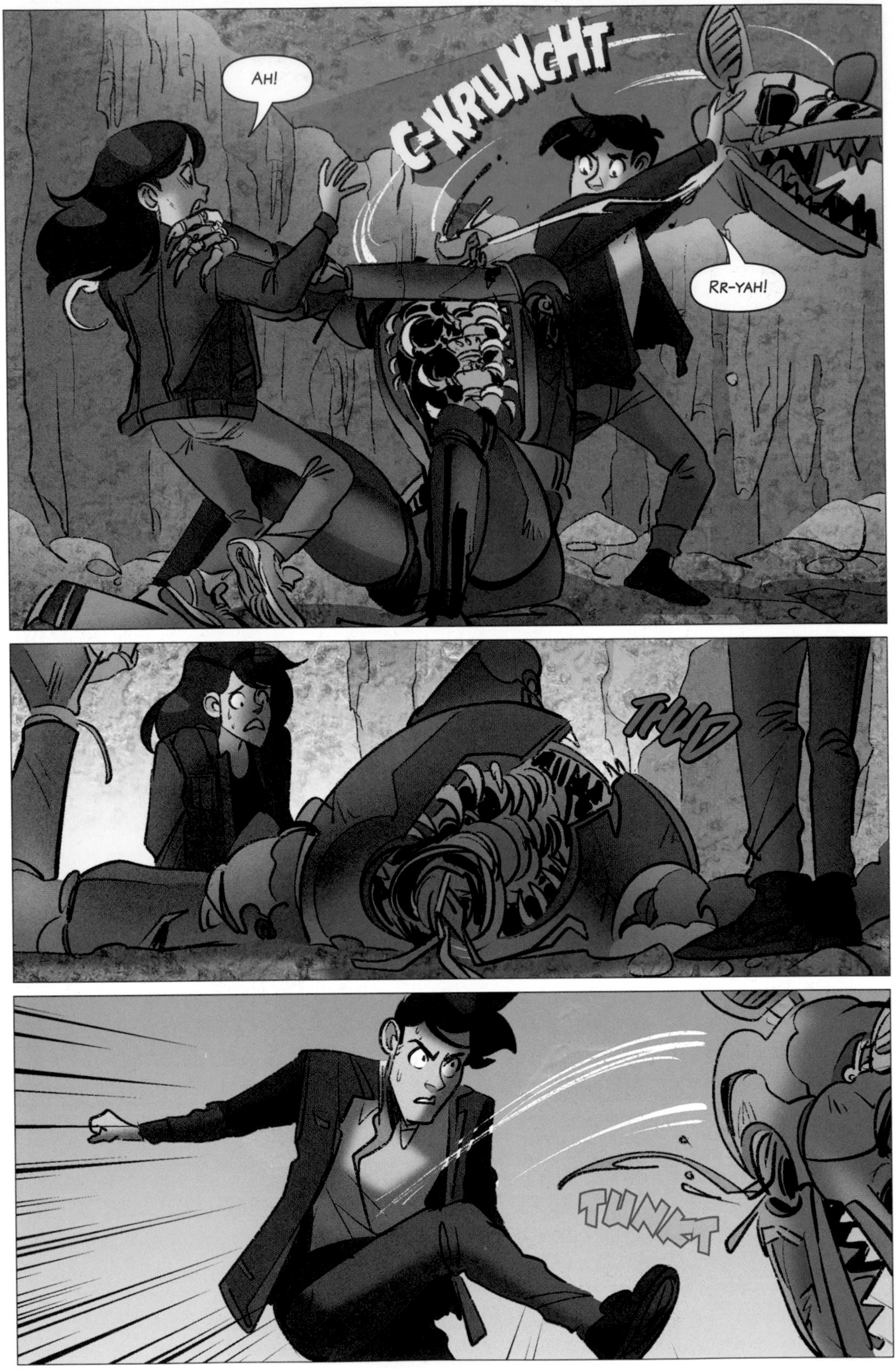
AH!
C-KRUNCHT
RR-YAH!
THUD
TUNKT

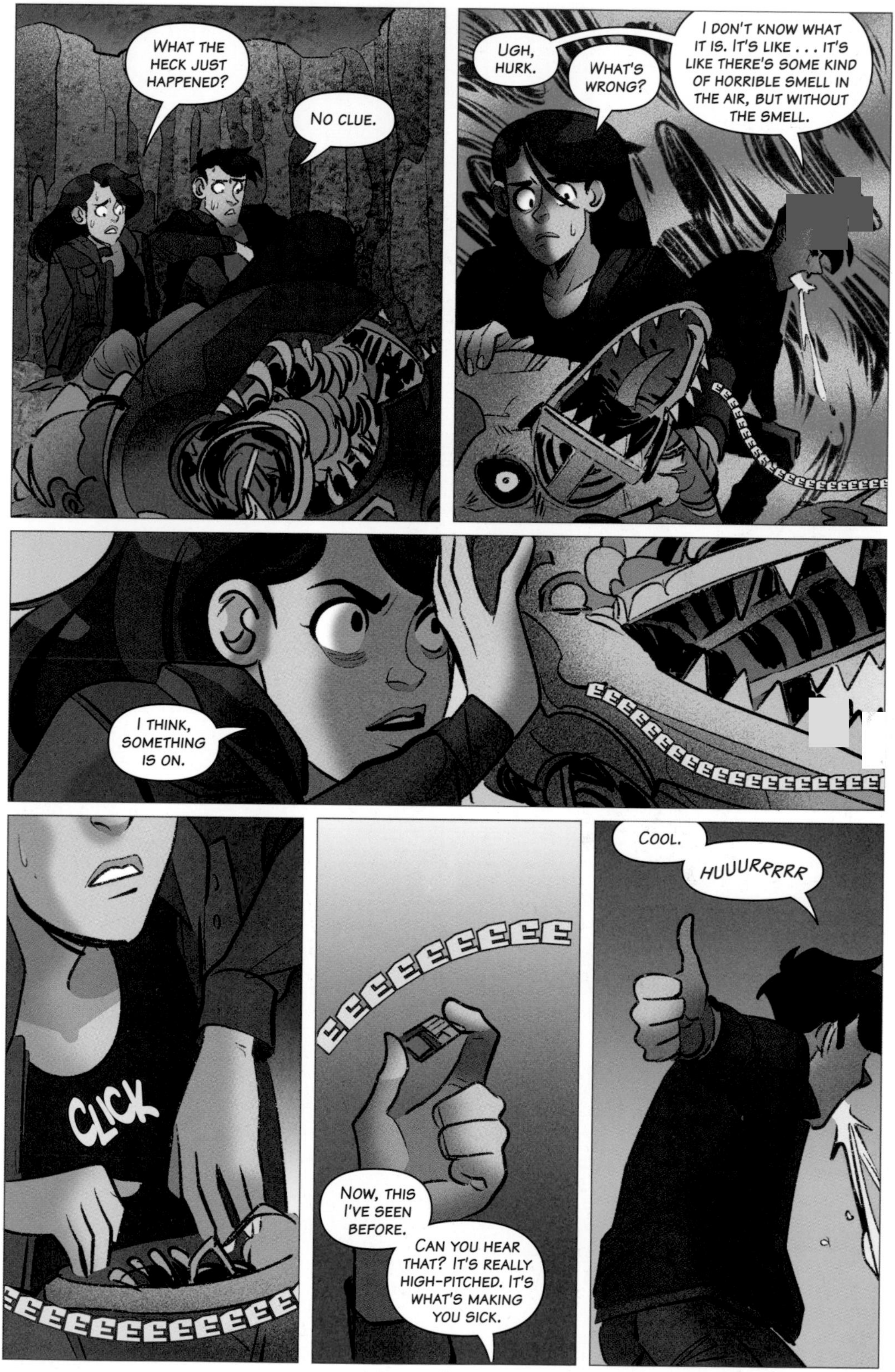
WHAT THE HECK JUST HAPPENED?
NO CLUE.
UGH, HURK.
WHAT'S WRONG?
I DON'T KNOW WHAT IT IS. IT'S LIKE . . . IT'S LIKE THERE'S SOME KIND OF HORRIBLE SMELL IN THE AIR, BUT WITHOUT THE SMELL.
EEEEEEEEEEEEEEEEEEEEE
I THINK, SOMETHING IS ON.
EEEEEEEEEEEEEEEEEEEEEEEE
CLICK
EEEEEEEEEEEEEE
EEEEEEEEEEEE
NOW, THIS I'VE SEEN BEFORE.
CAN YOU HEAR THAT? IT'S REALLY HIGH-PITCHED. IT'S WHAT'S MAKING YOU SICK.
COOL.
HUUURRRRR

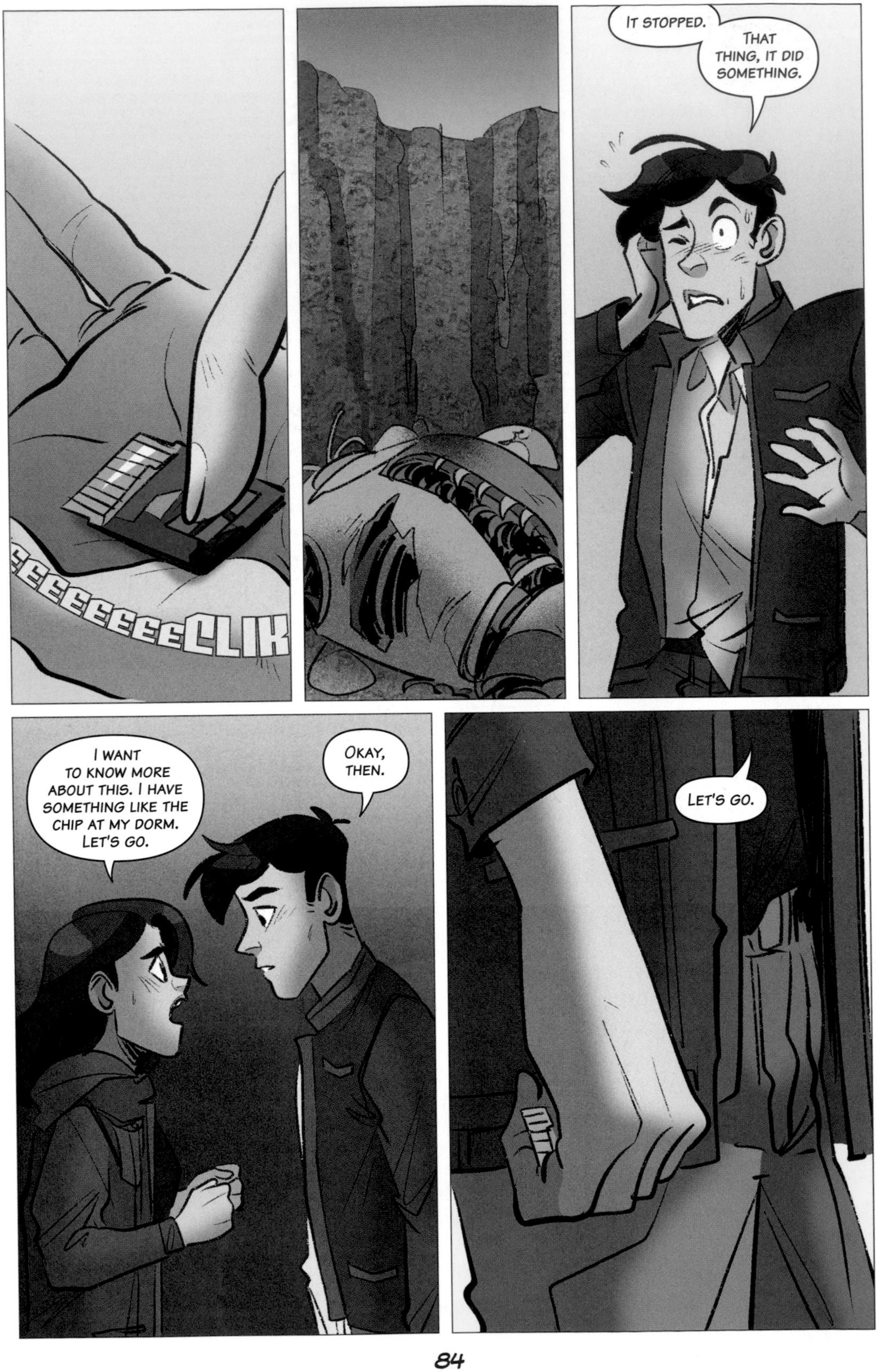

EEEEEEEEEECLIK
IT STOPPED.
THAT THING, IT DID SOMETHING.
I WANT TO KNOW MORE ABOUT THIS. I HAVE SOMETHING LIKE THE CHIP AT MY DORM. LET'S GO.
OKAY, THEN.
LET'S GO.

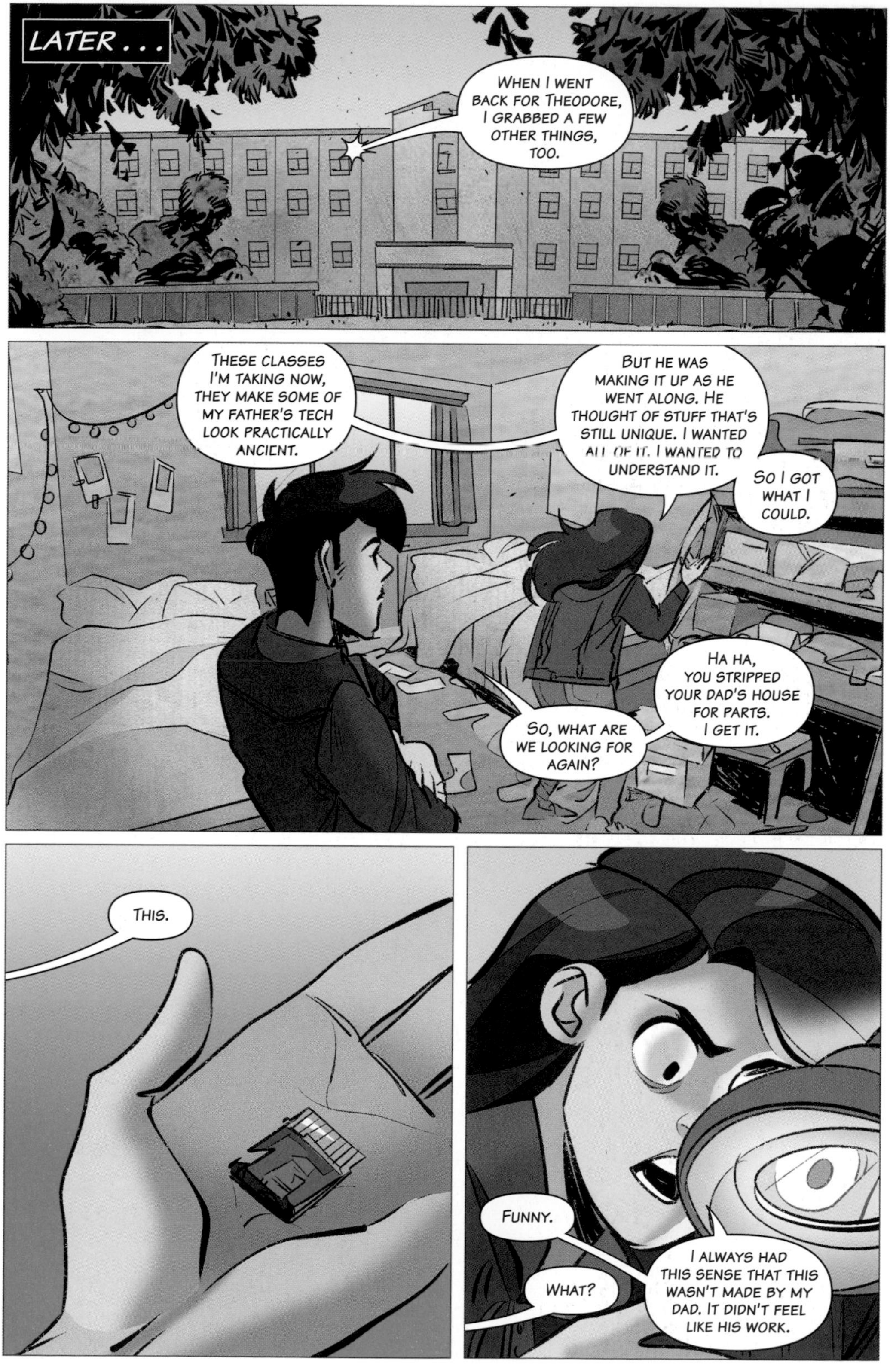
LATER . . .
WHEN I WENT BACK FOR THEODORE, I GRABBED A FEW OTHER THINGS, TOO.
THESE CLASSES I'M TAKING NOW, THEY MAKE SOME OF MY FATHER'S TECH LOOK PRACTICALLY ANCIENT.
BUT HE WAS MAKING IT UP AS HE WENT ALONG. HE THOUGHT OF STUFF THAT'S STILL UNIQUE. I WANTED ALL OF IT. I WANTED TO UNDERSTAND IT.
SO I GOT WHAT I COULD.
HA HA, YOU STRIPPED YOUR DAD'S HOUSE FOR PARTS. I GET IT.
SO, WHAT ARE WE LOOKING FOR AGAIN?
THIS.
FUNNY.
WHAT?
I ALWAYS HAD THIS SENSE THAT THIS WASN'T MADE BY MY DAD. IT DIDN'T FEEL LIKE HIS WORK.

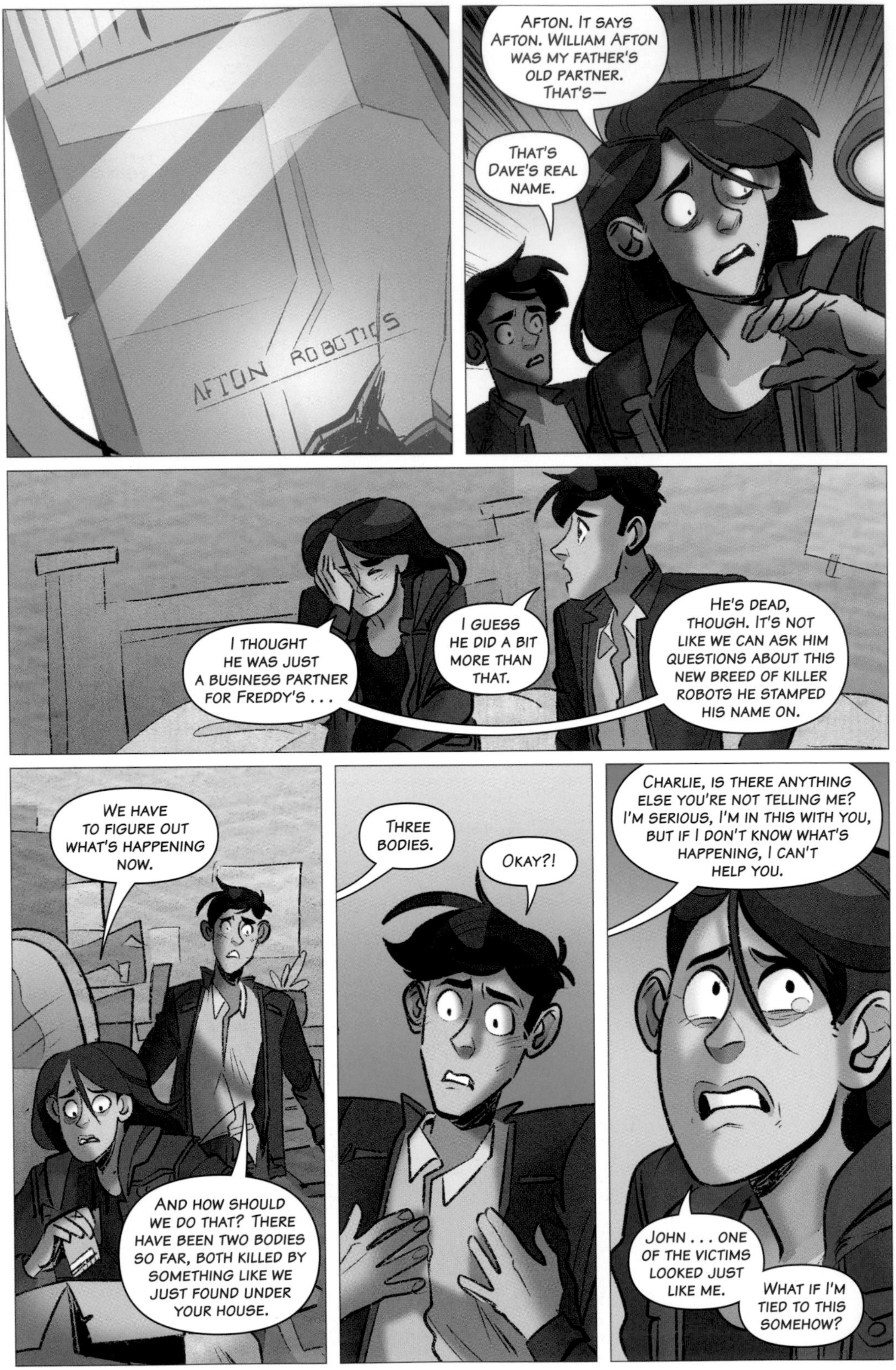
AFTON ROBOTICS
AFTON. IT SAYS AFTON. WILLIAM AFTON WAS MY FATHER'S OLD PARTNER. THAT'S—
THAT'S DAVE'S REAL NAME.
I THOUGHT HE WAS JUST A BUSINESS PARTNER FOR FREDDY'S . . .
I GUESS HE DID A BIT MORE THAN THAT.
HE'S DEAD, THOUGH. IT'S NOT LIKE WE CAN ASK HIM QUESTIONS ABOUT THIS NEW BREED OF KILLER ROBOTS HE STAMPED HIS NAME ON.
WE HAVE TO FIGURE OUT WHAT'S HAPPENING NOW.
AND HOW SHOULD WE DO THAT? THERE HAVE BEEN TWO BODIES SO FAR, BOTH KILLED BY SOMETHING LIKE WE JUST FOUND UNDER YOUR HOUSE.
THREE BODIES.
OKAY?!
CHARLIE, IS THERE ANYTHING ELSE YOU'RE NOT TELLING ME? I'M SERIOUS, I'M IN THIS WITH YOU, BUT IF I DON'T KNOW WHAT'S HAPPENING, I CAN'T HELP YOU.
JOHN . . . ONE OF THE VICTIMS LOOKED JUST LIKE ME.
WHAT IF I'M TIED TO THIS SOMEHOW?

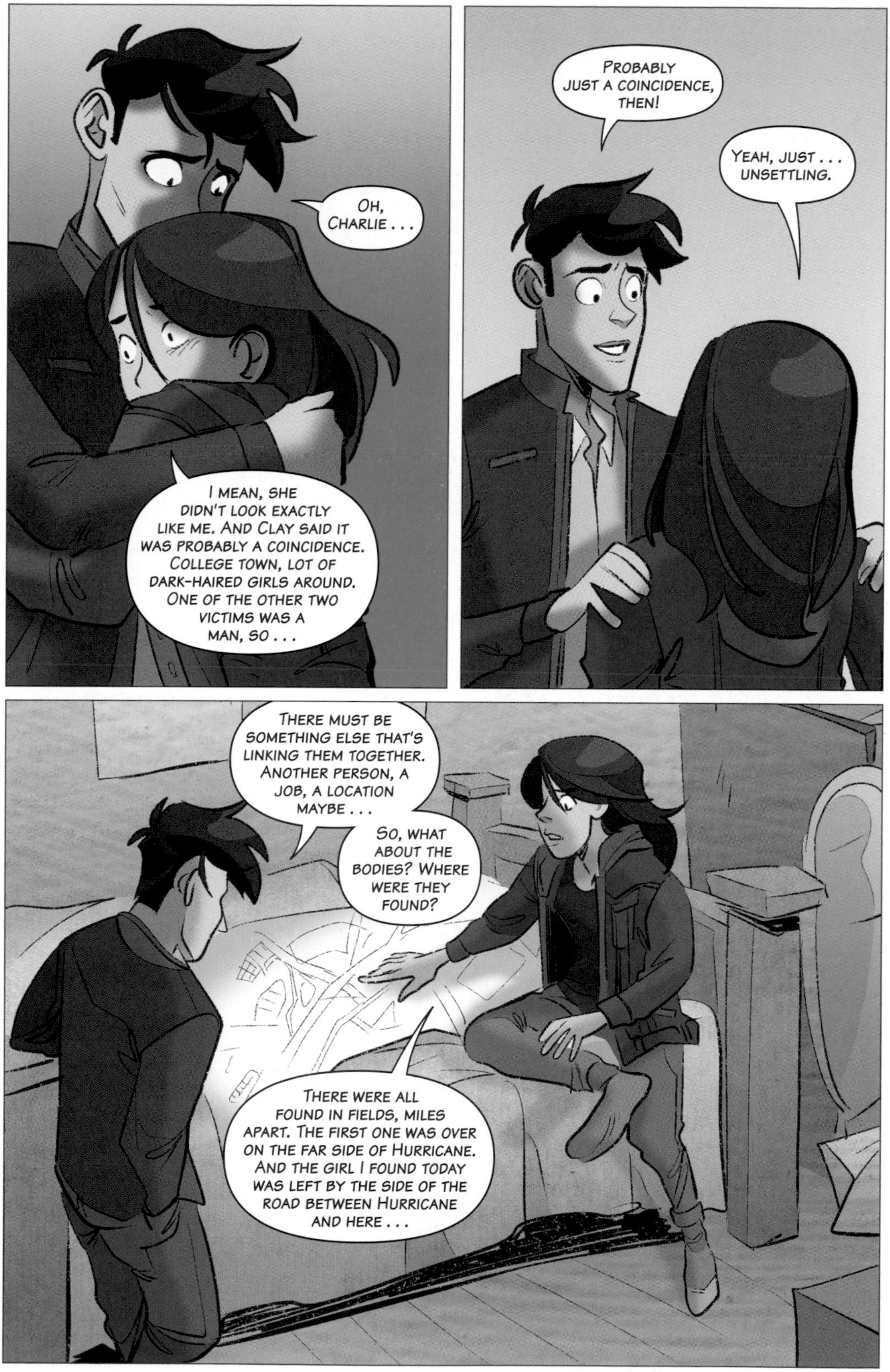
OH, CHARLIE . . .
I MEAN, SHE DIDN'T LOOK EXACTLY LIKE ME. AND CLAY SAID IT WAS PROBABLY A COINCIDENCE. COLLEGE TOWN, LOT OF DARK-HAIRED GIRLS AROUND. ONE OF THE OTHER TWO VICTIMS WAS A MAN, SO . . .
PROBABLY JUST A COINCIDENCE, THEN!
YEAH, JUST . . . UNSETTLING.
THERE MUST BE SOMETHING ELSE THAT'S LINKING THEM TOGETHER. ANOTHER PERSON, A JOB, A LOCATION MAYBE . . .
SO, WHAT ABOUT THE BODIES? WHERE WERE THEY FOUND?
THERE WERE ALL FOUND IN FIELDS, MILES APART. THE FIRST ONE WAS OVER ON THE FAR SIDE OF HURRICANE. AND THE GIRL I FOUND TODAY WAS LEFT BY THE SIDE OF THE ROAD BETWEEN HURRICANE AND HERE . . .

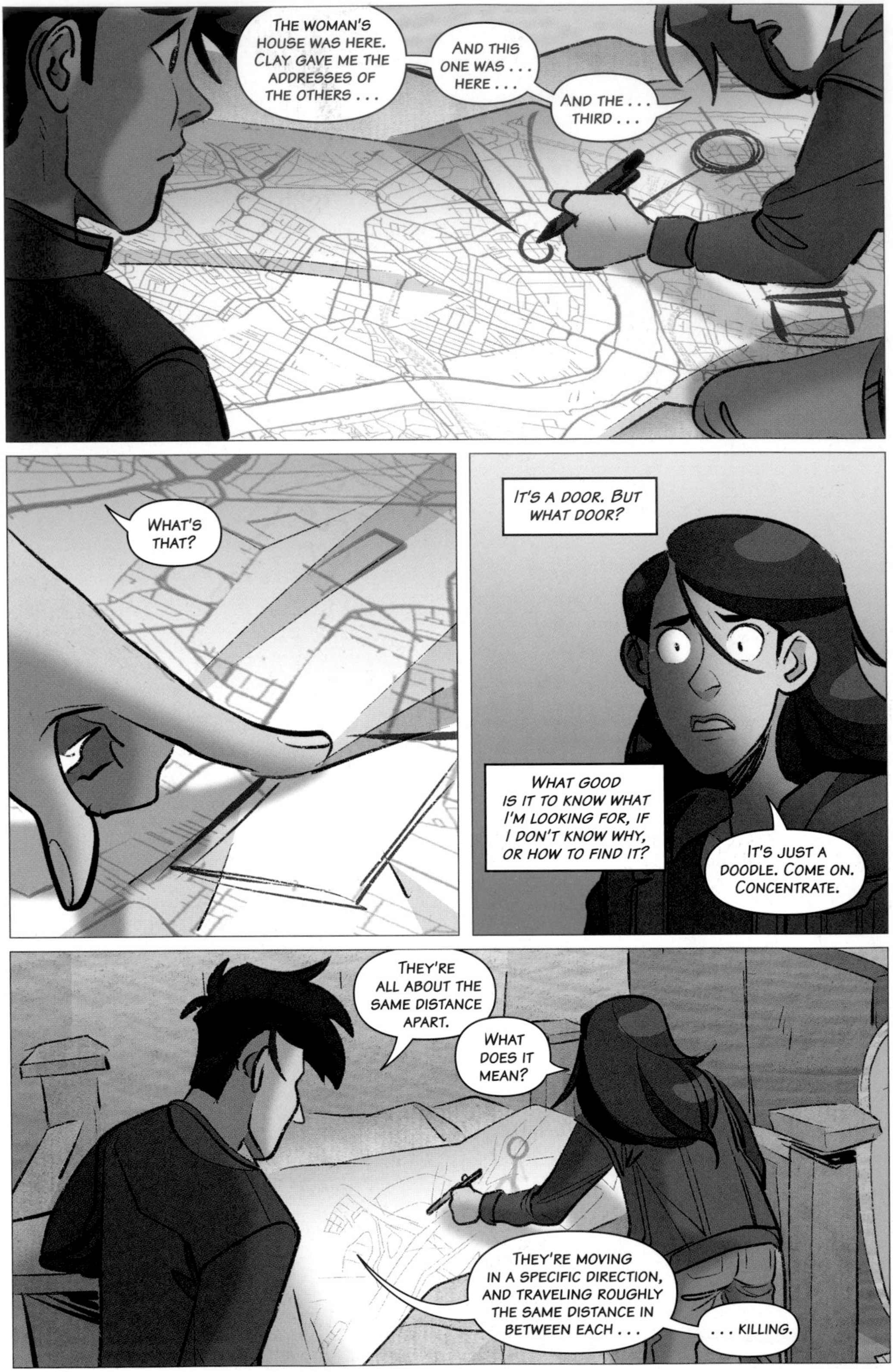
THE WOMAN'S HOUSE WAS HERE. CLAY GAVE ME THE ADDRESSES OF THE OTHERS . . .
AND THIS ONE WAS . . . HERE . . .
AND THE . . . THIRD . . .
WHAT'S THAT?
IT'S A DOOR. BUT WHAT DOOR?
WHAT GOOD IS IT TO KNOW WHAT I'M LOOKING FOR, IF I DON'T KNOW WHY, OR HOW TO FIND IT?
IT'S JUST A DOODLE. COME ON. CONCENTRATE.
THEY'RE ALL ABOUT THE SAME DISTANCE APART.
WHAT DOES IT MEAN?
THEY'RE MOVING IN A SPECIFIC DIRECTION, AND TRAVELING ROUGHLY THE SAME DISTANCE IN BETWEEN EACH . . .
. . . KILLING.

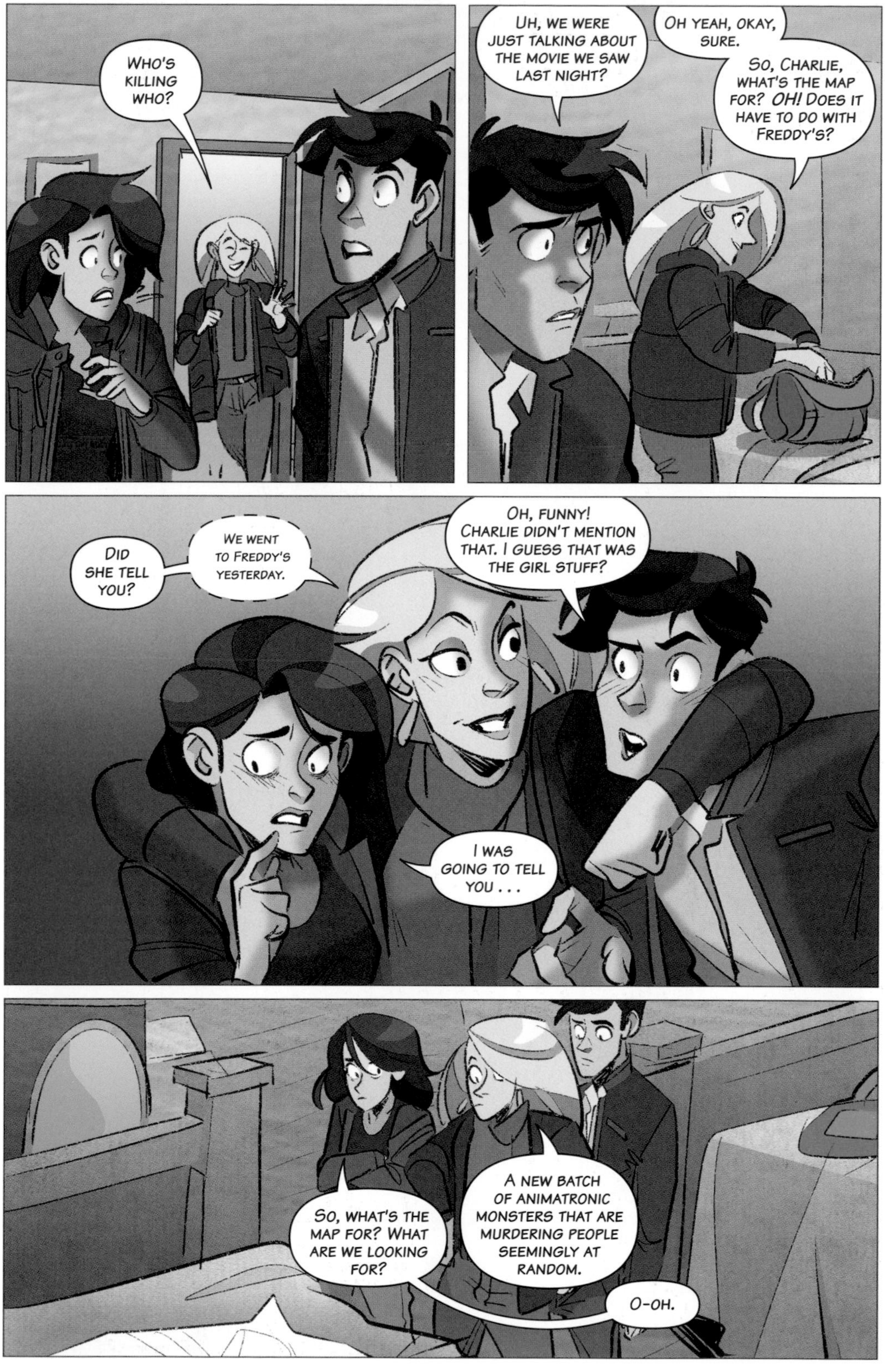
WHO'S KILLING WHO?
UH, WE WERE JUST TALKING ABOUT THE MOVIE WE SAW LAST NIGHT?
OH YEAH, OKAY, SURE.
SO, CHARLIE, WHAT'S THE MAP FOR? OH! DOES IT HAVE TO DO WITH FREDDY'S?
DID SHE TELL YOU?
WE WENT TO FREDDY'S YESTERDAY.
OH, FUNNY! CHARLIE DIDN'T MENTION THAT. I GUESS THAT WAS THE GIRL STUFF?
I WAS GOING TO TELL YOU . . .
SO, WHAT'S THE MAP FOR? WHAT ARE WE LOOKING FOR?
A NEW BATCH OF ANIMATRONIC MONSTERS THAT ARE MURDERING PEOPLE SEEMINGLY AT RANDOM.
O-OH.

HOW? WHERE DID THEY COME FROM? FREDDY'S?

NO, NOT FREDDY'S. THEY CAME FROM MY DAD'S HOUSE, WE THINK. BUT HE DIDN'T BUILD THEM!

IT WAS DAVE. OR AFTON. OR WHATEVER HIS NAME IS.

SHE MEANS—

NO, I GET IT . . . I WAS AT FREDDY'S LAST YEAR, TOO, REMEMBER? WHY DIDN'T YOU TELL ME?

I JUST DIDN'T WANT IT TO BE LIKE LAST TIME. THERE'S NO NEED TO PUT EVERYONE AT RISK.

YEAH, JUST ME.

SO, WHAT ARE WE DOING?

THERE'RE ABOUT THREE MILES BETWEEN EACH LOCATION.

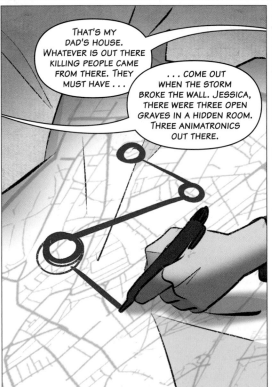

THAT'S MY DAD'S HOUSE. WHATEVER IS OUT THERE KILLING PEOPLE CAME FROM THERE. THEY MUST HAVE . . .

. . . COME OUT WHEN THE STORM BROKE THE WALL. JESSICA, THERE WERE THREE OPEN GRAVES IN A HIDDEN ROOM. THREE ANIMATRONICS OUT THERE.

IF WE AVERAGE OUT THIS PATH, WE CAN DRAW A STRAIGHT LINE . . .

IS THAT THE COLLEGE? IS THAT HERE?!

THAT WOMAN THAT LOOKED LIKE ME . . . IT WASN'T A COINCIDENCE.

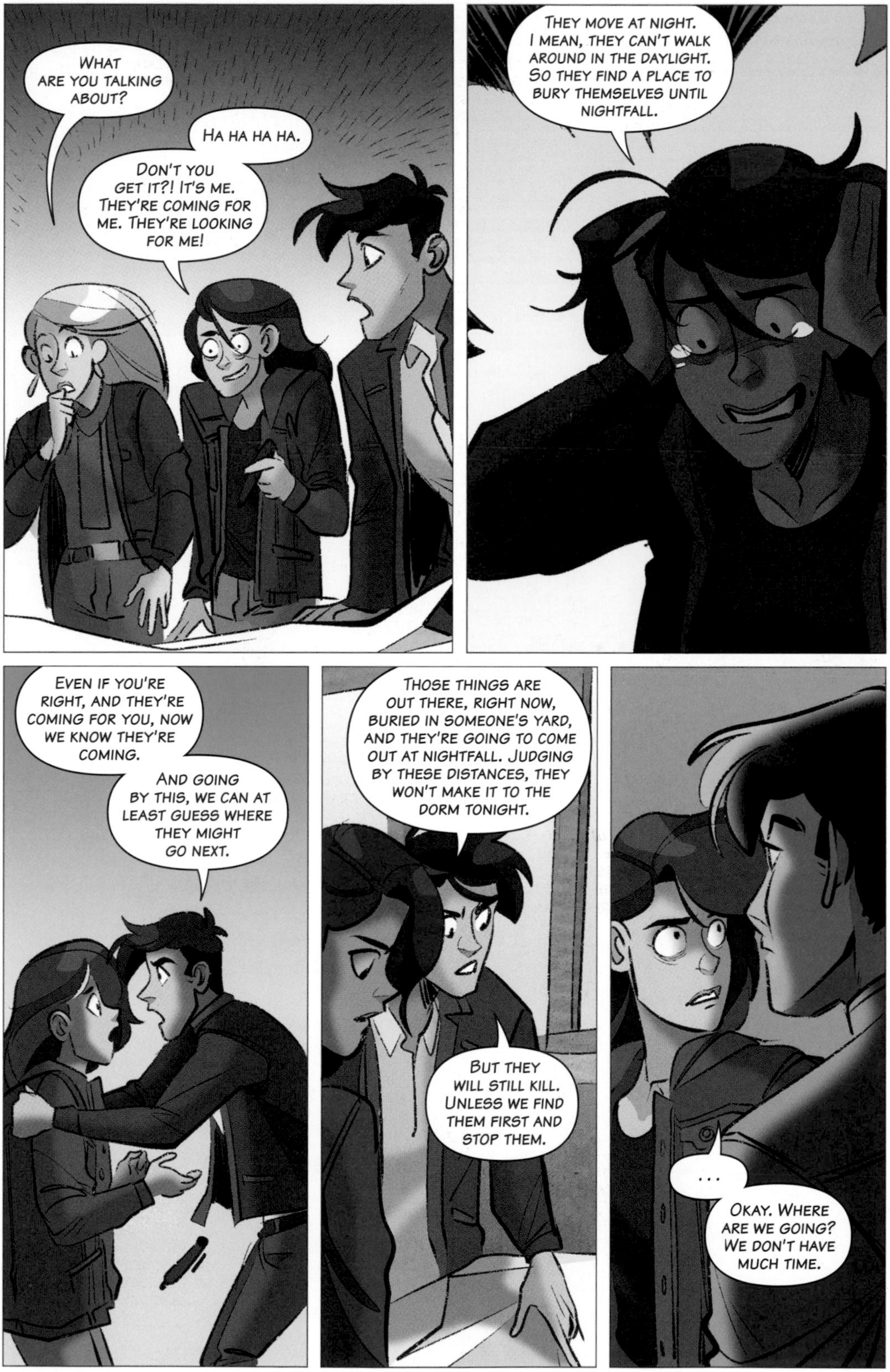
WHAT ARE YOU TALKING ABOUT?
HA HA HA HA.
DON'T YOU GET IT?! IT'S ME. THEY'RE COMING FOR ME. THEY'RE LOOKING FOR ME!
THEY MOVE AT NIGHT. I MEAN, THEY CAN'T WALK AROUND IN THE DAYLIGHT. SO THEY FIND A PLACE TO BURY THEMSELVES UNTIL NIGHTFALL.
EVEN IF YOU'RE RIGHT, AND THEY'RE COMING FOR YOU, NOW WE KNOW THEY'RE COMING.
AND GOING BY THIS, WE CAN AT LEAST GUESS WHERE THEY MIGHT GO NEXT.
THOSE THINGS ARE OUT THERE, RIGHT NOW, BURIED IN SOMEONE'S YARD, AND THEY'RE GOING TO COME OUT AT NIGHTFALL. JUDGING BY THESE DISTANCES, THEY WON'T MAKE IT TO THE DORM TONIGHT.
BUT THEY WILL STILL KILL. UNLESS WE FIND THEM FIRST AND STOP THEM.
...
OKAY. WHERE ARE WE GOING? WE DON'T HAVE MUCH TIME.

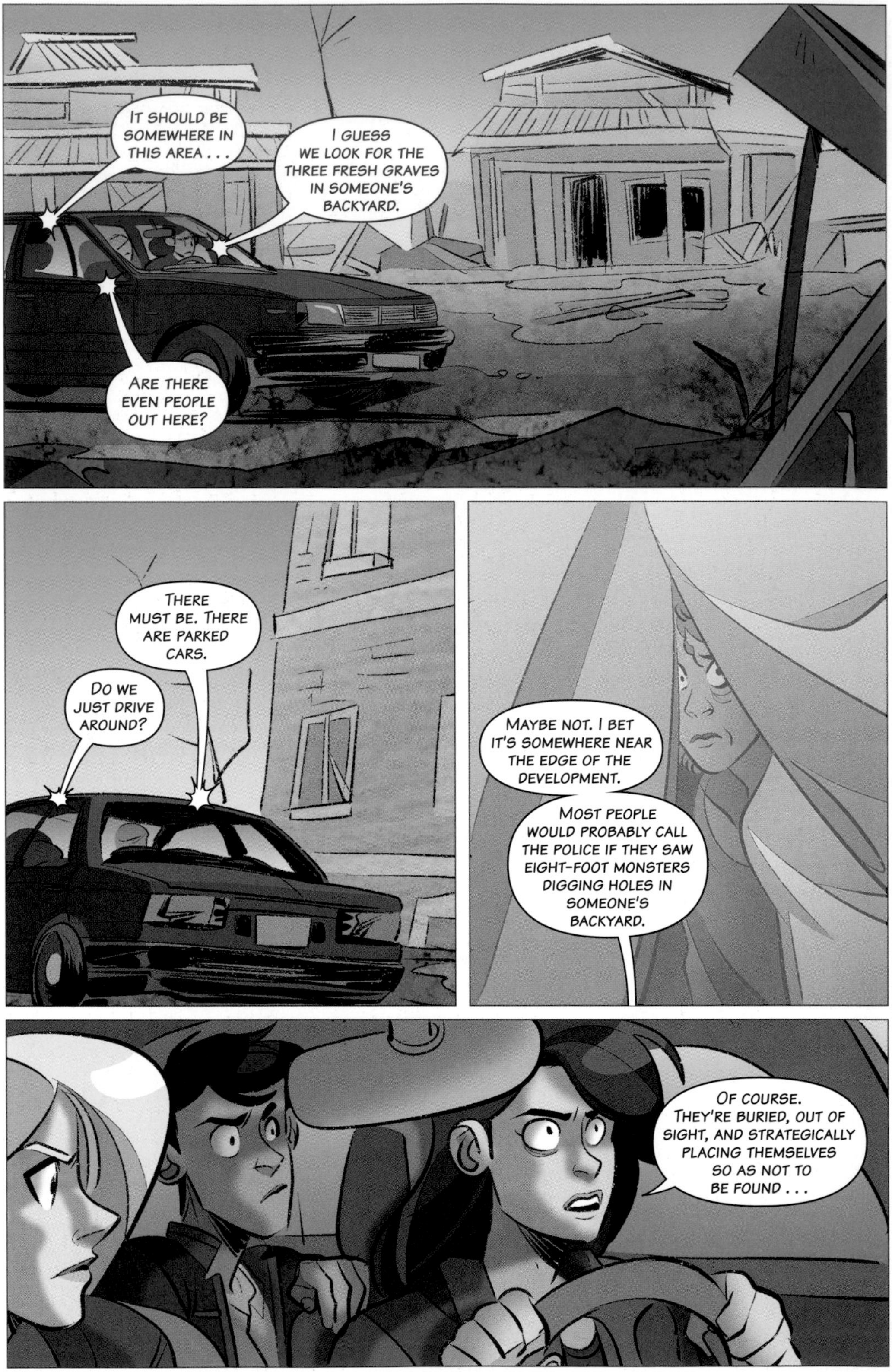
It should be somewhere in this area . . .
I guess we look for the three fresh graves in someone's backyard.
Are there even people out here?
Do we just drive around?
There must be. There are parked cars.
Maybe not. I bet it's somewhere near the edge of the development.
Most people would probably call the police if they saw eight-foot monsters digging holes in someone's backyard.
Of course. They're buried, out of sight, and strategically placing themselves so as not to be found . . .

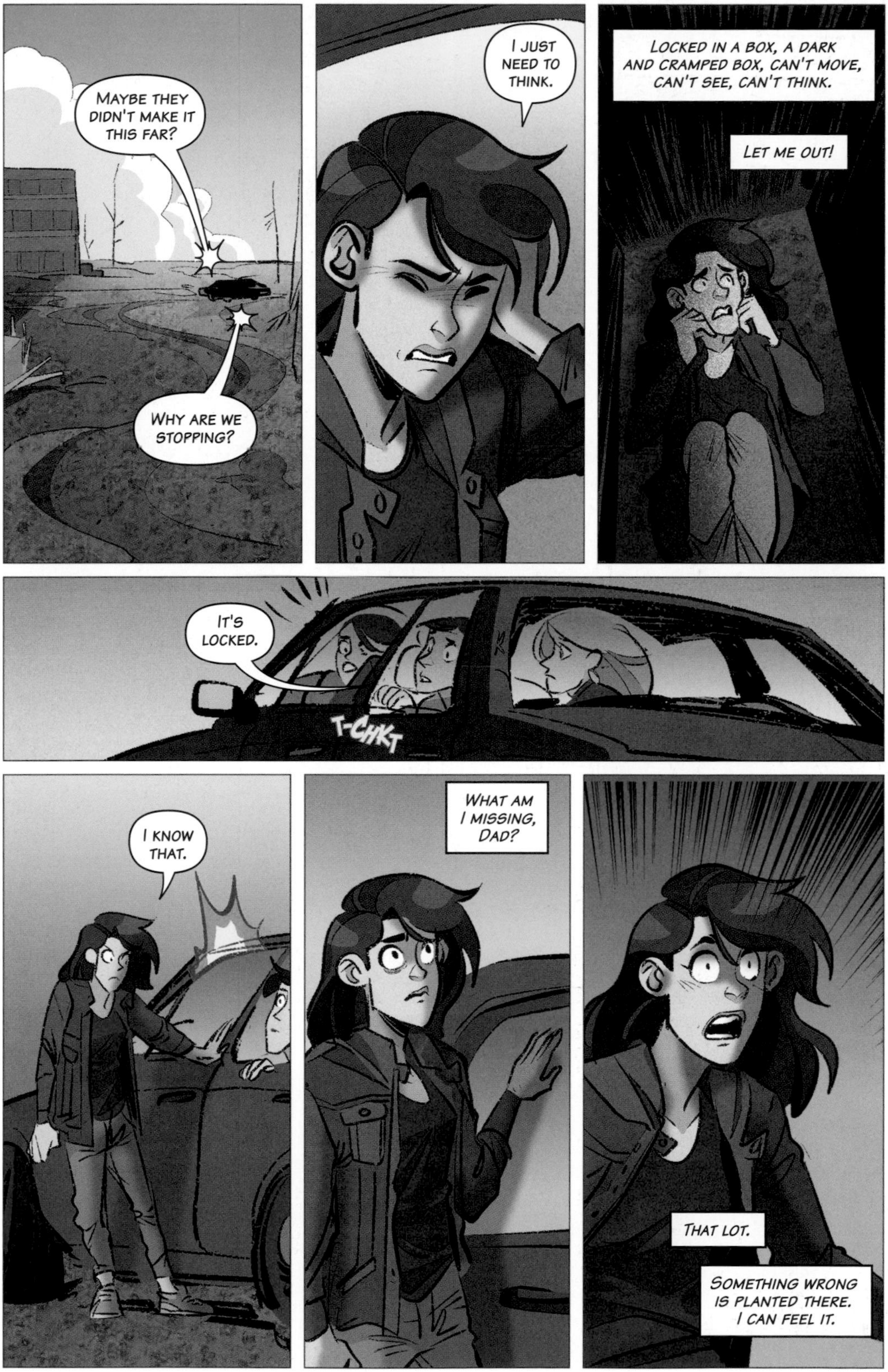
Maybe they didn't make it this far?
Why are we stopping?
I just need to think.
Locked in a box, a dark and cramped box, can't move, can't see, can't think.
Let me out!
It's locked.
T-CHKT
I know that.
What am I missing, Dad?
That lot.
Something wrong is planted there. I can feel it.

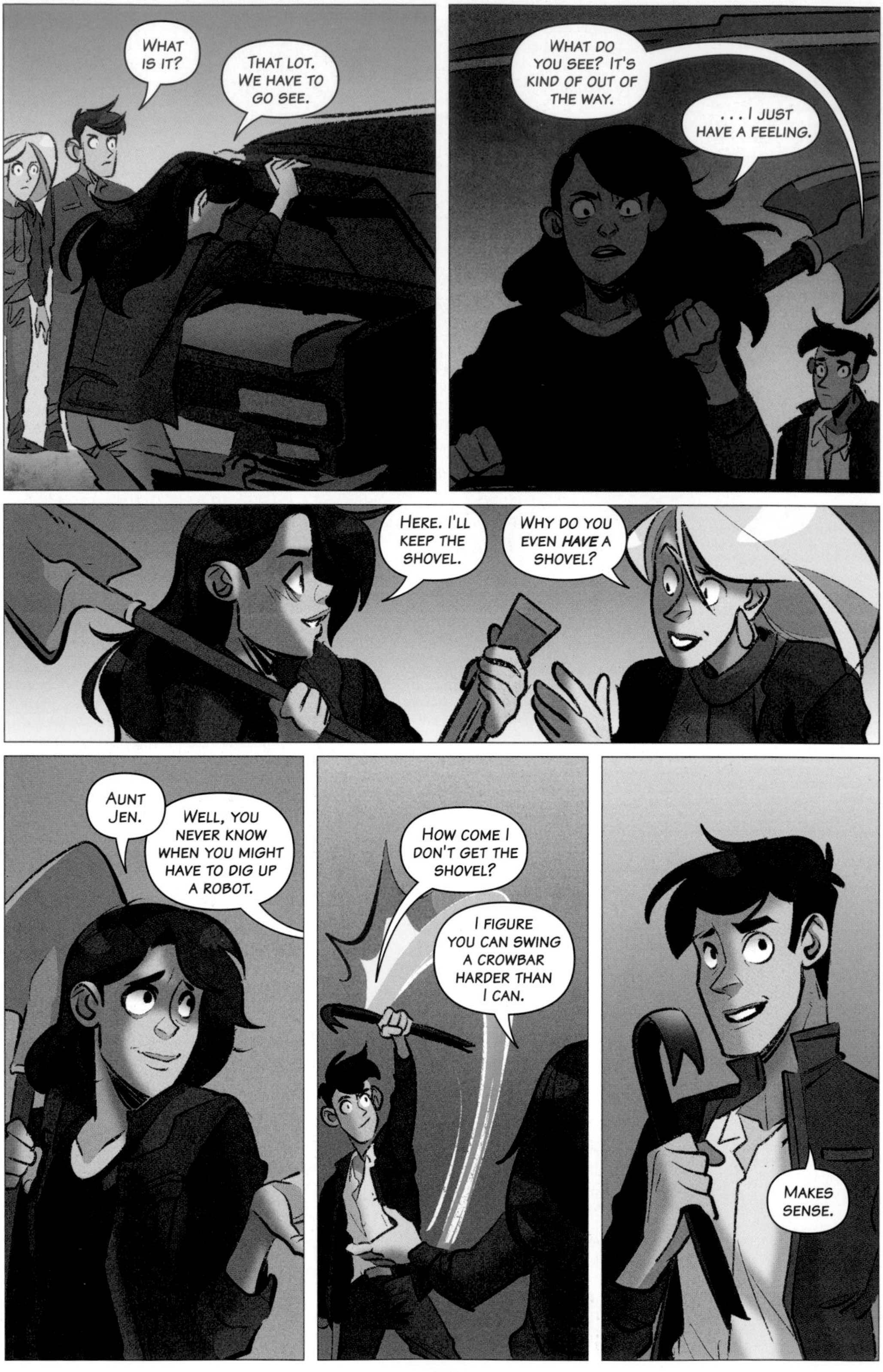
WHAT IS IT?
THAT LOT. WE HAVE TO GO SEE.
WHAT DO YOU SEE? IT'S KIND OF OUT OF THE WAY.
. . . I JUST HAVE A FEELING.
HERE. I'LL KEEP THE SHOVEL.
WHY DO YOU EVEN *HAVE* A SHOVEL?
AUNT JEN.
WELL, YOU NEVER KNOW WHEN YOU MIGHT HAVE TO DIG UP A ROBOT.
HOW COME I DON'T GET THE SHOVEL?
I FIGURE YOU CAN SWING A CROWBAR HARDER THAN I CAN.
MAKES SENSE.

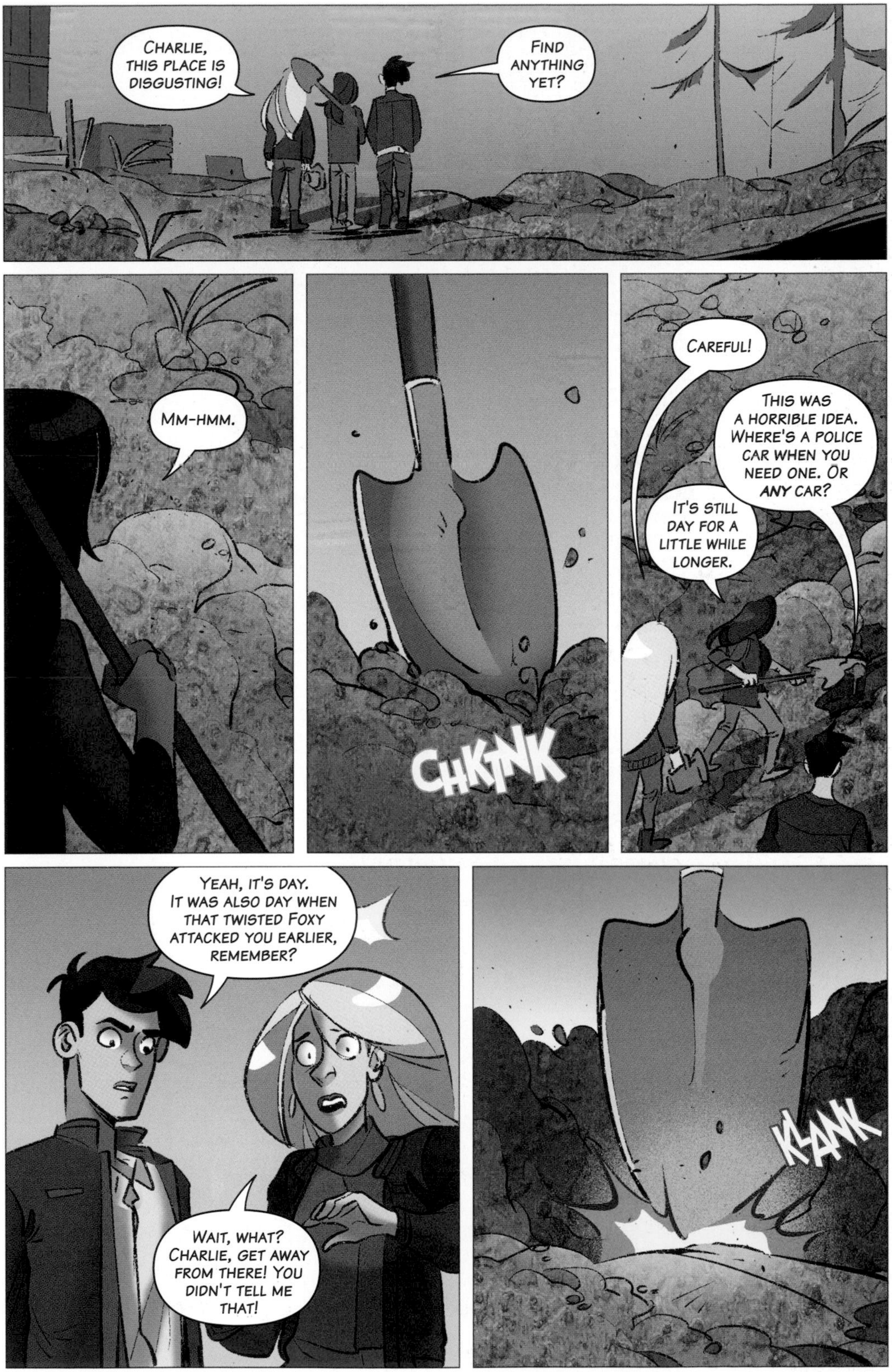
Charlie, this place is disgusting!
Find anything yet?
Mm-hmm.
CHKTINK
Careful!
This was a horrible idea. Where's a police car when you need one. Or any car?
It's still day for a little while longer.
Yeah, it's day. It was also day when that twisted Foxy attacked you earlier, remember?
Wait, what? Charlie, get away from there! You didn't tell me that!
KLANK

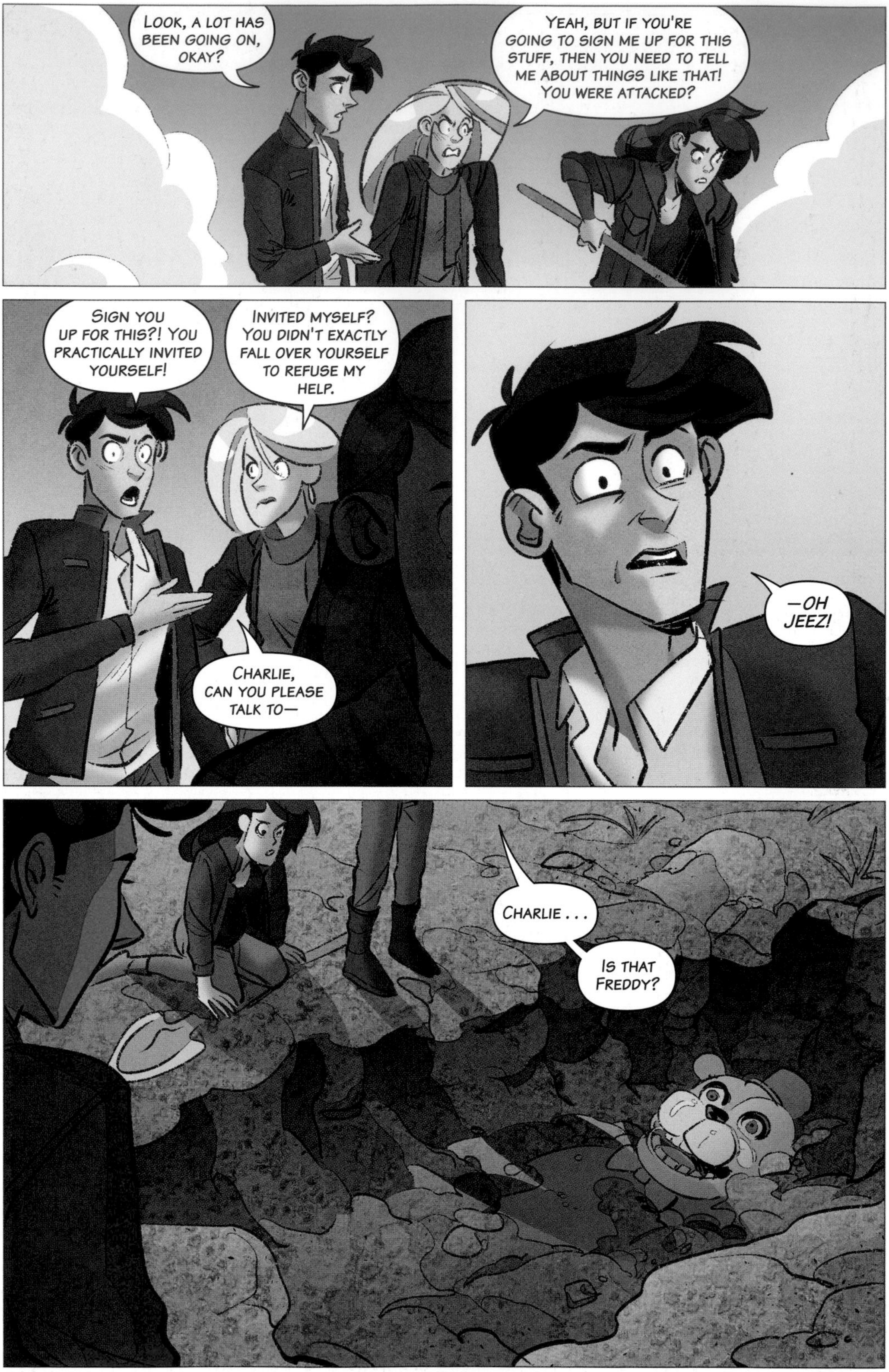
LOOK, A LOT HAS BEEN GOING ON, OKAY?
YEAH, BUT IF YOU'RE GOING TO SIGN ME UP FOR THIS STUFF, THEN YOU NEED TO TELL ME ABOUT THINGS LIKE THAT! YOU WERE ATTACKED?
SIGN YOU UP FOR THIS?! YOU PRACTICALLY INVITED YOURSELF!
INVITED MYSELF? YOU DIDN'T EXACTLY FALL OVER YOURSELF TO REFUSE MY HELP.
CHARLIE, CAN YOU PLEASE TALK TO—
—OH JEEZ!
CHARLIE . . .
IS THAT FREDDY?

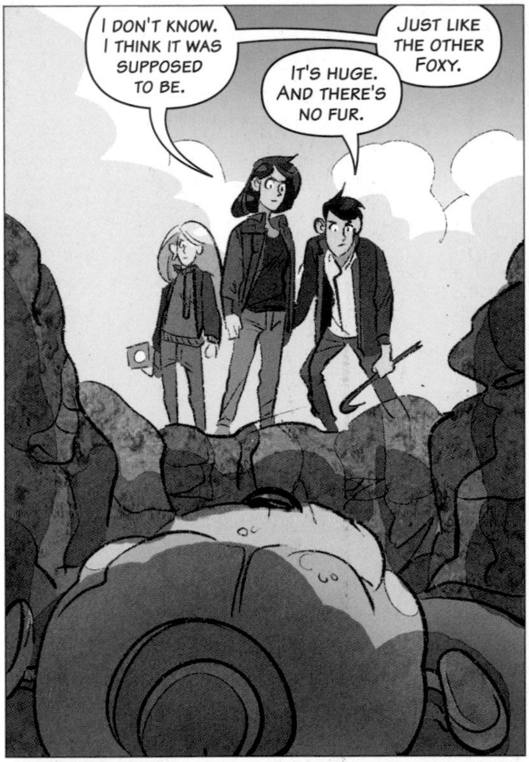
I DON'T KNOW. I THINK IT WAS SUPPOSED TO BE.
JUST LIKE THE OTHER FOXY.
IT'S HUGE. AND THERE'S NO FUR.

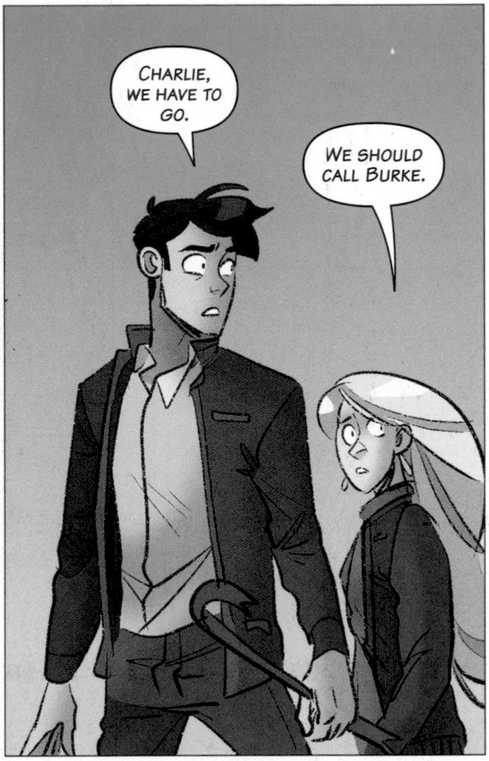
CHARLIE, WE HAVE TO GO.
WE SHOULD CALL BURKE.

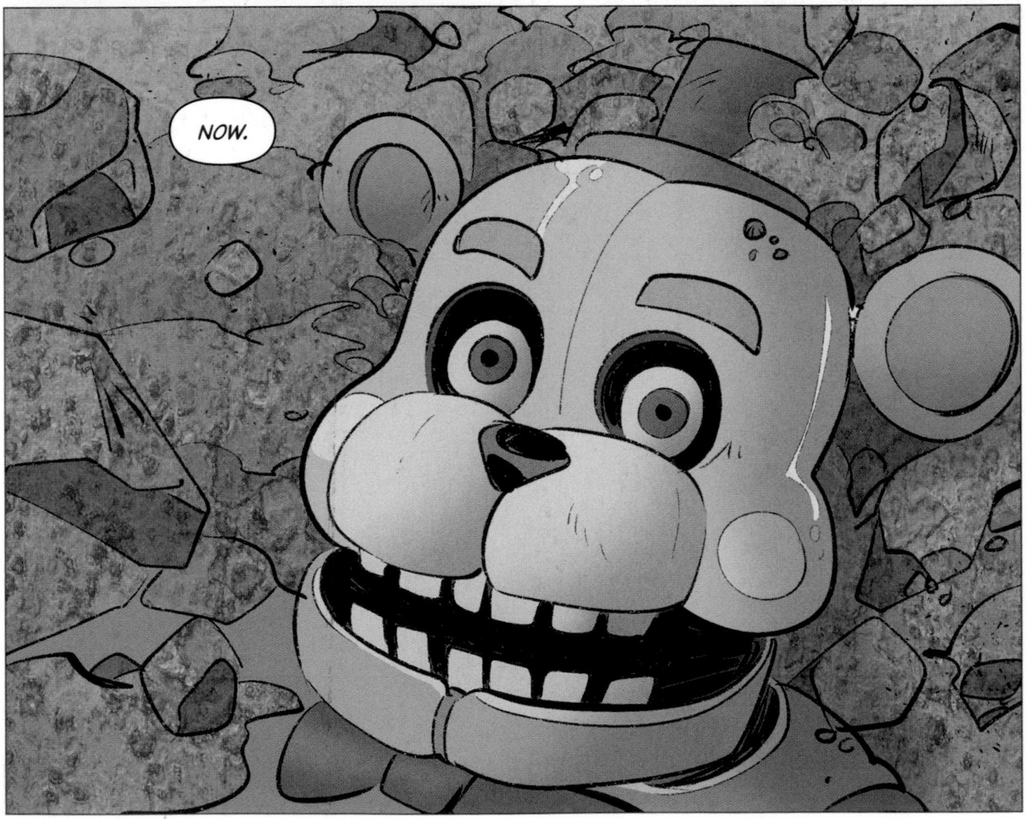
NOW.

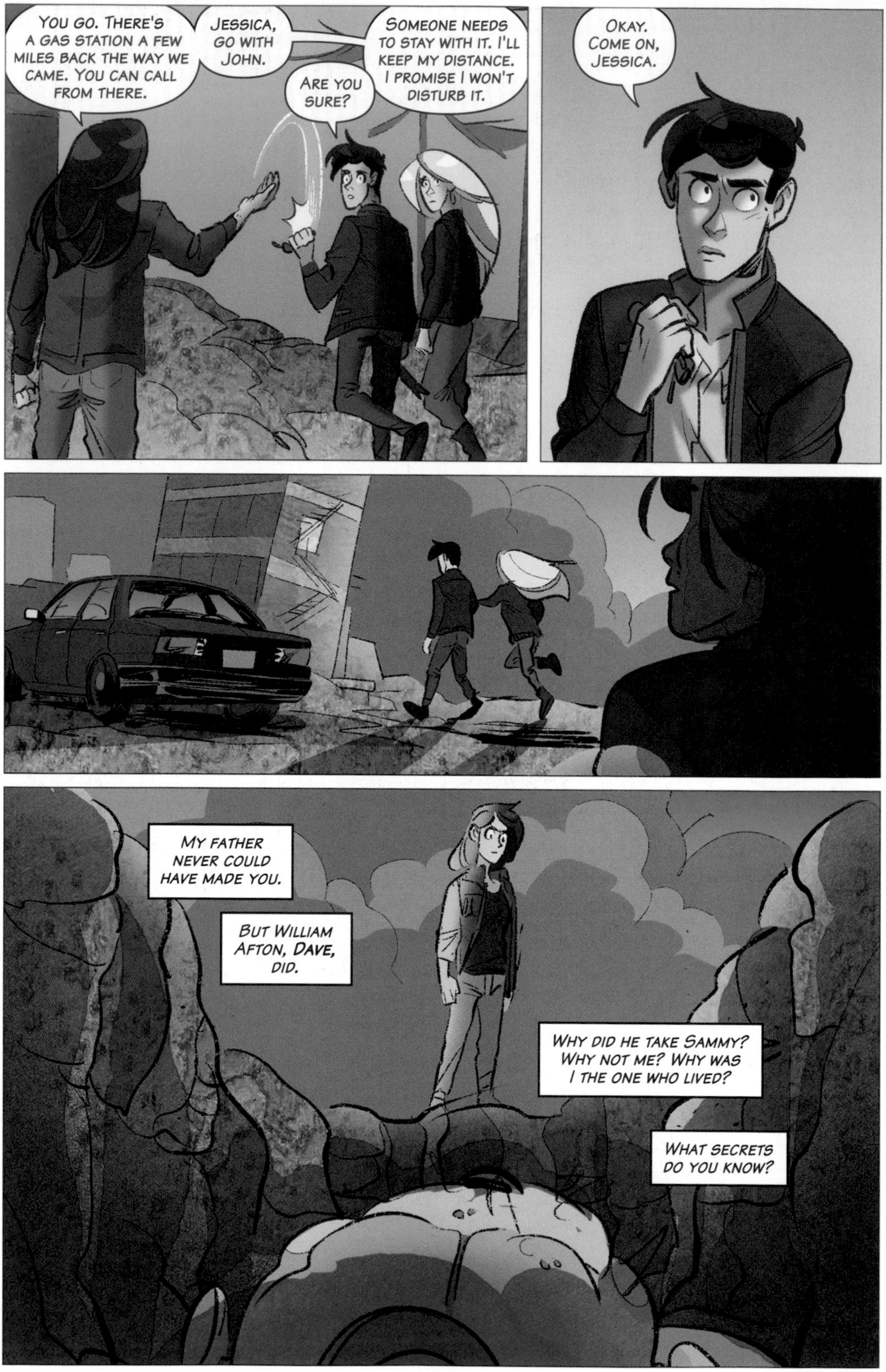
YOU GO. THERE'S A GAS STATION A FEW MILES BACK THE WAY WE CAME. YOU CAN CALL FROM THERE.
JESSICA, GO WITH JOHN.
ARE YOU SURE?
SOMEONE NEEDS TO STAY WITH IT. I'LL KEEP MY DISTANCE. I PROMISE I WON'T DISTURB IT.
OKAY. COME ON, JESSICA.
MY FATHER NEVER COULD HAVE MADE YOU.
BUT WILLIAM AFTON, DAVE, DID.
WHY DID HE TAKE SAMMY? WHY NOT ME? WHY WAS I THE ONE WHO LIVED?
WHAT SECRETS DO YOU KNOW?

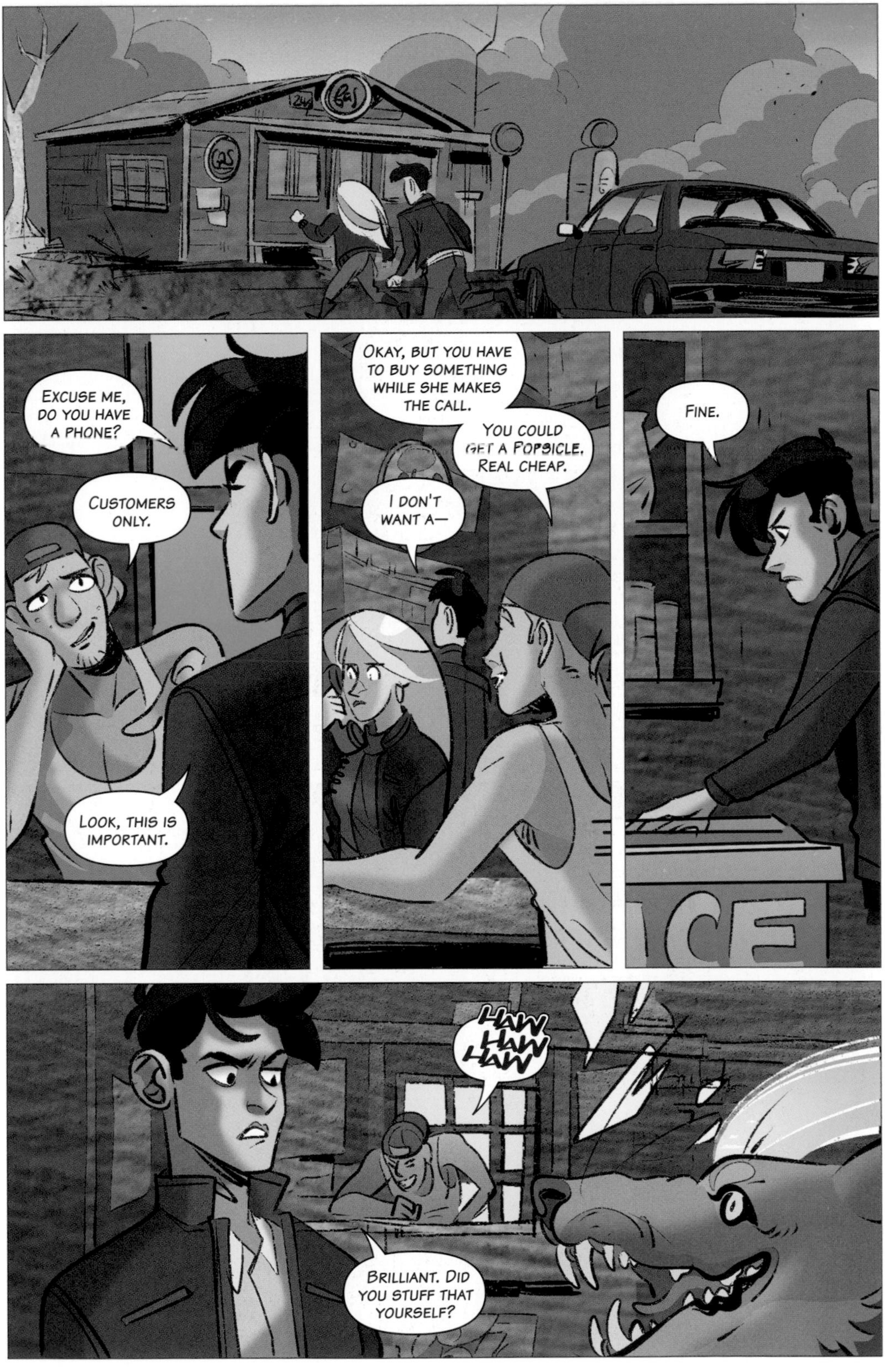

Excuse me, do you have a phone?
Customers only.
Look, this is important.
Okay, but you have to buy something while she makes the call.
You could get a Popsicle. Real cheap.
I don't want a—
Fine.
ICE
HAW HAW HAW
Brilliant. Did you stuff that yourself?

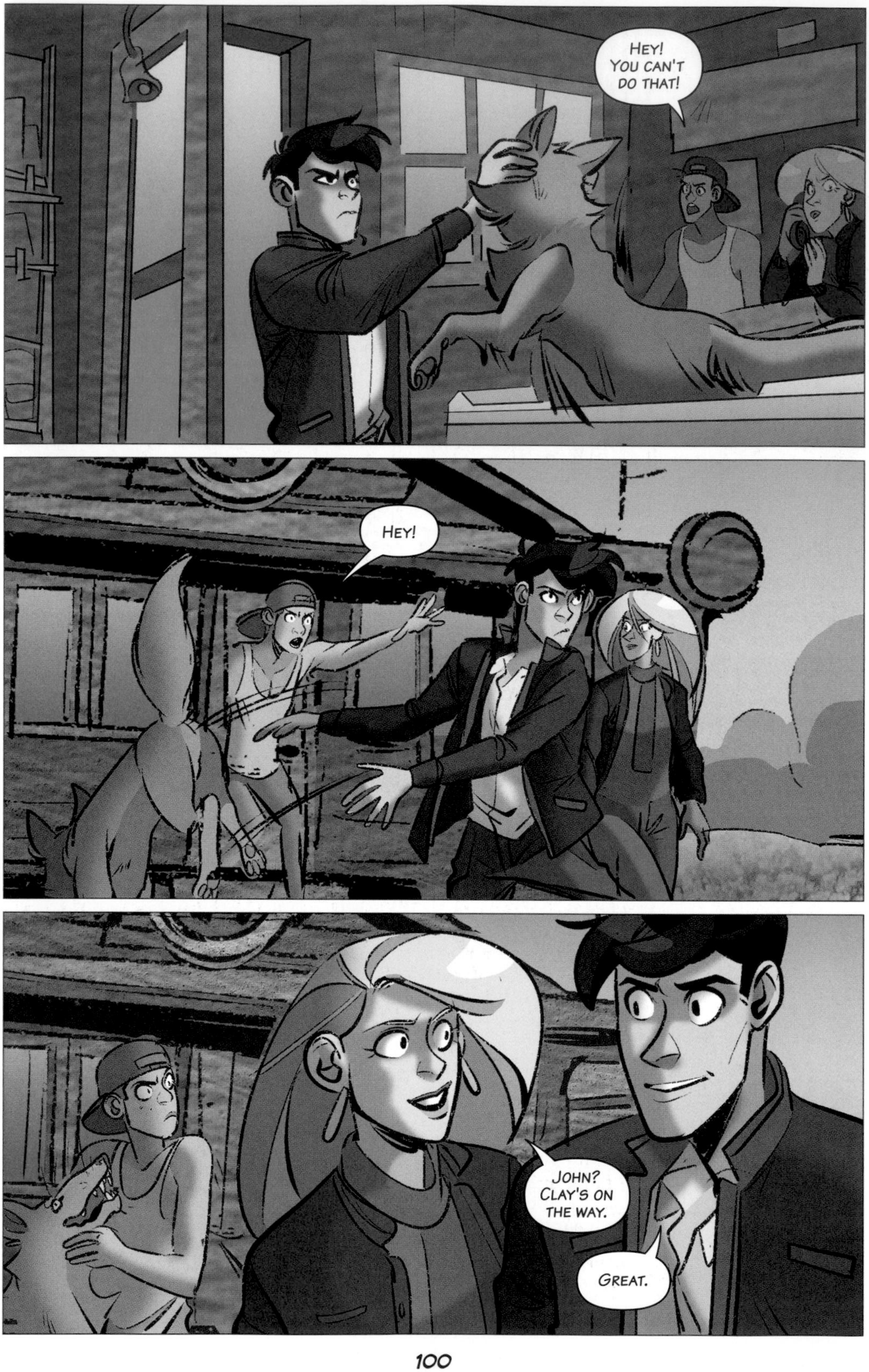
HEY!
YOU CAN'T
DO THAT!
HEY!
JOHN?
CLAY'S ON
THE WAY.
GREAT.

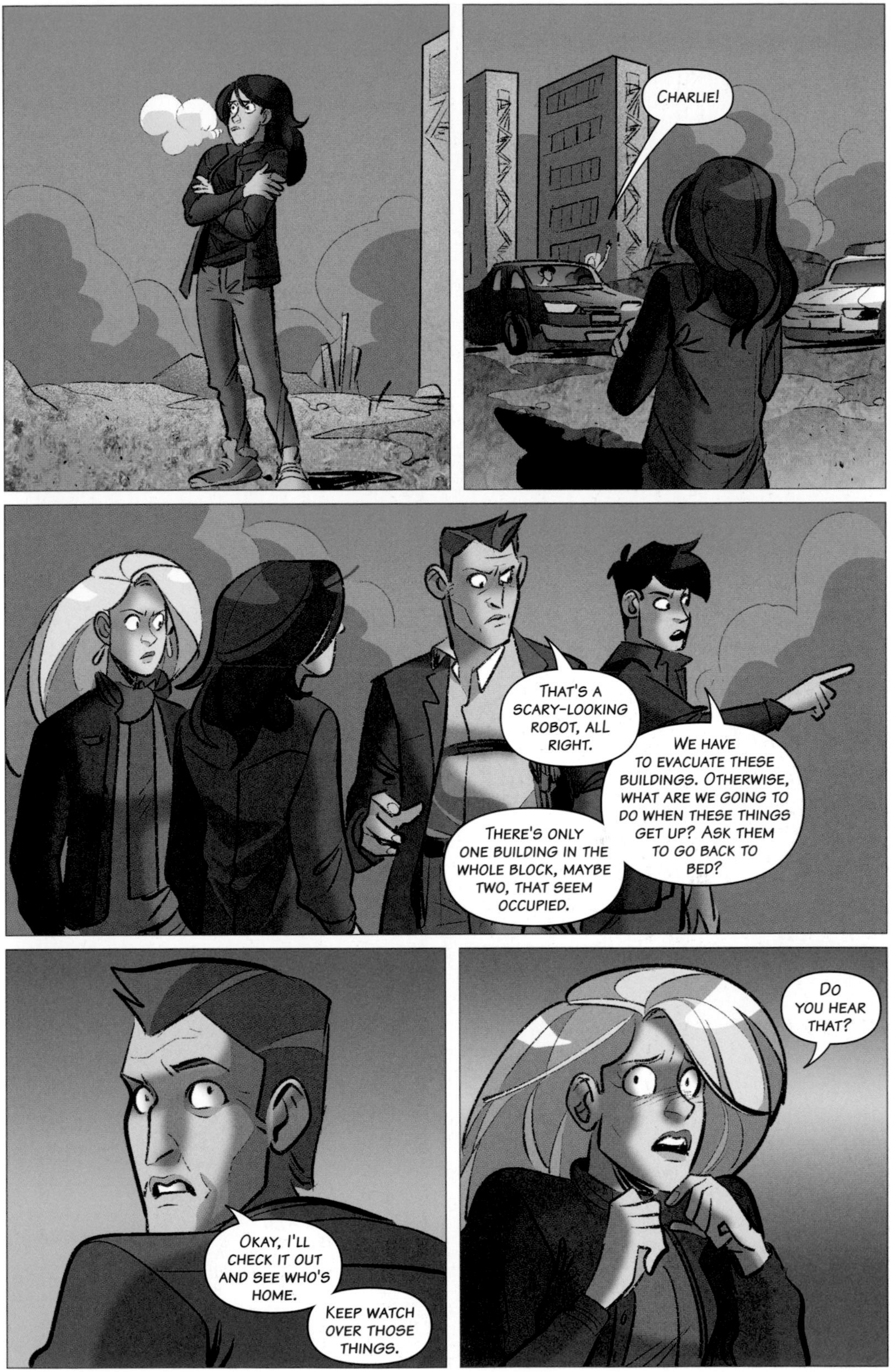
CHARLIE!
THAT'S A SCARY-LOOKING ROBOT, ALL RIGHT.
WE HAVE TO EVACUATE THESE BUILDINGS. OTHERWISE, WHAT ARE WE GOING TO DO WHEN THESE THINGS GET UP? ASK THEM TO GO BACK TO BED?
THERE'S ONLY ONE BUILDING IN THE WHOLE BLOCK, MAYBE TWO, THAT SEEM OCCUPIED.
OKAY, I'LL CHECK IT OUT AND SEE WHO'S HOME.
KEEP WATCH OVER THOSE THINGS.
DO YOU HEAR THAT?

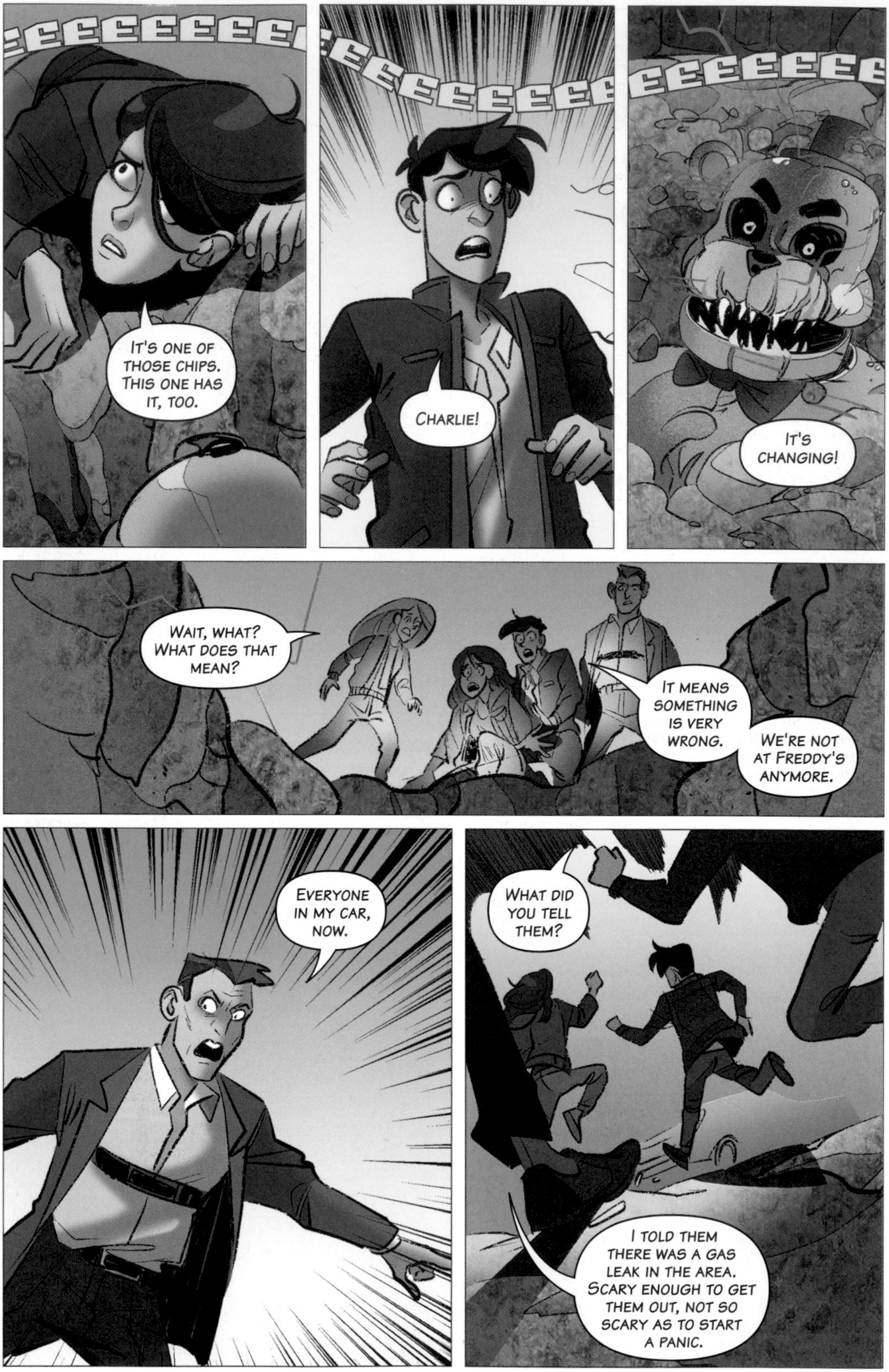
EEEEEEEEE
It's one of those chips. This one has it, too.
EEEEEEEEEE
Charlie!
EEEEEEEE
It's changing!
Wait, what? What does that mean?
It means something is very wrong.
We're not at Freddy's anymore.
Everyone in my car, now.
What did you tell them?
I told them there was a gas leak in the area. Scary enough to get them out, not so scary as to start a panic.

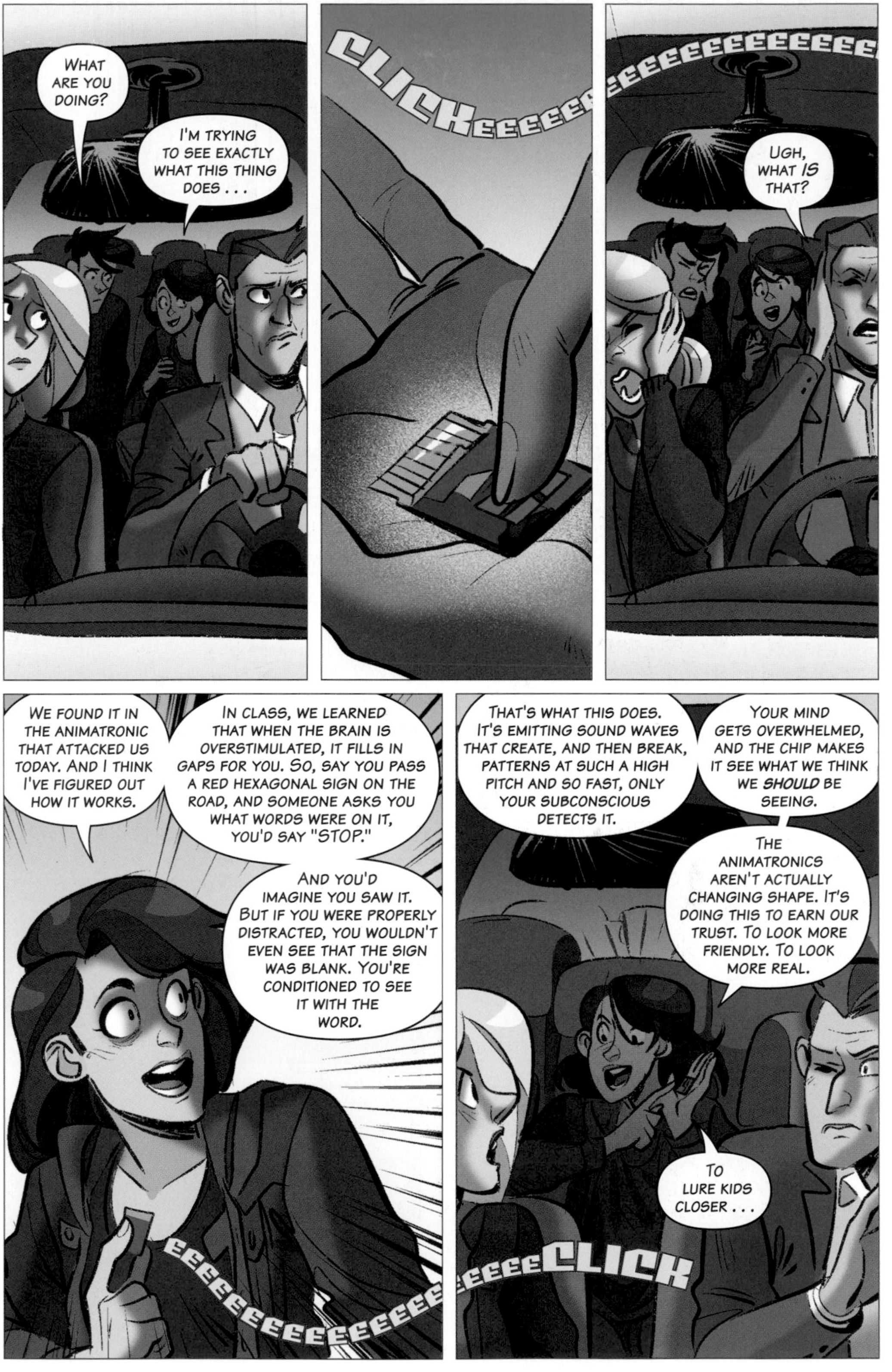

WHAT ARE YOU DOING?
I'M TRYING TO SEE EXACTLY WHAT THIS THING DOES . . .
CLICKEEEEEEEEEEEEEEEEEEEEEE
UGH, WHAT IS THAT?
WE FOUND IT IN THE ANIMATRONIC THAT ATTACKED US TODAY. AND I THINK I'VE FIGURED OUT HOW IT WORKS.
IN CLASS, WE LEARNED THAT WHEN THE BRAIN IS OVERSTIMULATED, IT FILLS IN GAPS FOR YOU. SO, SAY YOU PASS A RED HEXAGONAL SIGN ON THE ROAD, AND SOMEONE ASKS YOU WHAT WORDS WERE ON IT, YOU'D SAY "STOP."
AND YOU'D IMAGINE YOU SAW IT. BUT IF YOU WERE PROPERLY DISTRACTED, YOU WOULDN'T EVEN SEE THAT THE SIGN WAS BLANK. YOU'RE CONDITIONED TO SEE IT WITH THE WORD.
THAT'S WHAT THIS DOES. IT'S EMITTING SOUND WAVES THAT CREATE, AND THEN BREAK, PATTERNS AT SUCH A HIGH PITCH AND SO FAST, ONLY YOUR SUBCONSCIOUS DETECTS IT.
YOUR MIND GETS OVERWHELMED, AND THE CHIP MAKES IT SEE WHAT WE THINK WE SHOULD BE SEEING.
THE ANIMATRONICS AREN'T ACTUALLY CHANGING SHAPE. IT'S DOING THIS TO EARN OUR TRUST. TO LOOK MORE FRIENDLY. TO LOOK MORE REAL.
TO LURE KIDS CLOSER . . .
EEEEEEEEEEEEEEEEEEEEEEEEEECLICK

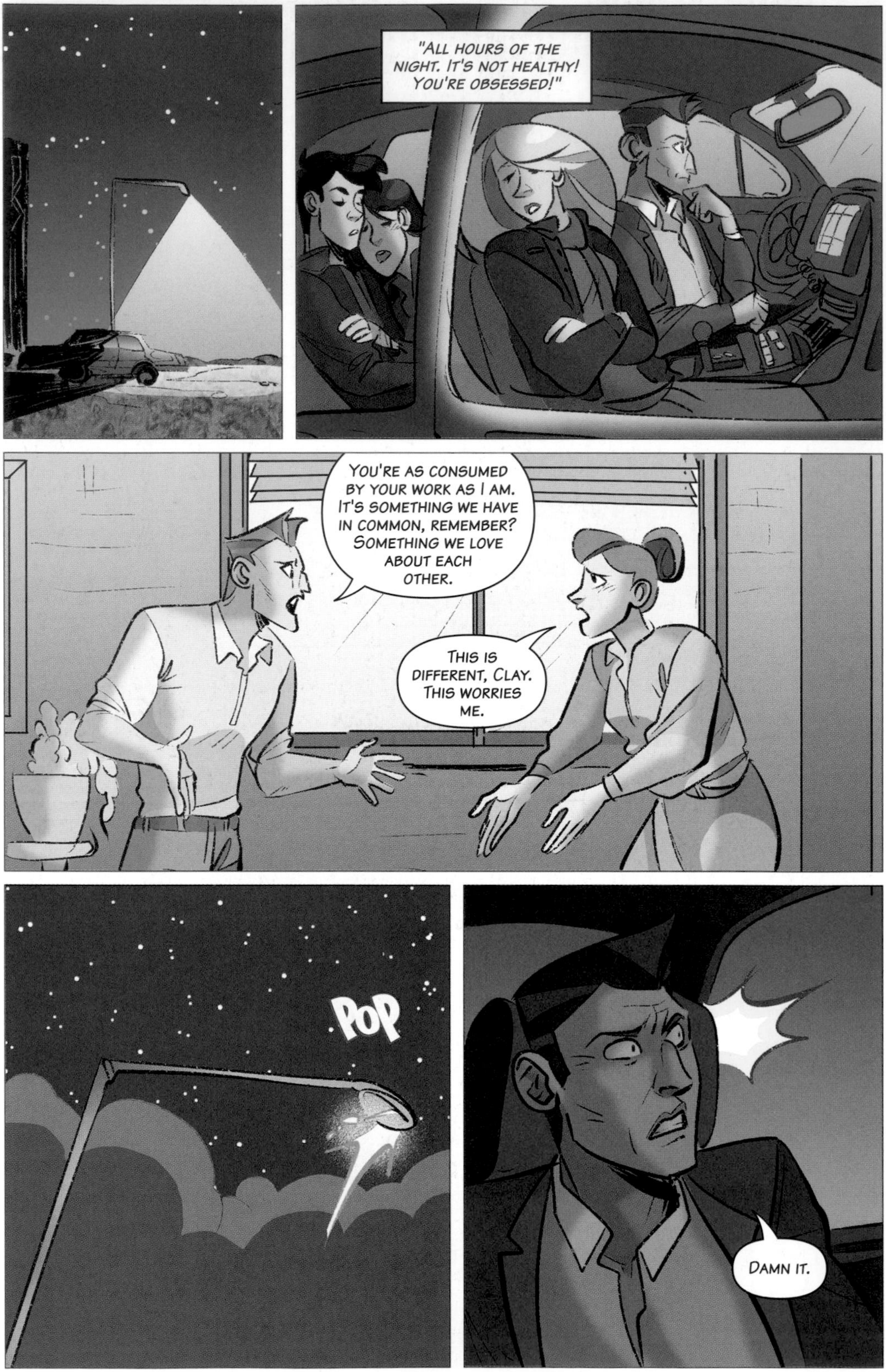
"All hours of the night. It's not healthy! You're obsessed!"
You're as consumed by your work as I am. It's something we have in common, remember? Something we love about each other.
This is different, Clay. This worries me.
POP
Damn it.

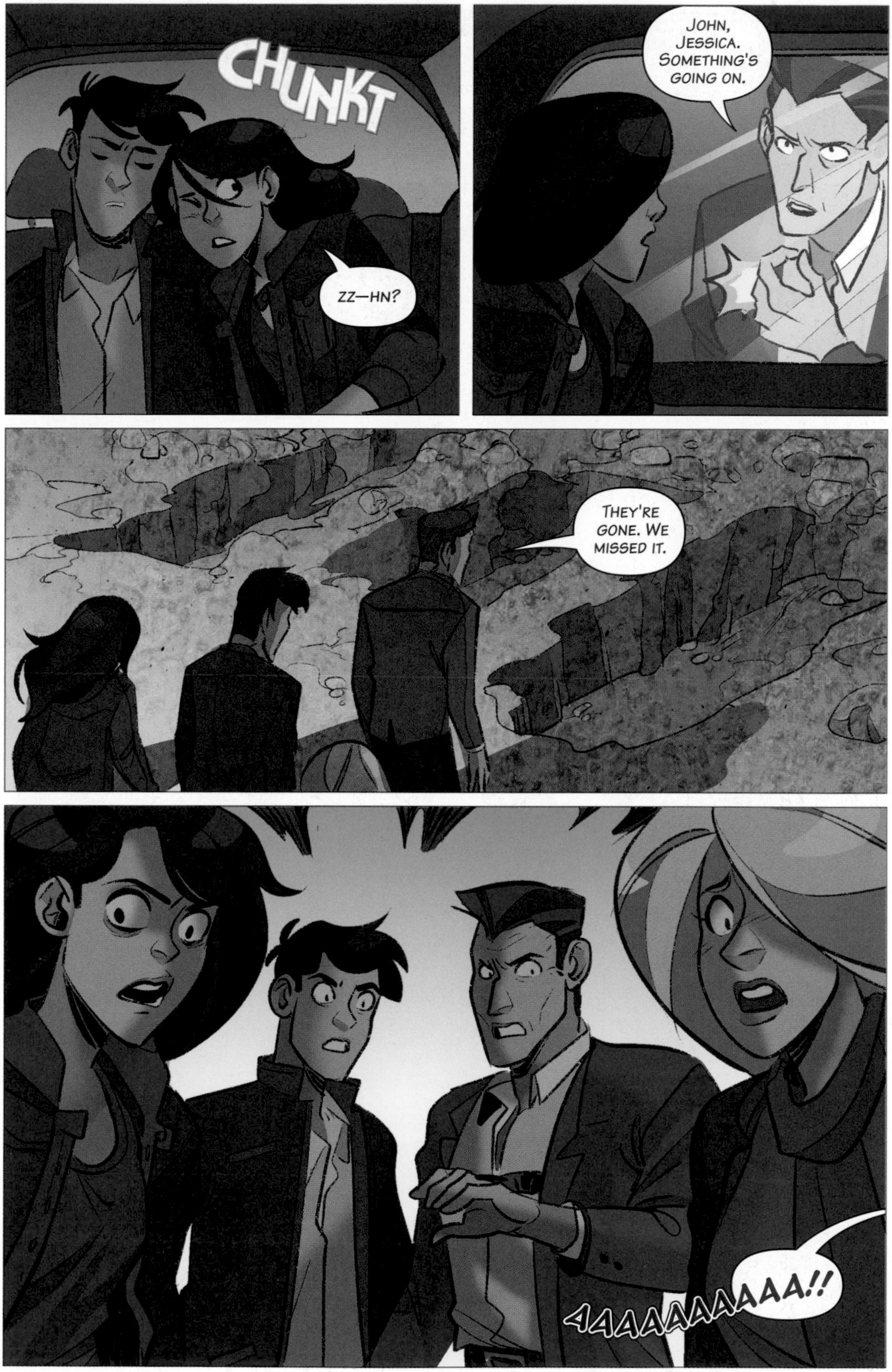
CHUNKT
ZZ—HN?
JOHN, JESSICA. SOMETHING'S GOING ON.
THEY'RE GONE. WE MISSED IT.
AAAAAAAAAAA!!

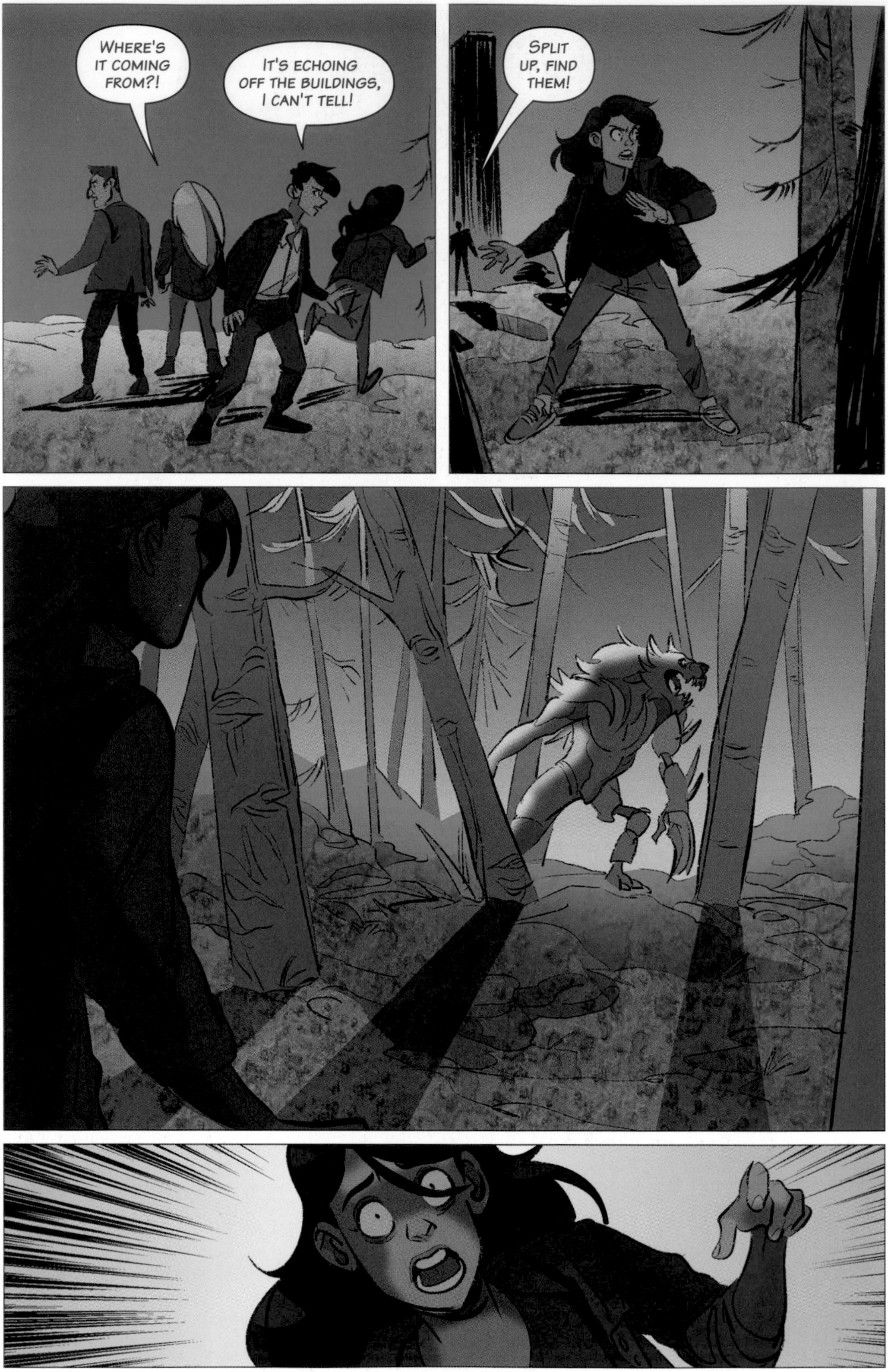

WHERE'S IT COMING FROM?!
IT'S ECHOING OFF THE BUILDINGS, I CAN'T TELL!
SPLIT UP, FIND THEM!

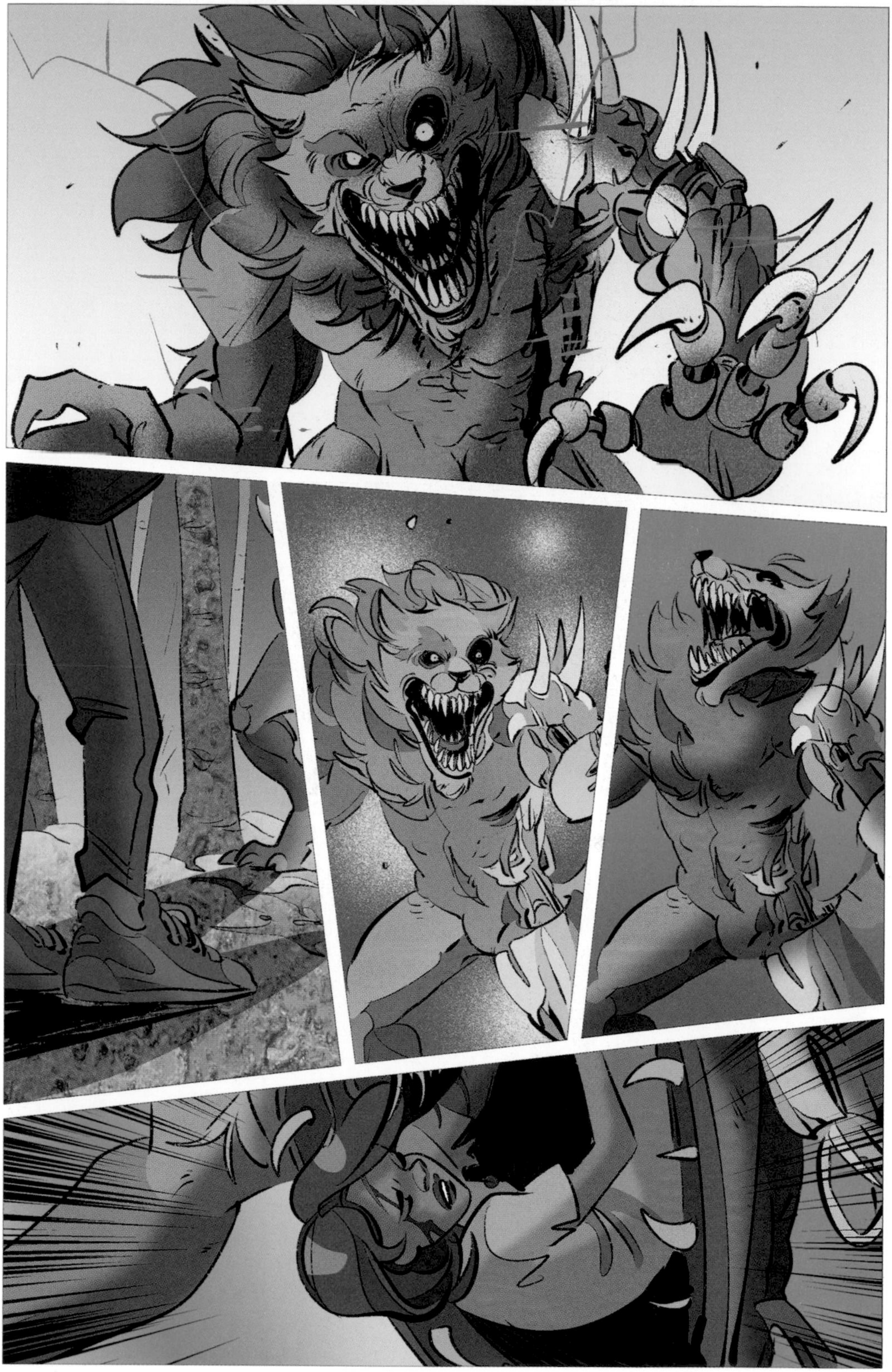

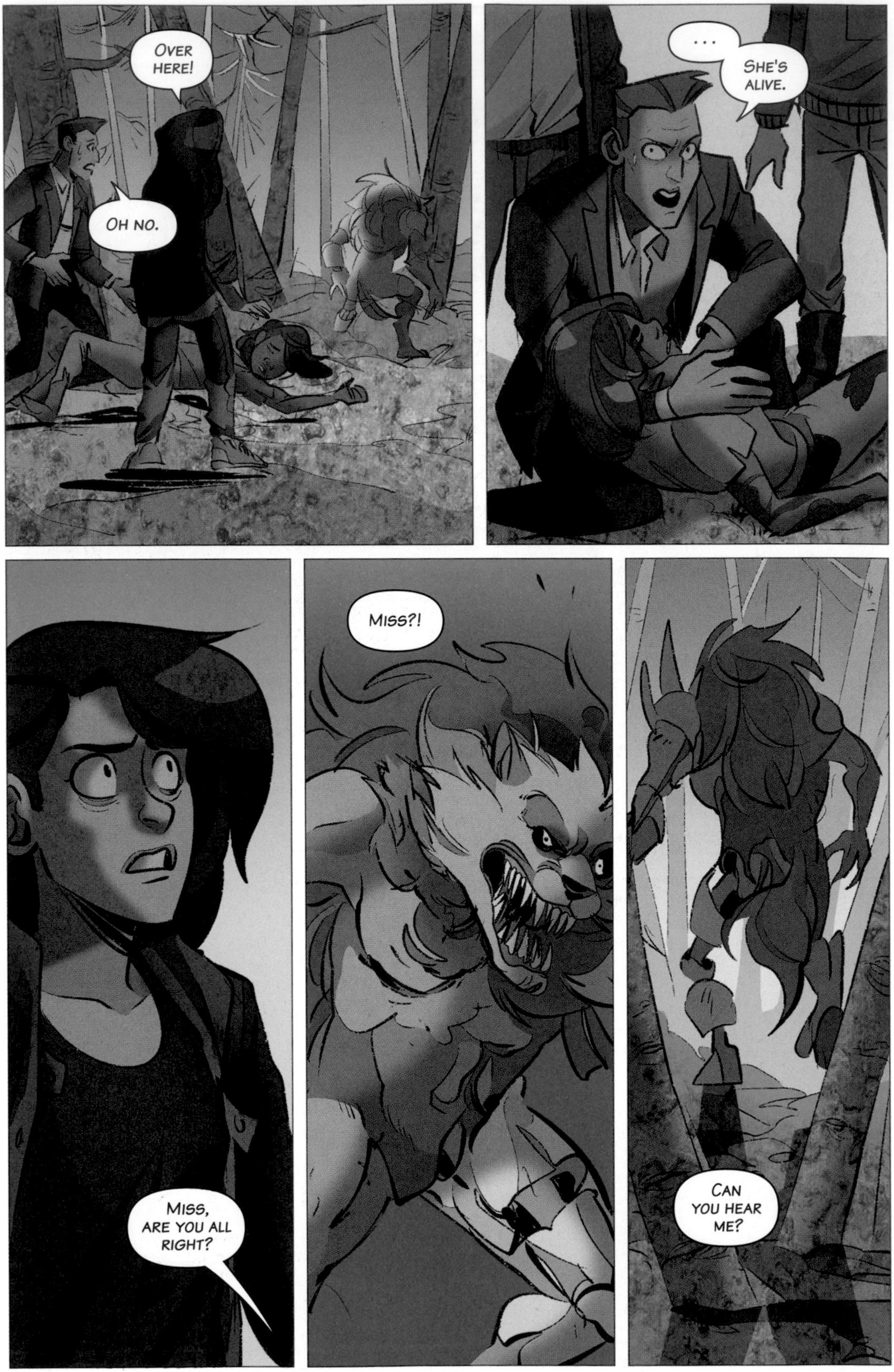
Over here!
Oh no.
...
She's alive.
Miss, are you all right?
Miss?!
Can you hear me?

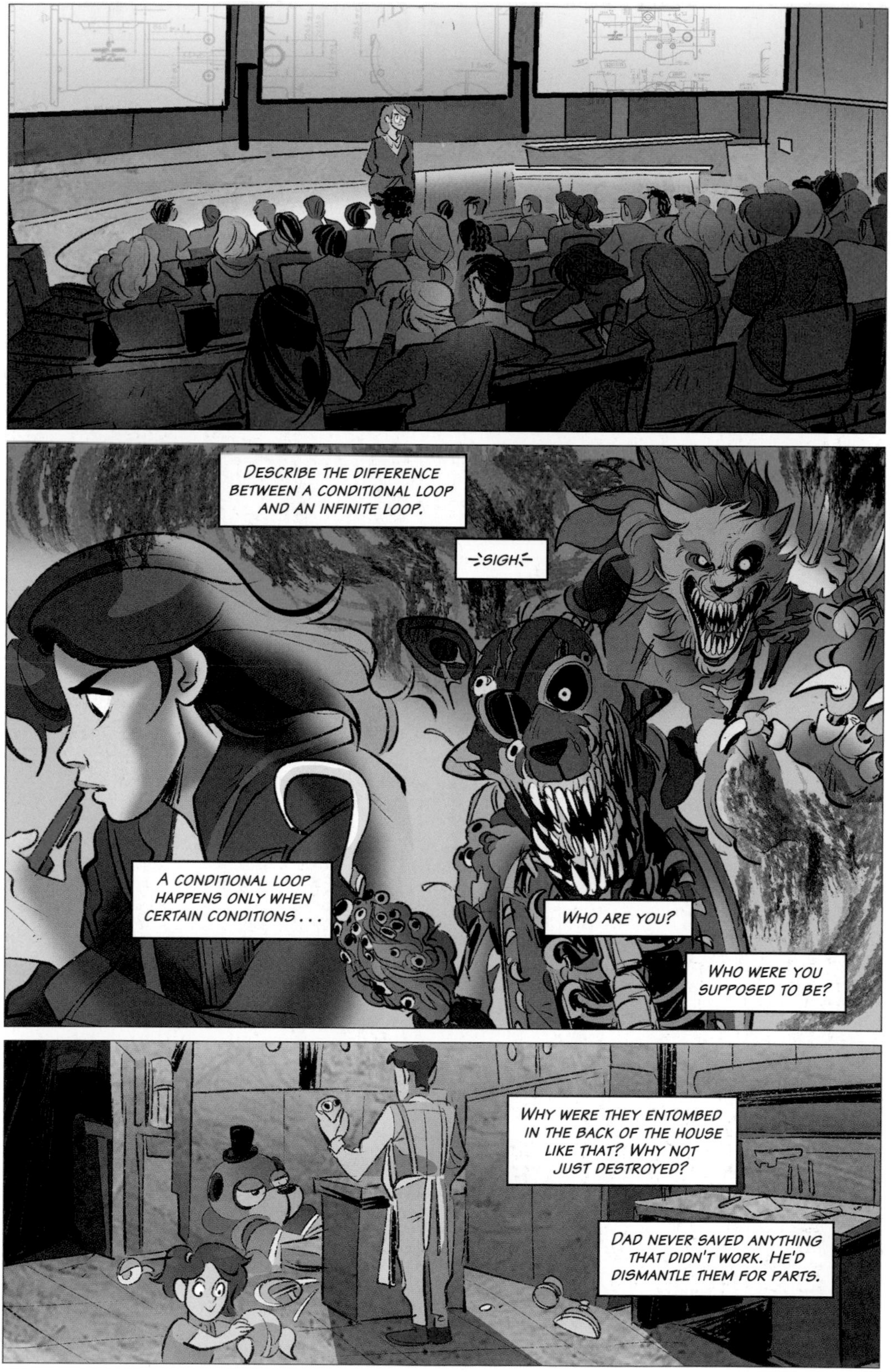
DESCRIBE THE DIFFERENCE BETWEEN A CONDITIONAL LOOP AND AN INFINITE LOOP.
SIGH
A CONDITIONAL LOOP HAPPENS ONLY WHEN CERTAIN CONDITIONS . . .
WHO ARE YOU?
WHO WERE YOU SUPPOSED TO BE?
WHY WERE THEY ENTOMBED IN THE BACK OF THE HOUSE LIKE THAT? WHY NOT JUST DESTROYED?
DAD NEVER SAVED ANYTHING THAT DIDN'T WORK. HE'D DISMANTLE THEM FOR PARTS.

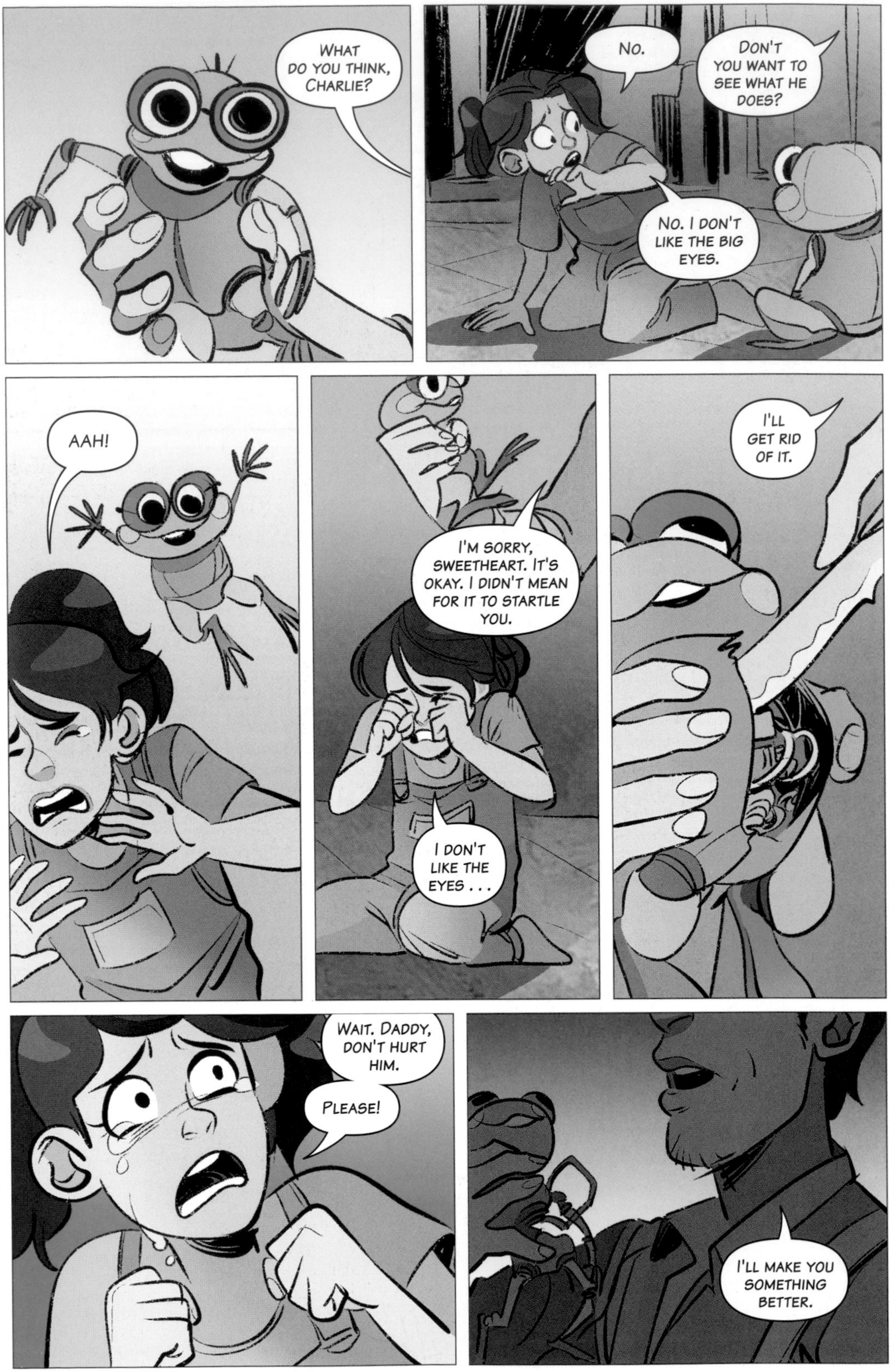
What do you think, Charlie?
No.
Don't you want to see what he does?
No. I don't like the big eyes.
AAH!
I'm sorry, sweetheart. It's okay. I didn't mean for it to startle you.
I don't like the eyes . . .
I'll get rid of it.
Wait. Daddy, don't hurt him.
Please!
I'll make you something better.

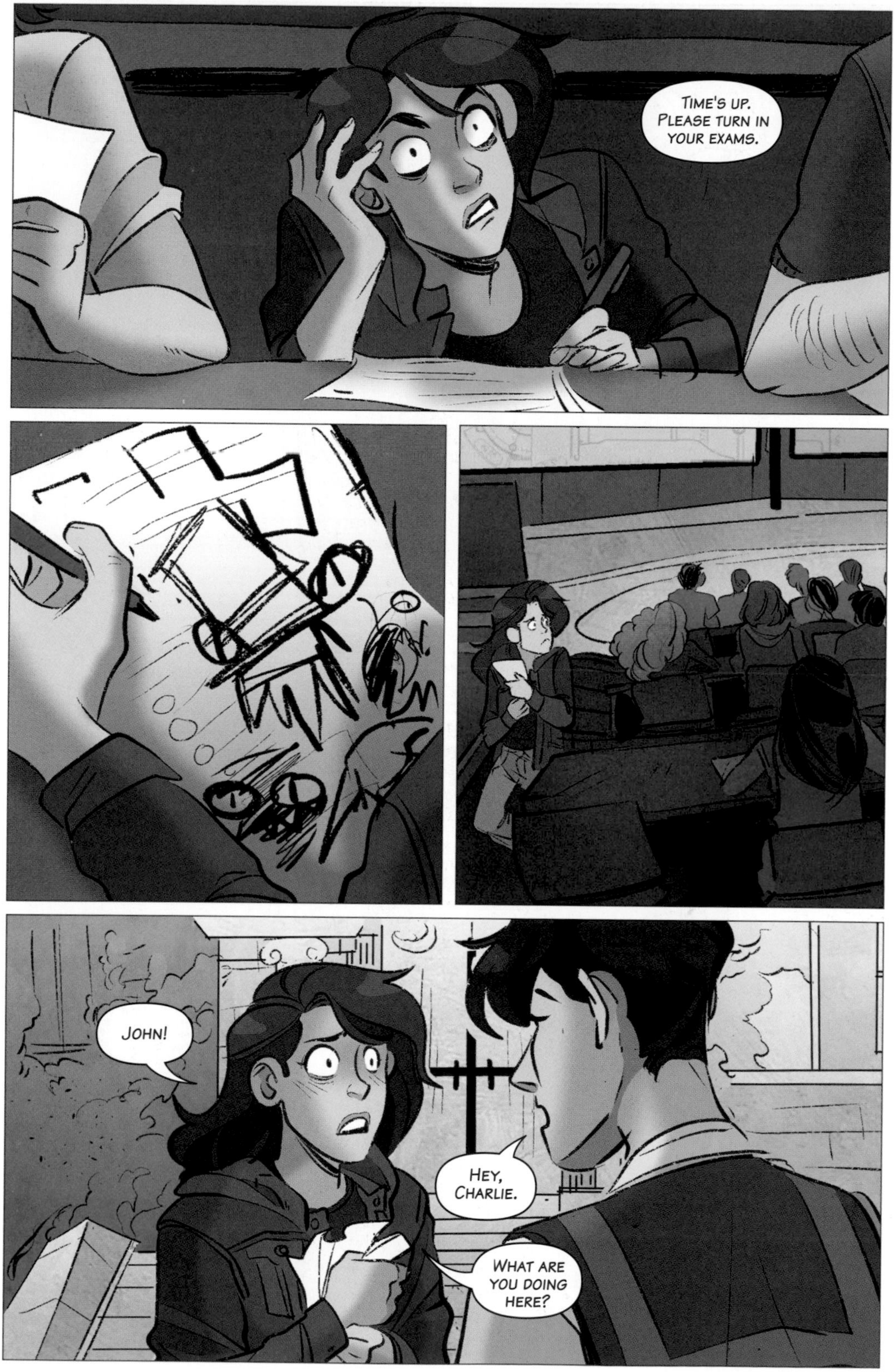
TIME'S UP. PLEASE TURN IN YOUR EXAMS.
JOHN!
HEY, CHARLIE.
WHAT ARE YOU DOING HERE?

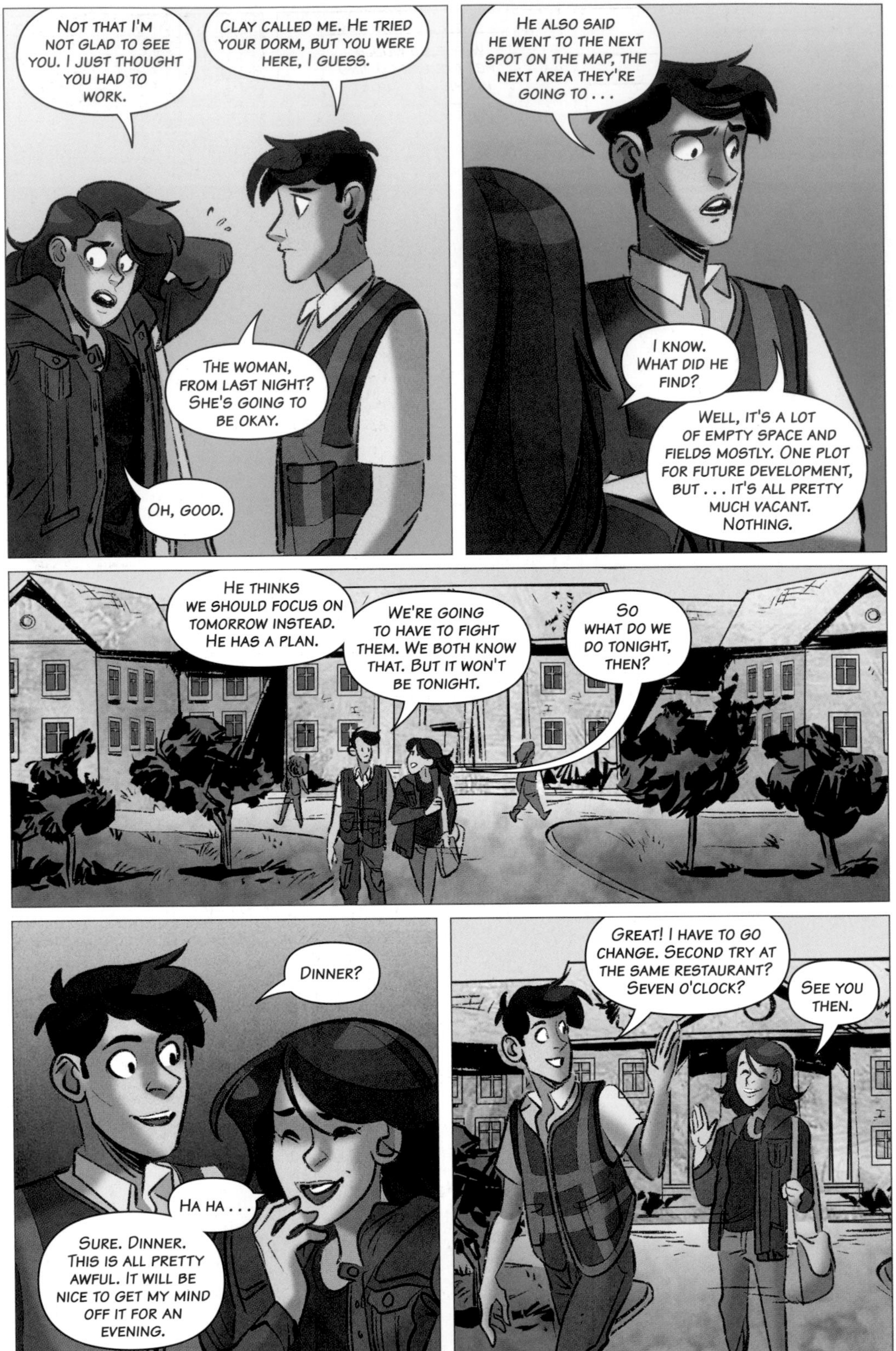
Not that I'm not glad to see you. I just thought you had to work.
Clay called me. He tried your dorm, but you were here, I guess.
The woman, from last night? She's going to be okay.
Oh, good.
He also said he went to the next spot on the map, the next area they're going to . . .
I know. What did he find?
Well, it's a lot of empty space and fields mostly. One plot for future development, but . . . it's all pretty much vacant. Nothing.
He thinks we should focus on tomorrow instead. He has a plan.
We're going to have to fight them. We both know that. But it won't be tonight.
So what do we do tonight, then?
Dinner?
Ha ha . . .
Sure. Dinner. This is all pretty awful. It will be nice to get my mind off it for an evening.
Great! I have to go change. Second try at the same restaurant? Seven o'clock?
See you then.

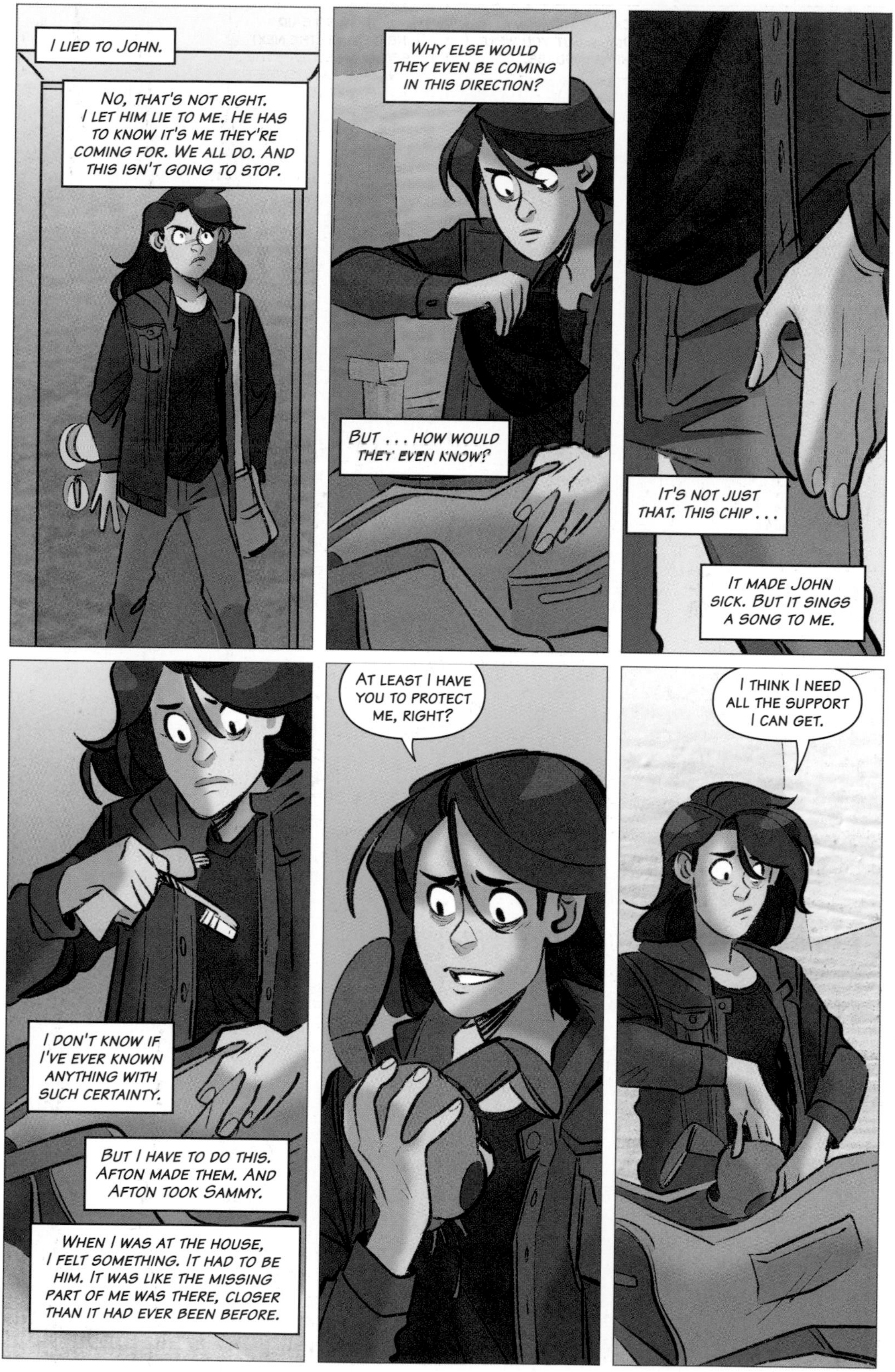
I LIED TO JOHN.
NO, THAT'S NOT RIGHT. I LET HIM LIE TO ME. HE HAS TO KNOW IT'S ME THEY'RE COMING FOR. WE ALL DO. AND THIS ISN'T GOING TO STOP.
WHY ELSE WOULD THEY EVEN BE COMING IN THIS DIRECTION?
BUT . . . HOW WOULD THEY EVEN KNOW?
IT'S NOT JUST THAT. THIS CHIP . . .
IT MADE JOHN SICK. BUT IT SINGS A SONG TO ME.
I DON'T KNOW IF I'VE EVER KNOWN ANYTHING WITH SUCH CERTAINTY.
BUT I HAVE TO DO THIS. AFTON MADE THEM. AND AFTON TOOK SAMMY.
WHEN I WAS AT THE HOUSE, I FELT SOMETHING. IT HAD TO BE HIM. IT WAS LIKE THE MISSING PART OF ME WAS THERE, CLOSER THAN IT HAD EVER BEEN BEFORE.
AT LEAST I HAVE YOU TO PROTECT ME, RIGHT?
I THINK I NEED ALL THE SUPPORT I CAN GET.

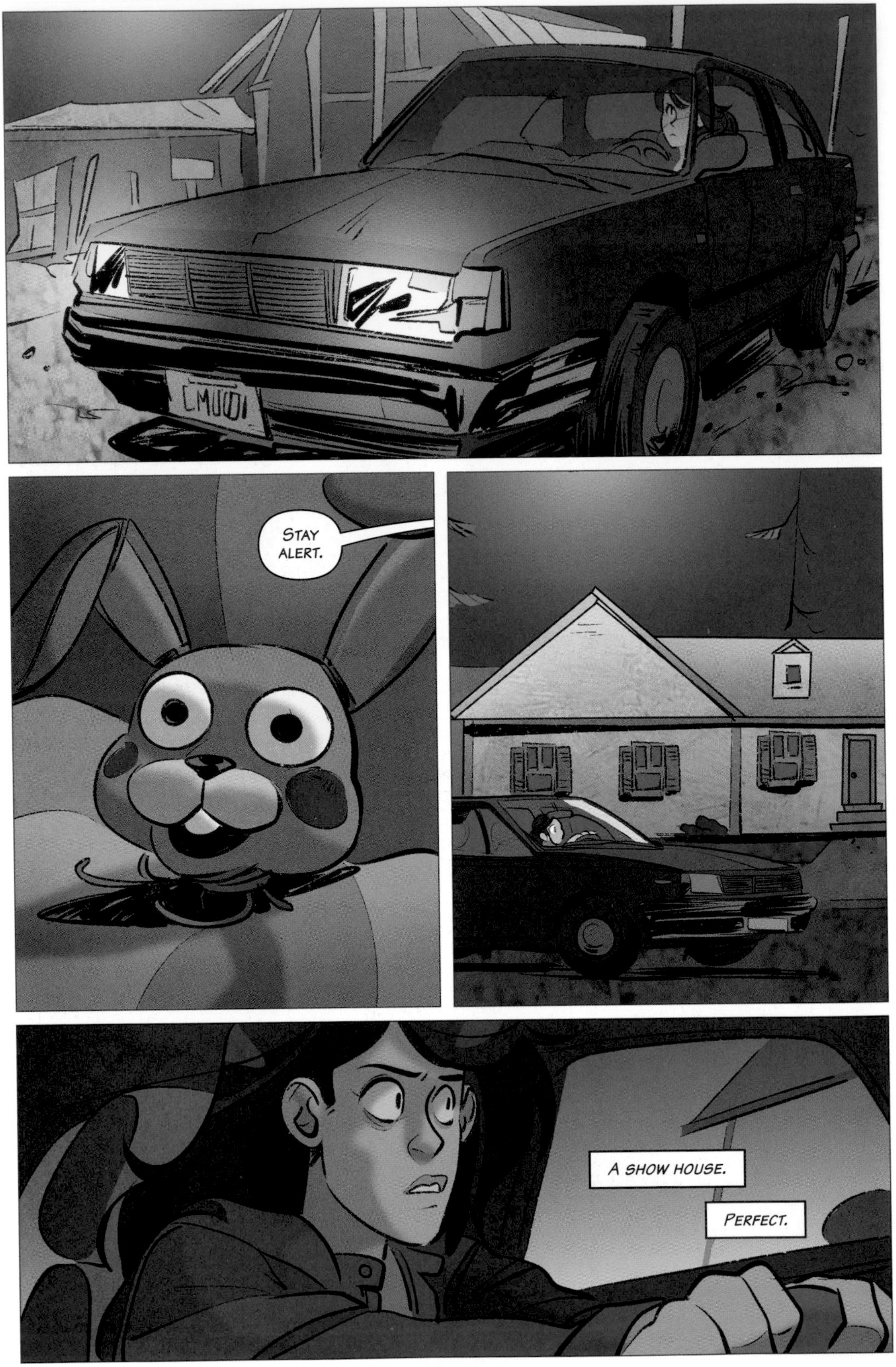
Stay alert.
A show house.
Perfect.

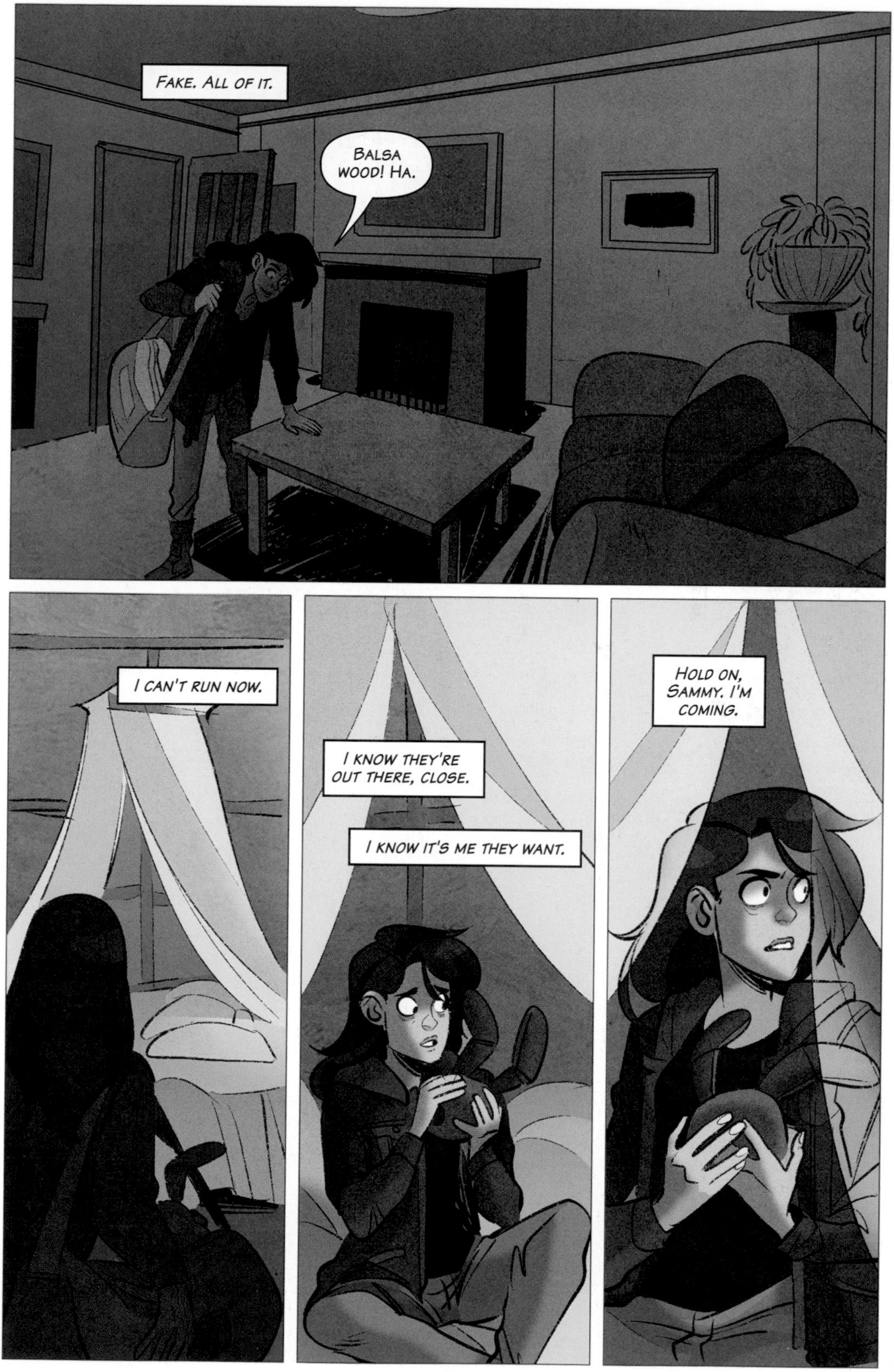
FAKE. ALL OF IT.
BALSA WOOD! HA.
I CAN'T RUN NOW.
I KNOW THEY'RE OUT THERE, CLOSE.
I KNOW IT'S ME THEY WANT.
HOLD ON, SAMMY. I'M COMING.

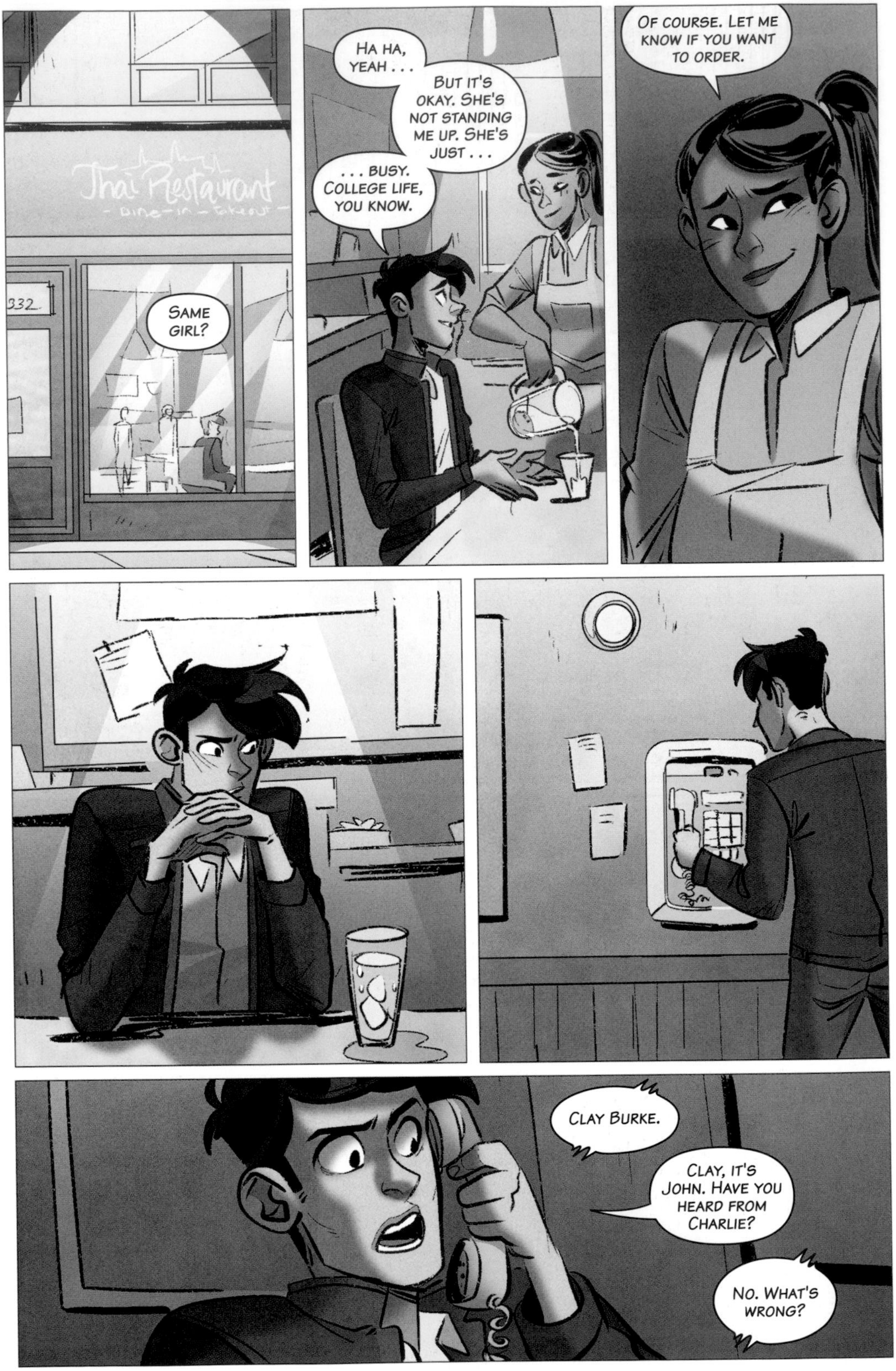
Thai Restaurant
- Dine-in - takeout -
332
Same girl?
Ha ha, yeah . . .
But it's okay. She's not standing me up. She's just . . .
. . . busy. College life, you know.
Of course. Let me know if you want to order.
Clay Burke.
Clay, it's John. Have you heard from Charlie?
No. What's wrong?

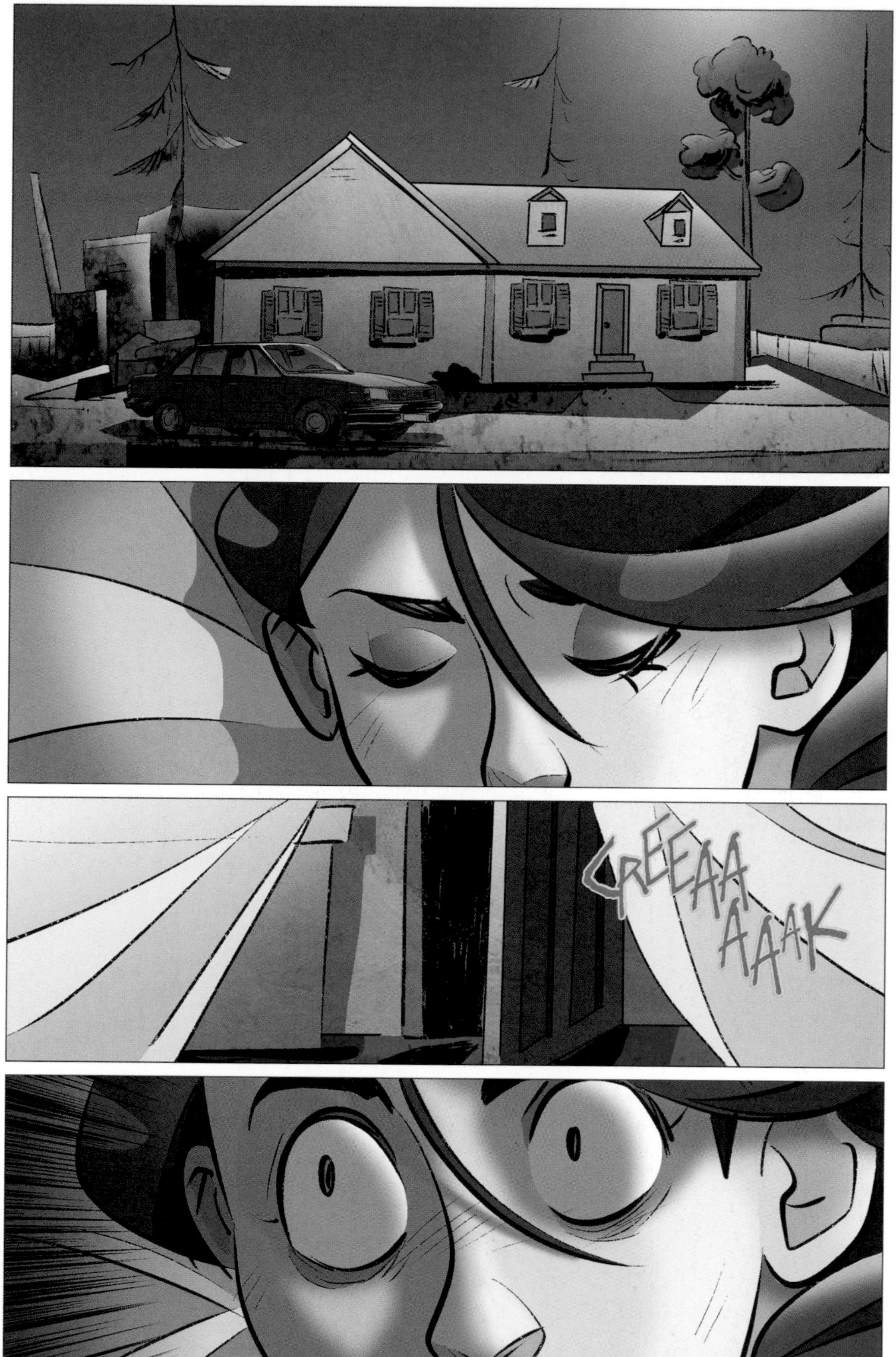
CREEAAAAAK

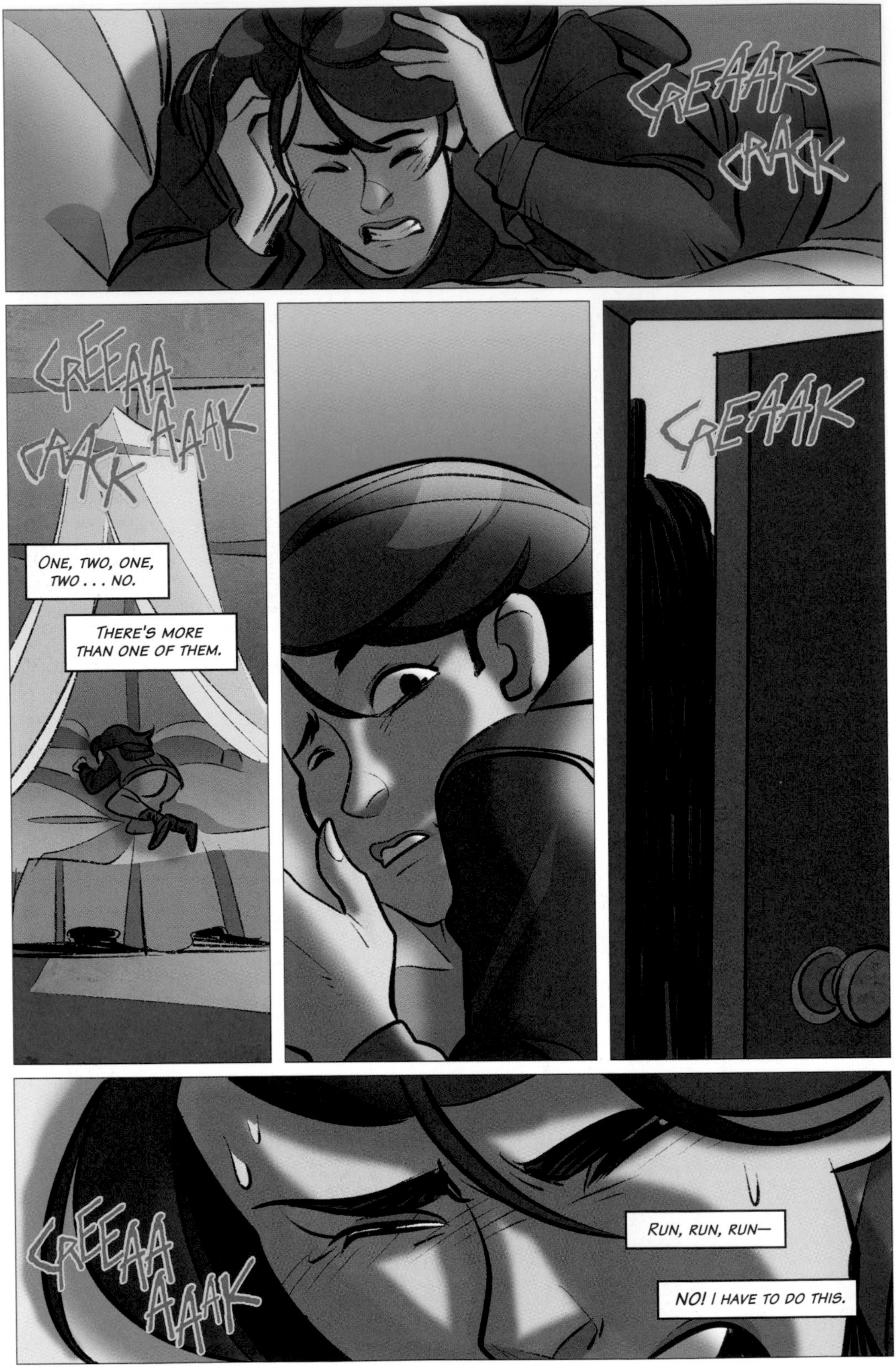
CREAAK
CRACK
CREEAA AAAK
CRACK
ONE, TWO, ONE, TWO . . . NO.
THERE'S MORE THAN ONE OF THEM.
CREAAK
CREEAA AAAK
RUN, RUN, RUN—
NO! I HAVE TO DO THIS.

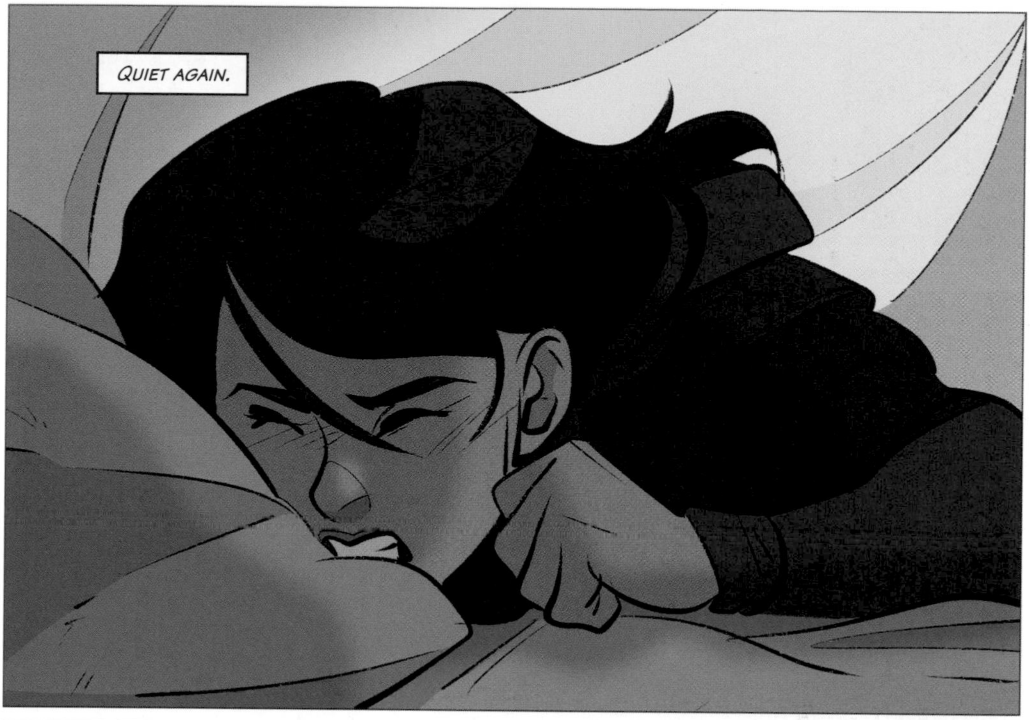
QUIET AGAIN.

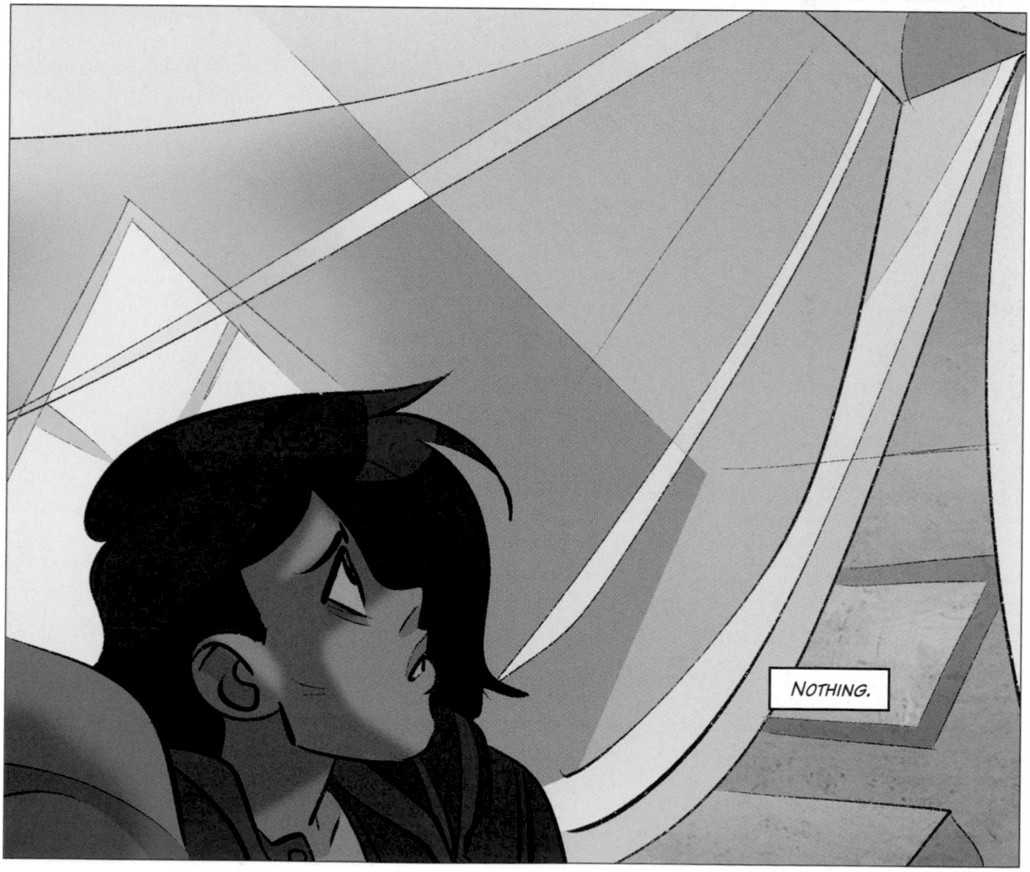
NOTHING.

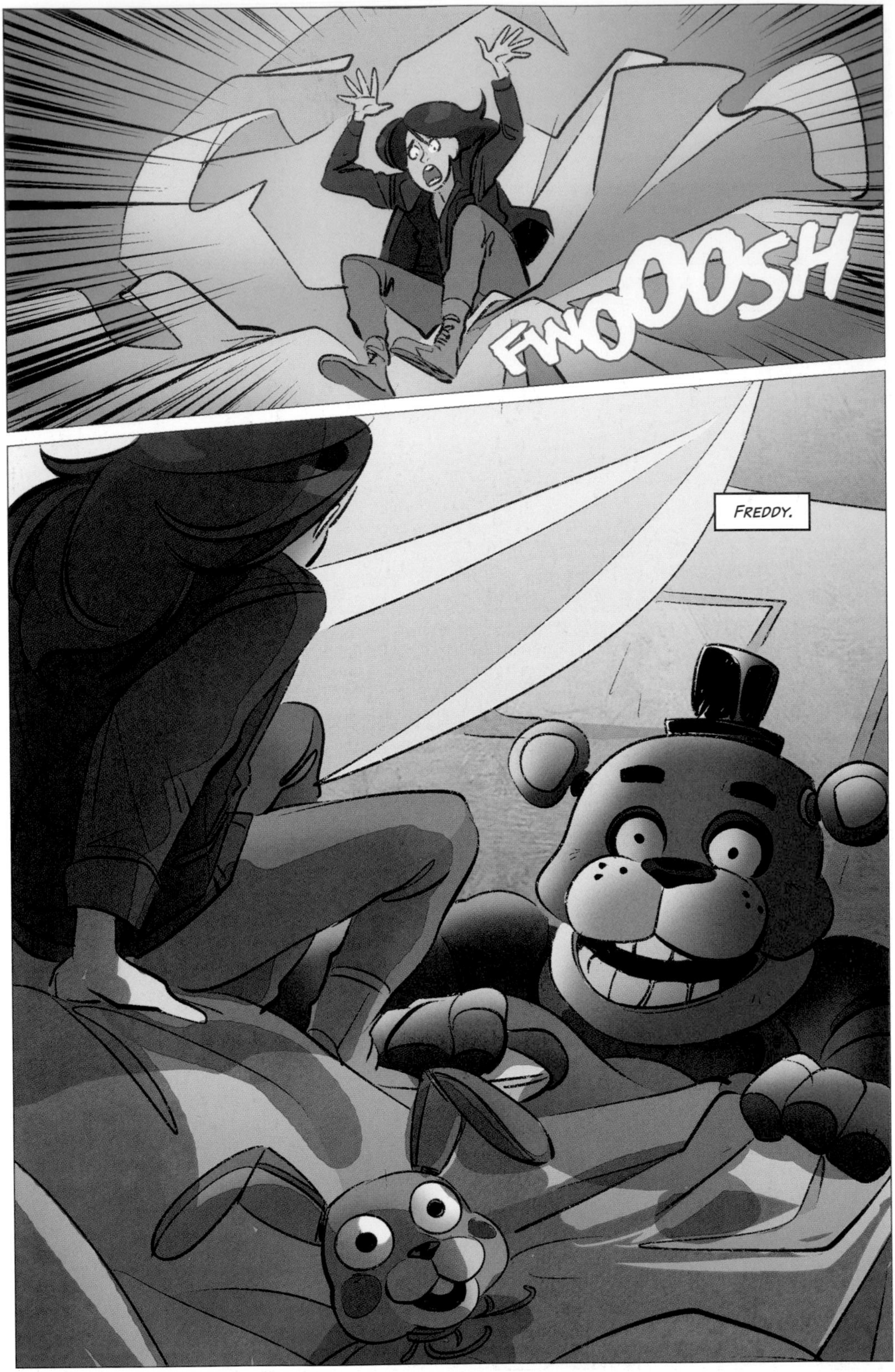
FWOOOOSH
FREDDY.

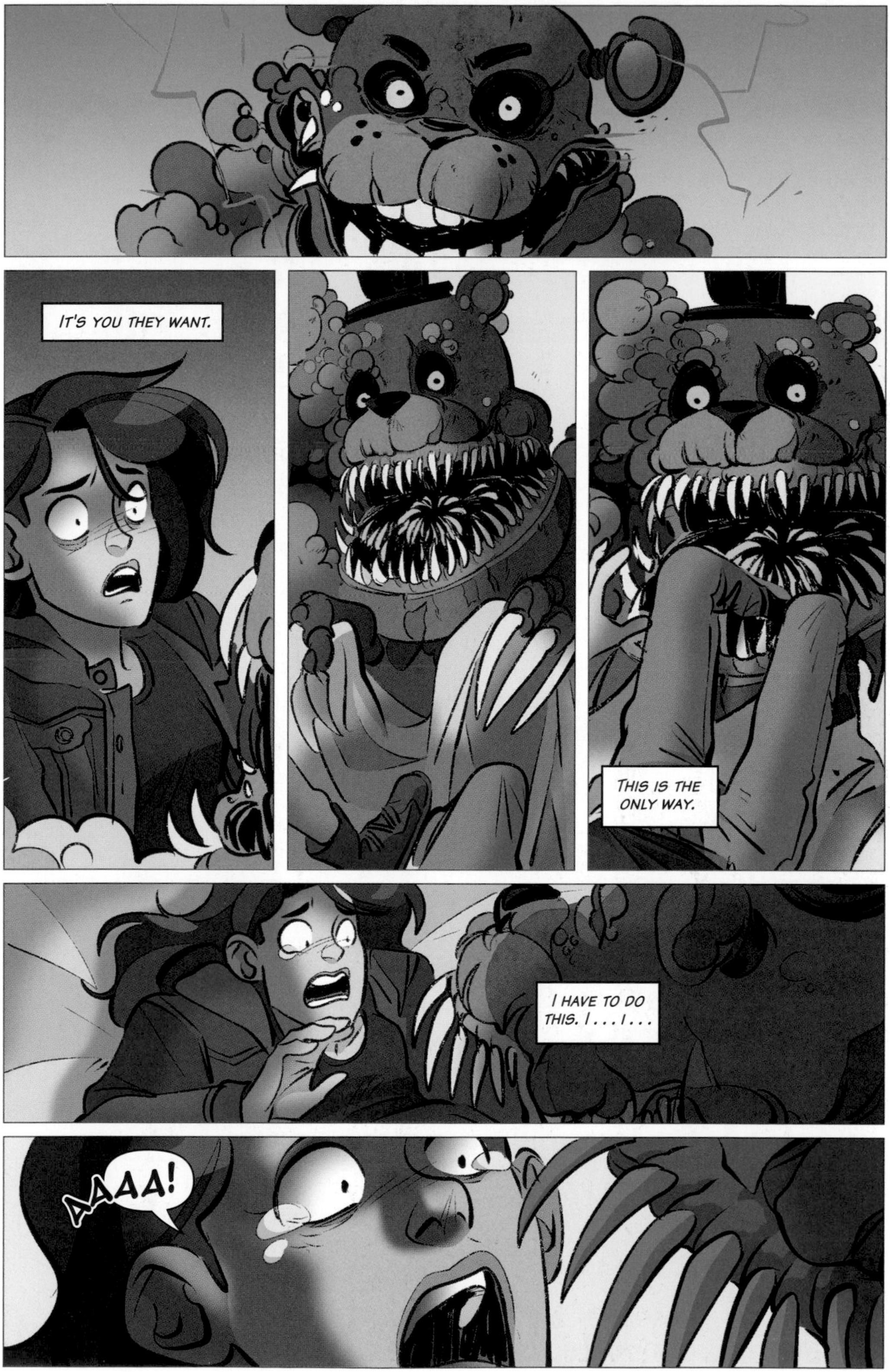
IT'S YOU THEY WANT.
THIS IS THE ONLY WAY.
I HAVE TO DO THIS. I . . . I . . .
AAAA!

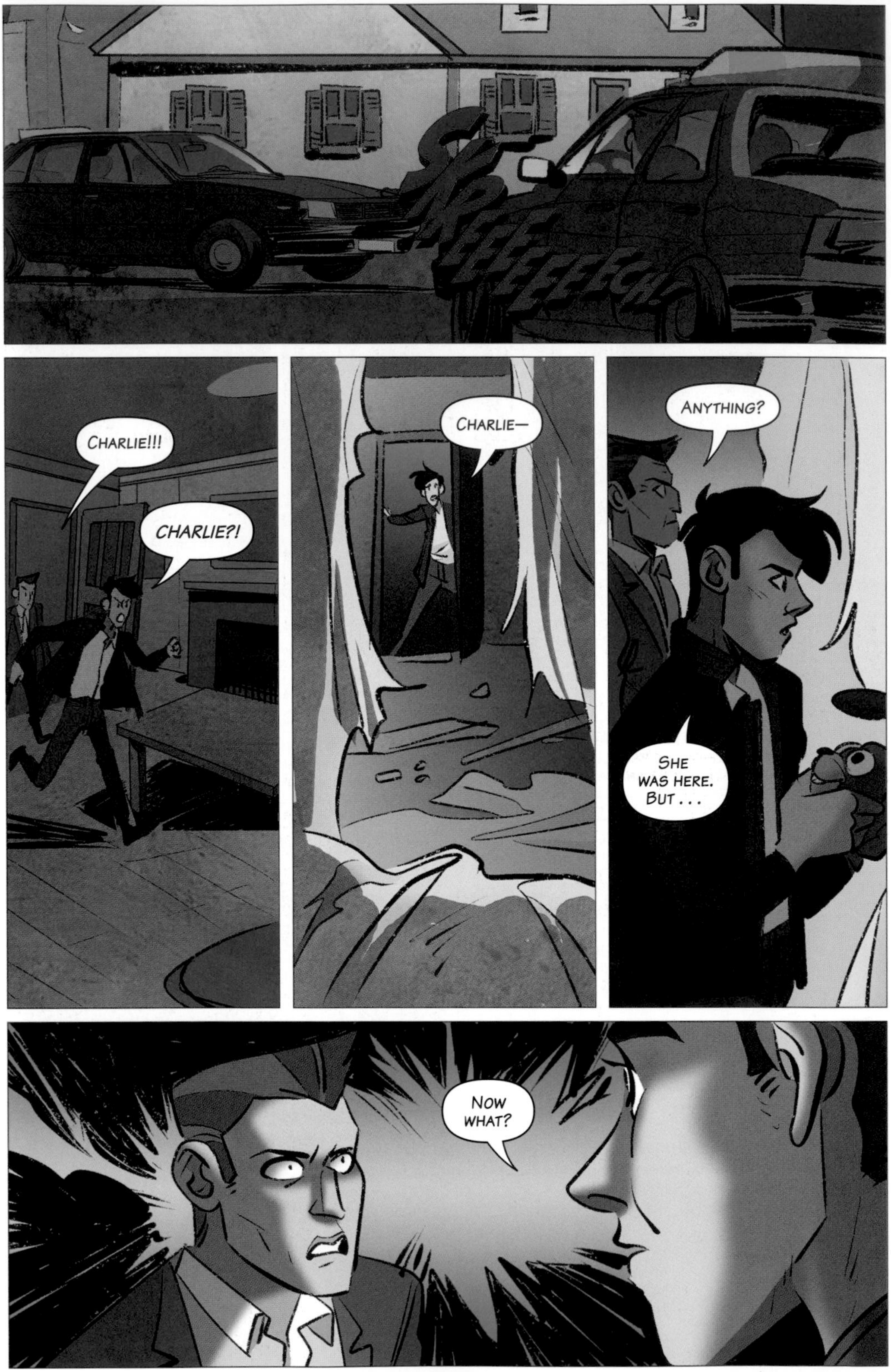
SKREEEEECH!
CHARLIE!!!
CHARLIE?!
CHARLIE—
ANYTHING?
SHE WAS HERE. BUT . . .
NOW WHAT?

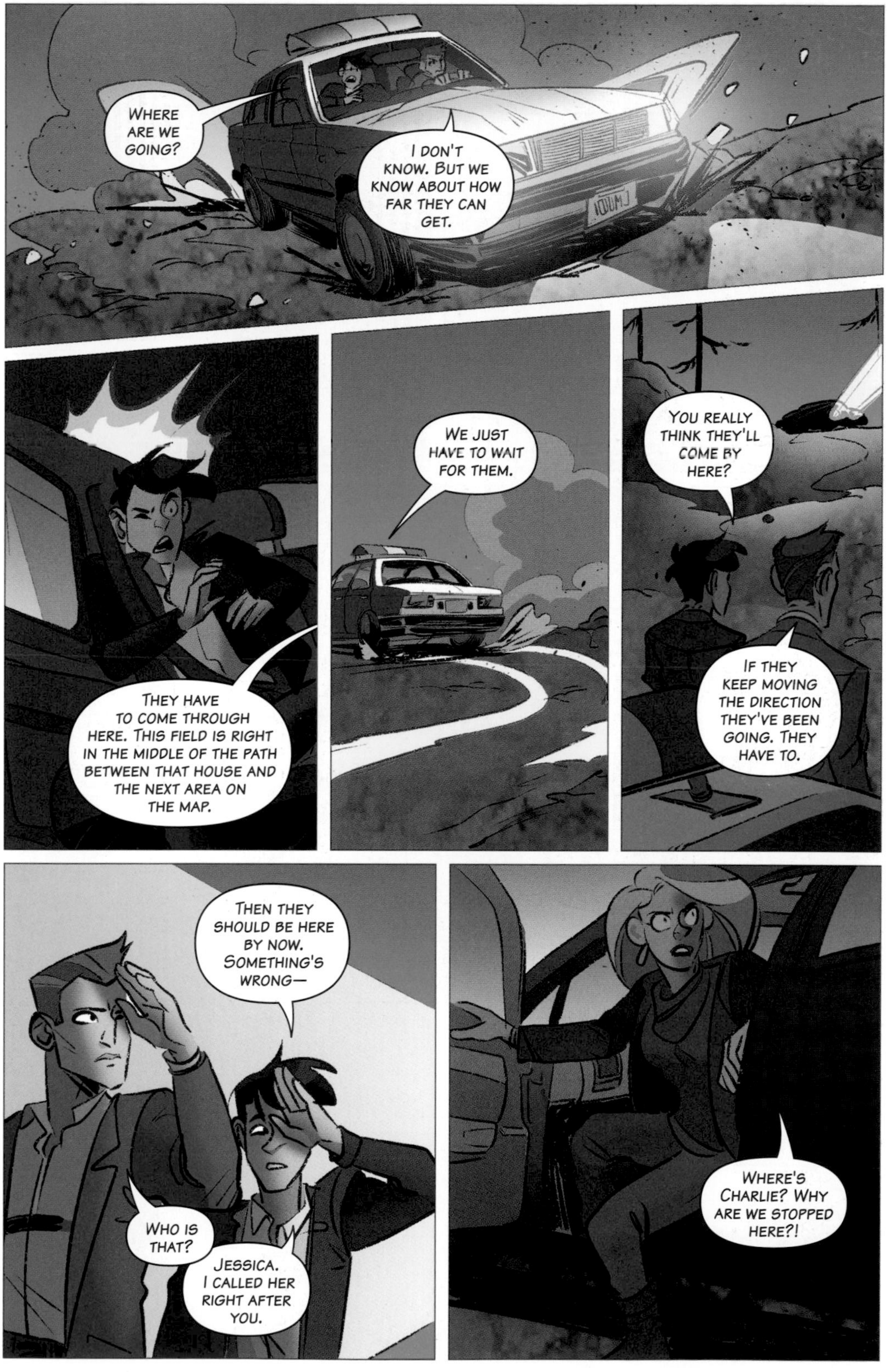

WHERE ARE WE GOING?
I DON'T KNOW. BUT WE KNOW ABOUT HOW FAR THEY CAN GET.
THEY HAVE TO COME THROUGH HERE. THIS FIELD IS RIGHT IN THE MIDDLE OF THE PATH BETWEEN THAT HOUSE AND THE NEXT AREA ON THE MAP.
WE JUST HAVE TO WAIT FOR THEM.
YOU REALLY THINK THEY'LL COME BY HERE?
IF THEY KEEP MOVING THE DIRECTION THEY'VE BEEN GOING. THEY HAVE TO.
THEN THEY SHOULD BE HERE BY NOW. SOMETHING'S WRONG—
WHO IS THAT?
JESSICA. I CALLED HER RIGHT AFTER YOU.
WHERE'S CHARLIE? WHY ARE WE STOPPED HERE?!

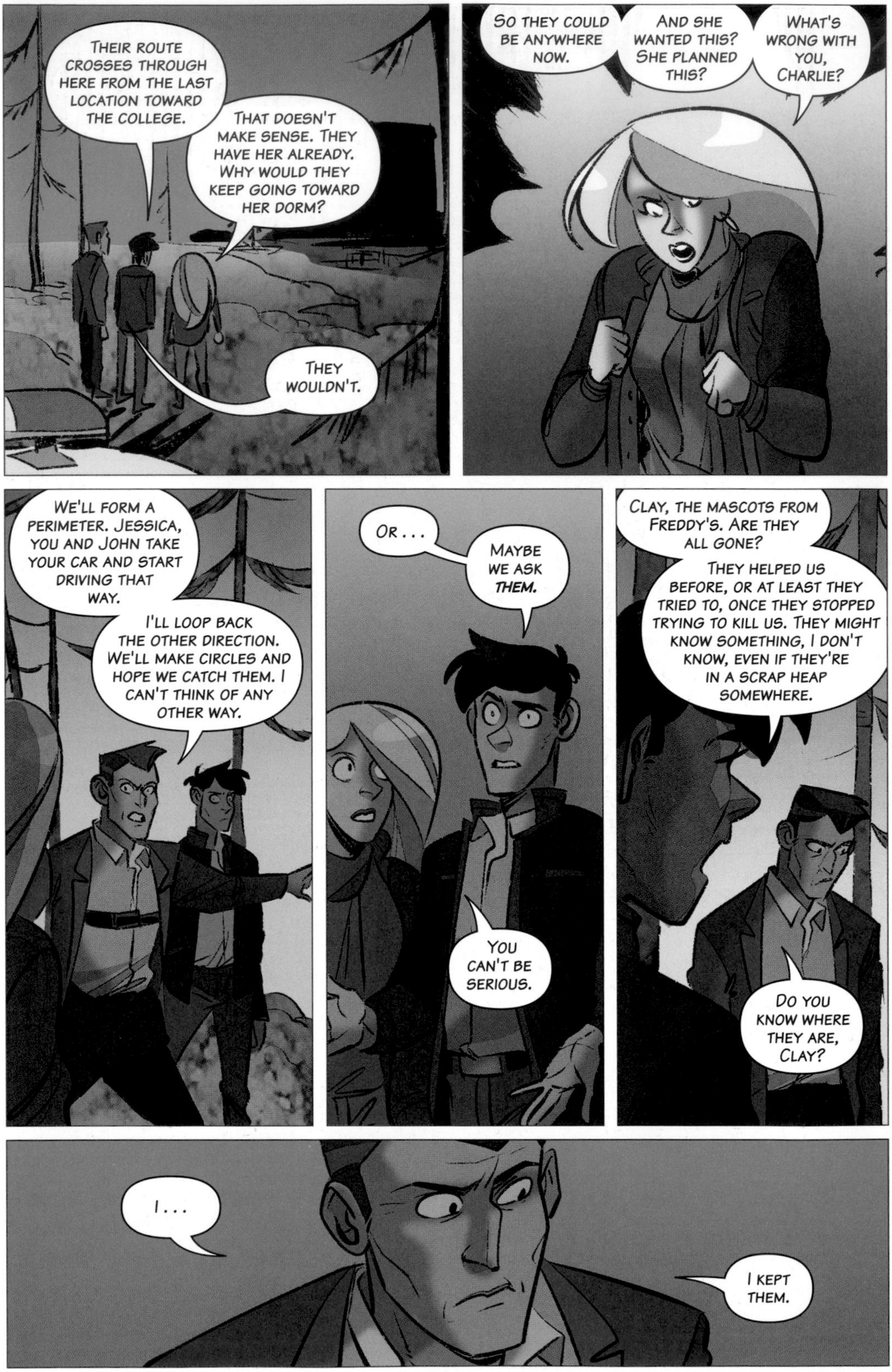
Their route crosses through here from the last location toward the college.
That doesn't make sense. They have her already. Why would they keep going toward her dorm?
They wouldn't.
So they could be anywhere now.
And she wanted this? She planned this?
What's wrong with you, Charlie?
We'll form a perimeter. Jessica, you and John take your car and start driving that way.
I'll loop back the other direction. We'll make circles and hope we catch them. I can't think of any other way.
Or . . .
Maybe we ask *them.*
You can't be serious.
Clay, the mascots from Freddy's. Are they all gone?
They helped us before, or at least they tried to, once they stopped trying to kill us. They might know something, I don't know, even if they're in a scrap heap somewhere.
Do you know where they are, Clay?
I . . .
I kept them.

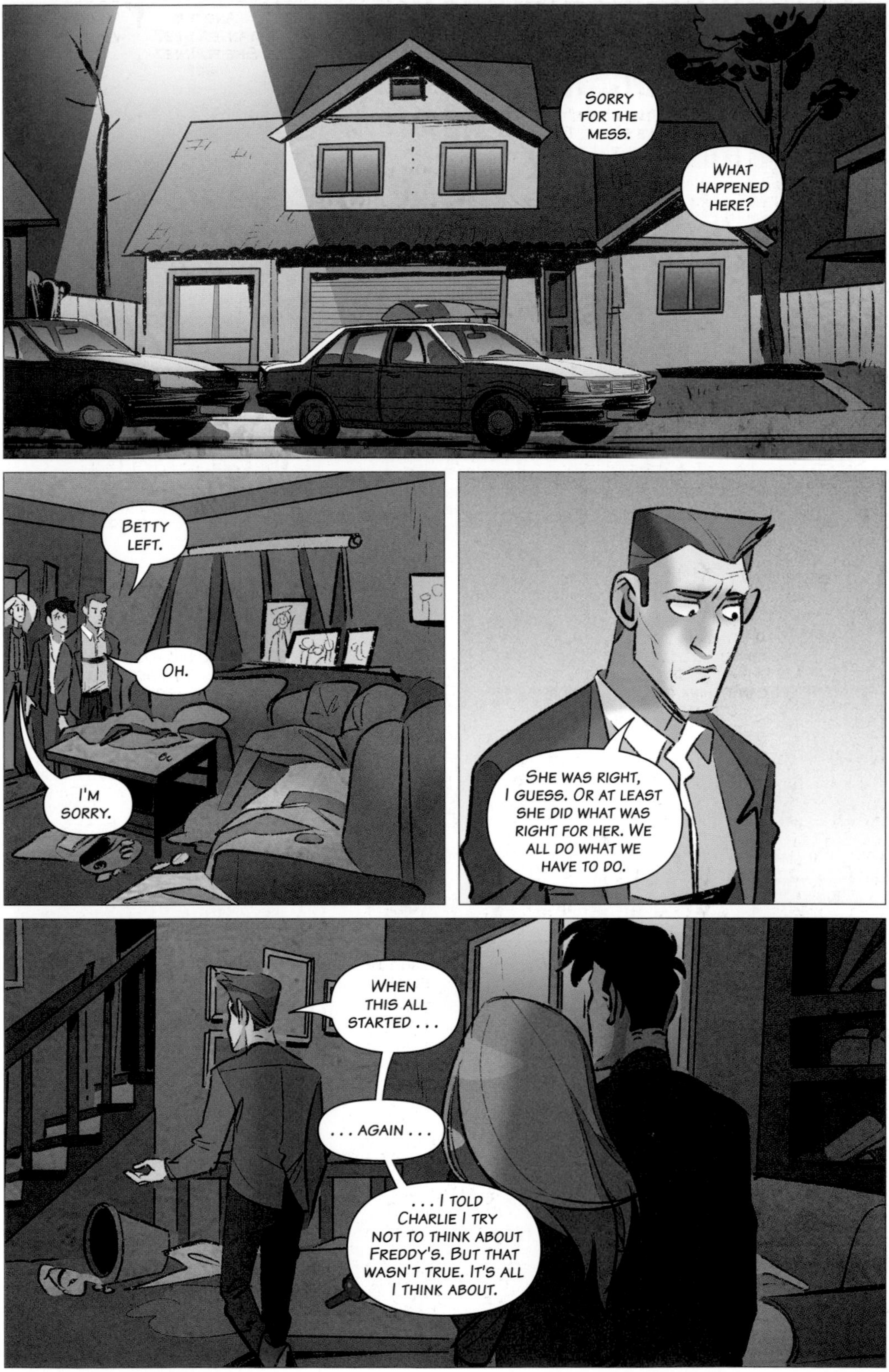
SORRY FOR THE MESS.
WHAT HAPPENED HERE?
BETTY LEFT.
OH.
I'M SORRY.
SHE WAS RIGHT, I GUESS. OR AT LEAST SHE DID WHAT WAS RIGHT FOR HER. WE ALL DO WHAT WE HAVE TO DO.
WHEN THIS ALL STARTED . . .
. . . AGAIN . . .
. . . I TOLD CHARLIE I TRY NOT TO THINK ABOUT FREDDY'S. BUT THAT WASN'T TRUE. IT'S ALL I THINK ABOUT.

"AFTER ALL OF YOU LEFT TOWN, I WENT BACK FOR THEM."

"WHEN I GOT INSIDE, THEY WERE ALL THERE, PILED TOGETHER IN THAT ROOM WITH A LITTLE STAGE, SITTING PATIENTLY, LIKE THEY WERE WAITING FOR ME."

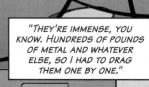

"THEY'RE IMMENSE, YOU KNOW. HUNDREDS OF POUNDS OF METAL AND WHATEVER ELSE, SO I HAD TO DRAG THEM ONE BY ONE."

"I LOADED THEM INTO THE TRUCK, CAME HERE, AND LOWERED THEM ONE BY ONE INTO THE CELLAR, ALL WITH NOBODY SEEING ME. IT WOULD HAVE NEVER WORKED IF IT WEREN'T FOR THE THUNDER AND LIGHTNING MASKING WHAT I WAS DOING."

"ALL I WANTED TO DO WAS FALL INTO BED, BUT I COULDN'T. I FELL ASLEEP IN FRONT OF THE BASEMENT DOOR, AND IN THE MORNING, THEY WERE EXACTLY AS I LEFT THEM."

"EVERY NIGHT AFTER THAT, I'D GO DOWN AND CHECK ON THEM WHILE BETTY WAS ASLEEP. THEY NEVER MOVED, THOUGH. THEY JUST SAT LIKE BROKEN DOLLS."

126

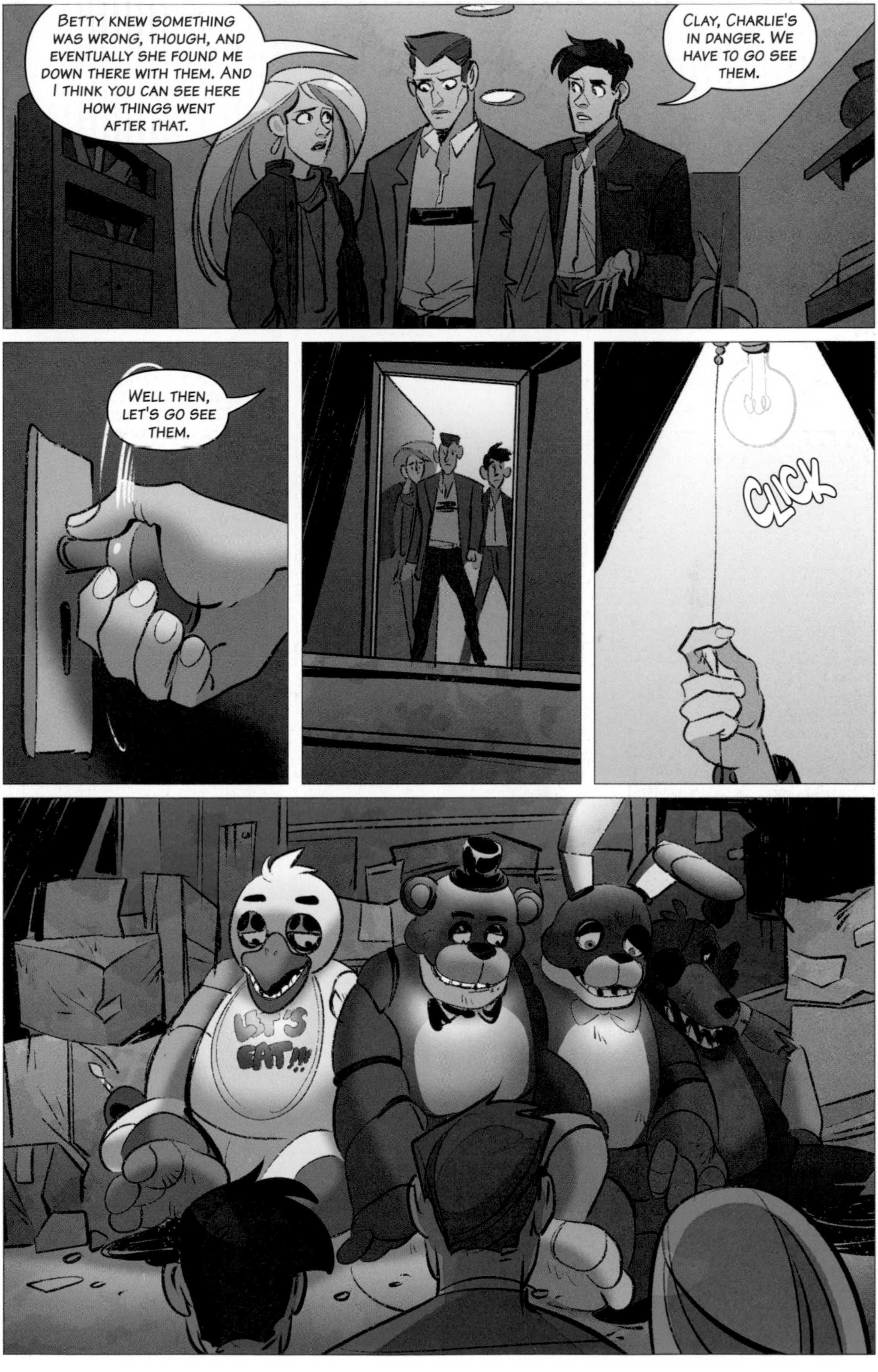
BETTY KNEW SOMETHING WAS WRONG, THOUGH, AND EVENTUALLY SHE FOUND ME DOWN THERE WITH THEM. AND I THINK YOU CAN SEE HERE HOW THINGS WENT AFTER THAT.
CLAY, CHARLIE'S IN DANGER. WE HAVE TO GO SEE THEM.
WELL THEN, LET'S GO SEE THEM.
CLICK
LET'S EAT!!

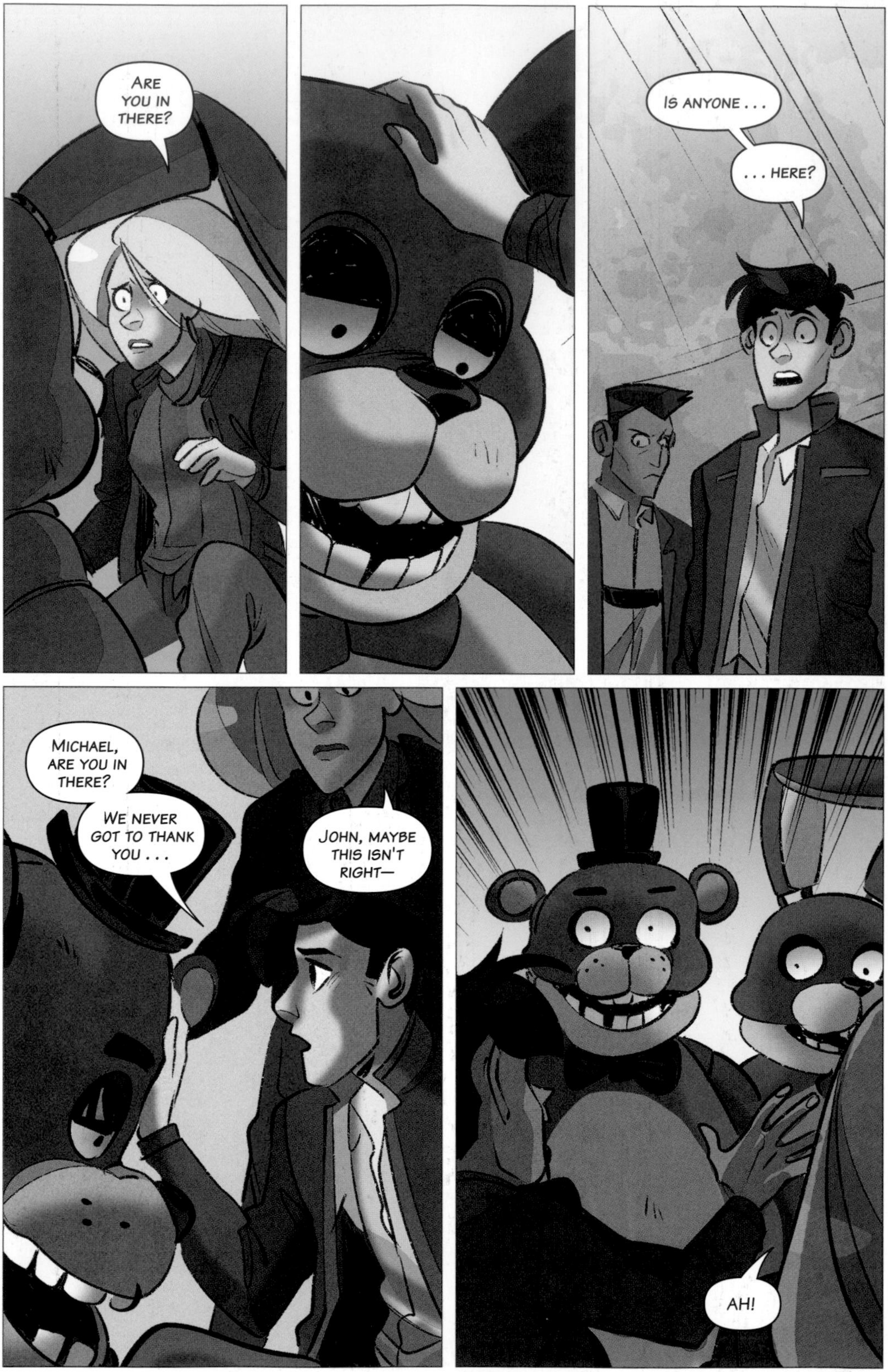

ARE YOU IN THERE?
IS ANYONE . . .
. . . HERE?
MICHAEL, ARE YOU IN THERE?
WE NEVER GOT TO THANK YOU . . .
JOHN, MAYBE THIS ISN'T RIGHT—
AH!

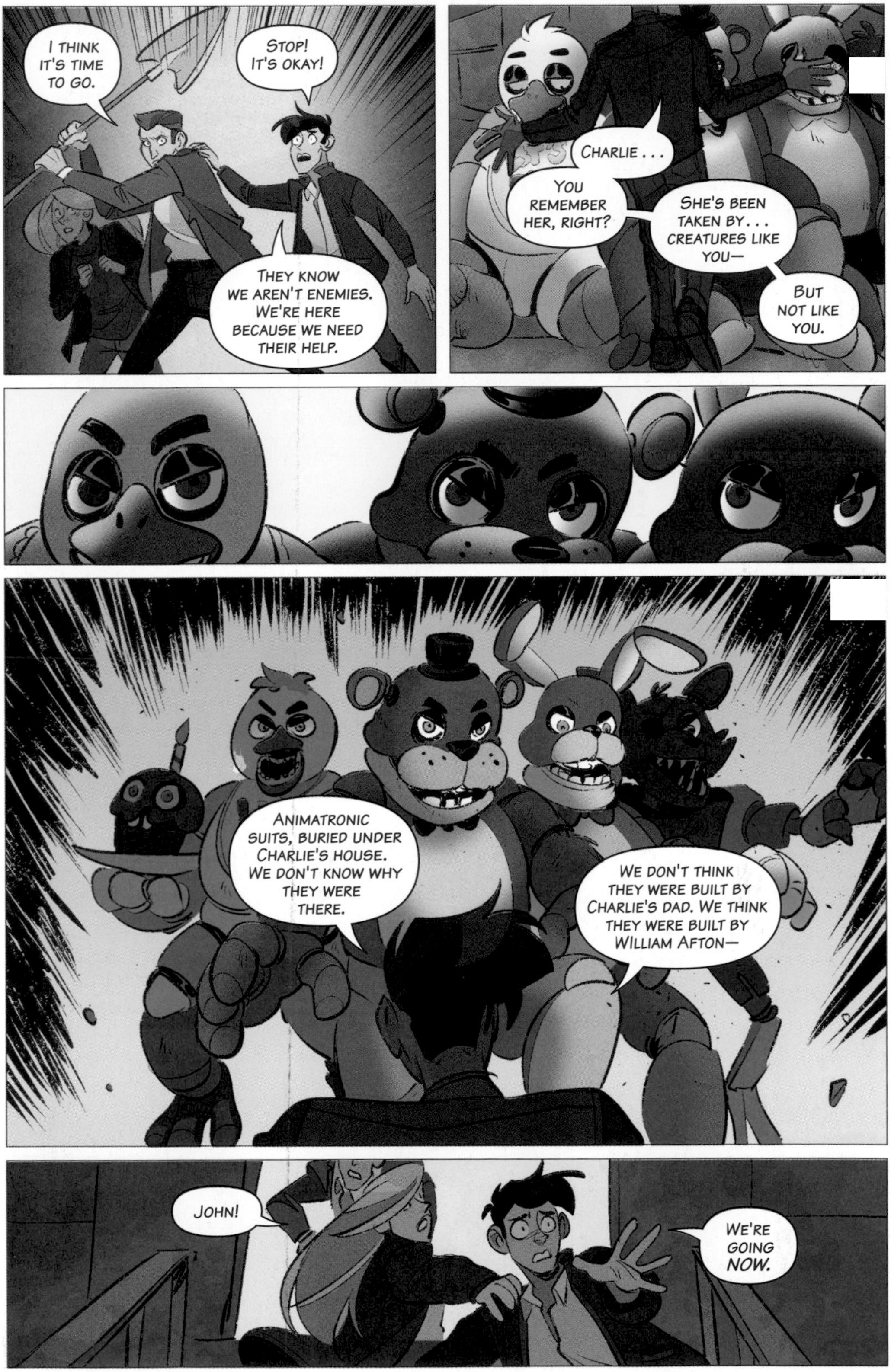
I THINK IT'S TIME TO GO.
STOP! IT'S OKAY!
THEY KNOW WE AREN'T ENEMIES. WE'RE HERE BECAUSE WE NEED THEIR HELP.
CHARLIE . . .
YOU REMEMBER HER, RIGHT?
SHE'S BEEN TAKEN BY . . . CREATURES LIKE YOU—
BUT NOT LIKE YOU.
ANIMATRONIC SUITS, BURIED UNDER CHARLIE'S HOUSE. WE DON'T KNOW WHY THEY WERE THERE.
WE DON'T THINK THEY WERE BUILT BY CHARLIE'S DAD. WE THINK THEY WERE BUILT BY WILLIAM AFTON—
JOHN!
WE'RE GOING NOW.

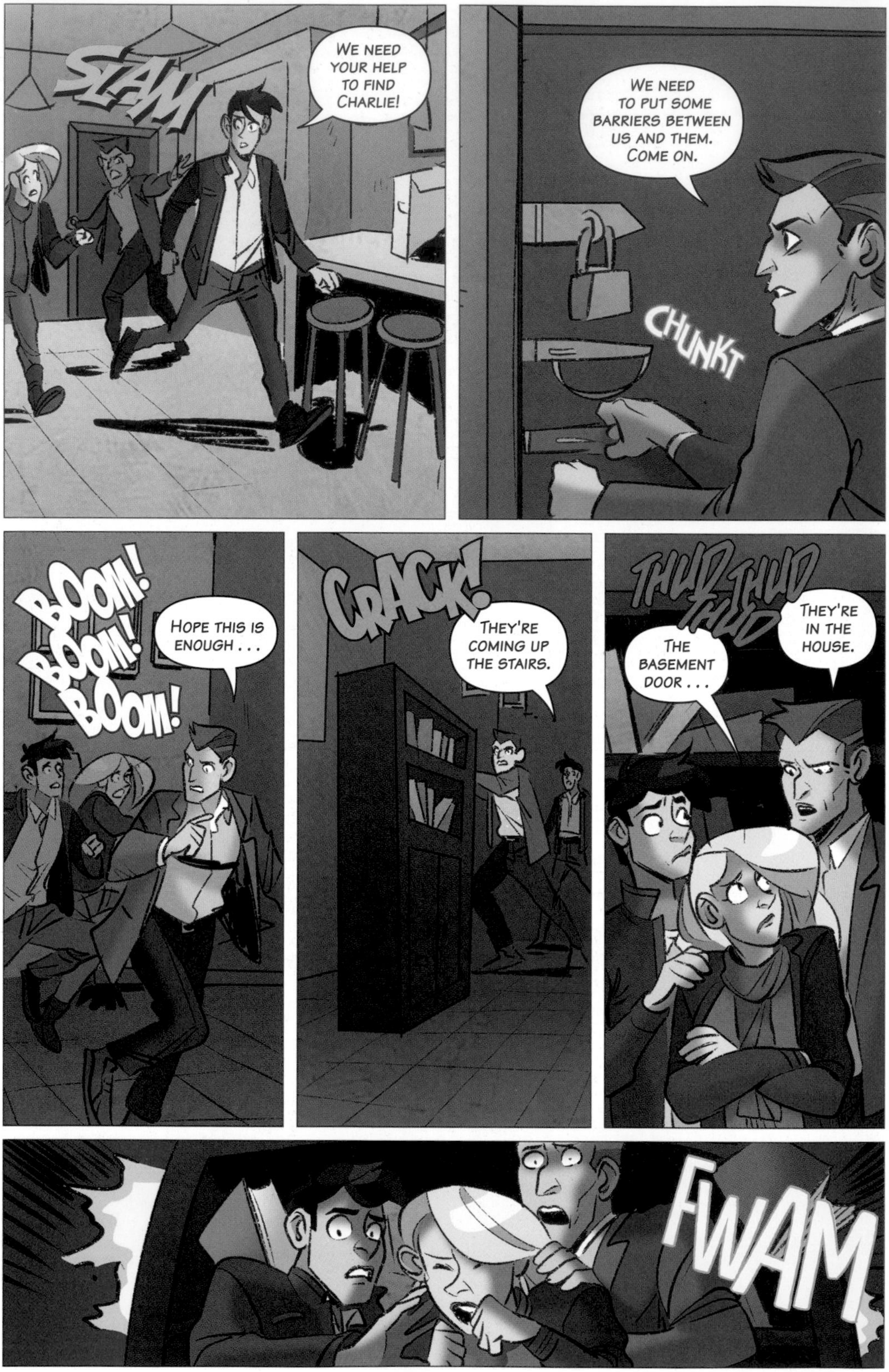
SLAM
WE NEED YOUR HELP TO FIND CHARLIE!
WE NEED TO PUT SOME BARRIERS BETWEEN US AND THEM. COME ON.
CHUNKT
BOOM! BOOM! BOOM!
HOPE THIS IS ENOUGH . . .
CRACK!
THEY'RE COMING UP THE STAIRS.
THUD THUD THUD
THE BASEMENT DOOR . . .
THEY'RE IN THE HOUSE.
FWAM

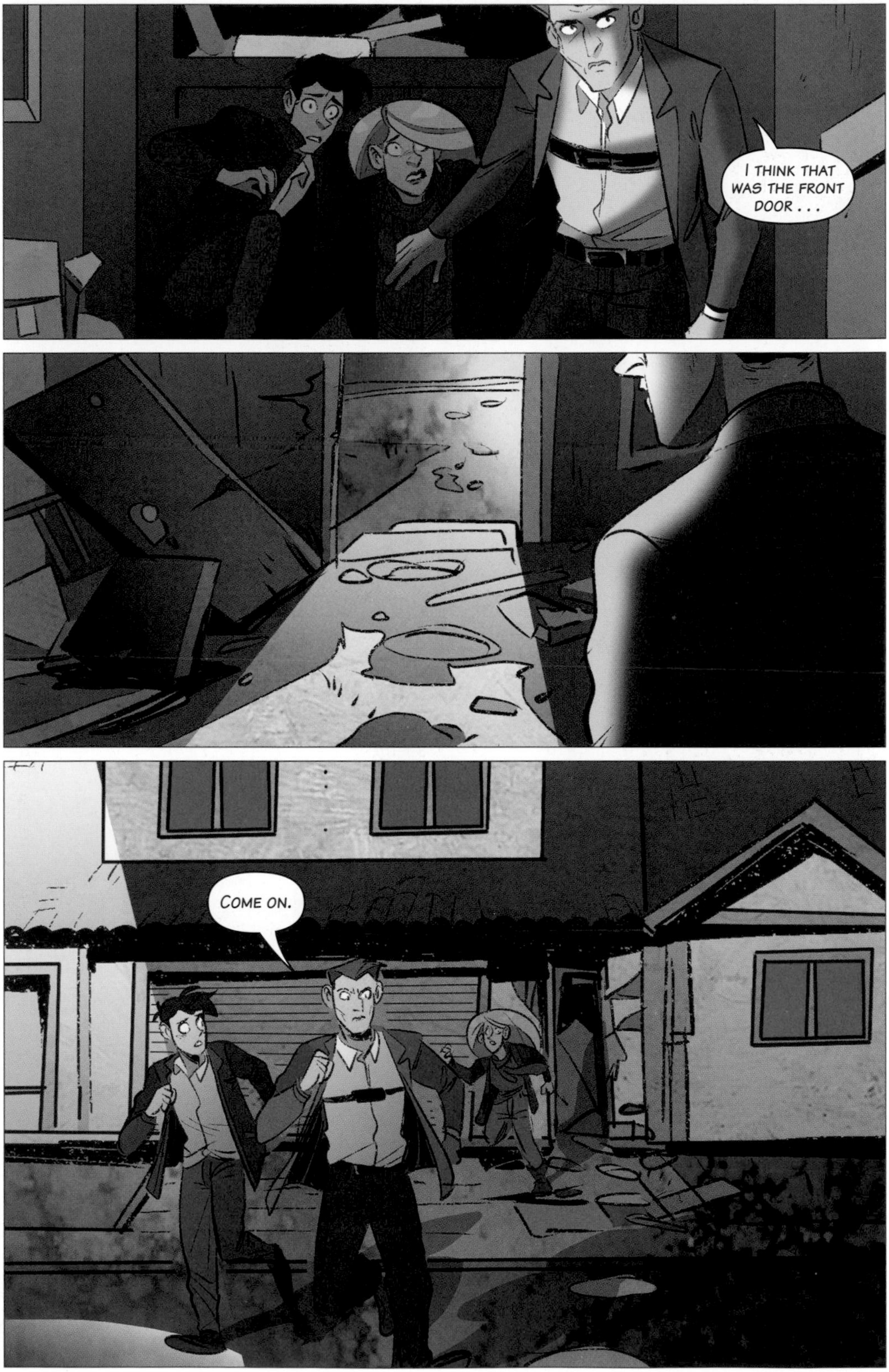
I THINK THAT WAS THE FRONT DOOR . . .
COME ON.

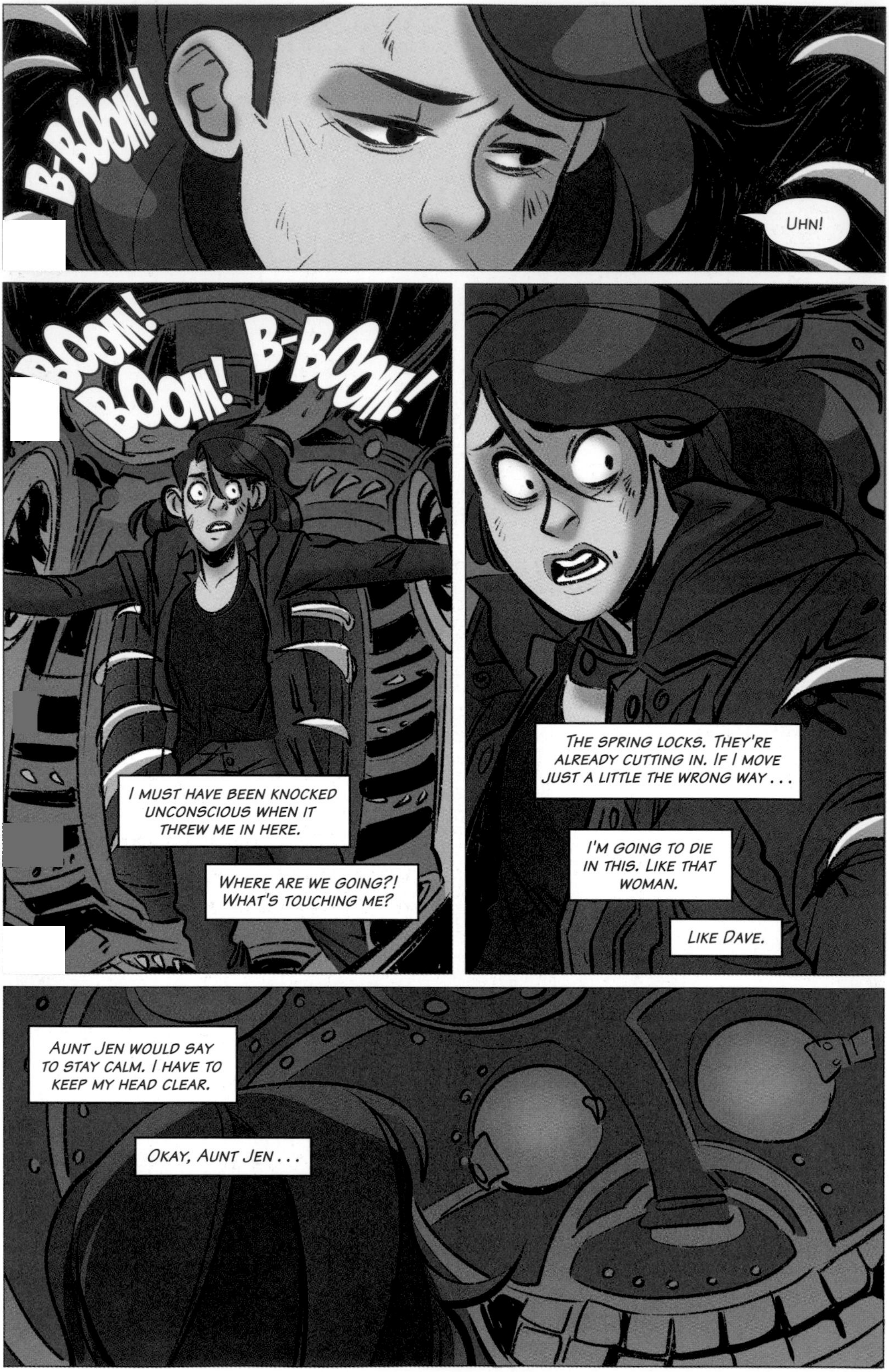
B-BOOM!
UHN!
BOOM!
BOOM!
B-BOOM!
I MUST HAVE BEEN KNOCKED UNCONSCIOUS WHEN IT THREW ME IN HERE.
WHERE ARE WE GOING?! WHAT'S TOUCHING ME?
THE SPRING LOCKS. THEY'RE ALREADY CUTTING IN. IF I MOVE JUST A LITTLE THE WRONG WAY . . .
I'M GOING TO DIE IN THIS. LIKE THAT WOMAN.
LIKE DAVE.
AUNT JEN WOULD SAY TO STAY CALM. I HAVE TO KEEP MY HEAD CLEAR.
OKAY, AUNT JEN . . .

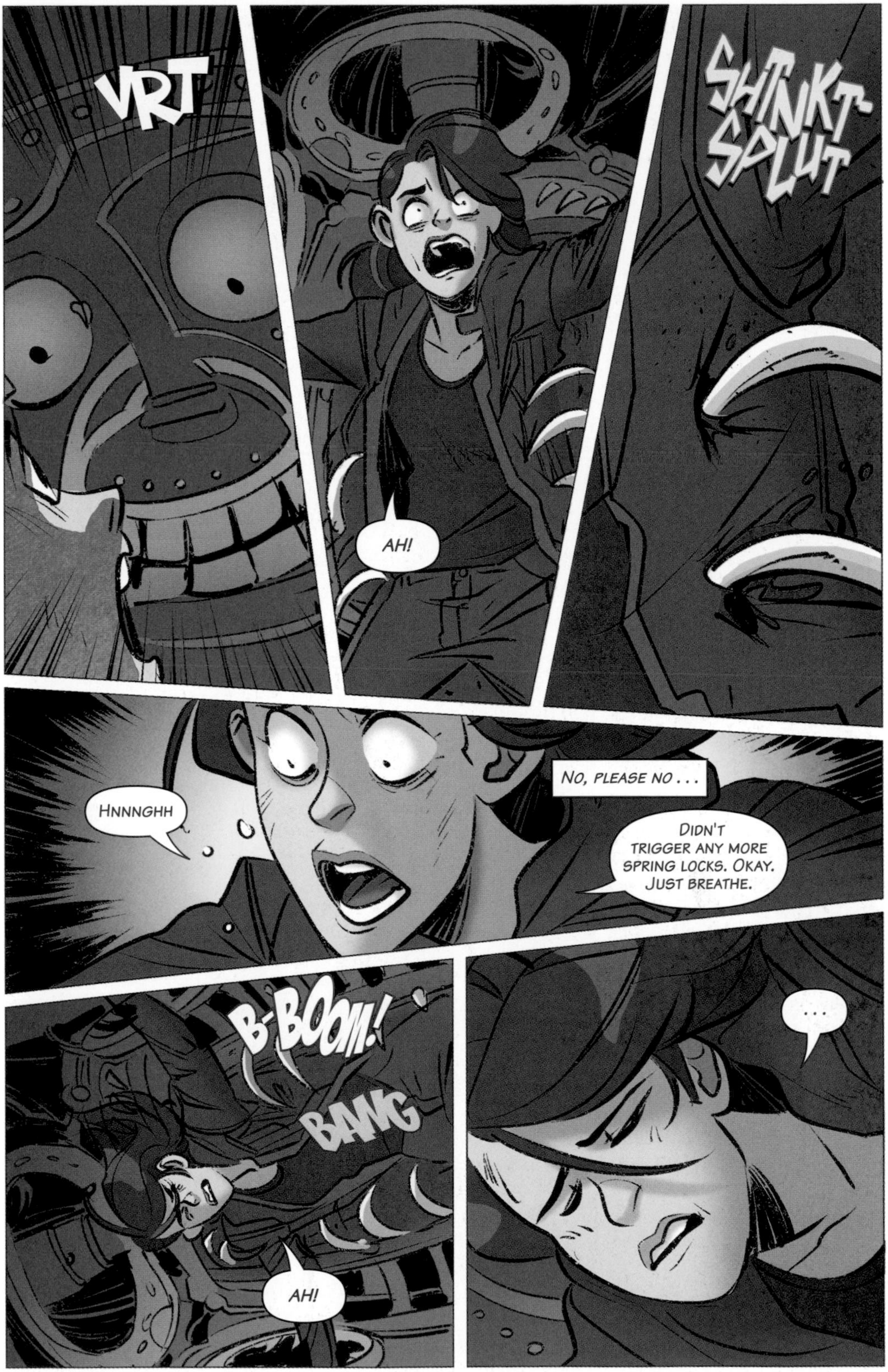
VRT
AH!
SHINKT-SPLUT
Hnnnghh
No, please no . . .
Didn't trigger any more spring locks. Okay. Just breathe.
B-BOOM!
BANG
AH!
. . .

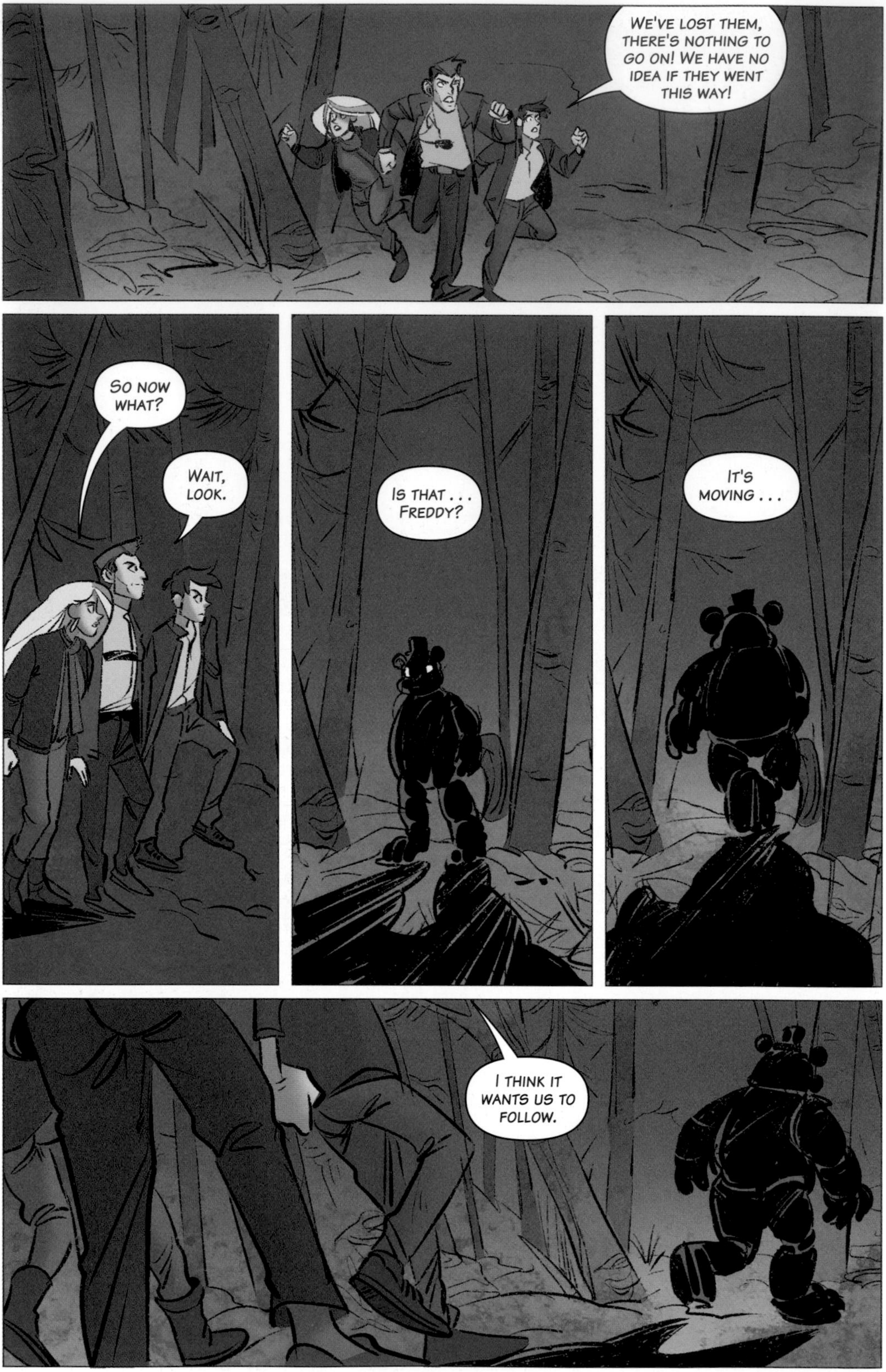
WE'VE LOST THEM, THERE'S NOTHING TO GO ON! WE HAVE NO IDEA IF THEY WENT THIS WAY!
SO NOW WHAT?
WAIT, LOOK.
IS THAT . . . FREDDY?
IT'S MOVING . . .
I THINK IT WANTS US TO FOLLOW.

I CAN'T BREATHE.

HACK HACK

COUGH

GASP

YOU'RE HYPERVENTILATING. YOU HAVE TO STOP. YOU HAVE TO CALM DOWN.

YOU HAVE TO GET YOUR ARMS FREE.

THERE'S SOMETHING AT THE SHOULDER JOINTS ON EITHER SIDE, AND A SPACE JUST BELOW. SPIKES IN A LINE ALL THE WAY DOWN TO MY ELBOW ON THE OUTSIDE AND . . .

. . . THOSE ARE THE SPRING LOCKS. OKAY, I'LL GET TO IT.

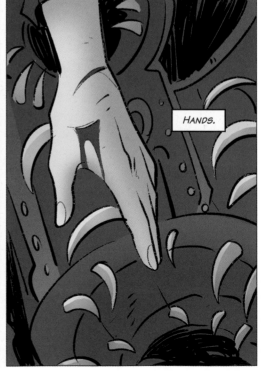

HANDS.

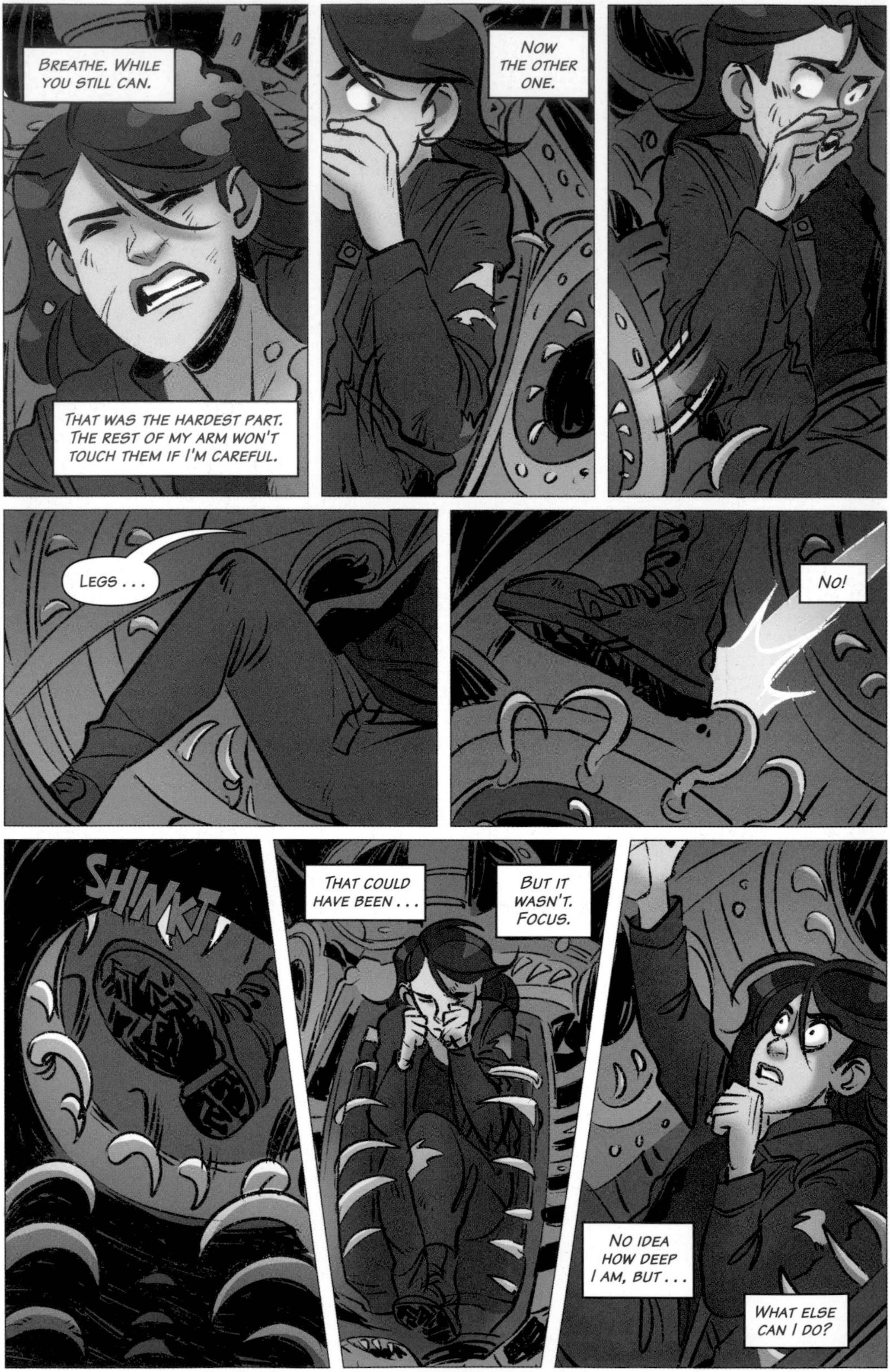
Breathe. While you still can.
That was the hardest part. The rest of my arm won't touch them if I'm careful.
Now the other one.
Legs . . .
No!
SHINKT
That could have been . . .
But it wasn't. Focus.
No idea how deep I am, but . . .
What else can I do?

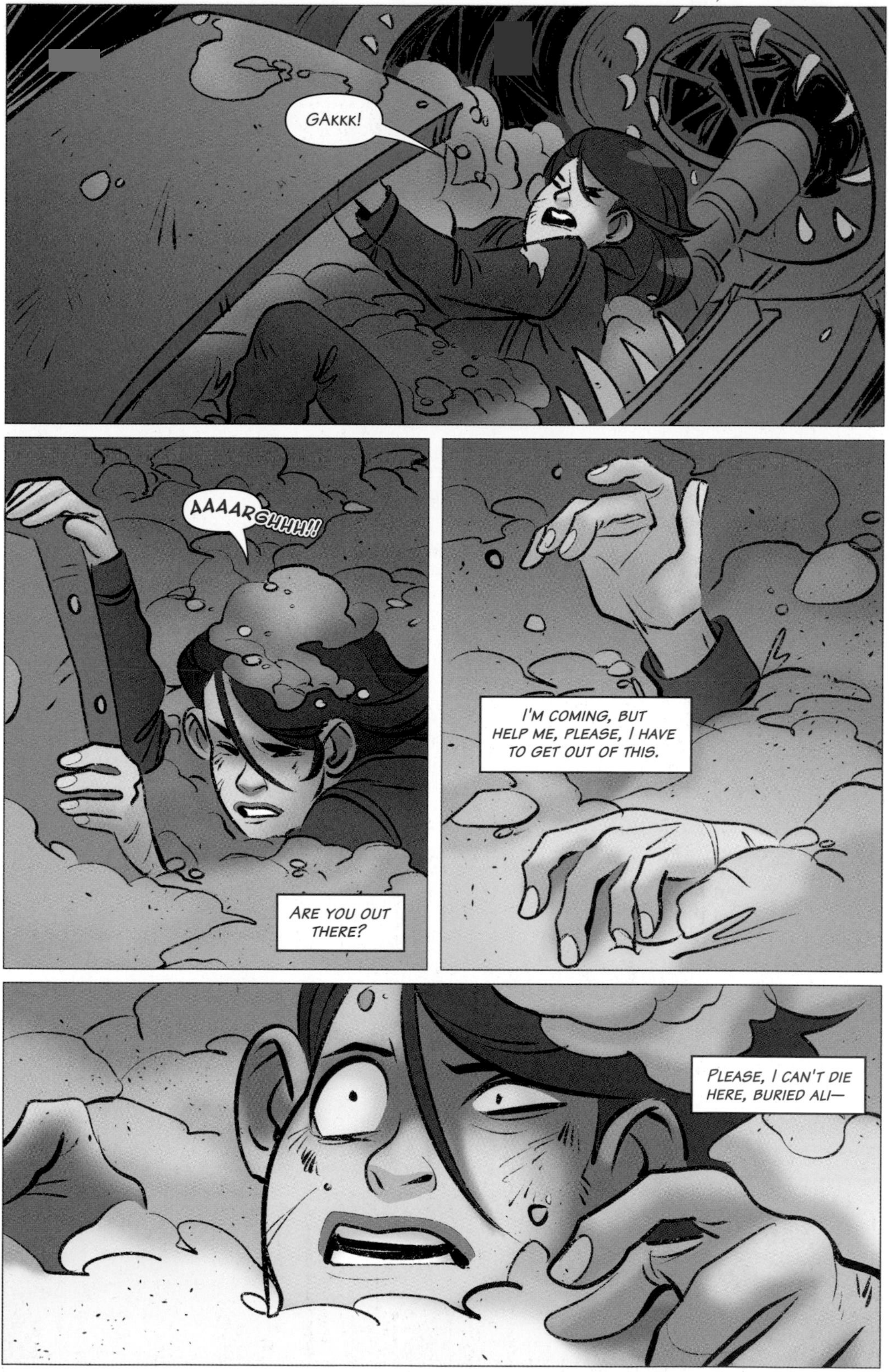
GAKKK!
AAAARGHHH!!
ARE YOU OUT THERE?
I'M COMING, BUT HELP ME, PLEASE, I HAVE TO GET OUT OF THIS.
PLEASE, I CAN'T DIE HERE, BURIED ALI—

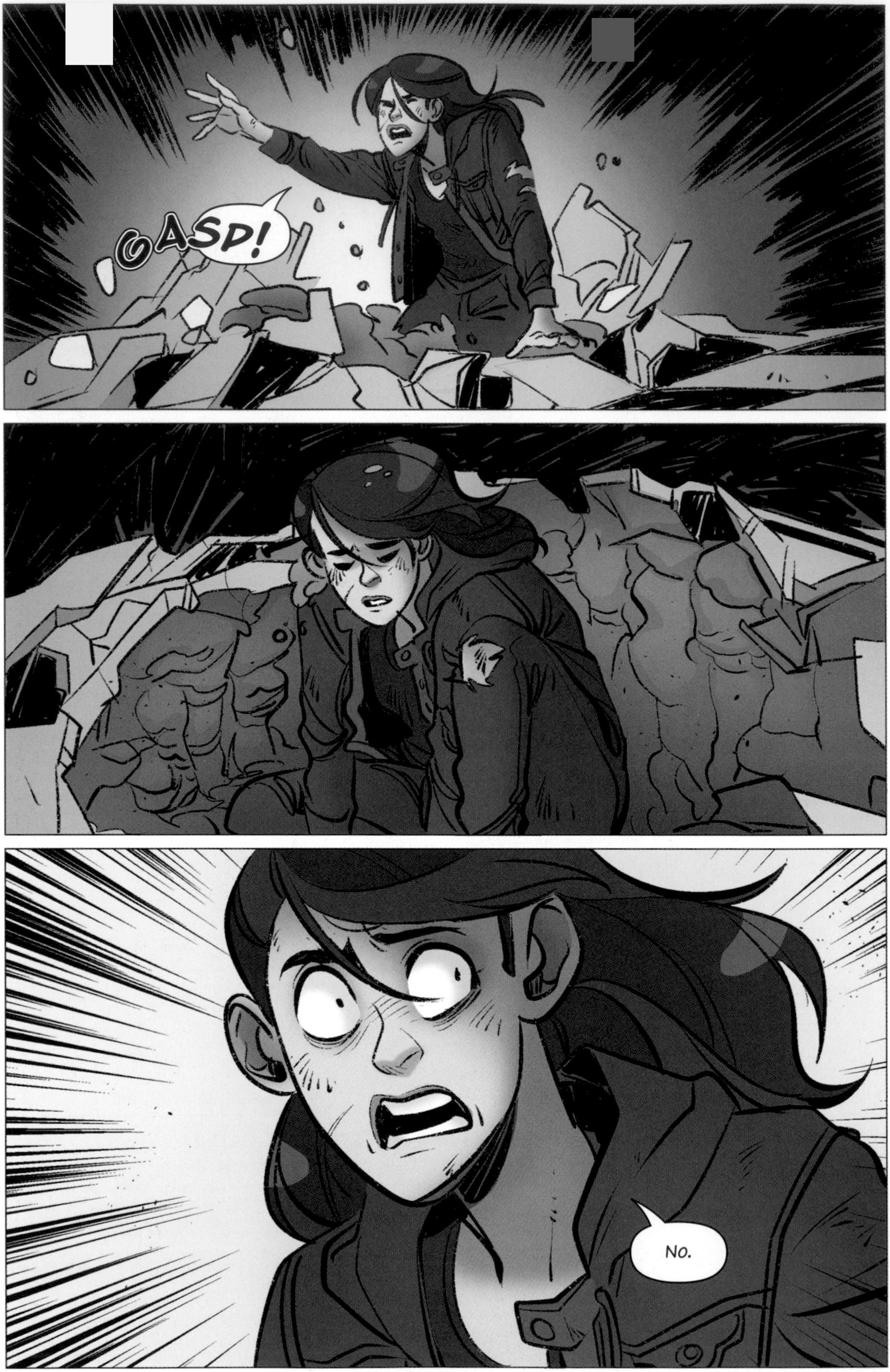
GASP!
No.

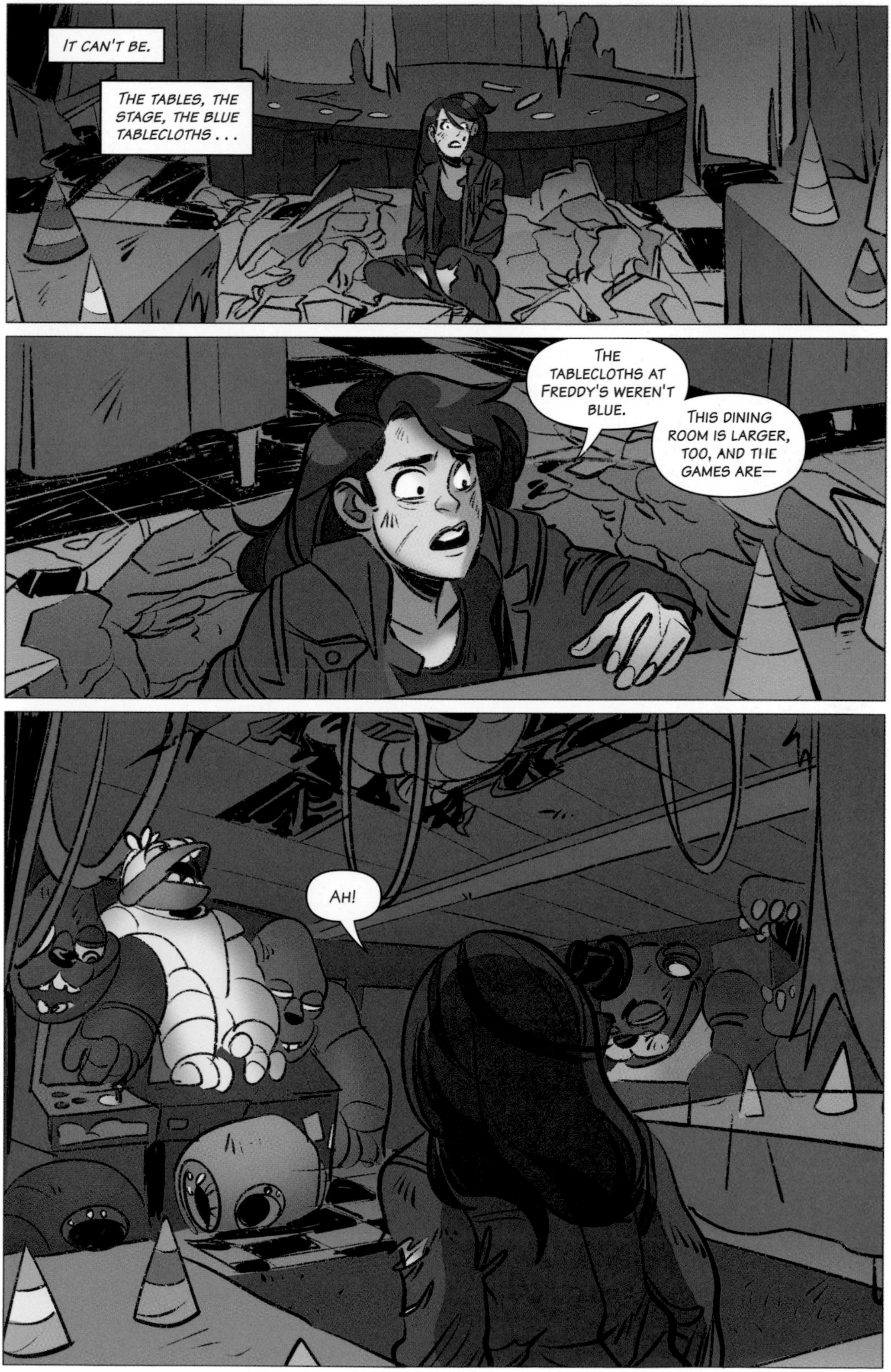
IT CAN'T BE.
THE TABLES, THE STAGE, THE BLUE TABLECLOTHS . . .
THE TABLECLOTHS AT FREDDY'S WEREN'T BLUE.
THIS DINING ROOM IS LARGER, TOO, AND THE GAMES ARE—
AH!

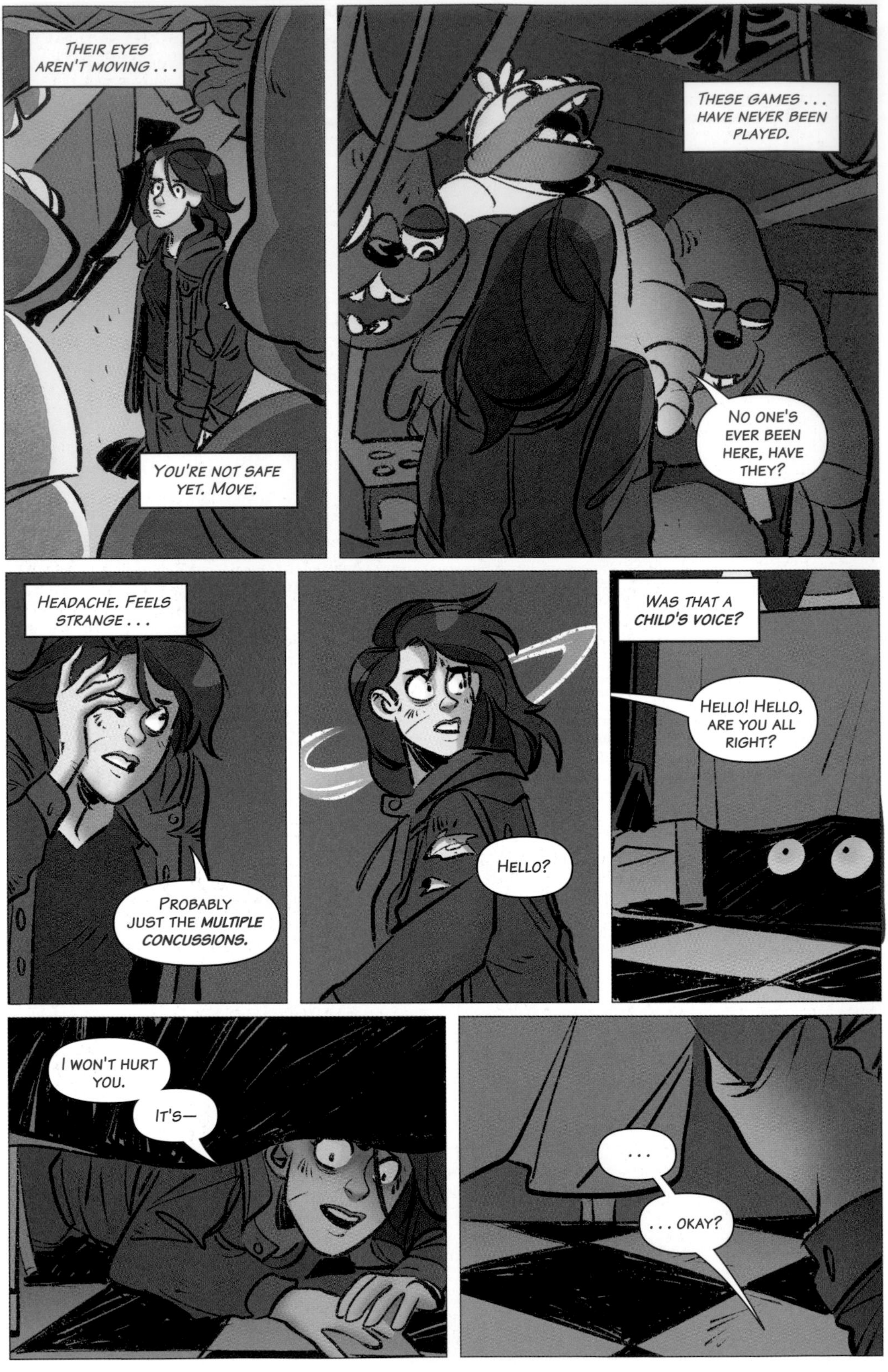
THEIR EYES AREN'T MOVING . . .
YOU'RE NOT SAFE YET. MOVE.
THESE GAMES . . . HAVE NEVER BEEN PLAYED.
NO ONE'S EVER BEEN HERE, HAVE THEY?
HEADACHE. FEELS STRANGE . . .
PROBABLY JUST THE MULTIPLE CONCUSSIONS.
HELLO?
WAS THAT A CHILD'S VOICE?
HELLO! HELLO, ARE YOU ALL RIGHT?
I WON'T HURT YOU.
IT'S—
. . .
. . . OKAY?

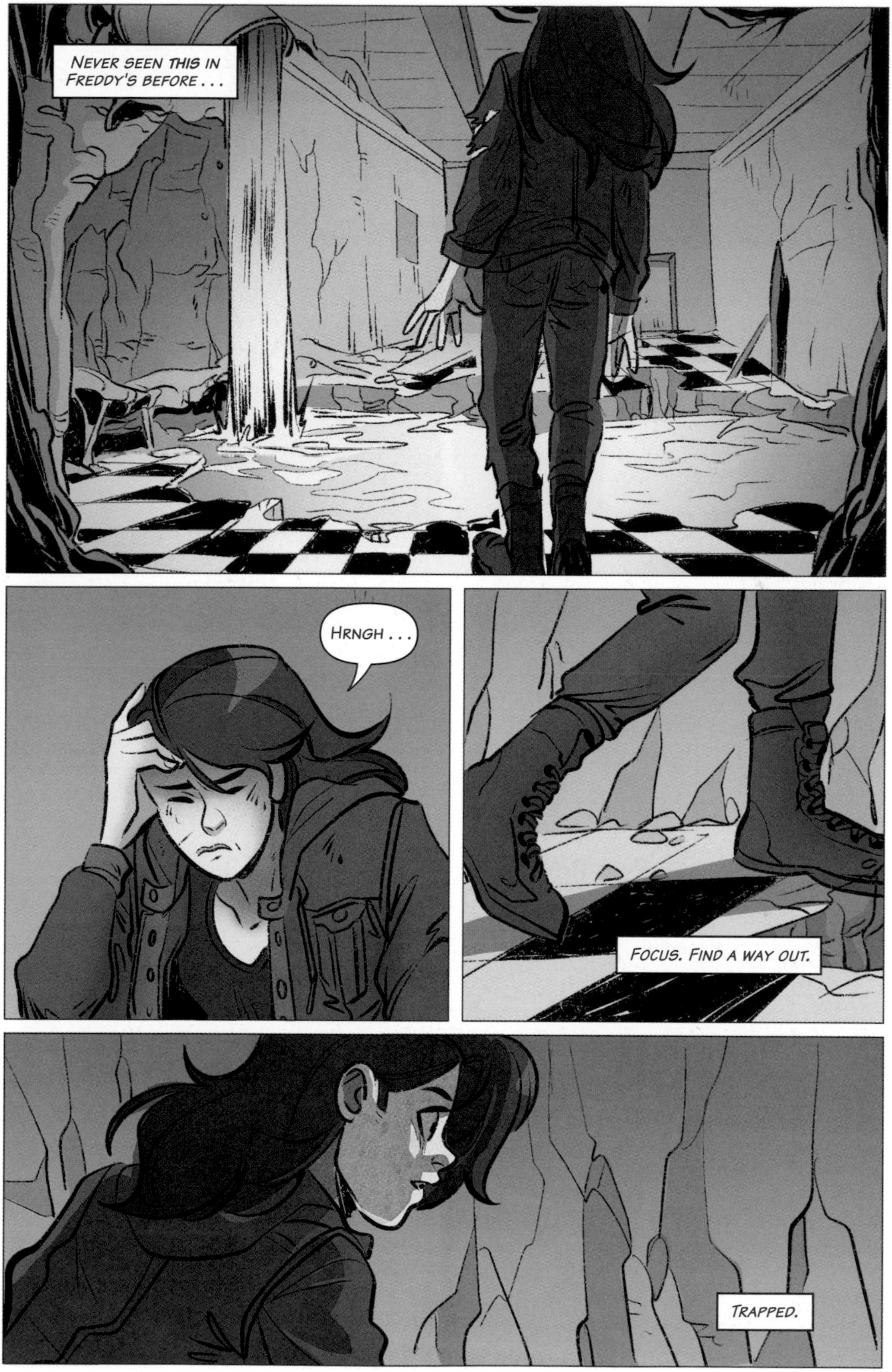
Never seen this in Freddy's before . . .
Hrngh . . .
Focus. Find a way out.
Trapped.

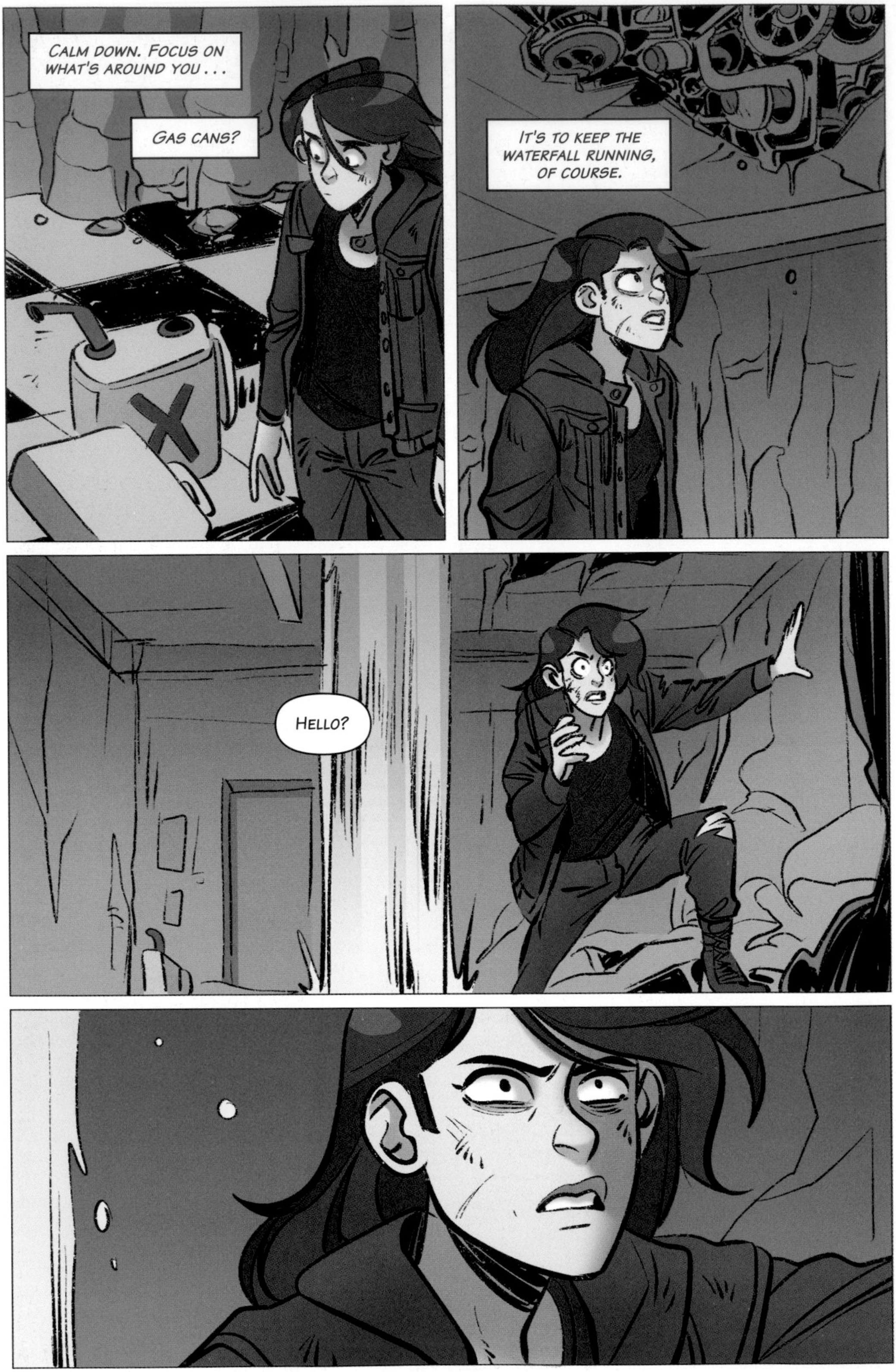
CALM DOWN. FOCUS ON WHAT'S AROUND YOU . . .
GAS CANS?
IT'S TO KEEP THE WATERFALL RUNNING, OF COURSE.
HELLO?

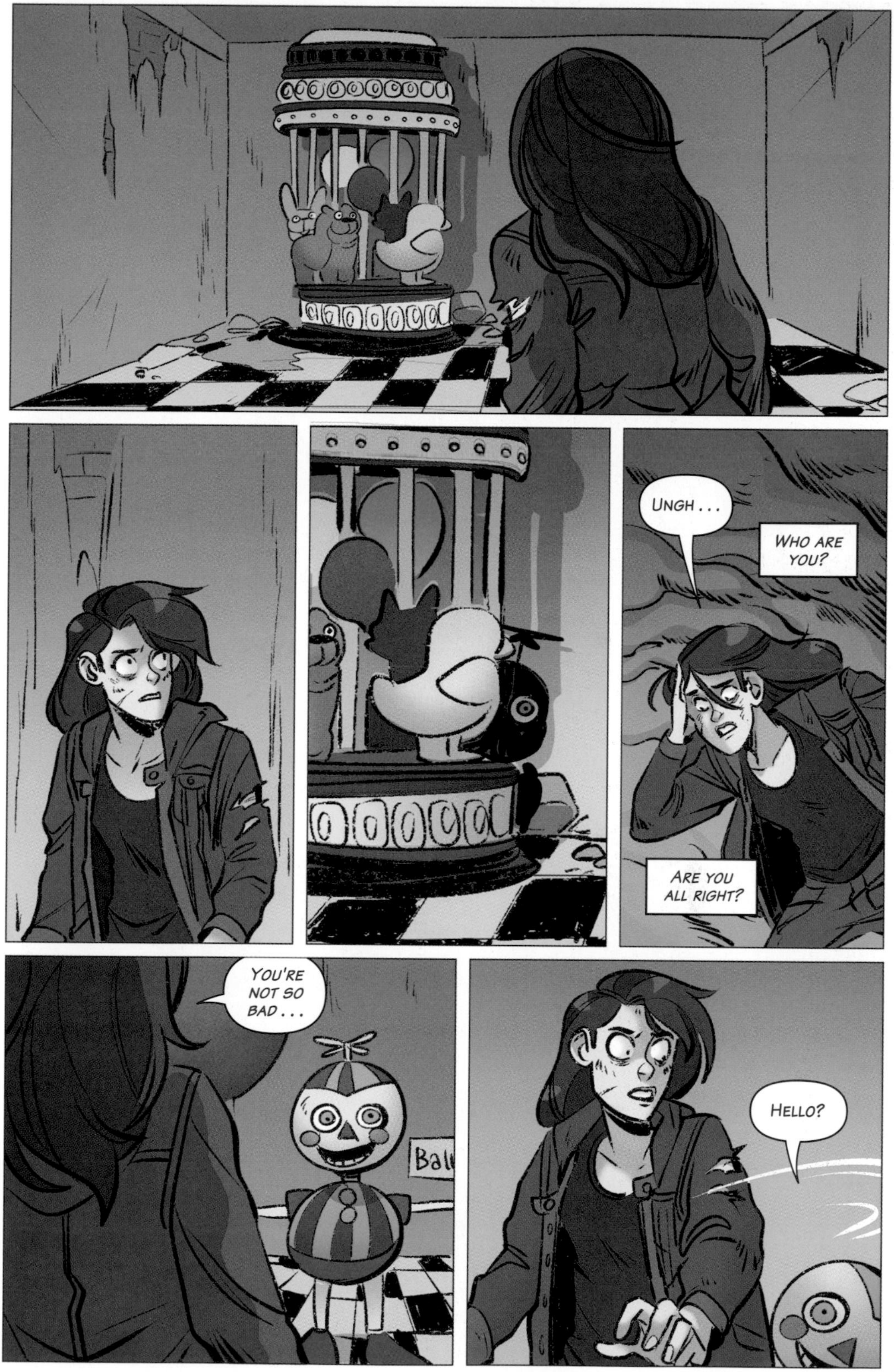
UNGH . . .
WHO ARE YOU?
ARE YOU ALL RIGHT?
YOU'RE NOT SO BAD . . .
Bal
HELLO?

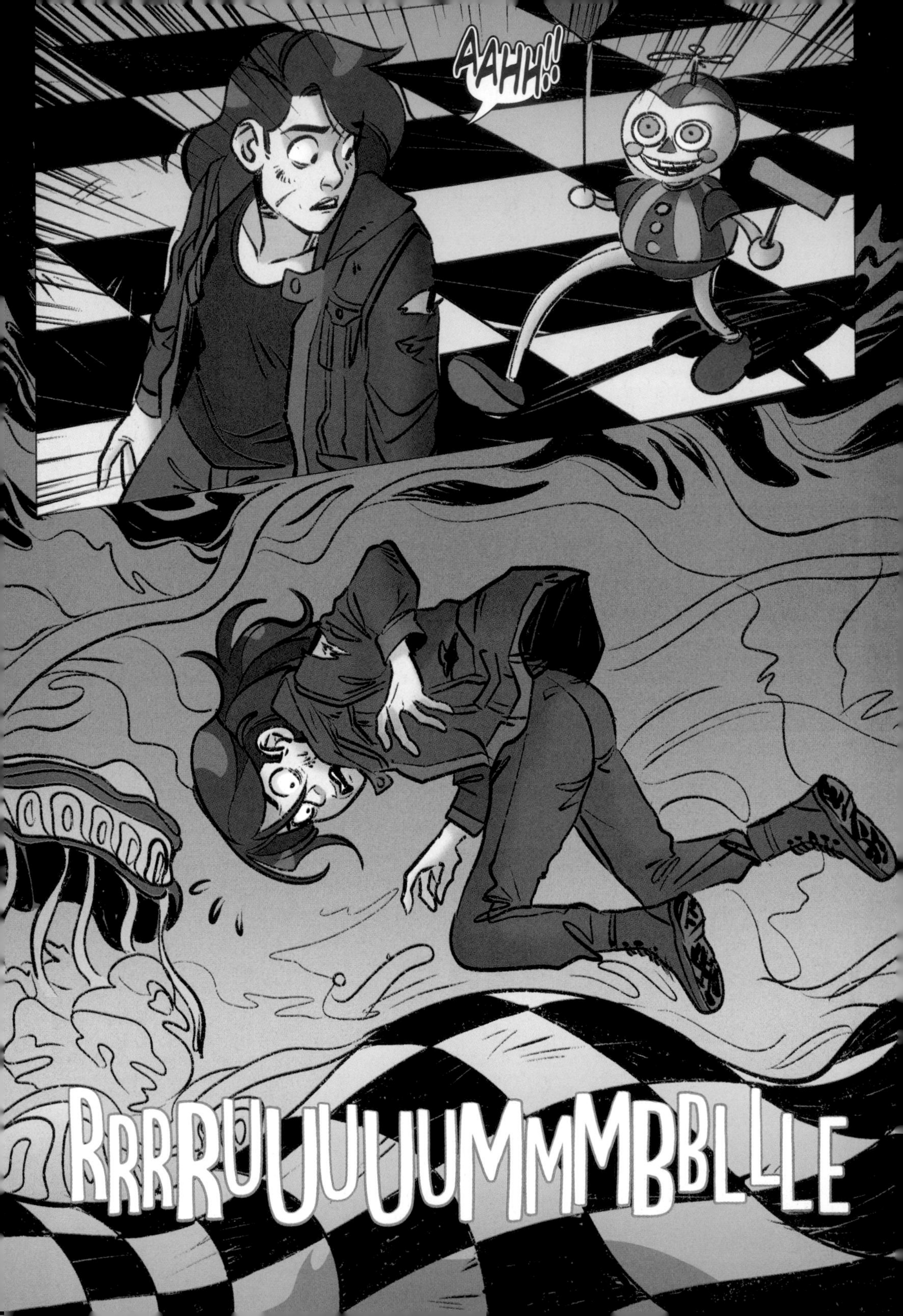
AAHH!!
RRRRUUUUUUMMMMBBLLLE

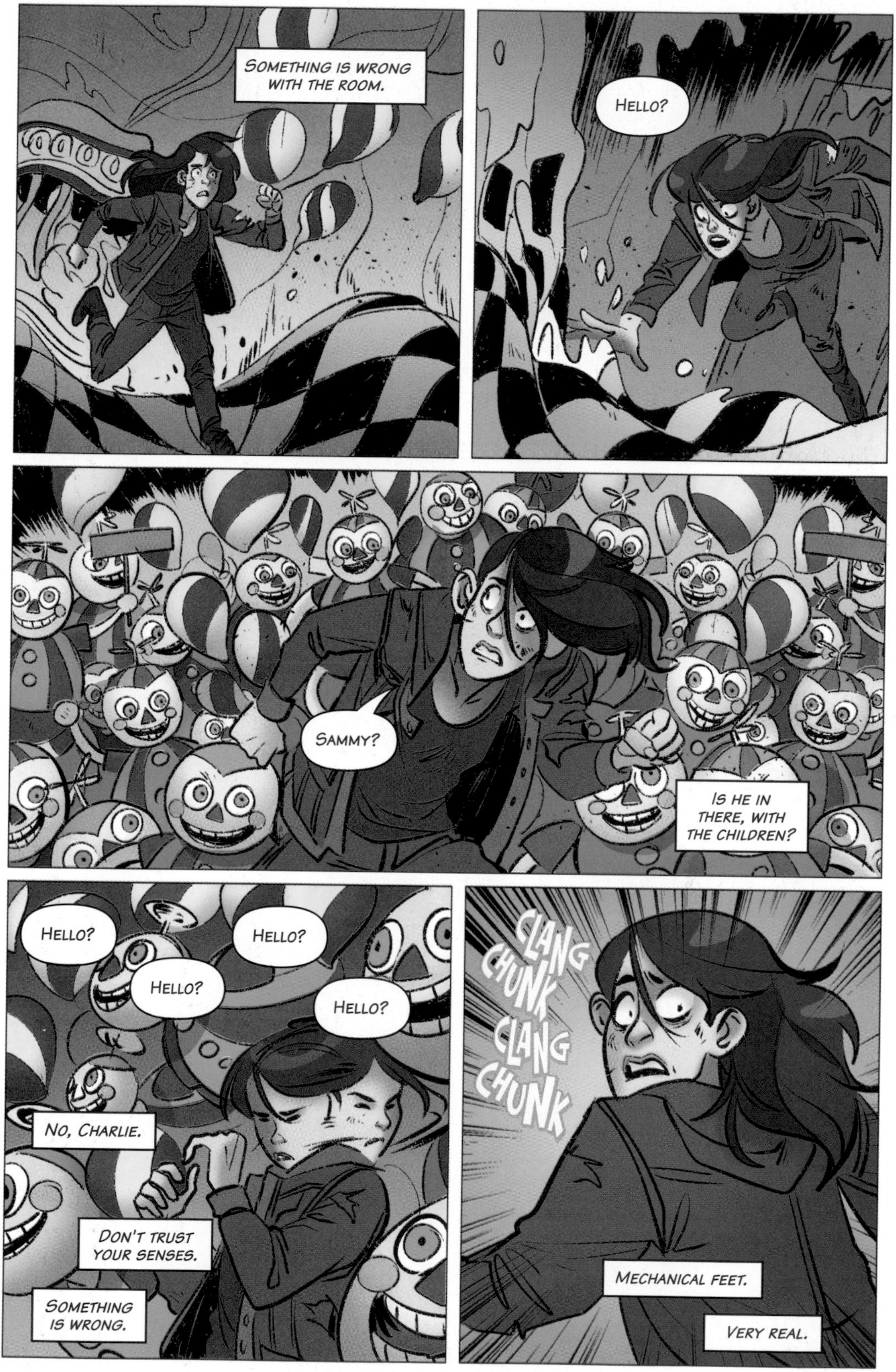
Something is wrong with the room.
Hello?
Sammy?
Is he in there, with the children?
Hello?
Hello?
Hello?
Hello?
No, Charlie.
Don't trust your senses.
Something is wrong.
CLANG
CHUNK
CLANG
CHUNK
Mechanical feet.
Very real.

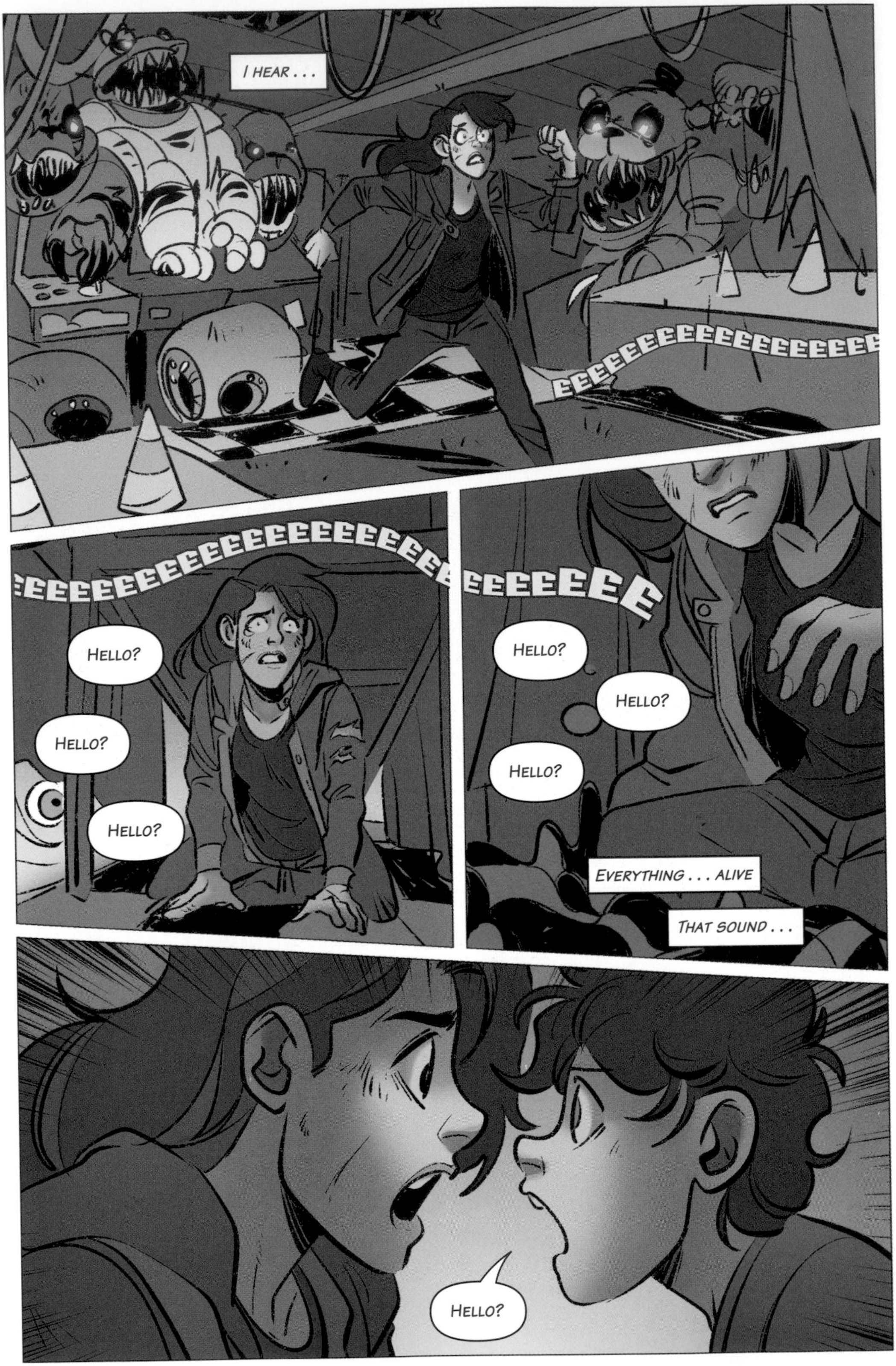
I HEAR . . .
EEEEEEEEEEEEEEEEEEEEE
EEEEEEEEEEEEEEEEEEEEEEEEEEEE
HELLO?
HELLO?
HELLO?
EEEEEEE
HELLO?
HELLO?
HELLO?
EVERYTHING . . . ALIVE
THAT SOUND . . .
HELLO?

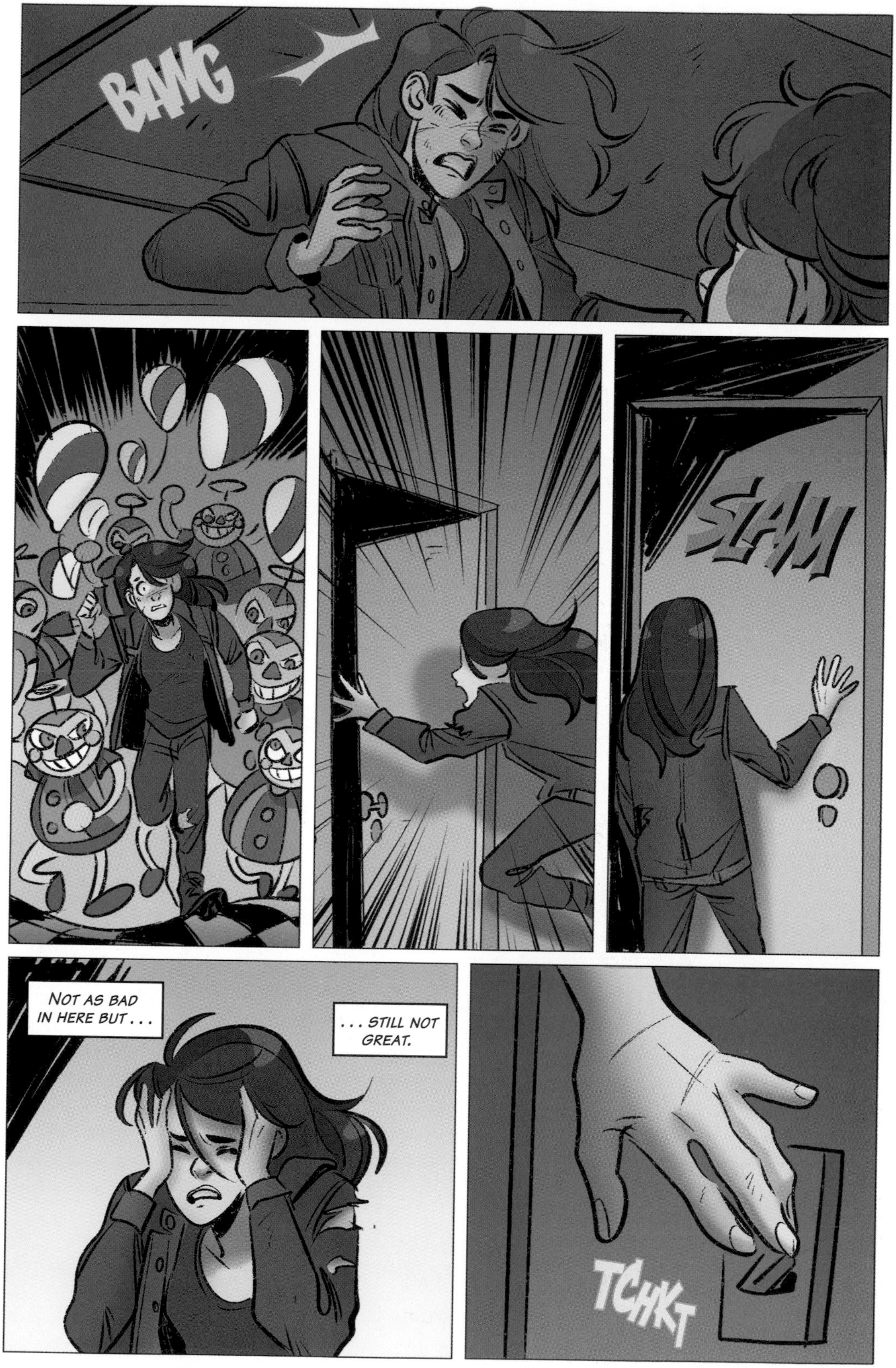
BANG
SLAM
NOT AS BAD IN HERE BUT . . .
. . . STILL NOT GREAT.
TCHKT

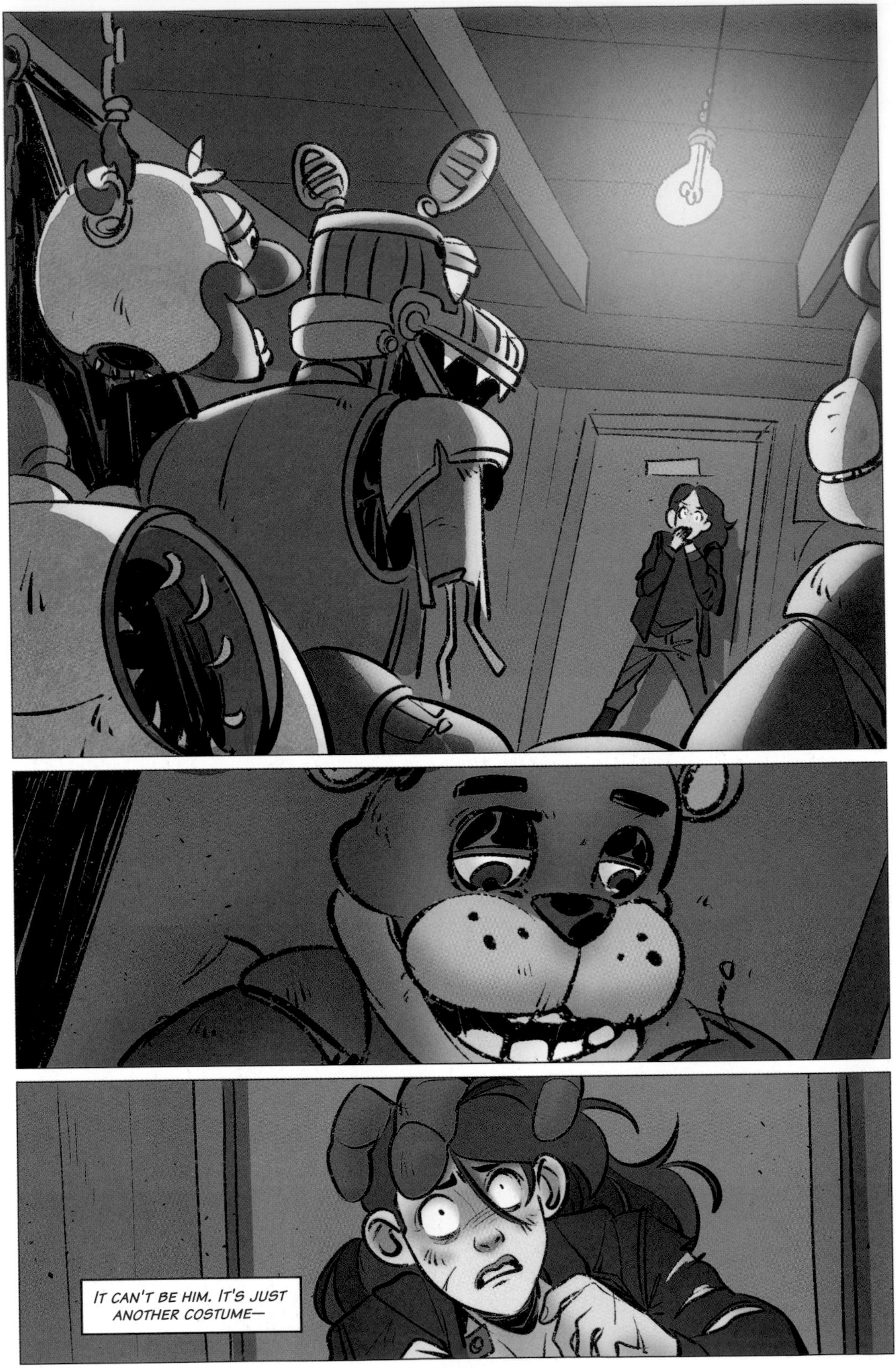

It can't be him. It's just another costume—

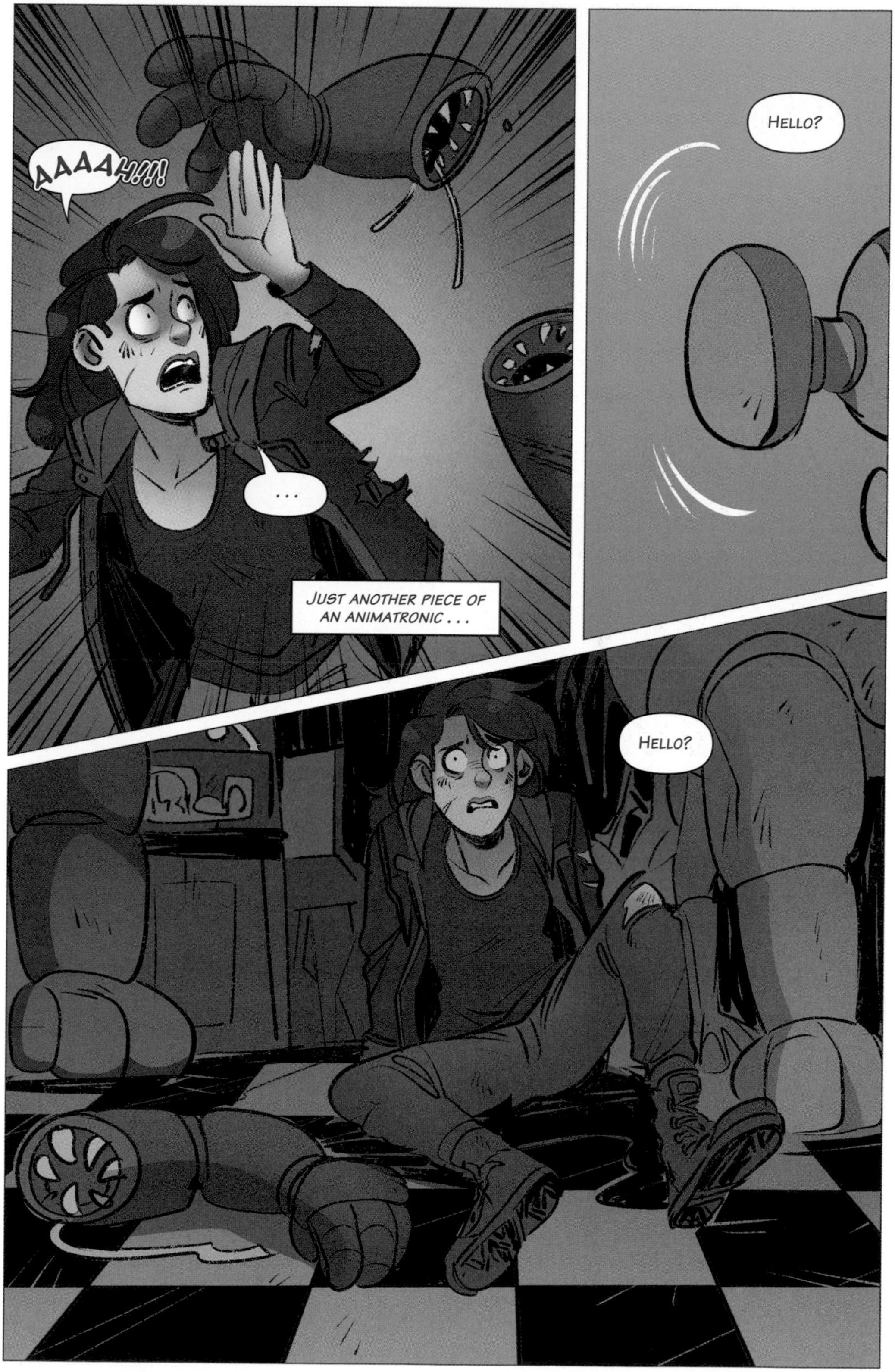
AAAAH!!!
...
JUST ANOTHER PIECE OF AN ANIMATRONIC . . .
HELLO?
HELLO?

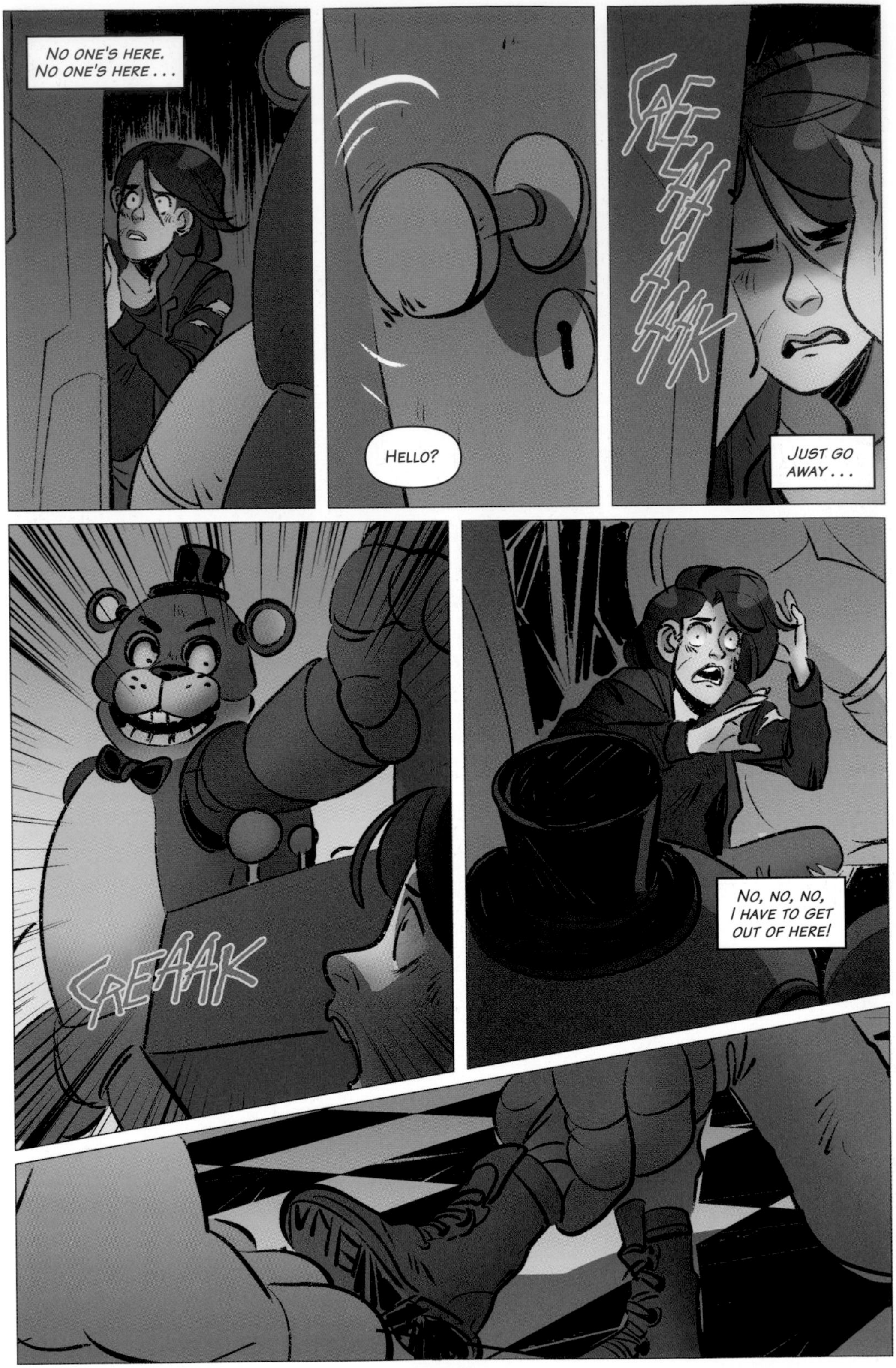
No one's here.
No one's here . . .
Hello?
CREEAAAAAK
Just go away . . .
CREAAK
No, no, no, I have to get out of here!

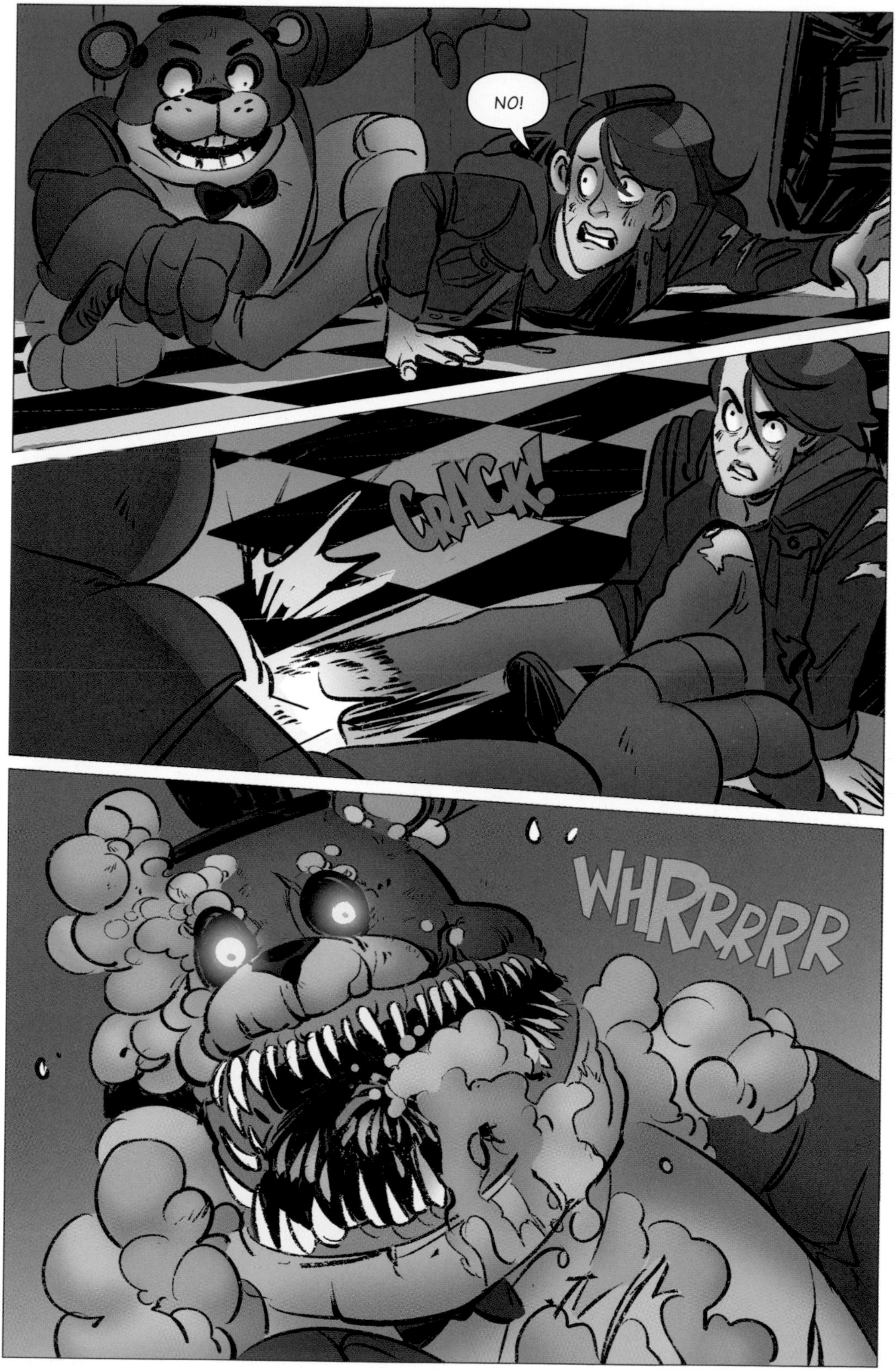
NO!
CRACK!
WHRRRRRR

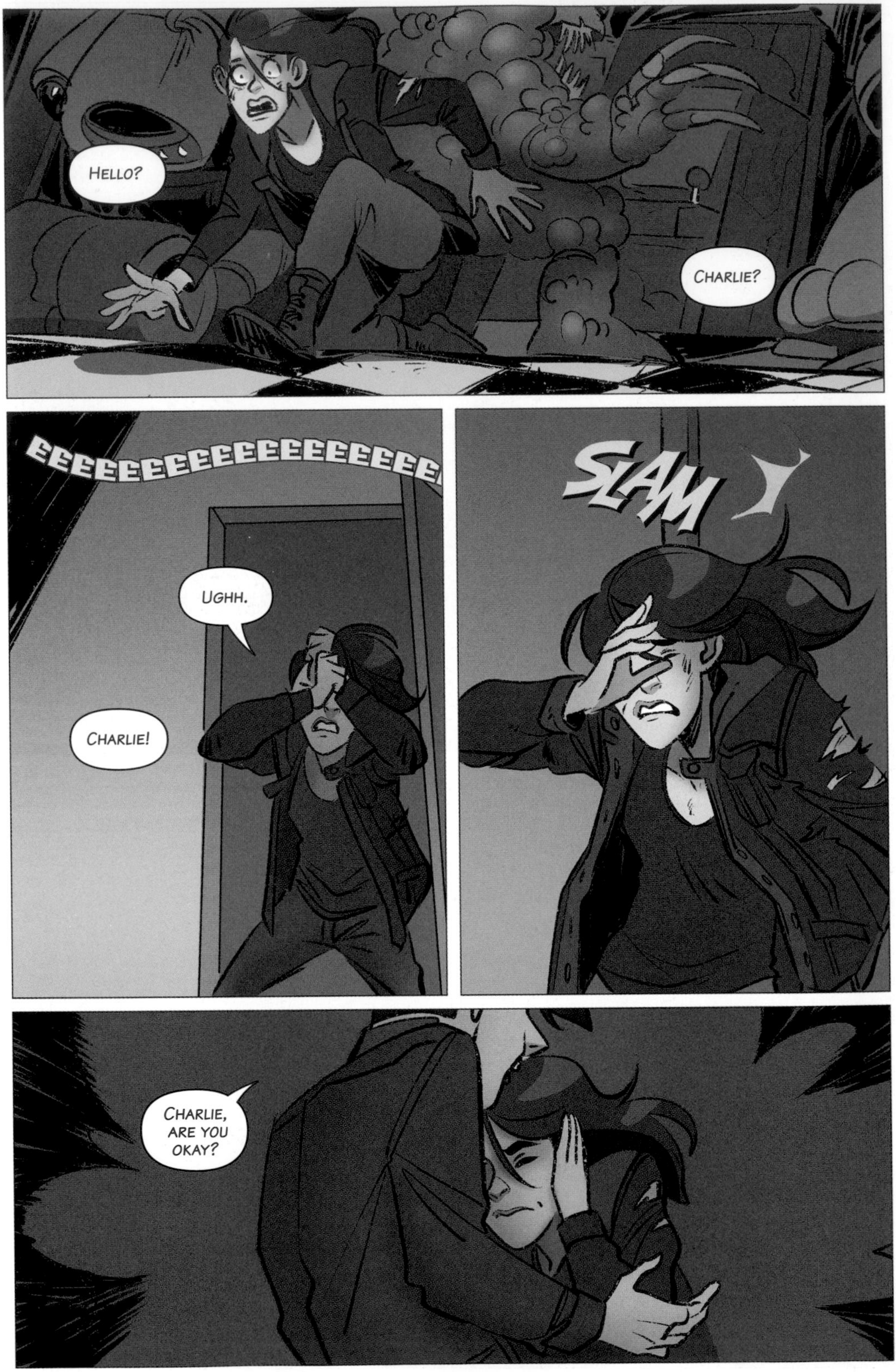
HELLO?
CHARLIE?
EEEEEEEEEEEEEEEEEE
UGHH.
CHARLIE!
SLAM
CHARLIE, ARE YOU OKAY?

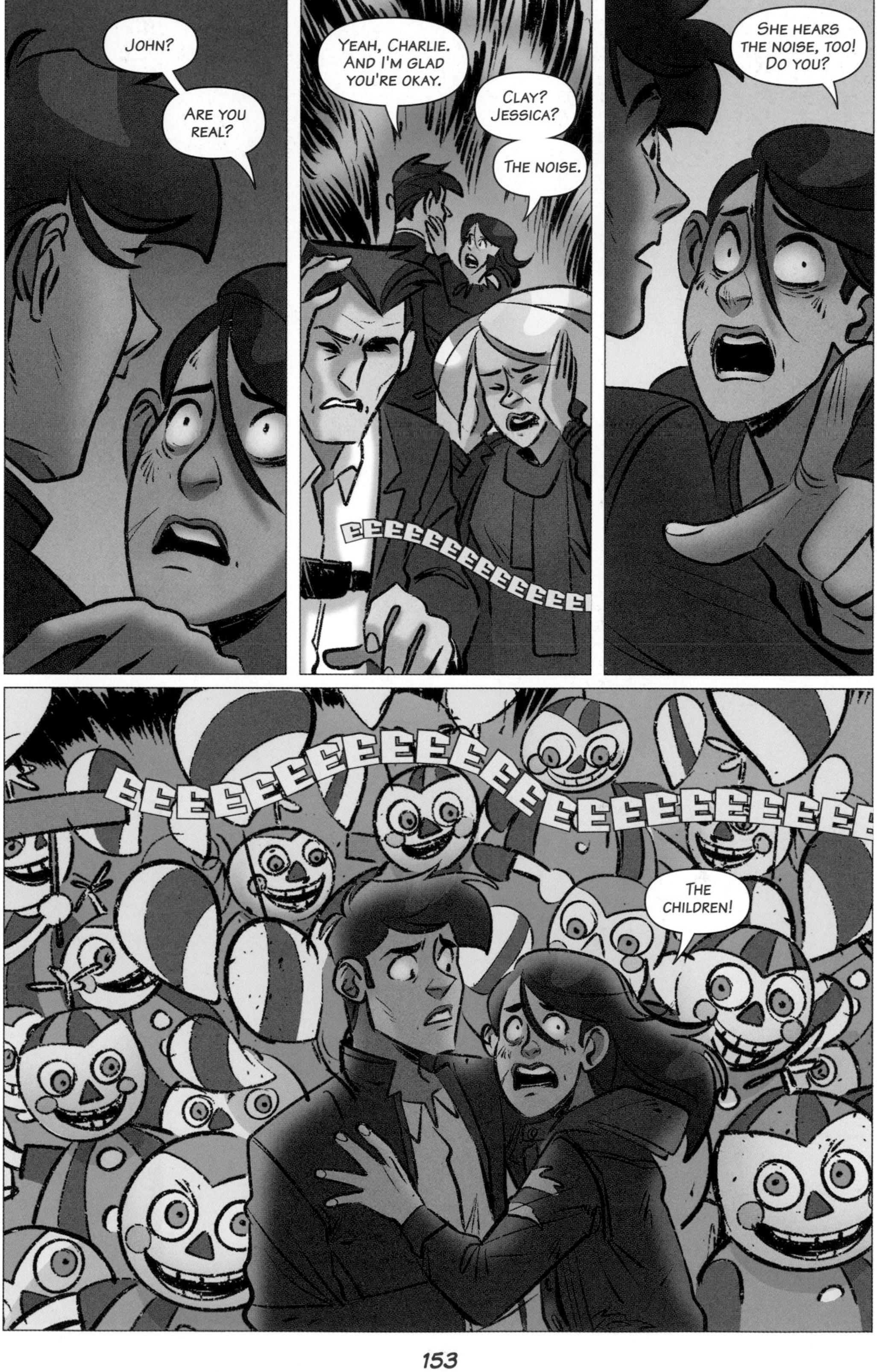

JOHN?
ARE YOU REAL?
YEAH, CHARLIE. AND I'M GLAD YOU'RE OKAY.
CLAY? JESSICA?
THE NOISE.
EEEEEEEEEEEEEEEEEE
SHE HEARS THE NOISE, TOO! DO YOU?
EEEEEEEEEEEEEEEEEEEEEEEEEE
THE CHILDREN!

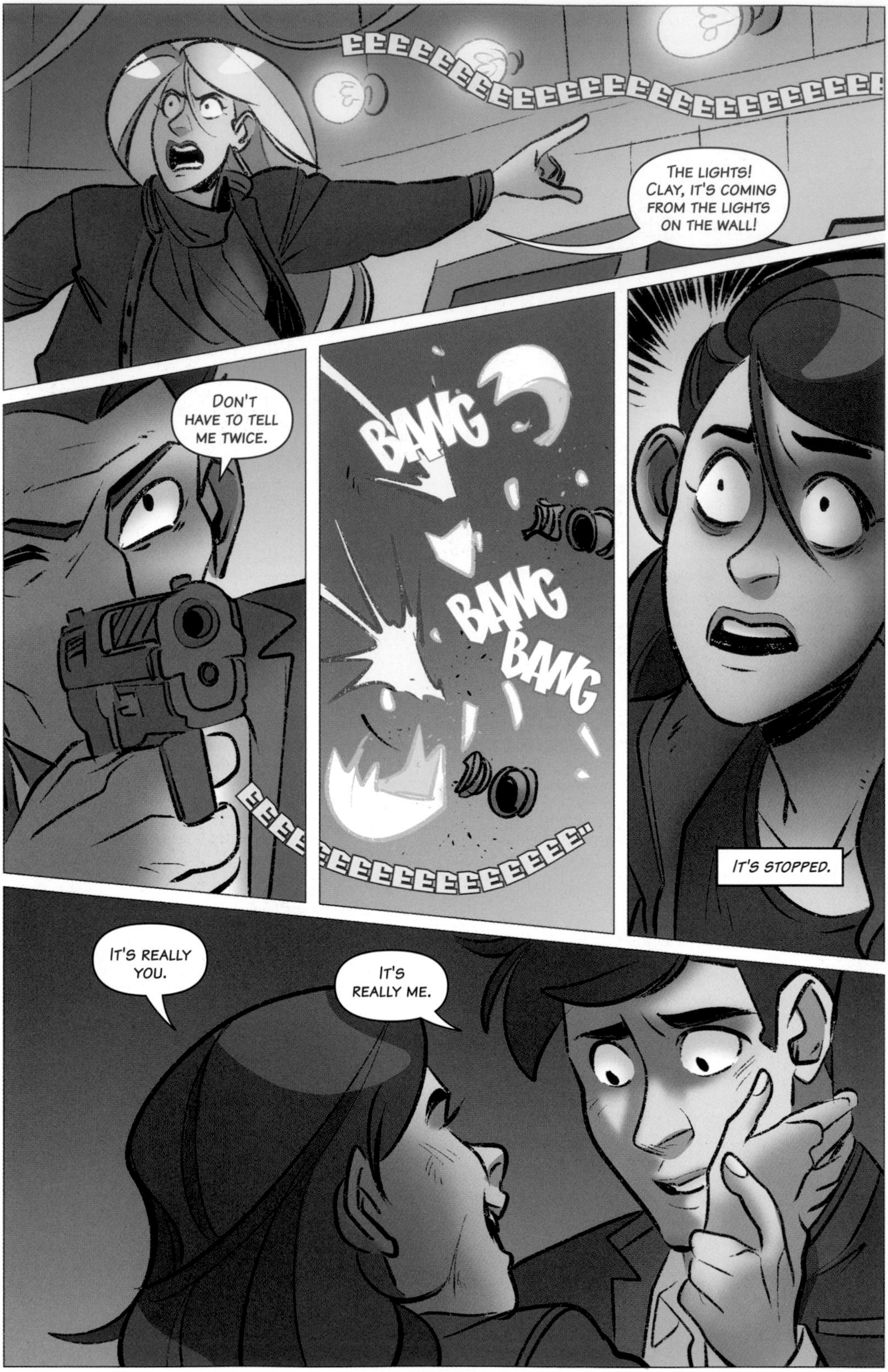
EEEEEEEEEEEEEEEEEEEEEEEEEEEEEE
THE LIGHTS! CLAY, IT'S COMING FROM THE LIGHTS ON THE WALL!
DON'T HAVE TO TELL ME TWICE.
BANG
BANG
BANG
EEEEEEEEEEEEEEEEEEEE..
IT'S STOPPED.
IT'S REALLY YOU.
IT'S REALLY ME.

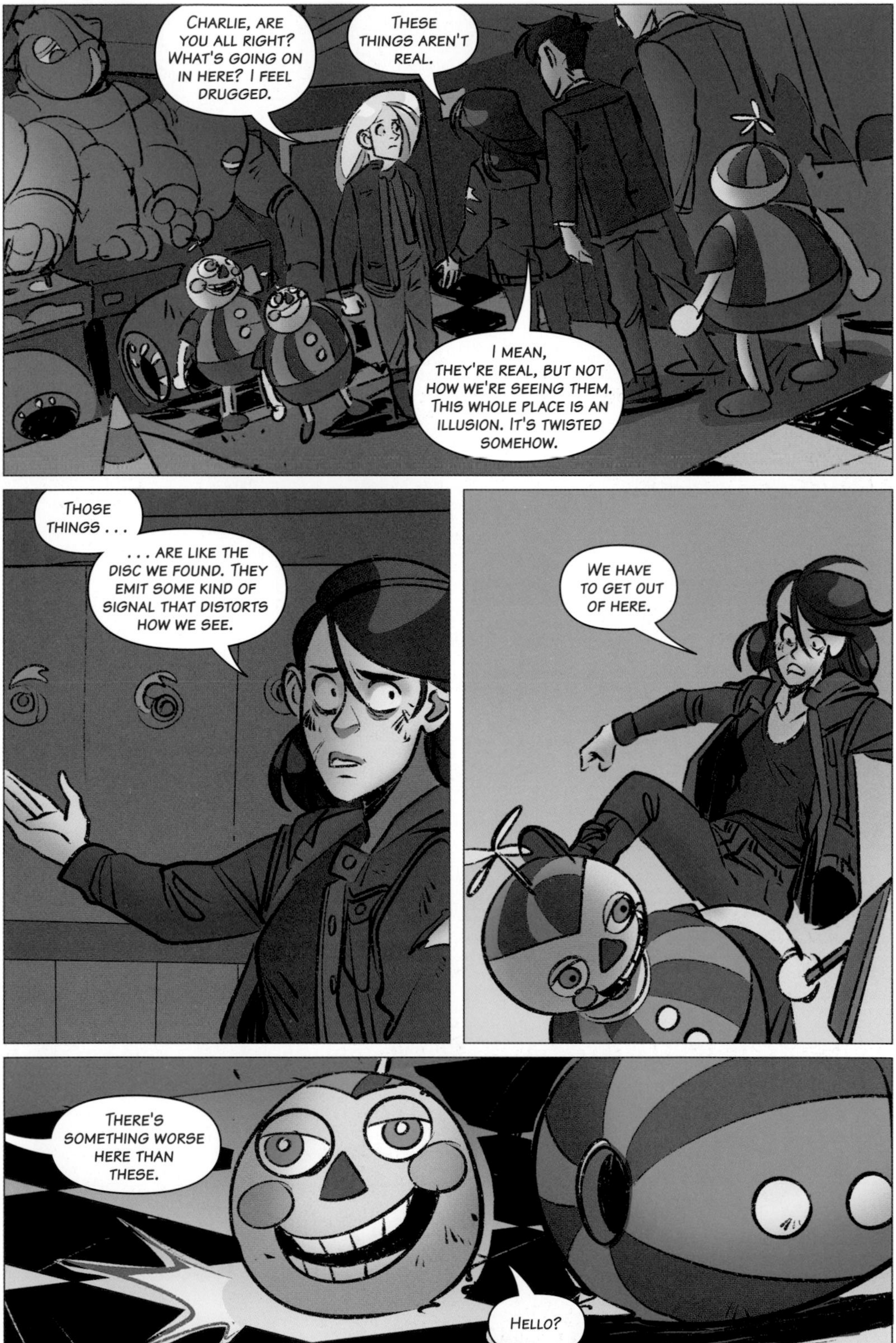
CHARLIE, ARE YOU ALL RIGHT? WHAT'S GOING ON IN HERE? I FEEL DRUGGED.
THESE THINGS AREN'T REAL.
I MEAN, THEY'RE REAL, BUT NOT HOW WE'RE SEEING THEM. THIS WHOLE PLACE IS AN ILLUSION. IT'S TWISTED SOMEHOW.
THOSE THINGS . . .
. . . ARE LIKE THE DISC WE FOUND. THEY EMIT SOME KIND OF SIGNAL THAT DISTORTS HOW WE SEE.
WE HAVE TO GET OUT OF HERE.
THERE'S SOMETHING WORSE HERE THAN THESE.
HELLO?

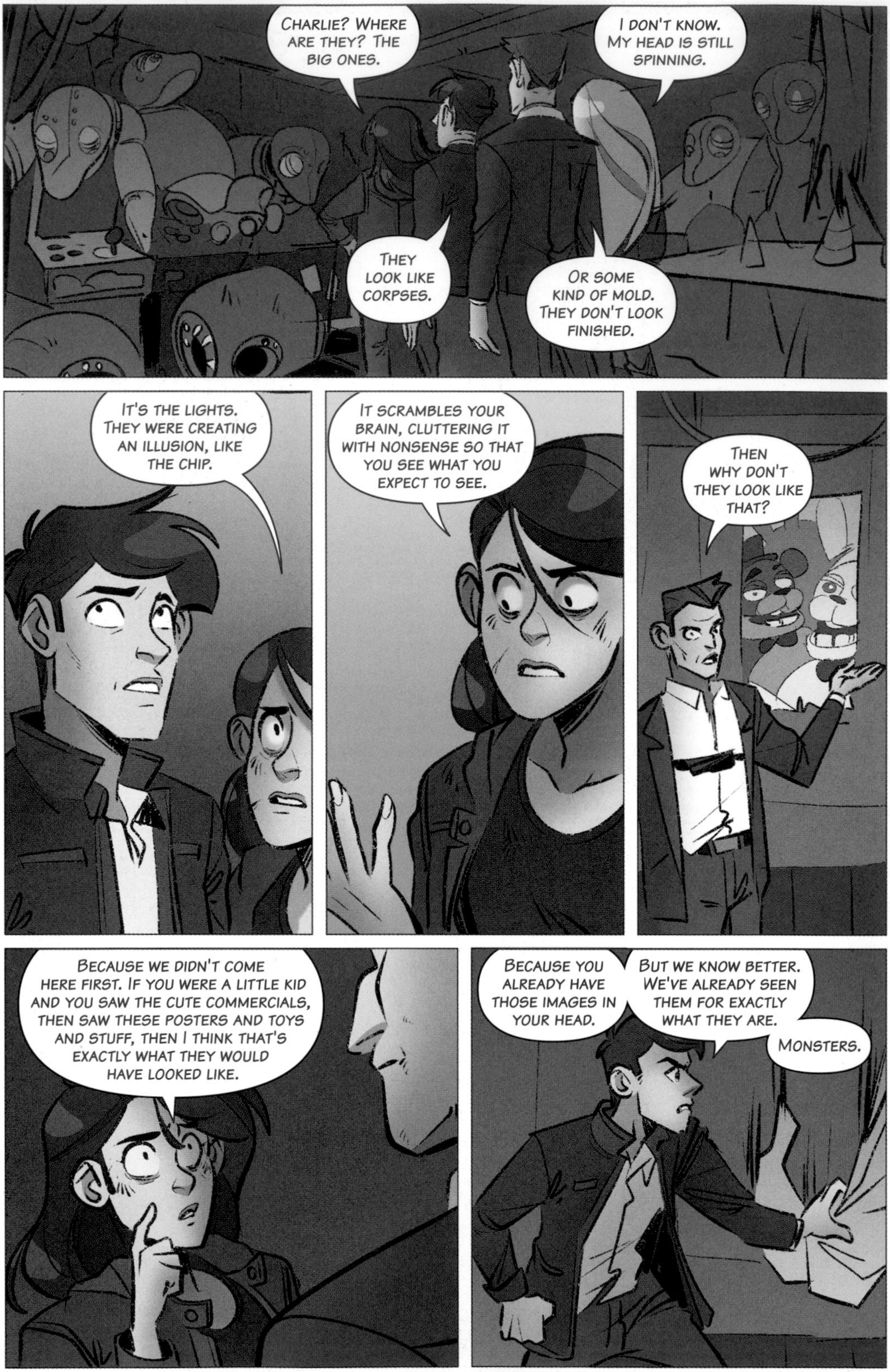
CHARLIE? WHERE ARE THEY? THE BIG ONES.
I DON'T KNOW. MY HEAD IS STILL SPINNING.
THEY LOOK LIKE CORPSES.
OR SOME KIND OF MOLD. THEY DON'T LOOK FINISHED.
IT'S THE LIGHTS. THEY WERE CREATING AN ILLUSION, LIKE THE CHIP.
IT SCRAMBLES YOUR BRAIN, CLUTTERING IT WITH NONSENSE SO THAT YOU SEE WHAT YOU EXPECT TO SEE.
THEN WHY DON'T THEY LOOK LIKE THAT?
BECAUSE WE DIDN'T COME HERE FIRST. IF YOU WERE A LITTLE KID AND YOU SAW THE CUTE COMMERCIALS, THEN SAW THESE POSTERS AND TOYS AND STUFF, THEN I THINK THAT'S EXACTLY WHAT THEY WOULD HAVE LOOKED LIKE.
BECAUSE YOU ALREADY HAVE THOSE IMAGES IN YOUR HEAD.
BUT WE KNOW BETTER. WE'VE ALREADY SEEN THEM FOR EXACTLY WHAT THEY ARE.
MONSTERS.

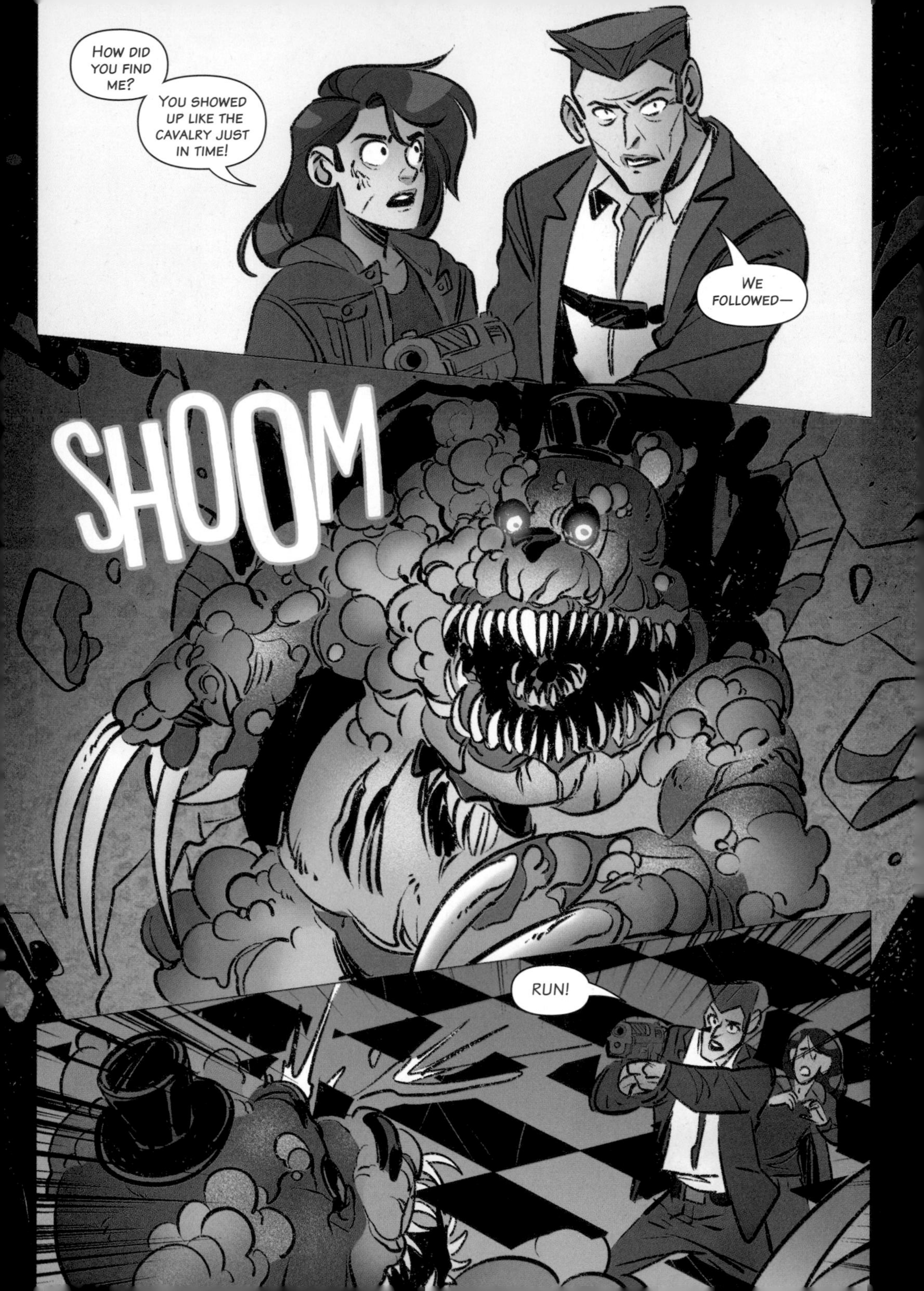
HOW DID YOU FIND ME?
YOU SHOWED UP LIKE THE CAVALRY JUST IN TIME!
WE FOLLOWED—
SHOOM
RUN!

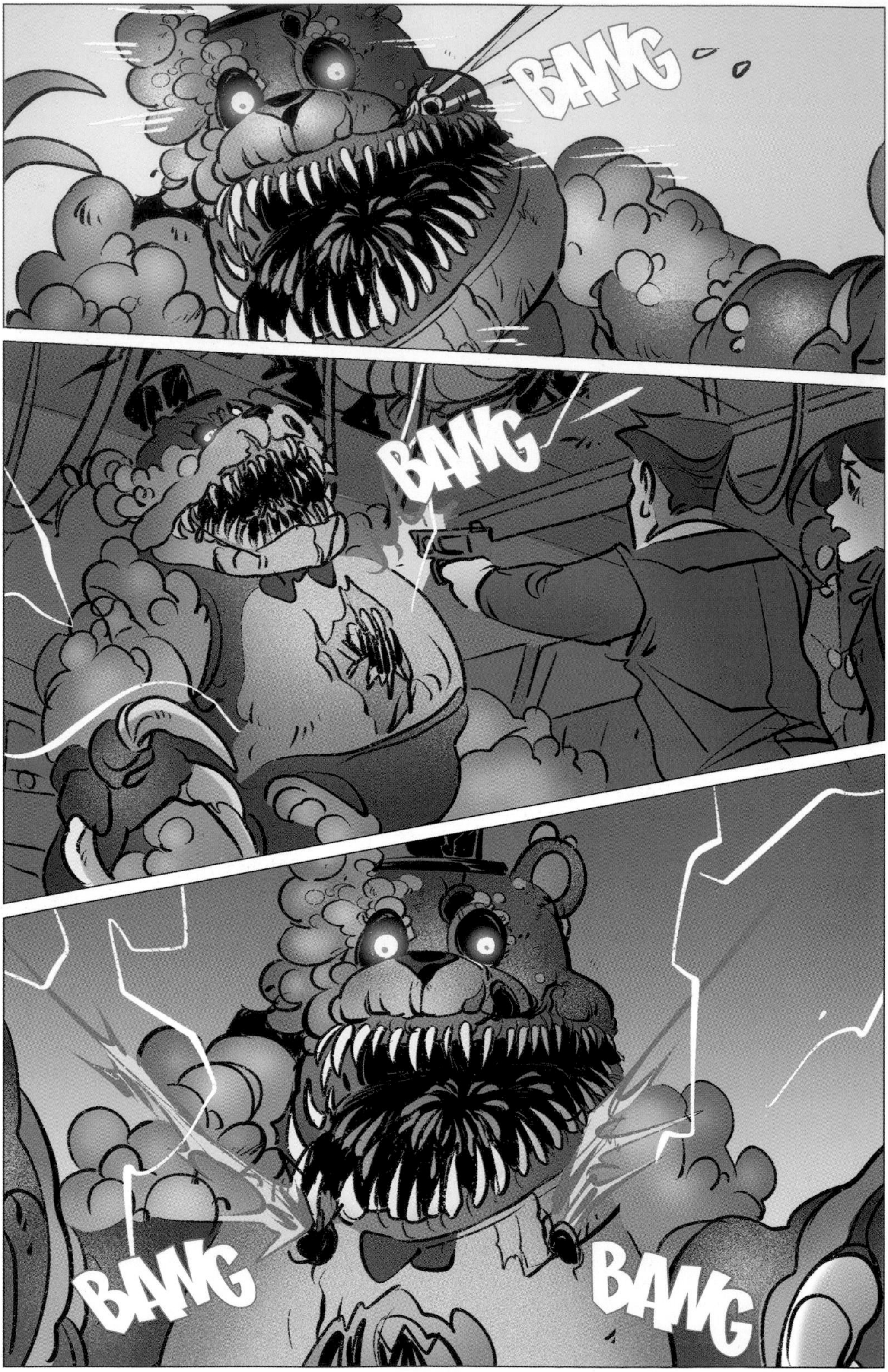
BANG
BANG
BANG
BANG

It's not like the other mascots from Freddy's.

These aren't made of fur and fabric, they're made of us, by twisting our minds.

Charlie . . .

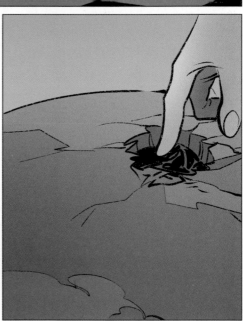

You shot the chip. You killed the illusion.

CLACK CLACK CLACK

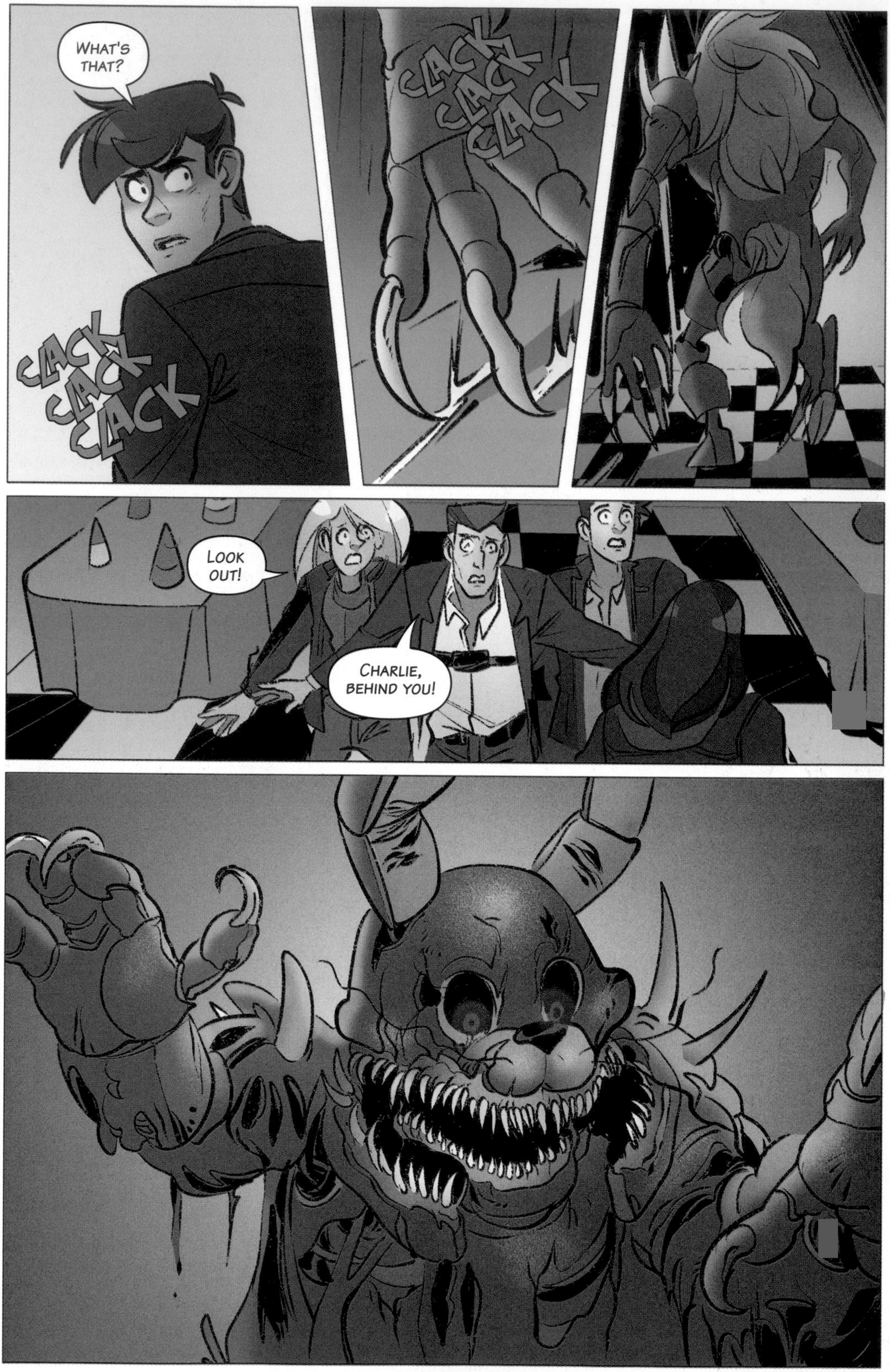
WHAT'S THAT?
CLACK CLACK CLACK
CLACK CLACK CLACK
LOOK OUT!
CHARLIE, BEHIND YOU!

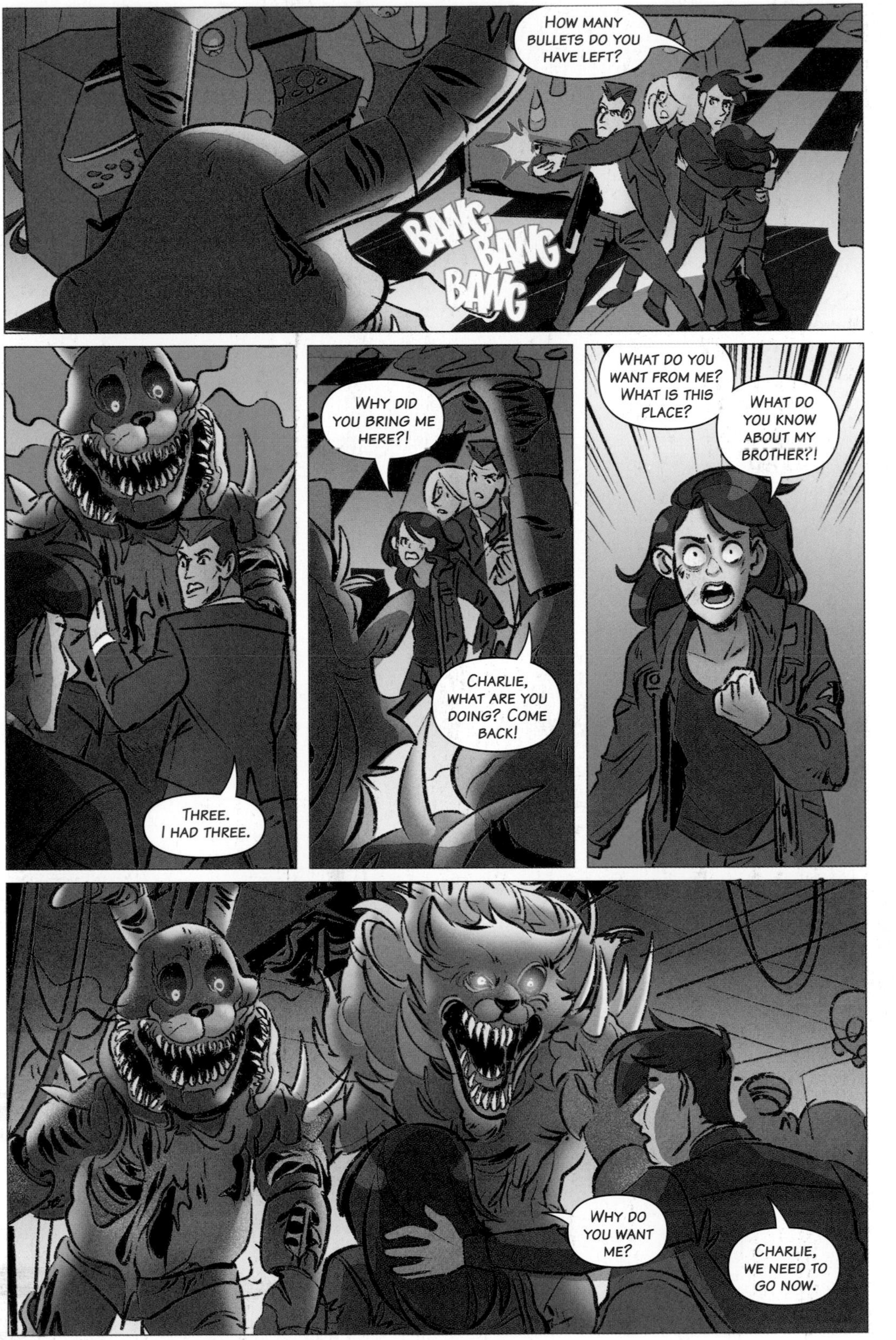
HOW MANY BULLETS DO YOU HAVE LEFT?
BANG BANG BANG
THREE. I HAD THREE.
WHY DID YOU BRING ME HERE?!
CHARLIE, WHAT ARE YOU DOING? COME BACK!
WHAT DO YOU WANT FROM ME? WHAT IS THIS PLACE?
WHAT DO YOU KNOW ABOUT MY BROTHER?!
WHY DO YOU WANT ME?
CHARLIE, WE NEED TO GO NOW.

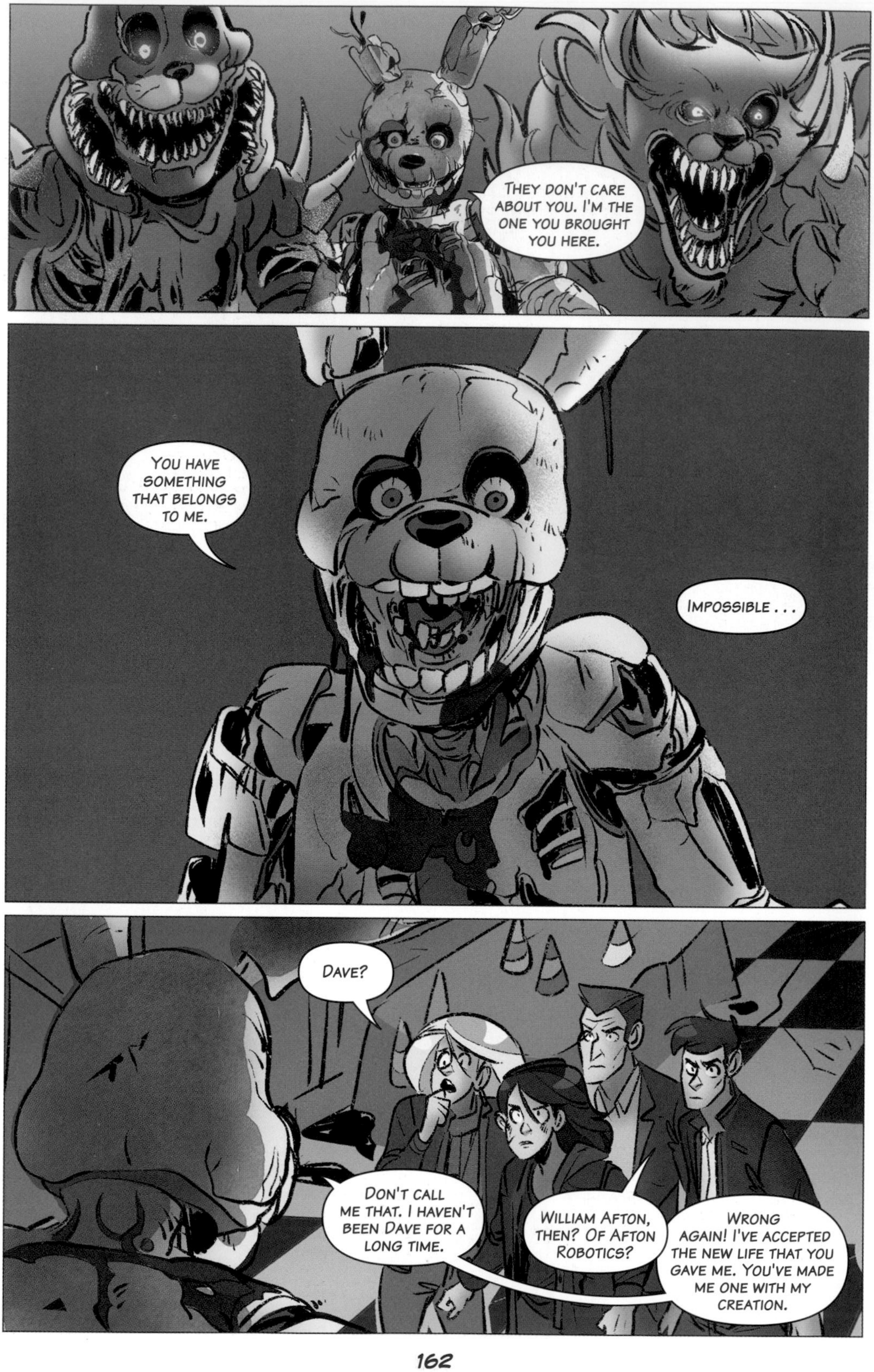

They don't care about you. I'm the one you brought you here.
You have something that belongs to me.
Impossible . . .
Dave?
Don't call me that. I haven't been Dave for a long time.
William Afton, then? Of Afton Robotics?
Wrong again! I've accepted the new life that you gave me. You've made me one with my creation.

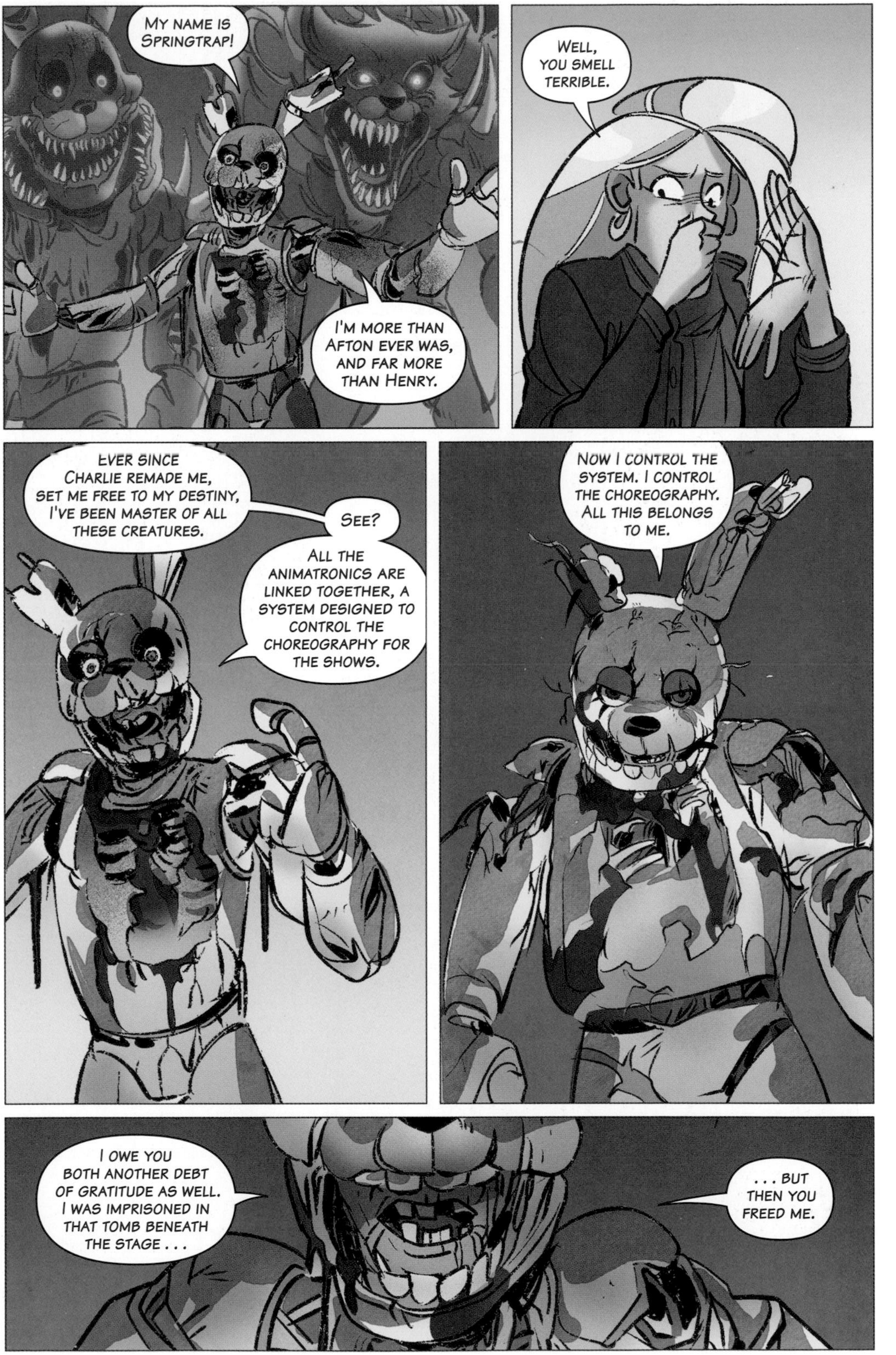
My name is Springtrap!
I'm more than Afton ever was, and far more than Henry.
Well, you smell terrible.
Ever since Charlie remade me, set me free to my destiny, I've been master of all these creatures.
See?
All the animatronics are linked together, a system designed to control the choreography for the shows.
Now I control the system. I control the choreography. All this belongs to me.
I owe you both another debt of gratitude as well. I was imprisoned in that tomb beneath the stage . . .
. . . but then you freed me.

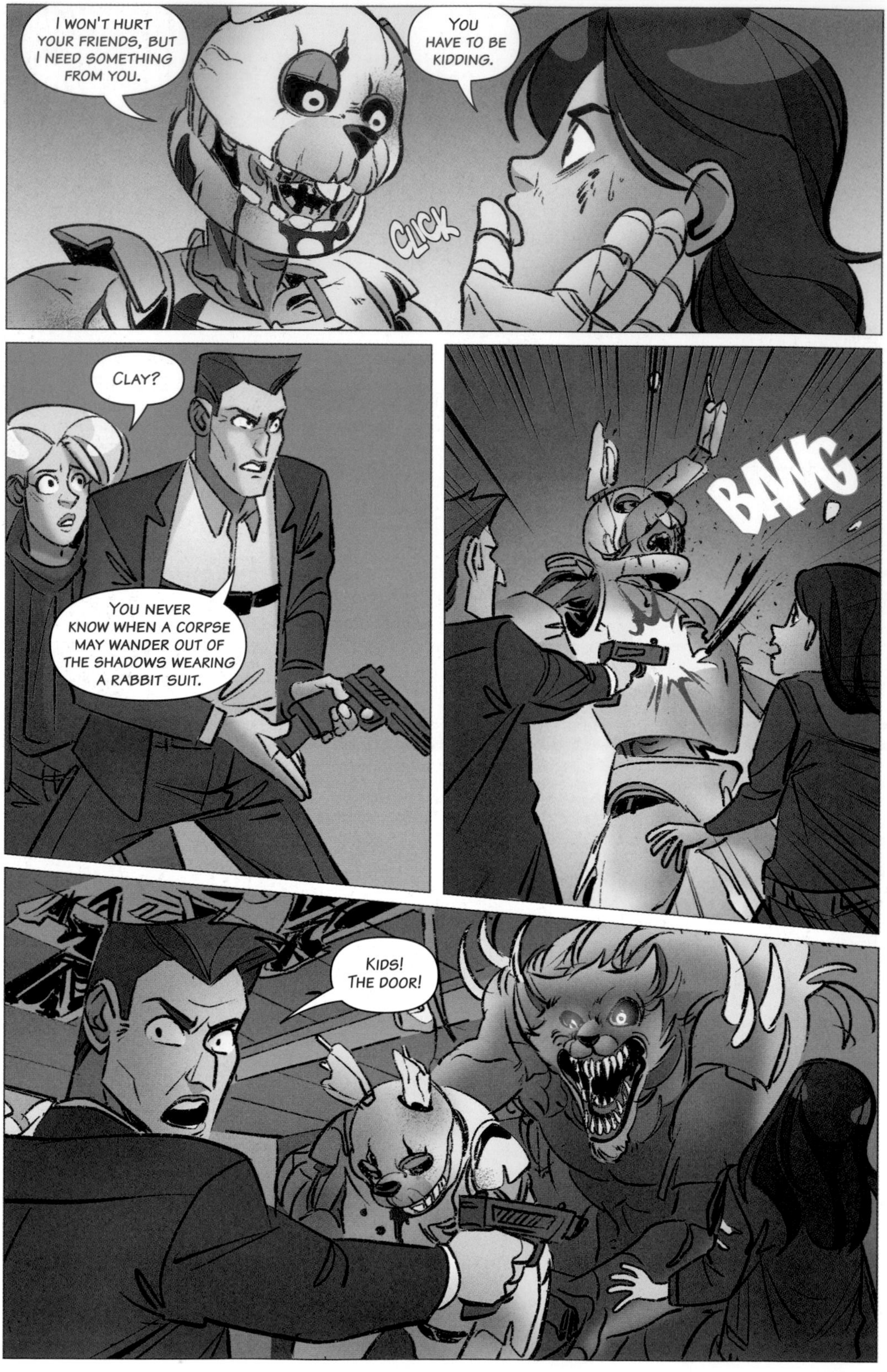
I WON'T HURT YOUR FRIENDS, BUT I NEED SOMETHING FROM YOU.
YOU HAVE TO BE KIDDING.
CLICK
CLAY?
YOU NEVER KNOW WHEN A CORPSE MAY WANDER OUT OF THE SHADOWS WEARING A RABBIT SUIT.
BANG
KIDS! THE DOOR!

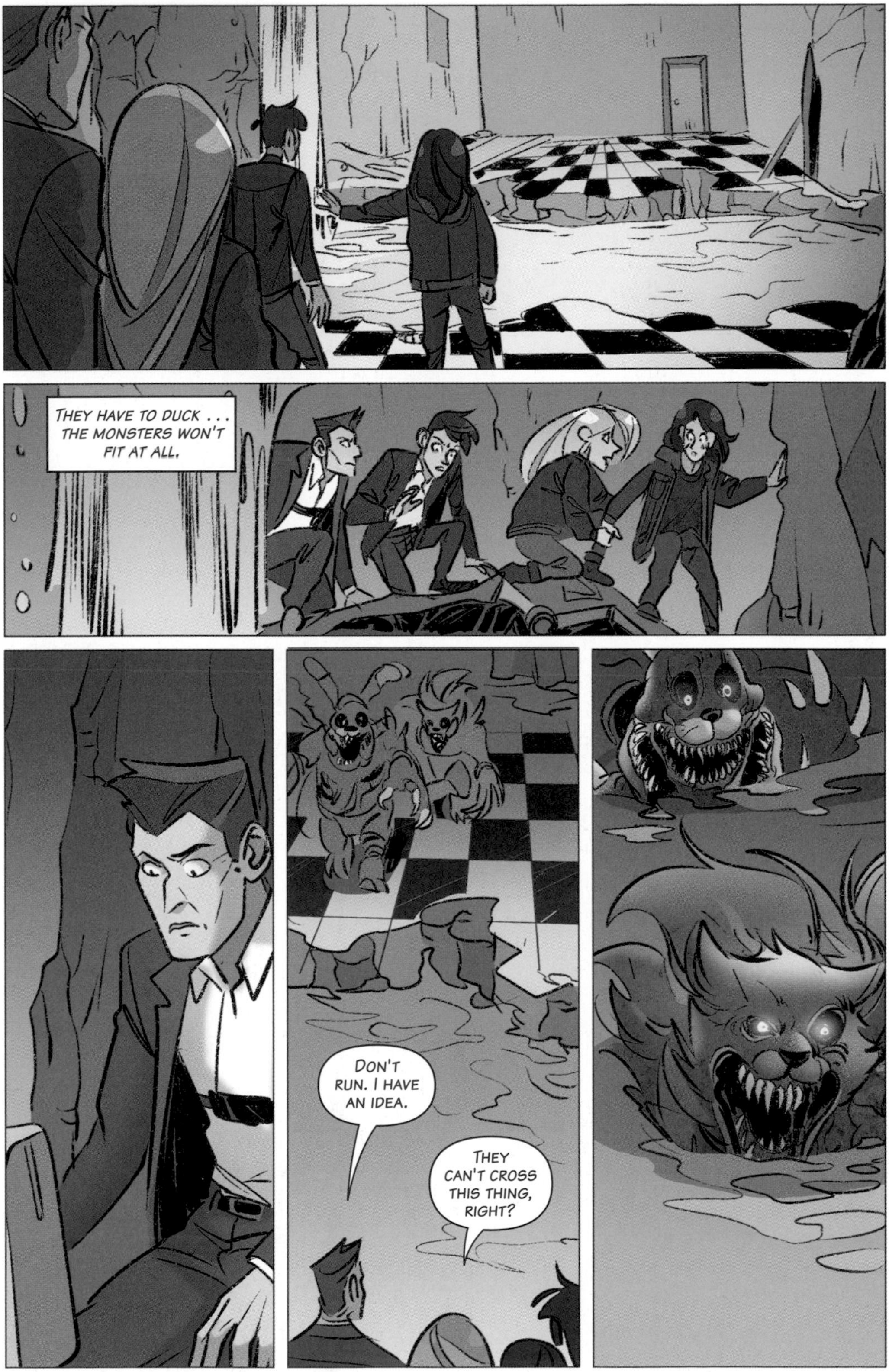
THEY HAVE TO DUCK . . . THE MONSTERS WON'T FIT AT ALL.
DON'T RUN. I HAVE AN IDEA.
THEY CAN'T CROSS THIS THING, RIGHT?

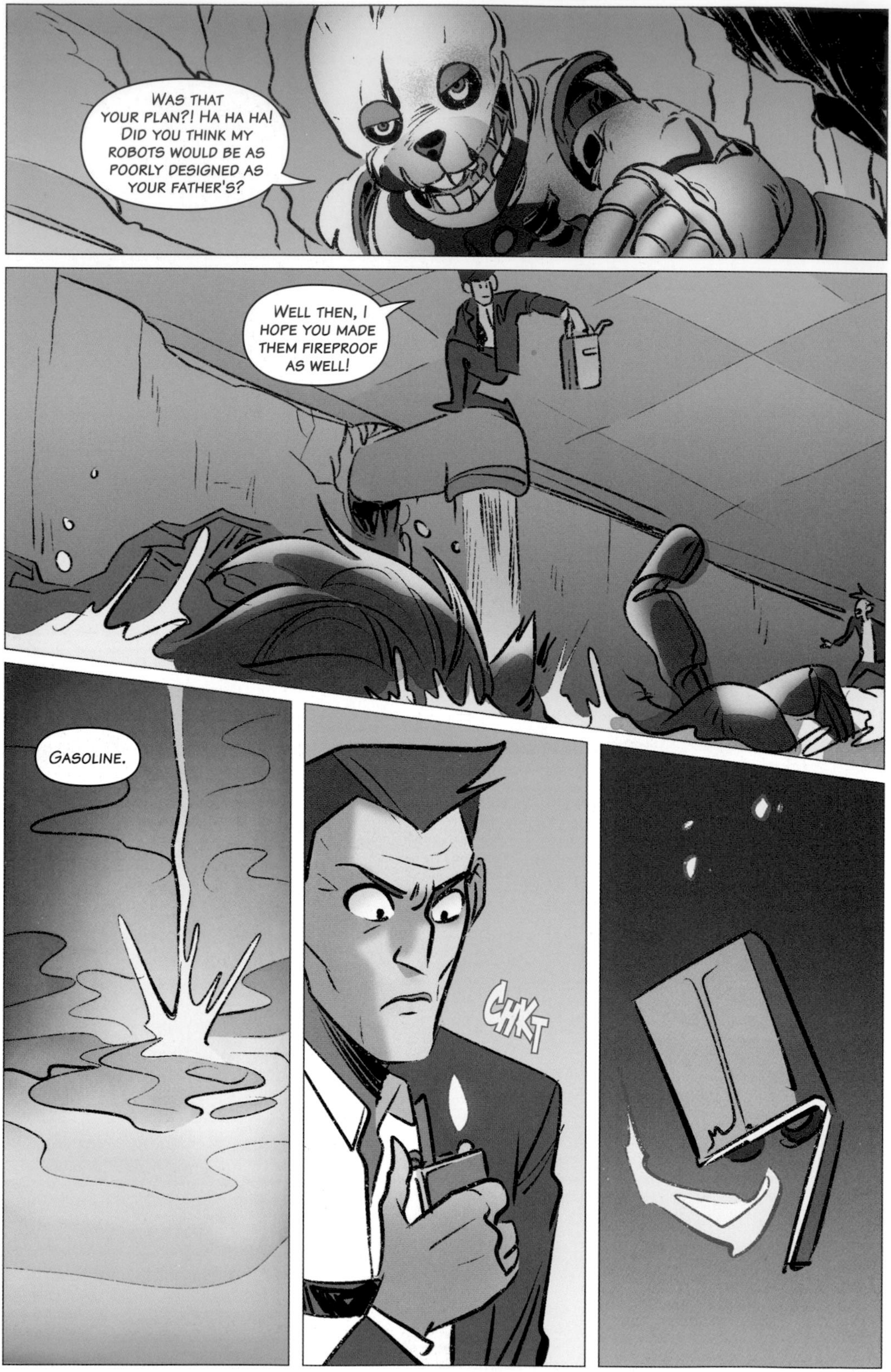
WAS THAT YOUR PLAN?! HA HA HA! DID YOU THINK MY ROBOTS WOULD BE AS POORLY DESIGNED AS YOUR FATHER'S?
WELL THEN, I HOPE YOU MADE THEM FIREPROOF AS WELL!
GASOLINE.
CHKT

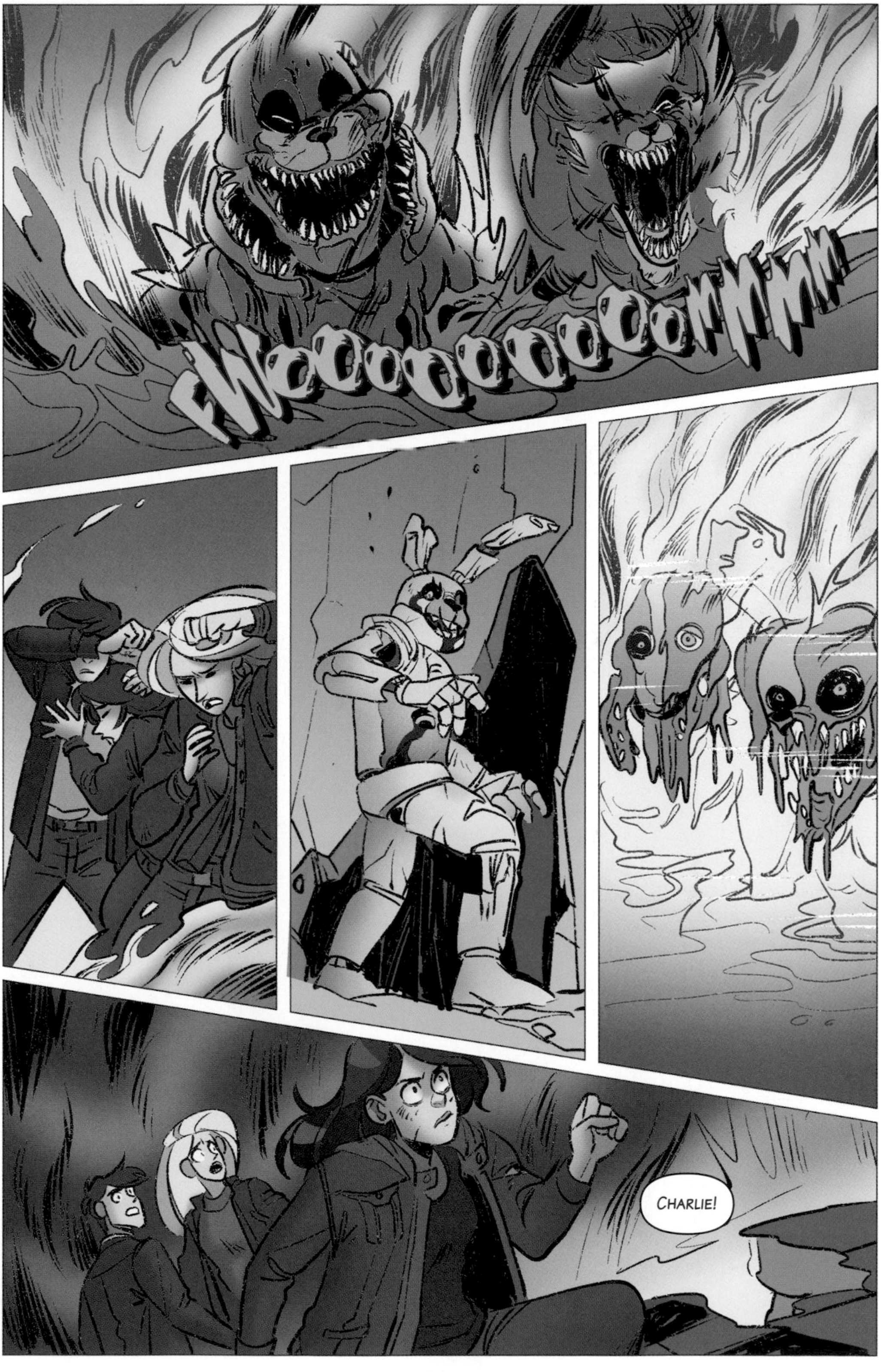
WOOOOOOOOOMMMM
CHARLIE!

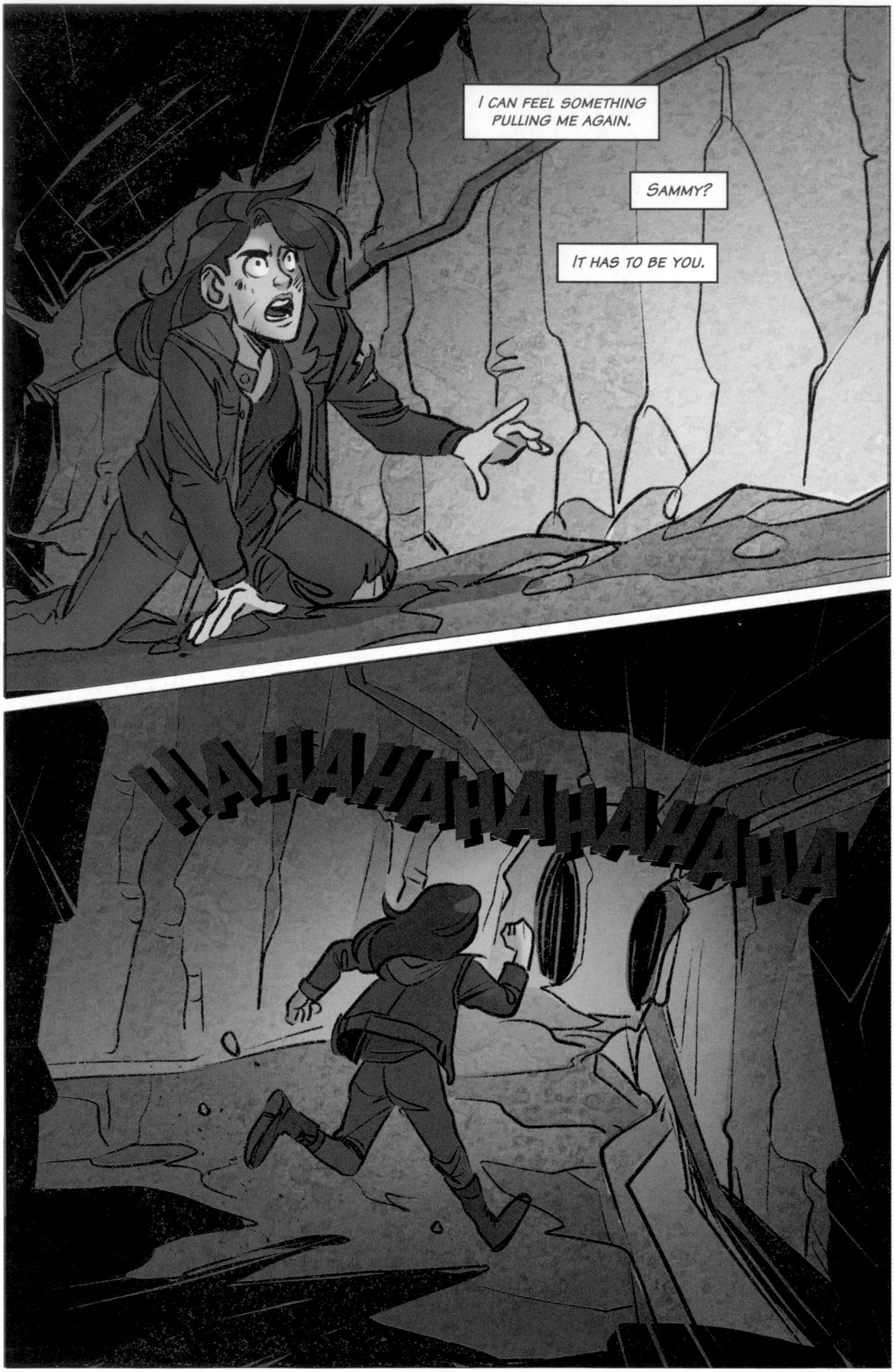
I CAN FEEL SOMETHING PULLING ME AGAIN.
SAMMY?
IT HAS TO BE YOU.
HAHAHAHAHAHAHAHAHAHA

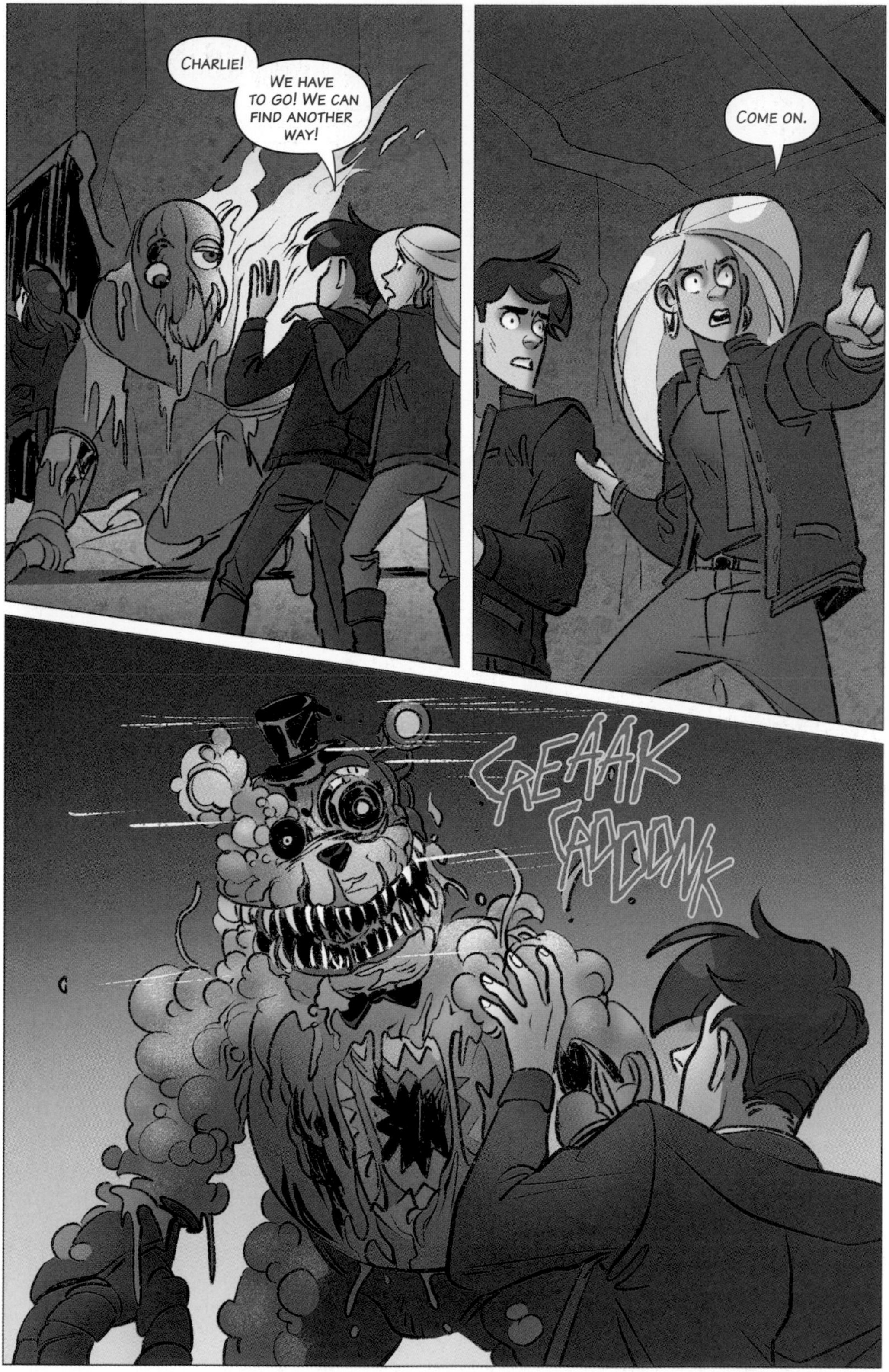
CHARLIE!
WE HAVE TO GO! WE CAN FIND ANOTHER WAY!
COME ON.
CREAAK
CADOONK

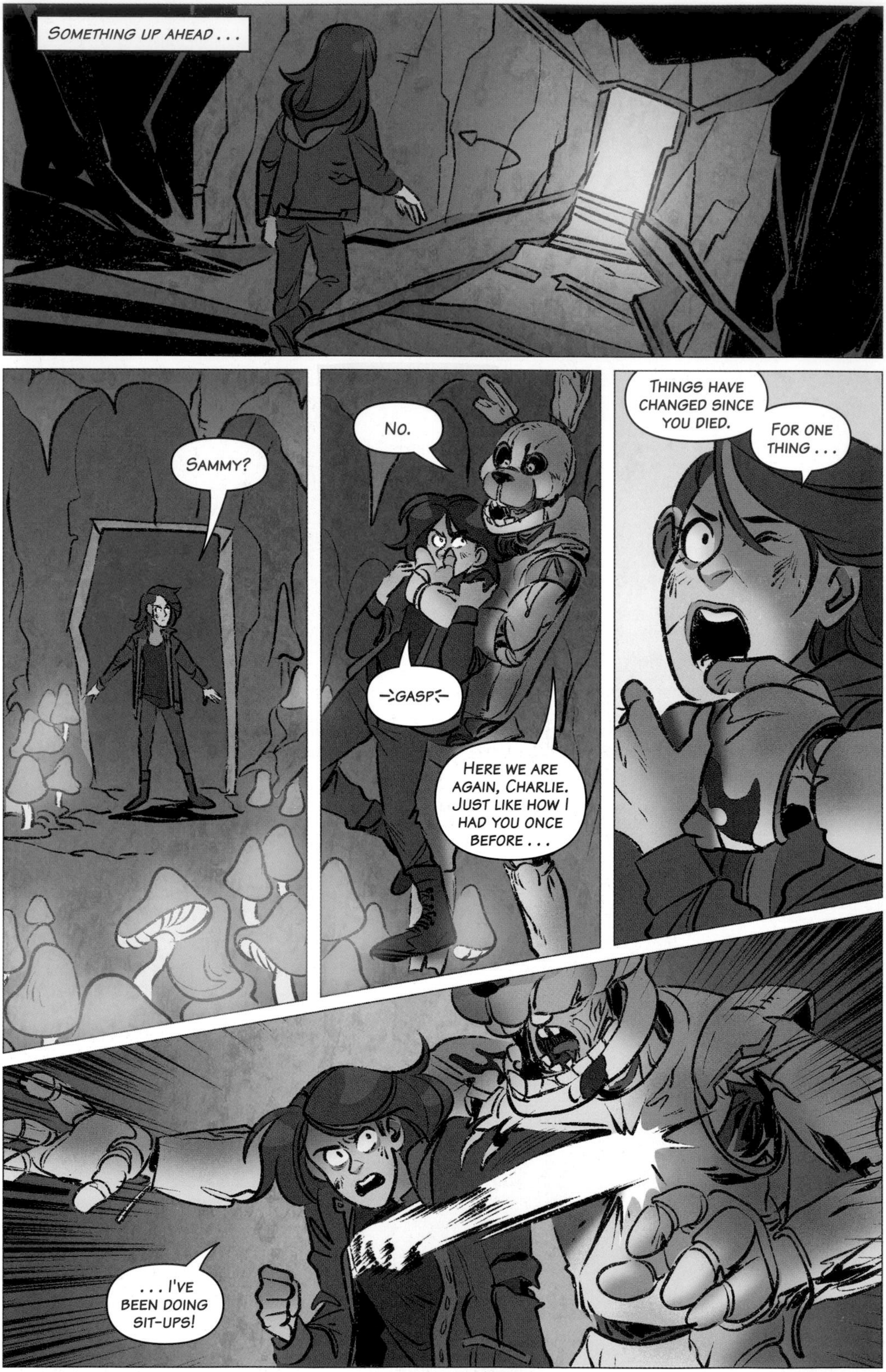
Something up ahead . . .
Sammy?
No.
-GASP-
Here we are again, Charlie. Just like how I had you once before . . .
Things have changed since you died.
For one thing . . .
. . . I've been doing sit-ups!

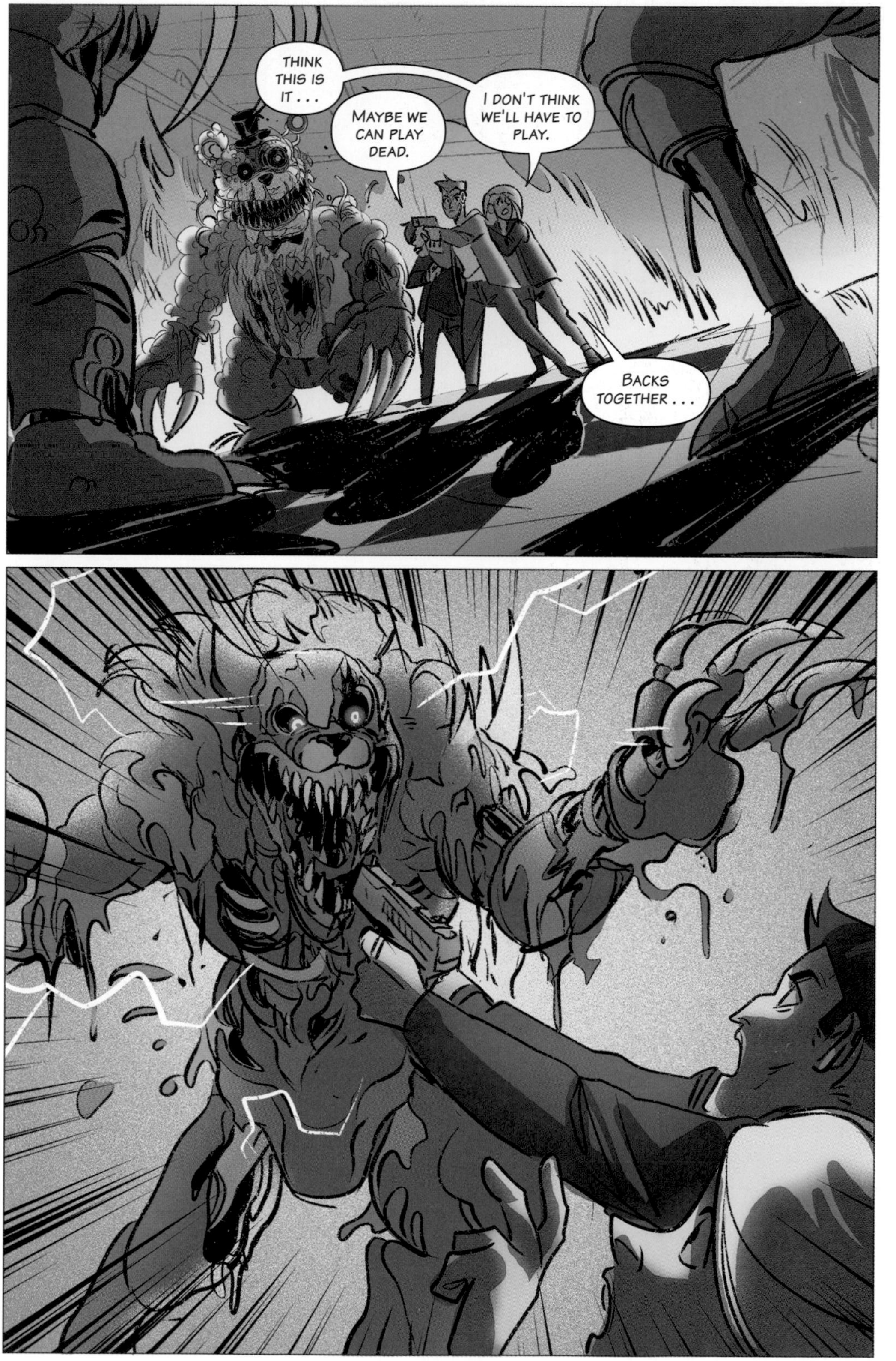
THINK THIS IS IT . . .
MAYBE WE CAN PLAY DEAD.
I DON'T THINK WE'LL HAVE TO PLAY.
BACKS TOGETHER . . .

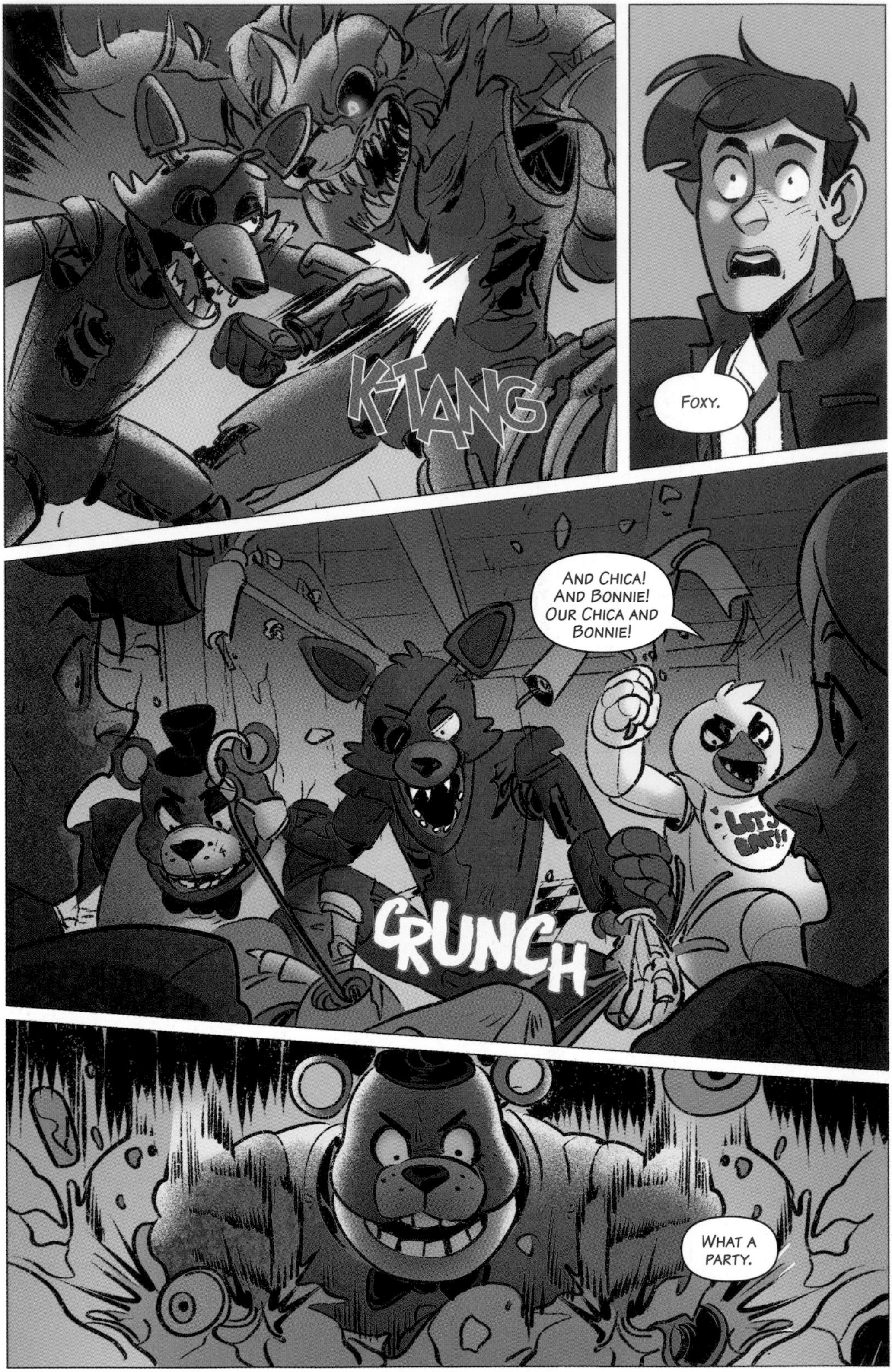
K-TANG
Foxy.
And Chica!
And Bonnie!
Our Chica and
Bonnie!
CRUNCH
What a
party.

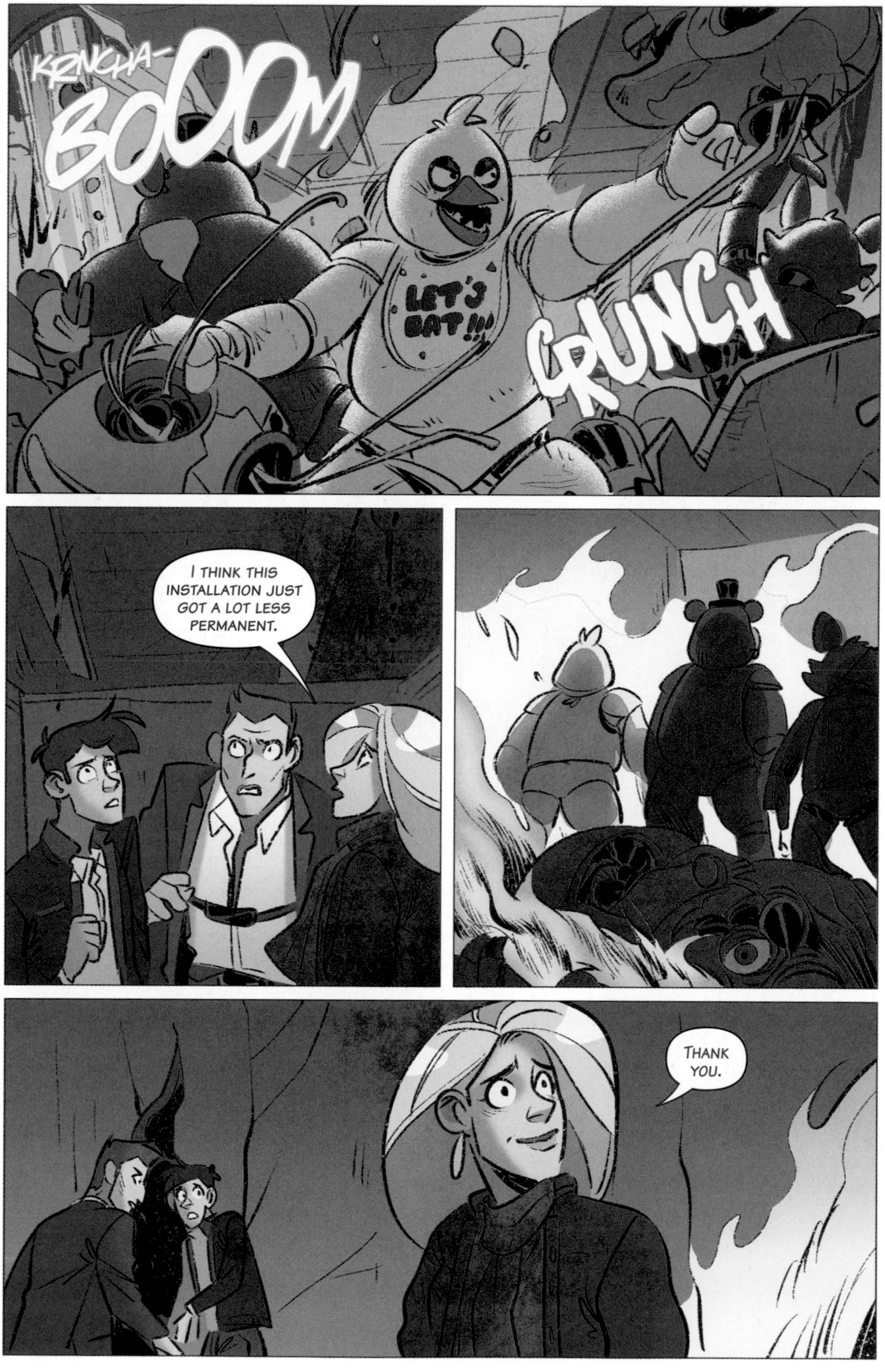
KRNCHA-
BOOOM
LET'S EAT!!!
CRUNCH
I THINK THIS INSTALLATION JUST GOT A LOT LESS PERMANENT.
THANK YOU.

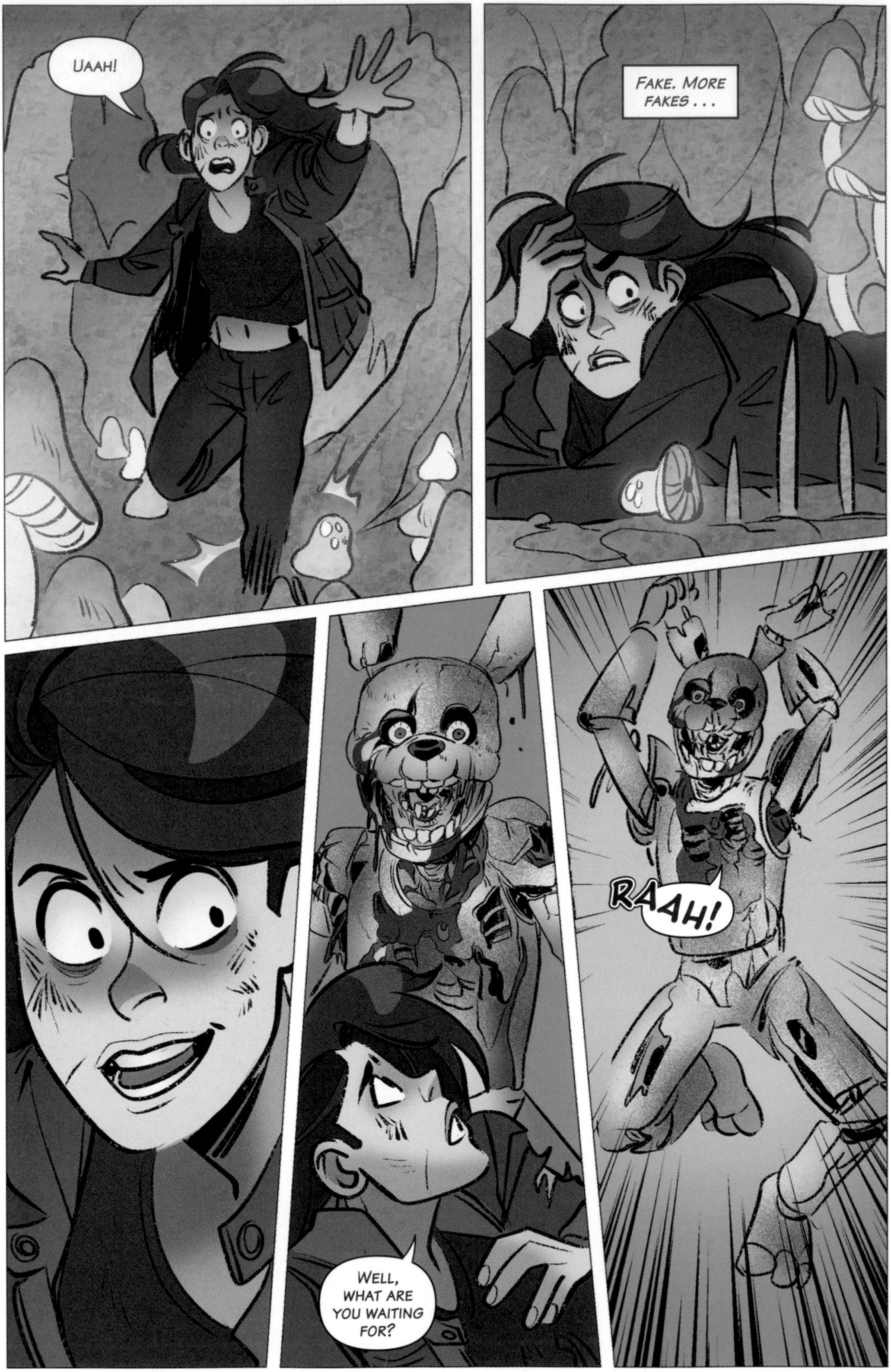
UAAH!
FAKE. MORE FAKES . . .
WELL, WHAT ARE YOU WAITING FOR?
RAAH!

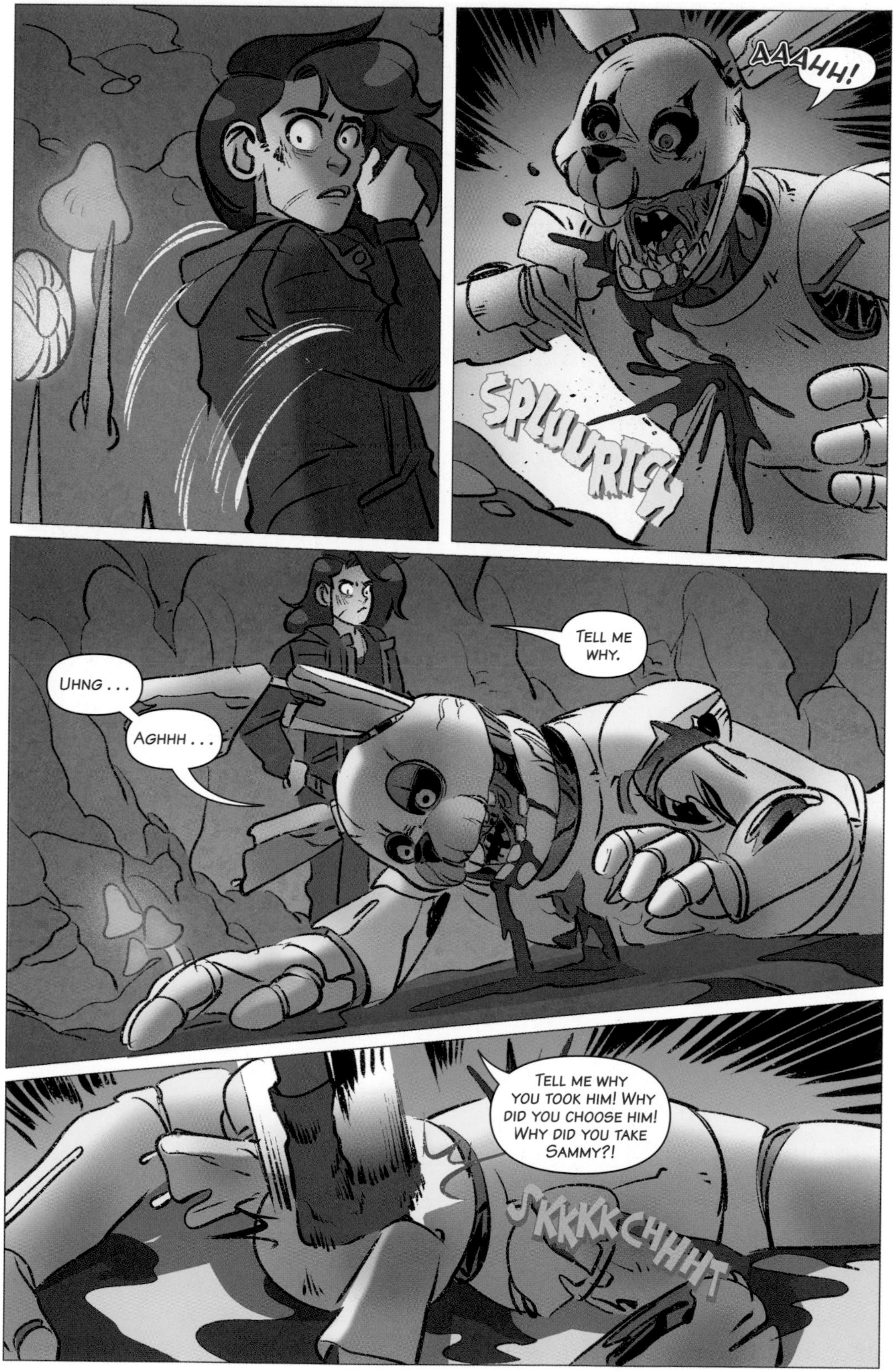
AAAHH!
SPLUURTCH
Tell me why.
Uhng . . .
Aghhh . . .
Tell me why you took him! Why did you choose him! Why did you take Sammy?!
SKKKKCHHHT

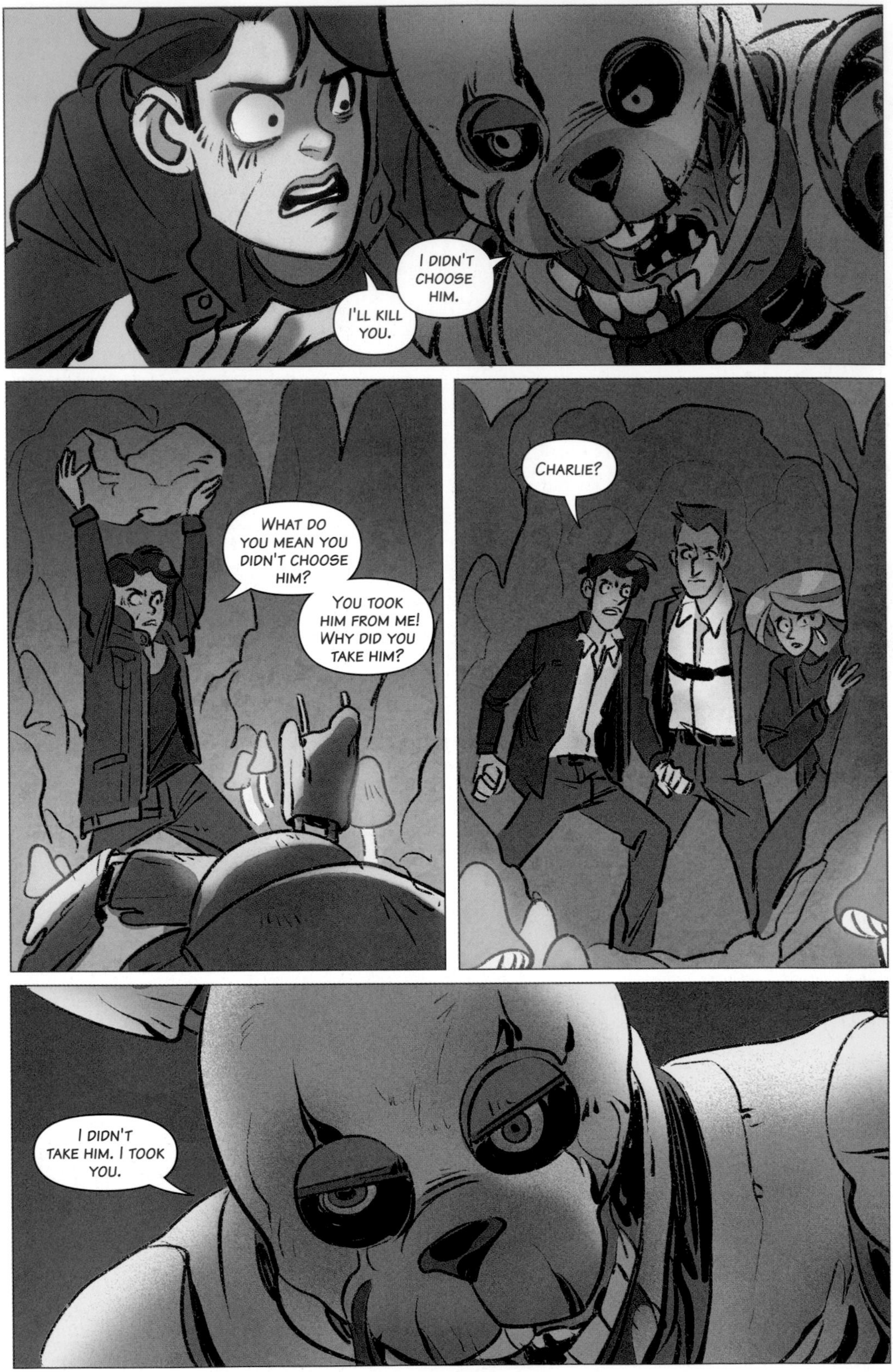
I'LL KILL YOU.
I DIDN'T CHOOSE HIM.
WHAT DO YOU MEAN YOU DIDN'T CHOOSE HIM?
YOU TOOK HIM FROM ME! WHY DID YOU TAKE HIM?
CHARLIE?
I DIDN'T TAKE HIM. I TOOK YOU.

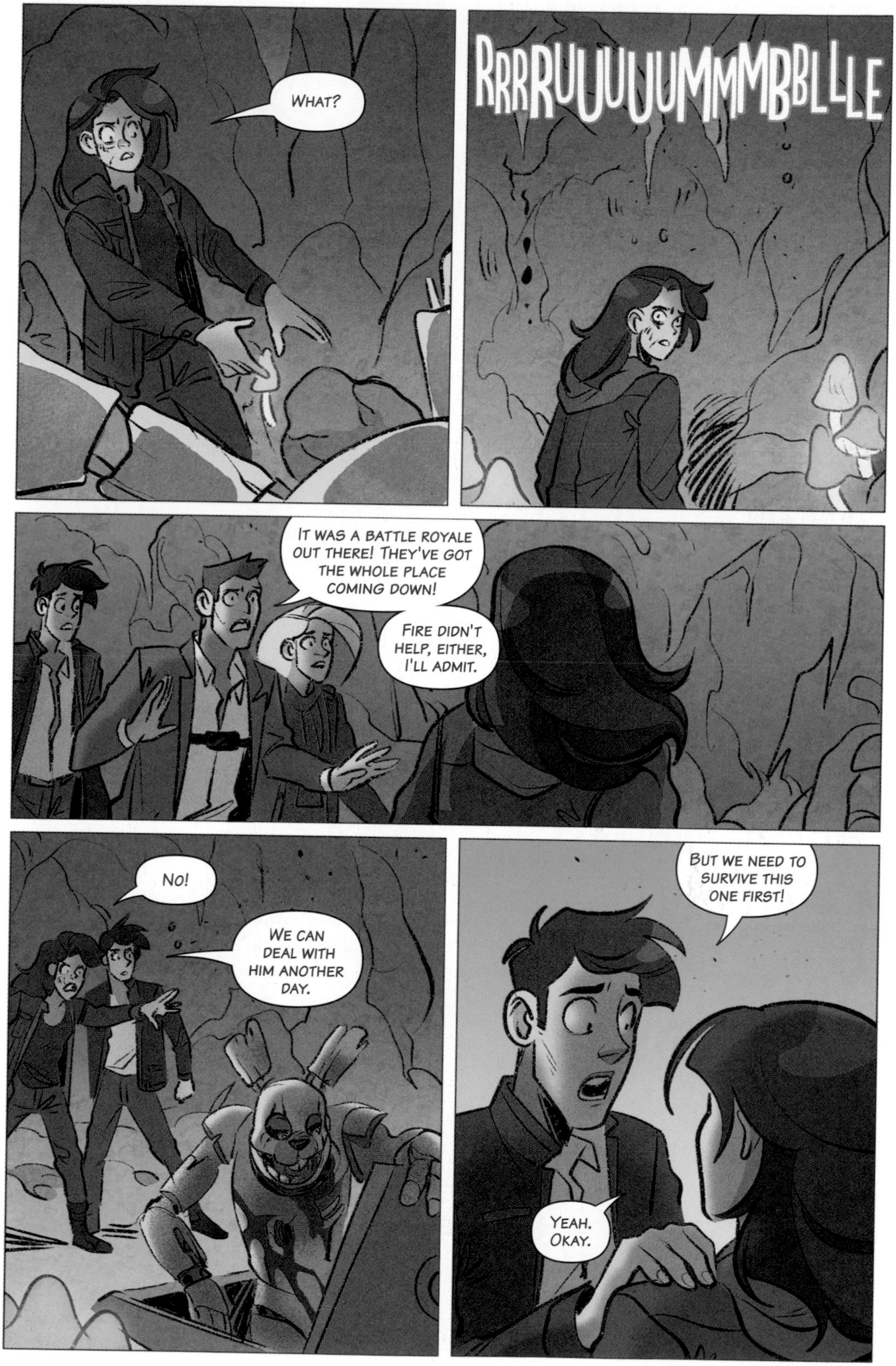
WHAT?
RRRRUUUUUMMMBBLLLE
IT WAS A BATTLE ROYALE OUT THERE! THEY'VE GOT THE WHOLE PLACE COMING DOWN!
FIRE DIDN'T HELP, EITHER, I'LL ADMIT.
NO!
WE CAN DEAL WITH HIM ANOTHER DAY.
BUT WE NEED TO SURVIVE THIS ONE FIRST!
YEAH. OKAY.

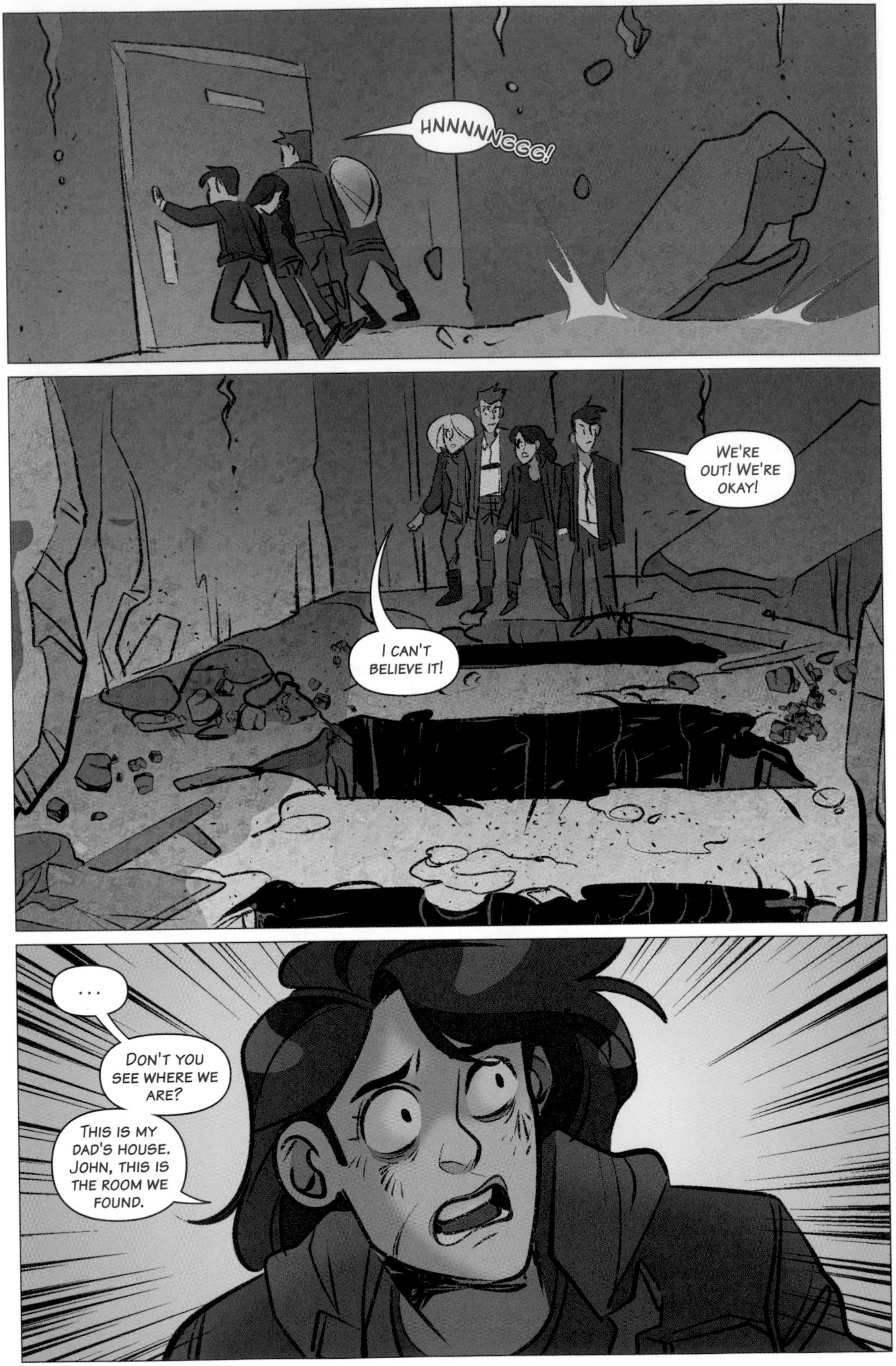
HNNNNNGGG!
WE'RE OUT! WE'RE OKAY!
I CAN'T BELIEVE IT!
...
DON'T YOU SEE WHERE WE ARE?
THIS IS MY DAD'S HOUSE. JOHN, THIS IS THE ROOM WE FOUND.

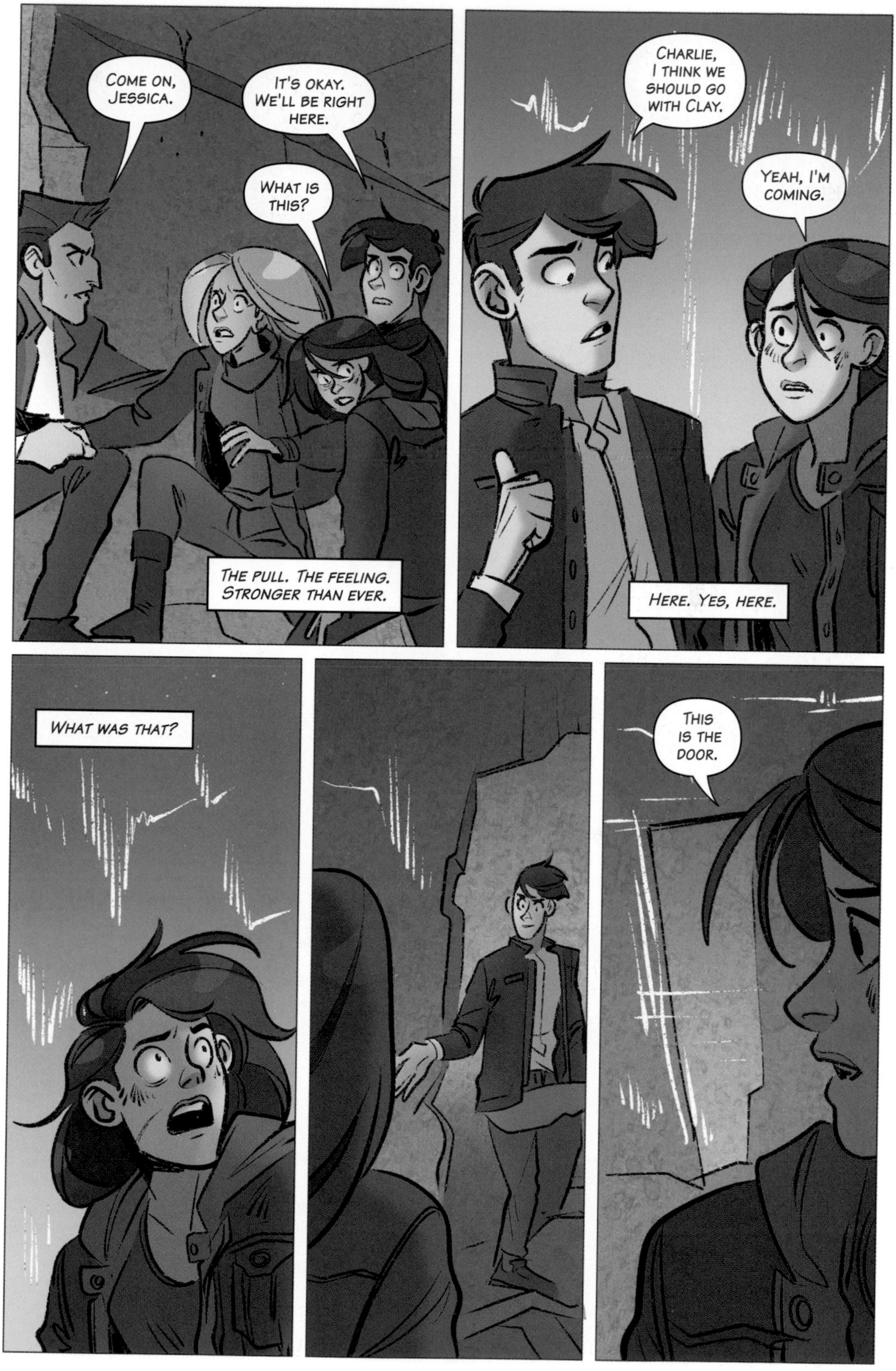
COME ON, JESSICA.
IT'S OKAY. WE'LL BE RIGHT HERE.
WHAT IS THIS?
THE PULL. THE FEELING. STRONGER THAN EVER.
CHARLIE, I THINK WE SHOULD GO WITH CLAY.
YEAH, I'M COMING.
HERE. YES, HERE.
WHAT WAS THAT?
THIS IS THE DOOR.

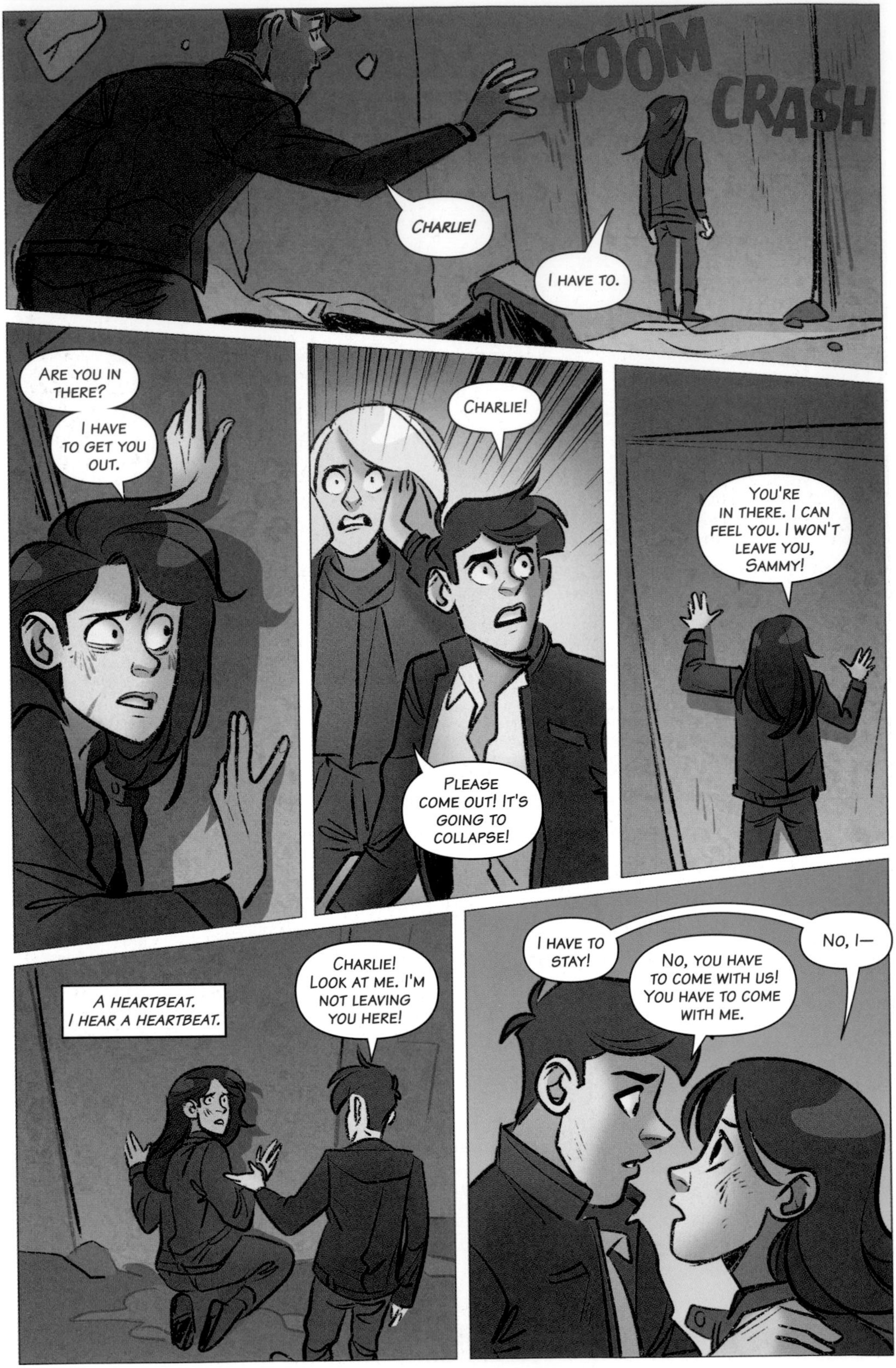
BOOM
CRASH
CHARLIE!
I HAVE TO.
ARE YOU IN THERE?
I HAVE TO GET YOU OUT.
CHARLIE!
PLEASE COME OUT! IT'S GOING TO COLLAPSE!
YOU'RE IN THERE. I CAN FEEL YOU. I WON'T LEAVE YOU, SAMMY!
A HEARTBEAT. I HEAR A HEARTBEAT.
CHARLIE! LOOK AT ME. I'M NOT LEAVING YOU HERE!
I HAVE TO STAY!
NO, YOU HAVE TO COME WITH US! YOU HAVE TO COME WITH ME.
NO, I—

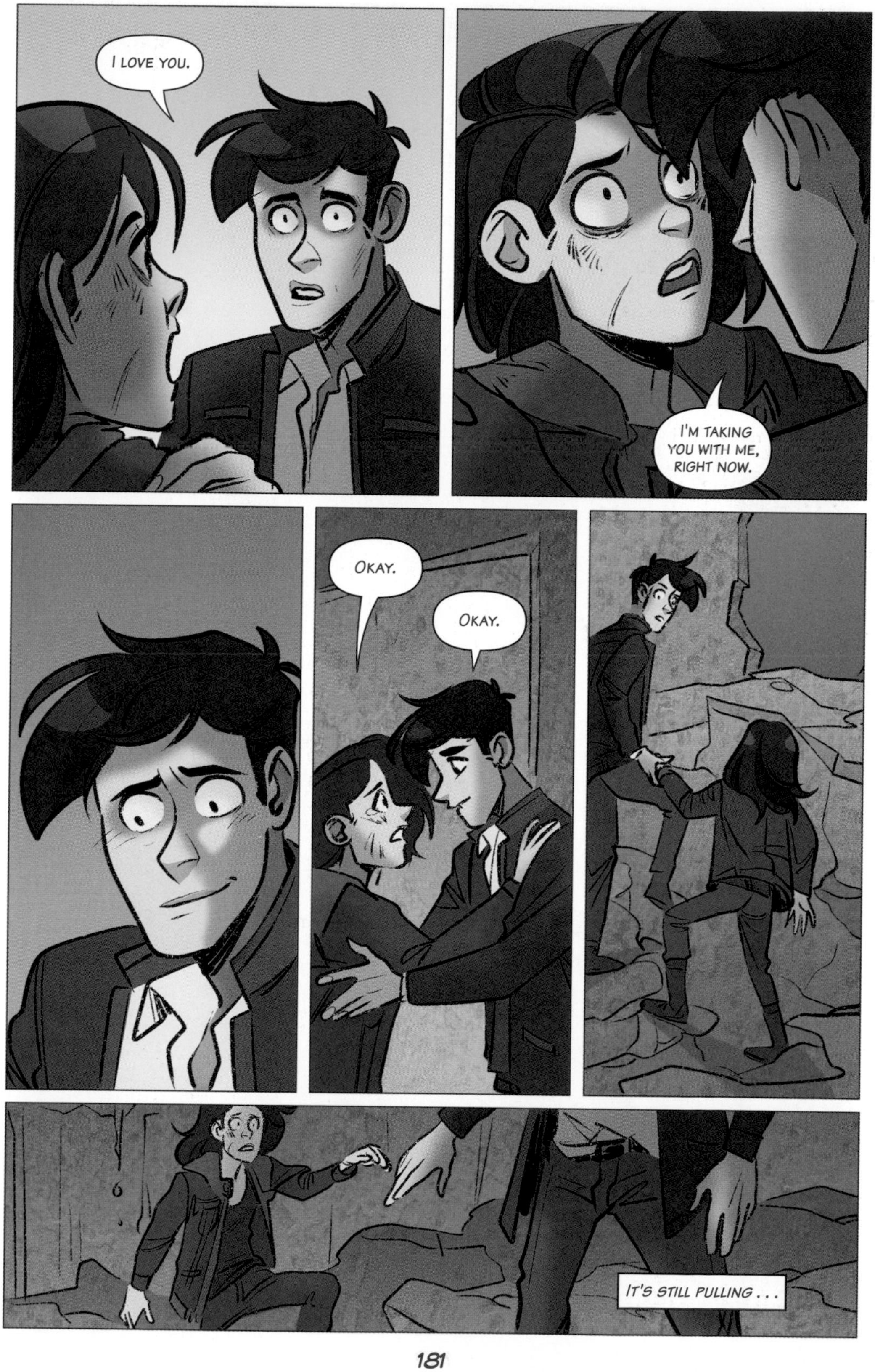

I LOVE YOU.
I'M TAKING YOU WITH ME, RIGHT NOW.
OKAY.
OKAY.
IT'S STILL PULLING . . .

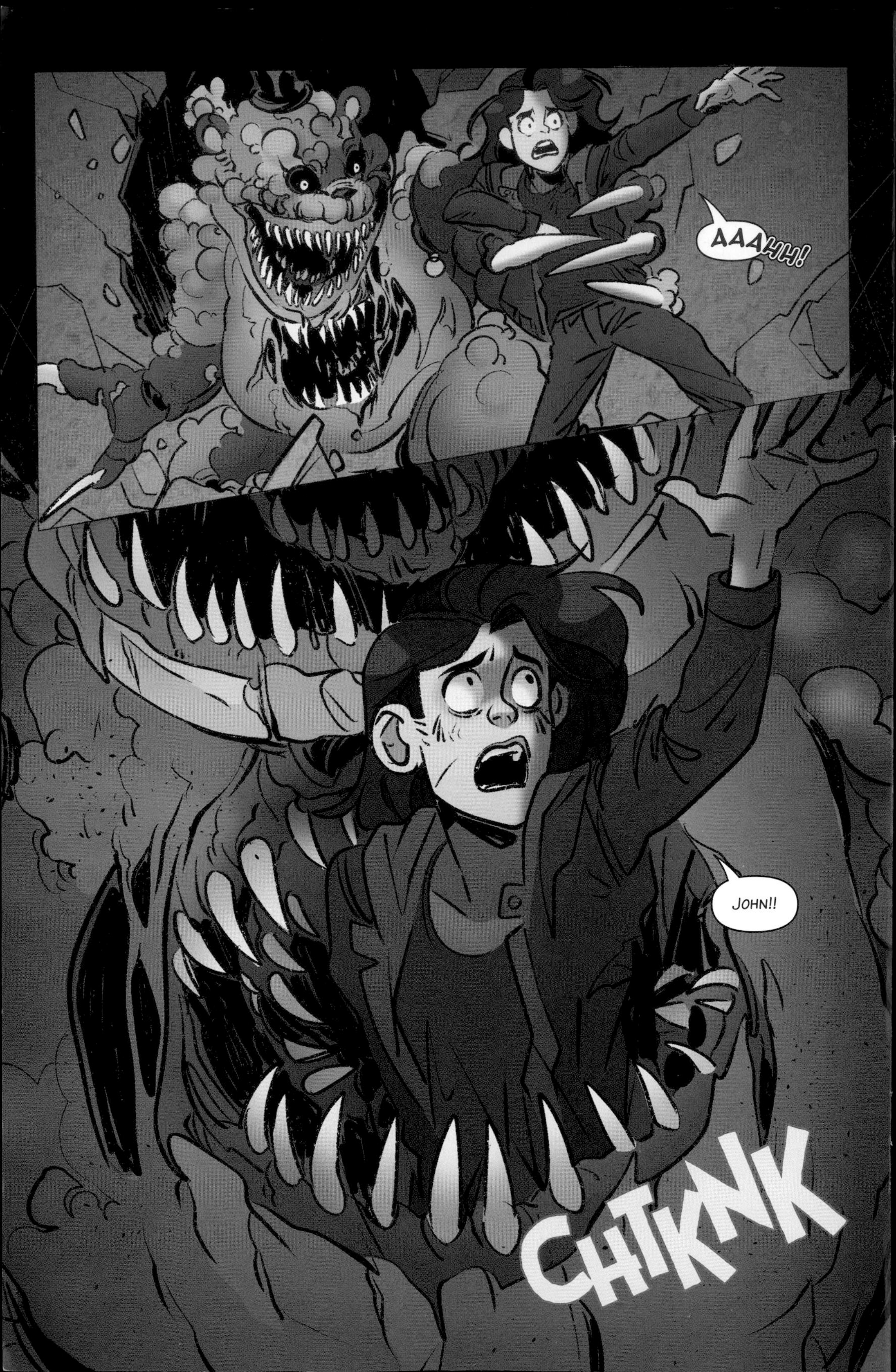
AAAHH!
JOHN!!
CHTKNK

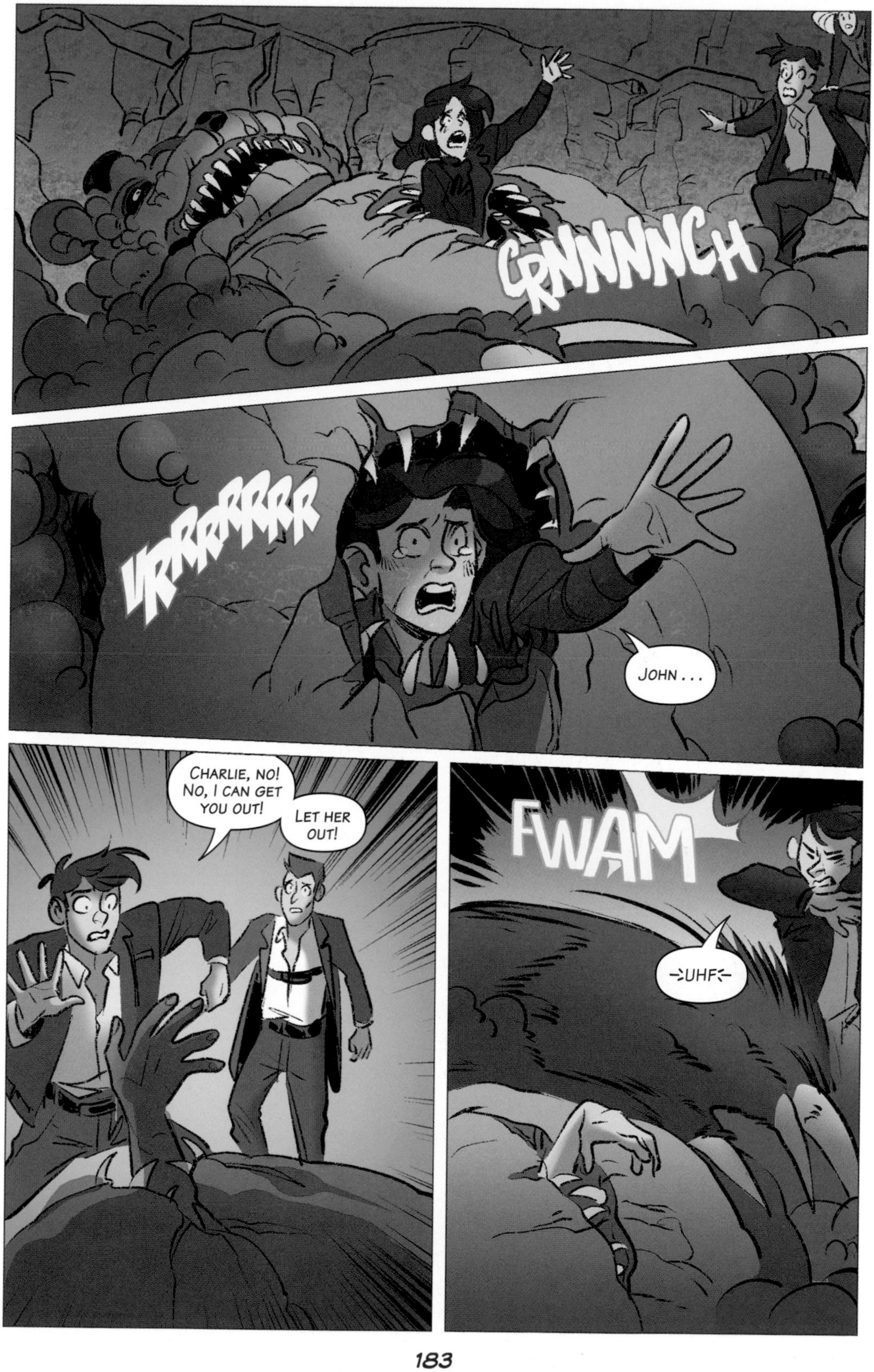
CRNNNNCH
URRRRRRR
JOHN . . .
CHARLIE, NO! NO, I CAN GET YOU OUT!
LET HER OUT!
FWAM
-UHF-

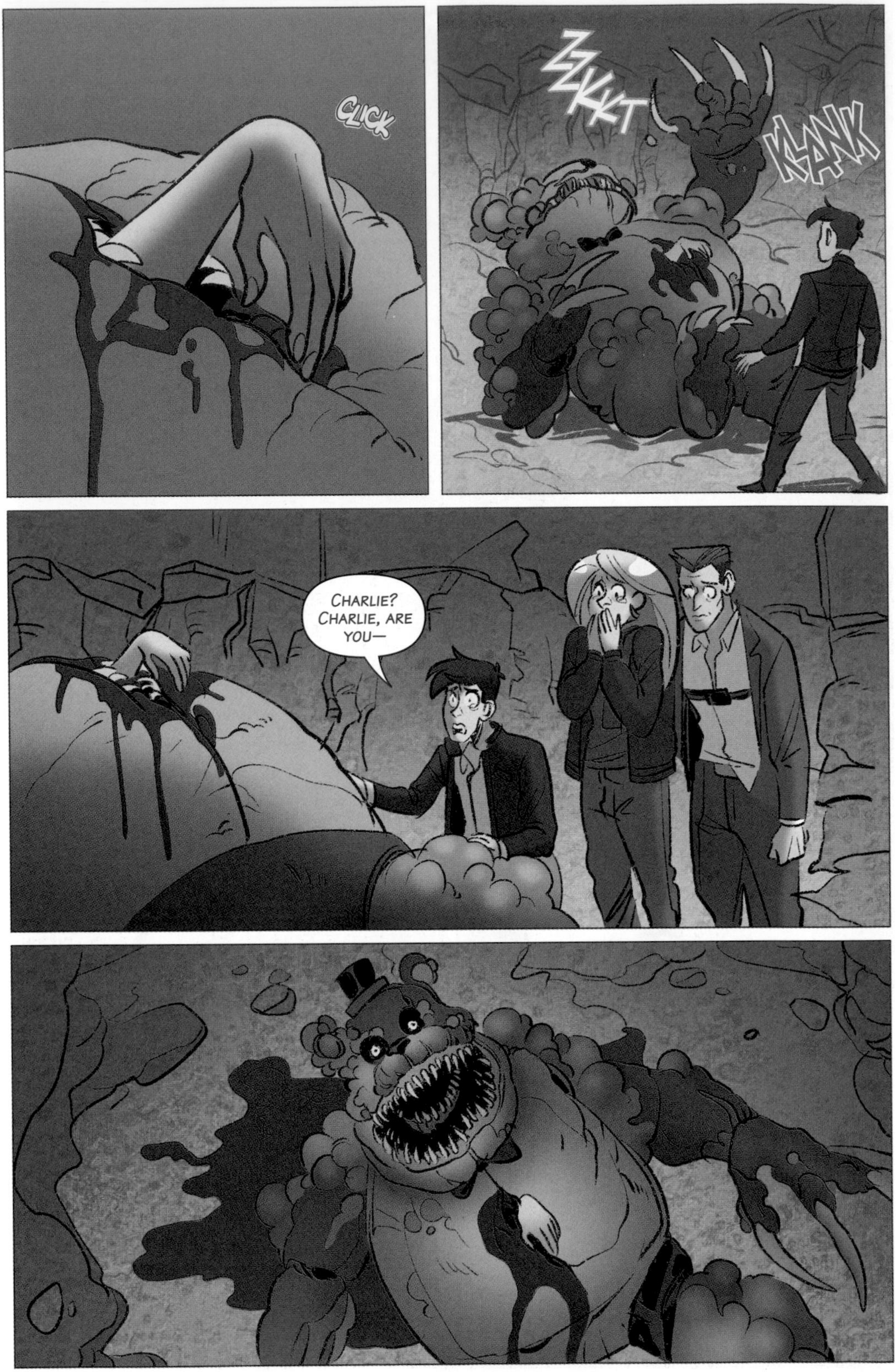
CLICK
ZZKKKT
KLANK
CHARLIE? CHARLIE, ARE YOU—

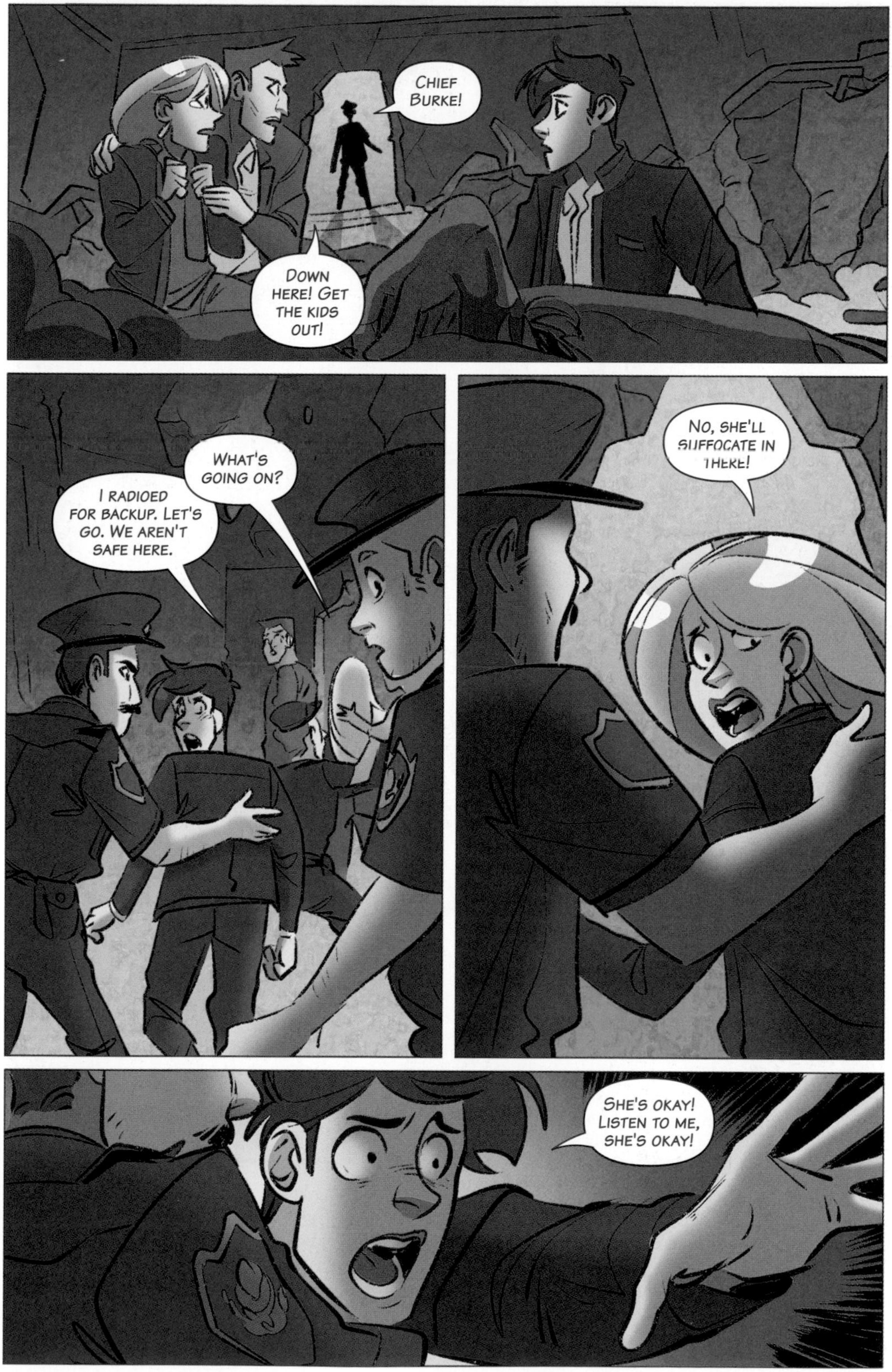
CHIEF BURKE!
DOWN HERE! GET THE KIDS OUT!
I RADIOED FOR BACKUP. LET'S GO. WE AREN'T SAFE HERE.
WHAT'S GOING ON?
NO, SHE'LL SUFFOCATE IN THERE!
SHE'S OKAY! LISTEN TO ME, SHE'S OKAY!

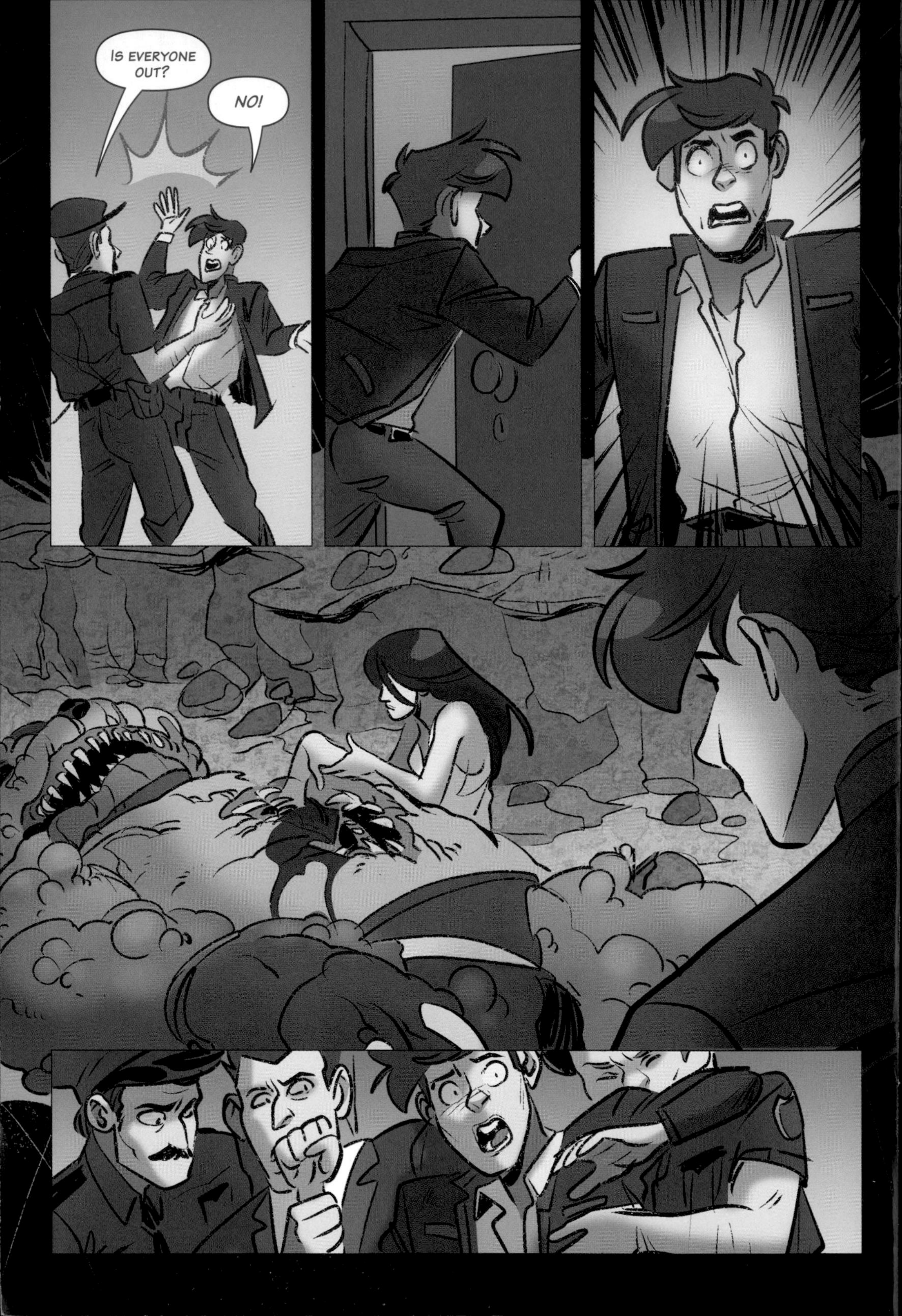
IS EVERYONE OUT?
NO!

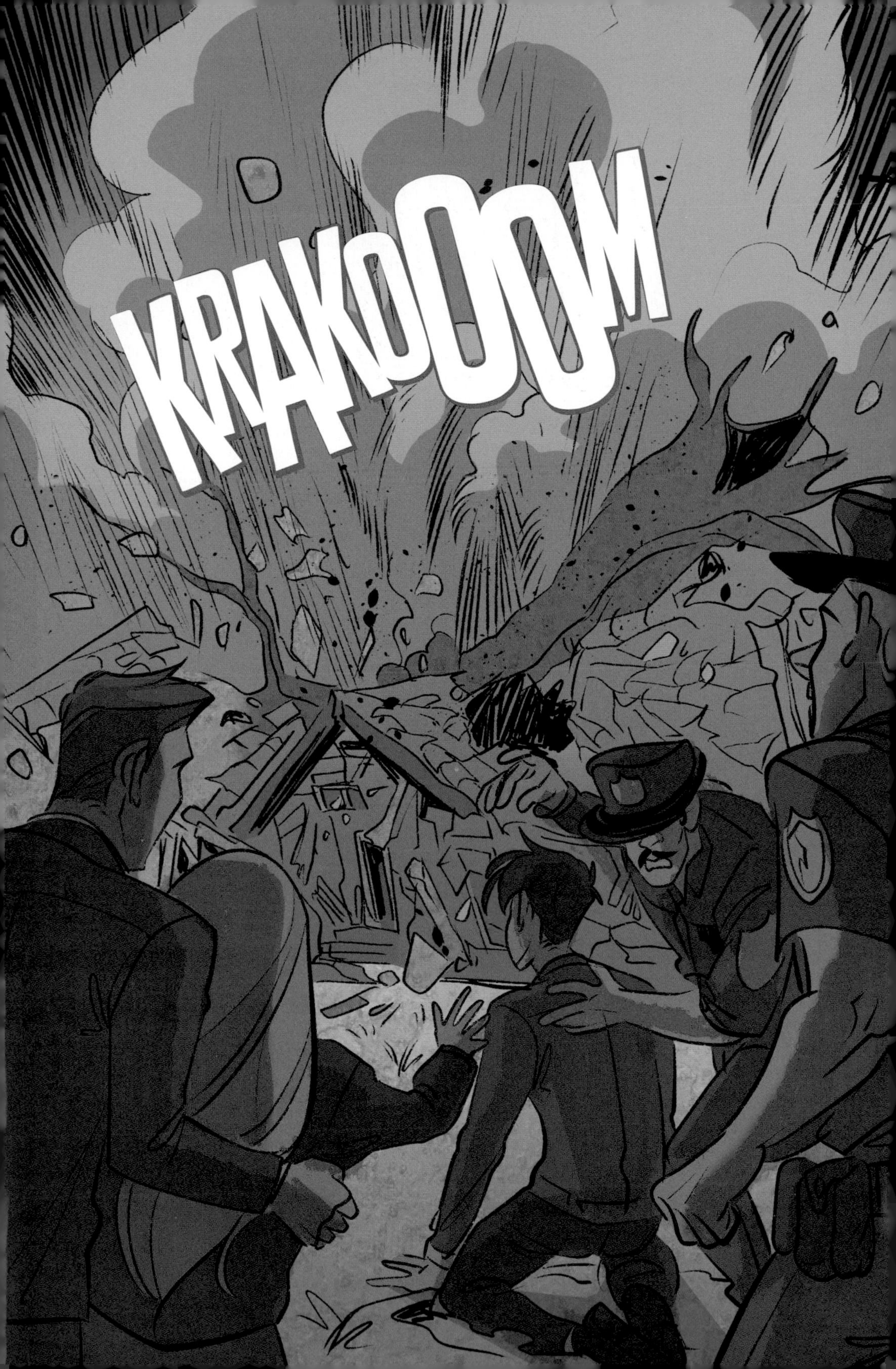
KRAKOOOM

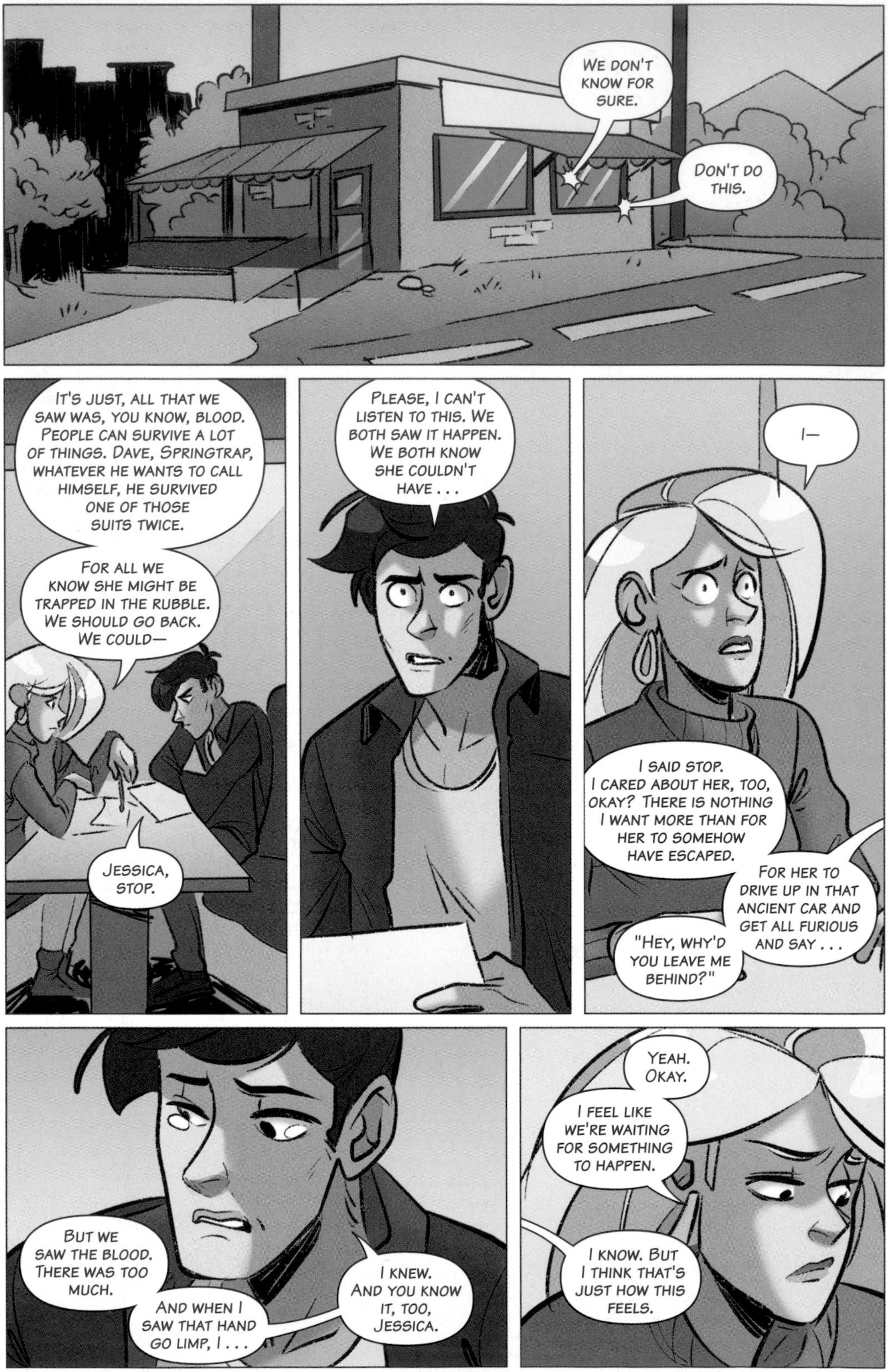

WE DON'T KNOW FOR SURE.
DON'T DO THIS.
IT'S JUST, ALL THAT WE SAW WAS, YOU KNOW, BLOOD. PEOPLE CAN SURVIVE A LOT OF THINGS. DAVE, SPRINGTRAP, WHATEVER HE WANTS TO CALL HIMSELF, HE SURVIVED ONE OF THOSE SUITS TWICE.
FOR ALL WE KNOW SHE MIGHT BE TRAPPED IN THE RUBBLE. WE SHOULD GO BACK. WE COULD—
JESSICA, STOP.
PLEASE, I CAN'T LISTEN TO THIS. WE BOTH SAW IT HAPPEN. WE BOTH KNOW SHE COULDN'T HAVE . . .
I—
I SAID STOP. I CARED ABOUT HER, TOO, OKAY? THERE IS NOTHING I WANT MORE THAN FOR HER TO SOMEHOW HAVE ESCAPED.
FOR HER TO DRIVE UP IN THAT ANCIENT CAR AND GET ALL FURIOUS AND SAY . . .
"HEY, WHY'D YOU LEAVE ME BEHIND?"
BUT WE SAW THE BLOOD. THERE WAS TOO MUCH.
AND WHEN I SAW THAT HAND GO LIMP, I . . .
I KNEW. AND YOU KNOW IT, TOO, JESSICA.
YEAH. OKAY.
I FEEL LIKE WE'RE WAITING FOR SOMETHING TO HAPPEN.
I KNOW. BUT I THINK THAT'S JUST HOW THIS FEELS.

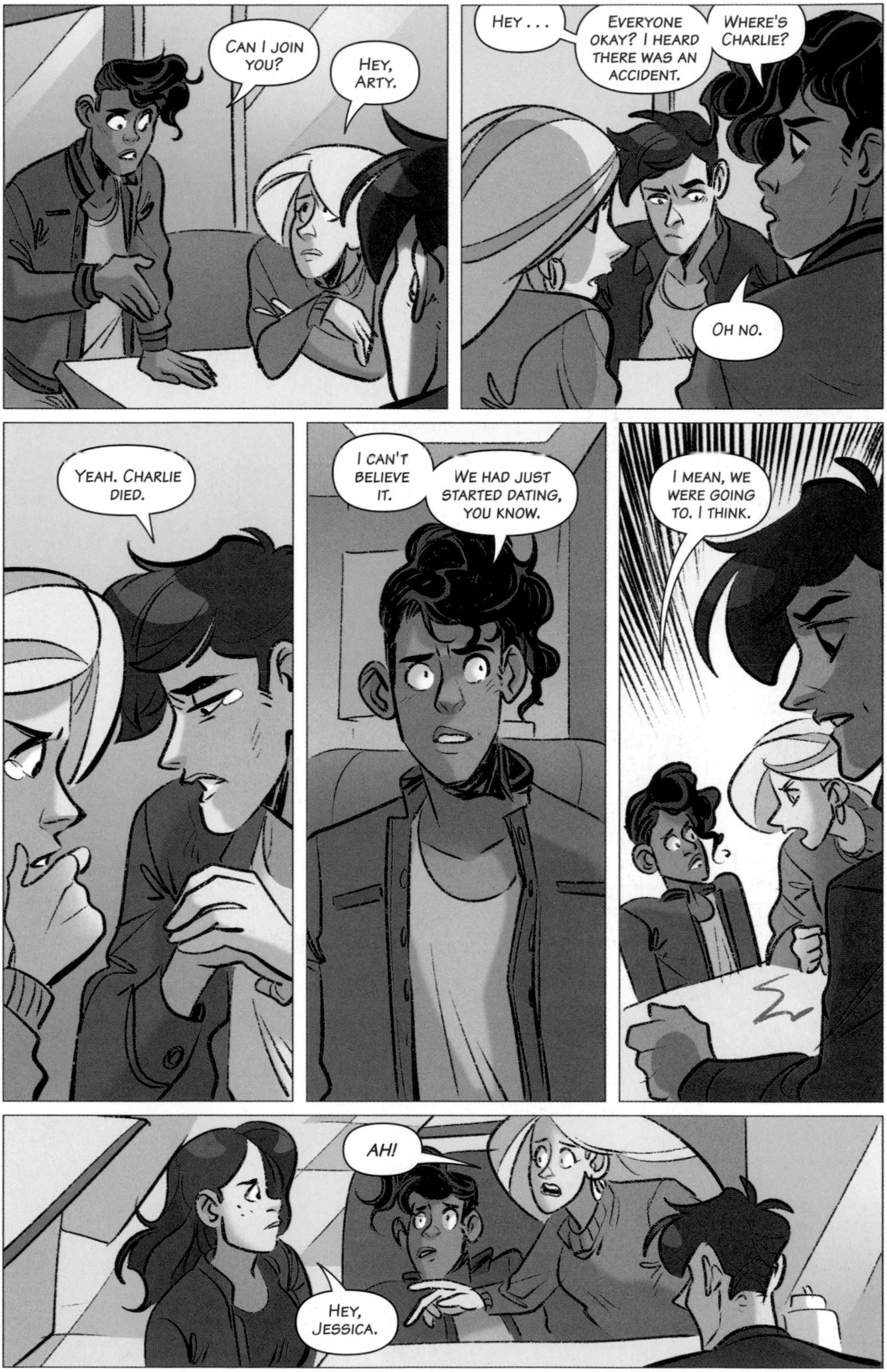
CAN I JOIN YOU?
HEY, ARTY.
HEY . . .
EVERYONE OKAY? I HEARD THERE WAS AN ACCIDENT.
WHERE'S CHARLIE?
OH NO.
YEAH. CHARLIE DIED.
I CAN'T BELIEVE IT.
WE HAD JUST STARTED DATING, YOU KNOW.
I MEAN, WE WERE GOING TO. I THINK.
AH!
HEY, JESSICA.

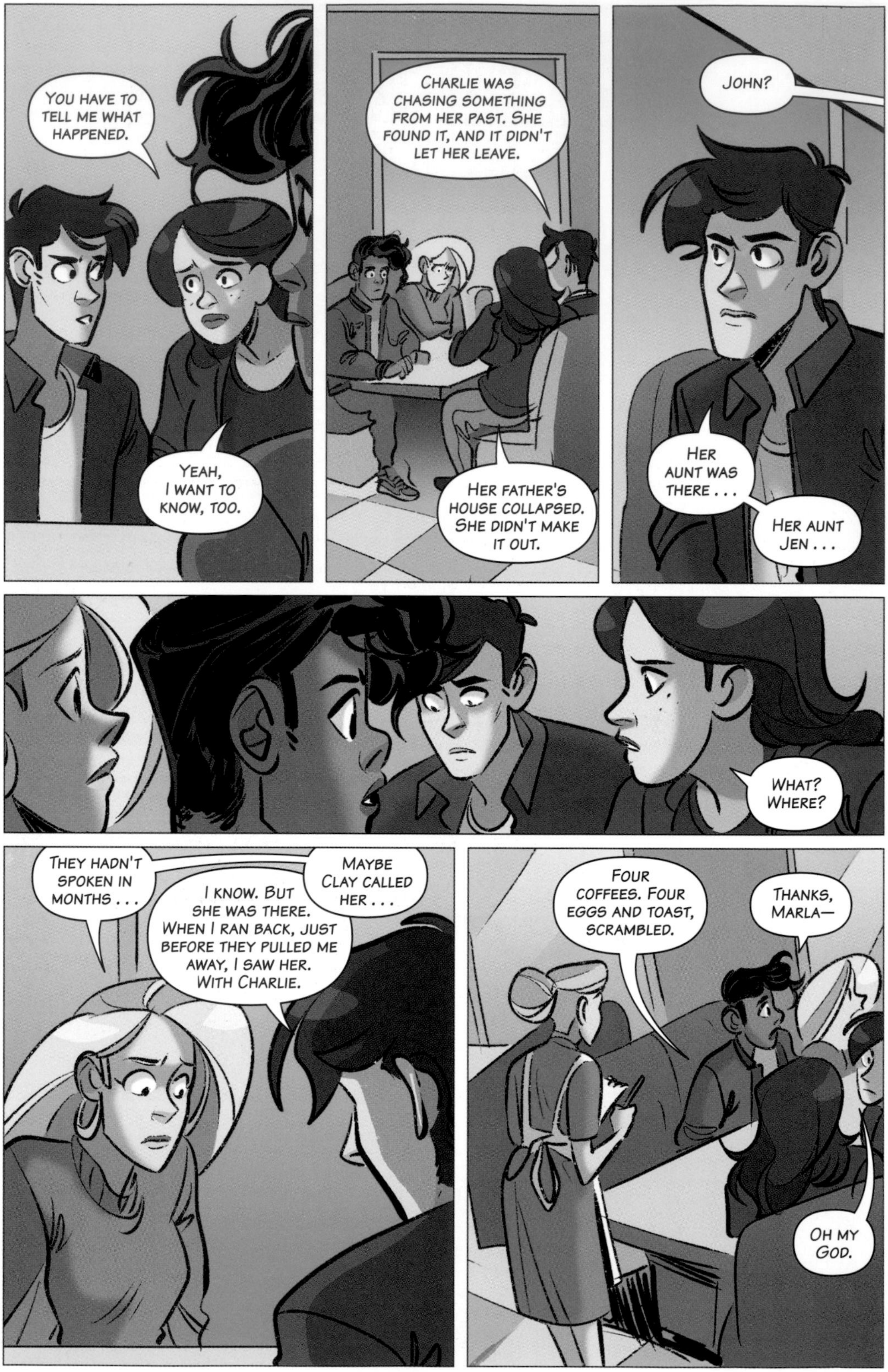
You have to tell me what happened.
Yeah, I want to know, too.
Charlie was chasing something from her past. She found it, and it didn't let her leave.
Her father's house collapsed. She didn't make it out.
John?
Her aunt was there . . .
Her aunt Jen . . .
What? Where?
They hadn't spoken in months . . .
Maybe Clay called her . . .
I know. But she was there. When I ran back, just before they pulled me away, I saw her. With Charlie.
Four coffees. Four eggs and toast, scrambled.
Thanks, Marla—
Oh my God.

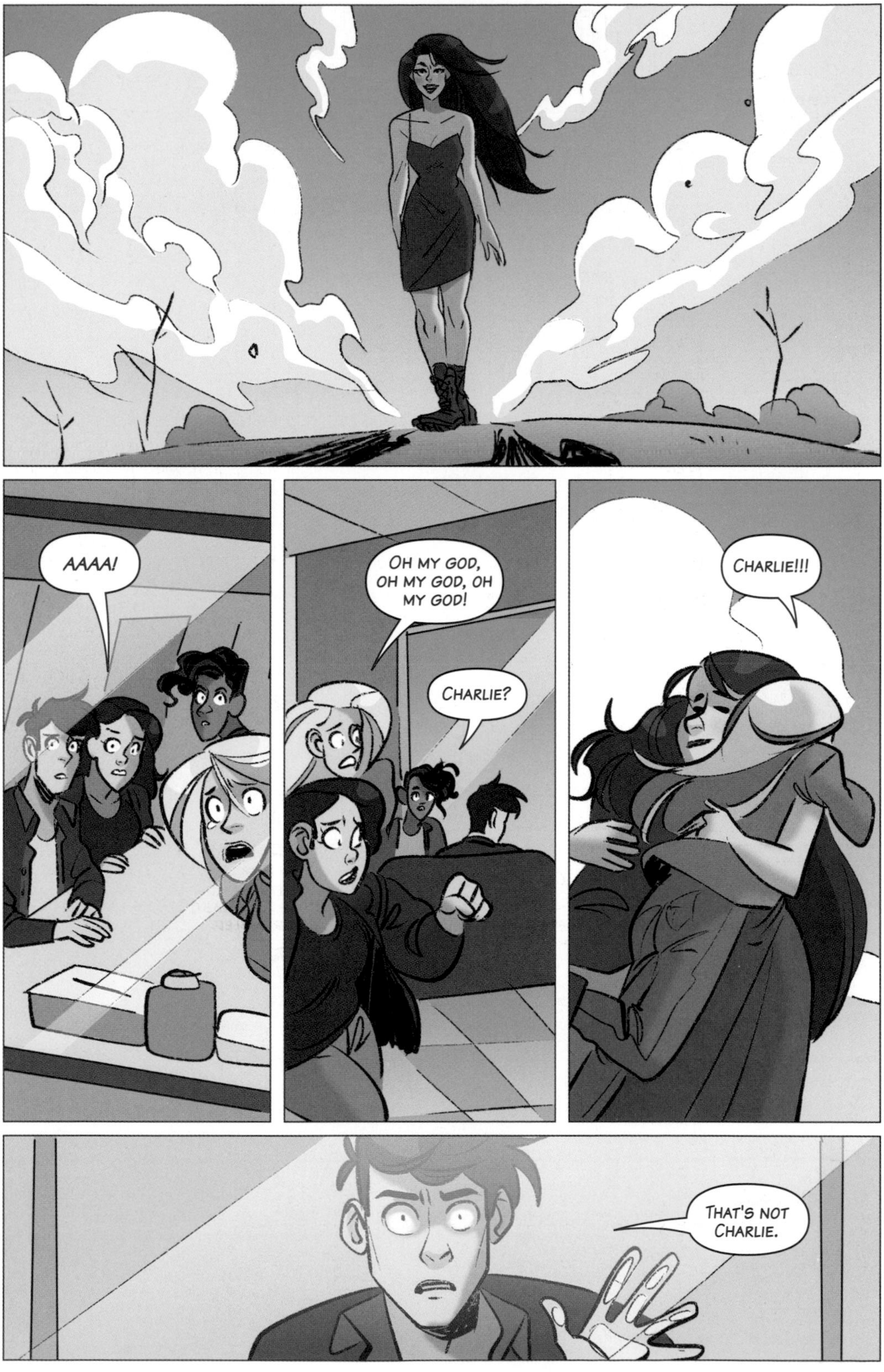
AAAA!
OH MY GOD, OH MY GOD, OH MY GOD!
CHARLIE?
CHARLIE!!!
THAT'S NOT CHARLIE.